D1706850

Masters' Escape

OTHER BOOKS BY JAMIE SCHULZ

Jake's Redemption
Masters' Mistress: The Angel Eyes Series Book 1

UPCOMING BOOKS

Masters' Promise: The Angel Eyes Series Book 3
Masters' Rebellion: The Angel Eyes Series Book 4
Masters' Betrayal: The Angel Eyes Series Book 5
Masters' Freedom: The Angel Eyes Series Book 6

Masters' Escape

The Angel Eyes Series Book 2

Jamie Schulz

COPYRIGHT

For the real *Angel and Monica...with all my love, always.*

AUTHOR'S NOTE

Dear Reader,

Masters' Escape is Book Two in the Angel Eyes Series. I highly recommend that you read Book One before diving into *Masters' Escape*. The prequel would also help in understanding this world that is complex, often cruel, and surprisingly sweet at times. Every book in the series will reveal a little more, not only between the characters themselves, but in the outside world, their small, local society, and how the characters' interact within them.

Bret and Angel's overarching story continues throughout all the books, but it's important to get a base for the setting and rules to this complicated yet compelling story.

Thank you,

Jamie

The Escape

1

BRET MASTERS STORMED into the dark, one-room apartment he shared with his best friend Jake Nichols and slammed the door behind him. Pent up fury roared through his veins and pounded in his ears. He wanted to break something, tear it apart piece by piece with his bare hands. But that wouldn't make him feel any better, and it wouldn't solve his dilemma.

As he'd made his way downstairs, his chest had tightened until he could hardly breathe. Now, raking trembling hands through his raven-black hair, Bret glanced around and discovered himself alone with the enormous weight of his hurt and anger. He stared at his roommate's undisturbed bed and felt another level of pressure inside his ribs, building like a volcano about to erupt. It took him less than five seconds to guess why Jake was not lying there asleep. The thought of his friend enjoying the warm company of a willing partner pricked Bret's already soaring temper.

"What the *hell* are you doing here?" Angel's high-pitched demand from only minutes ago rang inside Bret's mind. He tried to ignore it, but the memory wouldn't leave, replaying the whole conversation in painful detail.

"I was invited," he had replied as the smile slid off his face and a pang of foreboding clamped like a vise around his vulnerable heart.

For a moment, she'd actually looked confused as her wide-eyed gaze traveled over his naked body to settle on the white bedsheet draped low over his hips. She shook her head in denial. "I wouldn't have done that." Her voice was adamant, but her eyes, when they snapped back to his, told a different story.

"Well, darlin'," he had drawled, disappointed but unwilling to give in so easily; he lay on his side watching her and grinning again, "I hate to break it to you, but you did. Maybe not in so many words, but the meaning was the same."

She squeezed her eyes closed, shutting him out as crimson stained her cheeks, clearly regretting what had happened between them.

Remembering that conversation now brought a growl rumbling through his constricted throat. His fisted fingers pulled at his short-cropped hair in frustration, but a heartbeat later, he let his arms fall to his sides with a resigned sigh. It was probably better Jake wasn't there to witness his exasperated display. Jake would undoubtedly want to know why Bret was so upset and that wasn't something he would willingly discuss. Whether Bret revealed the soft-feeling, sweet-smelling, curly-haired cause of his displeasure or not, the subject would eventually lead to an argument, and he didn't want Jake to become an inadvertent target.

He wasn't angry with Jake, but he was furious and utterly disappointed with himself.

Once again, he'd trusted the wrong woman; believed that the beyond-the-physical-connection he'd felt with Angel was mutual. It sure seemed that way last night, right up to the point when she'd fallen asleep in his arms.

He should've known better than to allow hope to grow inside him. That particular sentiment had always been his downfall.

"You're an idiot," he told himself as he quickly stripped out of the white dress shirt and black slacks he'd worn to Angel's birthday party the night before. He wadded up the clothes and tossed them onto the heap near the door. Then, still fuming, he crawled into the cool sheets of his bed to attempt another hour or two of sleep. Laying on his back with one hand tucked under his head and the other flat on his chest, he reminisced about the wonders of the previous evening. But even that was tainted by this morning's gut-wrenching disappointment.

"Why did you come back to the dining hall last night?" she had asked softly when her shining eyes finally met his again. "Why couldn't you just stay away?"

He lifted one shoulder in an indifferent shrug. "I heard someone playing the piano. I didn't know it was you."

She looked away, her jaw clenched and her body curved inward defensively.

"Why did you apologize?" she asked without meeting his gaze.

He'd blinked in surprise at that. Did she think he was so cold that causing someone pain didn't affect him? "Because I felt I should, and you accepted."

"And the dance?" she said, pinning him again with her wary blue-gray stare.

"It was your birthday, and you looked sad, disappointed even. I just wanted to make you smile."

She huffed and turned away, dismissing him. "You need to leave before anyone sees you."

Even though a part of him had suspected it was coming, that statement had hit him like a slap to the face—not to mention what it did to his stubborn pride.

"What?" He had tried to laugh it off. "Are you actually throwing me out?"

Her lips thinned. "Yes."

"Angel," he started and reached for her hand, intent on soothing whatever troubled her, but she pulled away and scowled at him.

"Get out! I don't want you here. I don't *need* you here." Her expression softened suddenly, and her eyes seemed to plead with him. "Please...just...leave."

"So, that's how it is?" he asked as the hope he'd felt only a few hours before dwindled and burned to dust under the white-hot fury that burst to life inside him.

Pain. Women always caused him pain. Why did he keep believing it could be different?

"What does that mean?"

"You got what you wanted and now you're throwing me out?" He scoffed. "I thought you didn't use your breeders?"

"I don't."

"You did last night."

She glared at him.

"What's wrong?" he asked spitefully. "Did you get tired of using your old breeders and decided to play with the new toy?"

"That's not what happened."

"Isn't it?" He sat up. Bending one knee, he draped a forearm across it and met her frown with his own.

Angel's eyes had followed the sheet as it slipped down to puddle in his lap. Appreciation and something like fear or disgust passed over her face. Not that he cared what she thought of him…not anymore.

"No!" she replied, yanking her eyes back to his.

"Then what *did* happen?"

She paused and then seemed to slump as she shrugged. "You seduced me."

He barked a short, sardonic laugh. "Oh, no, honey. *You* seduced *me!*"

Angel sighed and surprised him with an affirming nod. "I shouldn't have done that. You should've stopped me."

He chuckled dryly. "I tried. Several times."

"You should've tried harder."

"I did, but you were insistent. Good God, how much restraint do you think I have? I knew you wanted me, there's no denying that. I just didn't expect such a passionate response to a simple kiss."

"What kiss?"

His eyes shifted from her gaze to her lips and back again. She had wanted him, badly. Why was she still denying it? "You know what kiss."

With a slight shift of her head, she had tried to refute his statement, but Bret wouldn't have that.

He locked her with a hard stare and leaned in closer. "Maybe I should remind you."

"Please don't," she'd squeaked and scooted a little farther away. "Please go, Bret. This can't happen again and no one can know."

"Why?" he asked, hurt infusing his words. "Am I so below you that being with me is an embarrassment?"

She sighed and shook her head. "It's not that."

"Then what?"

It took her a minute to answer, but when she did, she seemed to be holding something back.

"I've made a lot of enemies," she said, then explained that, with the current laws, her adversaries could take him from her. If those women learned of what had happened between them last night, their attempts to acquire him would only increase. "And when they get their hands on you—and they will with your temper—they'll hurt you to force me to do what they want. If that happened, they'd gain more power than I could ever overcome without an all-out civil war. I can't do that, Bret. I can't!"

He sat frowning at her for a long minute, weighing her answer and searching her face. When he saw the telltale flicker in her pretty azure eyes, he knew the truth. *She's not telling me something.*

"That's bullshit," he said as he kicked off the sheet and got to his feet, spurred as much by her response as by his internal demons.

"I don't understand," she said, confusion plain on her face. "You got what you wanted, so why are you so upset?"

He stopped in the middle of pulling his underwear up to glance at her before jerking the garment into place. With his hands on his hips and his slacks clenched in his fist, he directed a furious scowl at her. "Exactly what is it you think I wanted?"

"Last night you told me you wanted to sleep with me. You got what you wanted. So, what do you have to be angry about?"

He gave a short, humorless laugh. "And you think that's all I wanted?"

She lowered her chin in an almost imperceptible nod.

He snorted and shook his head as disappointment tightened his chest. "You don't think much of me, do you?"

"That's not true," she said as he jerked on his slacks. "I am...fond of you."

"Fond?" He laughed again, derisively this time. "That's one way to describe it, though not very accurate."

"What are you talking about?"

"You *used* me, Angel," he said harshly as he fastened the closure on his slacks and zipped them up. "You had an itch you needed scratched and there I was, a stupid, horny bastard you could easily seduce because I told you what I wanted." His voice had held a sad and sour note as he snatched his shirt off the floor. "Well, ma'am," he'd drawled with a mocking bow and a gallant wave of his hand, "I'm glad to have been of service, but I'll be off now."

When she'd fallen asleep in his arms, hope for something better—for a future with Angel by his side—had spread through his chest like an out of control wildfire. Then she'd smashed all those idiotic dreams and his heart along with them. Her rejection burned in his brain, his belly, his heart. Now, he lay in his room with a crushing weight on his chest, unable to sleep.

Last night, she'd given every indication of wanting more than just a one-night stand. Even before that, she'd melted at his touch and practically went up in flames every time he kissed her. And last night...

God, he groaned at the memories dancing through his mind, *last night she'd nearly had me begging!*

Despite everything—her rejection and lies about protecting him from enemies he had yet to ascertain—he still wanted her. He couldn't deny it, not when just the thought of her soft, silky body, warm and yielding beneath him, heated his blood and brought his body to rigid awareness.

What the hell happened? He clenched his fist and slammed it against the mattress in pure frustration. Everything she'd said and done the night before told Bret that more lay hidden beneath her cool outer shell, just waiting for him to discover it. Everything from her reaction to his touch to her admission that she wanted him had been enough to set them both on fire. But this morning, the minute she realized he was warming the bed beside her, she turned to ice. Still, her gaze had lingered on his body as he jerked on his clothes. He knew she was attracted to him. He knew she wanted him, but apparently, she didn't want more from him than the use of his body. His heart squeezed tight. *Just like all the others.*

Last night he'd told himself it didn't matter.

This morning was a different story.

Her actions had flayed him deeply and it had gotten worse when he tried to leave.

For a second, when she'd stopped his hasty departure at her bedroom door, he'd thought maybe she regretted throwing him out. But she'd smashed that hope too.

"I need to know you're not going to talk about this," she'd said in a quiet rush. "You can't, not with anyone, not even Jake."

Happy best described his state of mind when he fell asleep with Angel in his arms; a sentiment he hadn't experienced for a very long time. It shocked him now that her cold dismissal after such a wonderful night could hurt as badly as it did. He rubbed at the raw ache in his chest, not wanting to admit that it had anything to do with Angel. His heart was too well protected for that, but even so, he had to admit, she'd cut him deeply—deeper than anyone had before—and the lonely idiot he was still wanted her.

At her unequivocal final rejection, his uncle's voice, as it often did, had begun taunting him in his head. *See, boy, no woman'll want you for anything but a good fuck!*

On the heels of that old insult, memories of the last woman he had once loved to distraction slammed into his mind like an old Mac truck. Right before everything in his already sorry life went totally wrong, Amy Hensford had uttered hurtful words that sounded too much like the ones Uncle Vince had once tormented him with.

Lying in bed now, thinking back, Bret could recall everything about that early morning when Amy had shown her true colors. The cool chill of the mountain air, the dark shadows of the evergreens surrounding their camp, the Raiders with their whips in hand, and he and Jake on their knees. Bret remembered the sharp twinge in his heart when, out of the corner of his eye, he'd seen Jake's worried glance.

"Why did you betray me?" Bret had asked, completely stunned by what Amy had done.

Mirth had twinkled in Amy's dark eyes as she laughed in his face. "You're a sappy fool, Bret," she said, giggling as Bret stared up at her in shock. "I don't care for you. I never did. I just liked your looks. Your talents in bed were quite a pleasing surprise. Both are qualities that'll increase your price at auction. Though, I'll hate to lose access to your…" her eyes had drifted over his body, assessing his worth and making Bret's skin crawl, "exceptional assets, I might get lucky in that regard."

She touched his face with a greedy caress and his breath caught in his throat. For a brief moment, hope that it had all been a very bad joke had bloomed inside him. Then his stomach roiled, sickened by how much her touch affected him, even after her betrayal.

When he pulled away, she smiled at him. "You do have such a pretty face, but no brains in your head," she said and then chuckled at his fulminating look. She told him that no woman would want him now…no self-respecting, decent woman anyway. Then she taunted him with the threat of making him a slave and that terrible possibility had awakened his fury.

A growl had ripped from his chest as he surged to his feet, all of his animosity focused on Amy. To his surprise, Jake and several others had joined him. During the fray, Amy struck at Bret, nearly sinking a long-bladed knife into his back. Instead, she landed a glancing blow that left a long, shallow gash. As he rolled away, he saw someone had tackled her, but in the dim light of pre-dawn, he didn't recognize his savior and there'd been no time to dwell on it.

"Run!" he'd shouted at the others as he made his own escape.

Bret had retreated to their predetermined rendezvous point, only Jake never showed. Too late, he realized Jake had been his savior. If he'd known—which Bret still felt he should have—he would never have left Jake. His stomach cramped at the thought of the horrors his friend must've faced. If he had known Jake was the man who'd taken Amy down, Bret wanted to believe that he'd have risked becoming a slave himself before condemning Jake to that fate.

Bret lost everything that day, including his self-respect. All because he'd wanted a woman's love so desperately that he'd ignored all the warning signs and Jake's better judgment.

He had promised himself he would never be that naive again.

But he *did* do it again. With his eyes wide open this time. Now, he suffered the heartache of being wrong once more. His stupidity made him furious. Not only with Angel but himself as well, and he'd reacted accordingly by storming out of the room. Well, he would've stormed out if she hadn't stopped him with her demand for his silence.

He had tried to be snide, to pretend her wanting to forget everything that had happened between them didn't hurt like severing a limb, but the pain was far worse than that, deeper and more damning.

"Bret, please…"

He had frowned and looked away, unable to meet Angel's pleading gaze. Molten heat had filled his body and his blood pounded in his ears, making him want to lash out, but he struggled to contain the burst of rage that struck him. Then his eyes fell on the big four-poster bed where they'd spent a substantial portion of the night making love, and everything in him went cold—and then hot all over again. She wanted to pretend their coupling had never happened. That was impossible, at least for him. Something did happen between them that went beyond the physical. He'd felt the connection and had thought she did too, but then, he'd been wrong before.

Unable to block out the emotions crashing through him, he'd closed his eyes and shook his head. *God dammit! Why do I keep doing this to myself?*

Standing beside Angel's bedroom door staring at her bed, he had gathered the tatters of his defenses back around his wounded heart. When he'd met Angel's worried gaze once more, the hurt and anger became more acute. He didn't believe she was concerned for him, but he could be nothing less than who he was. So, he had reassured her that no one else would ever know and escaped her room as fast as she would let him.

Their relationship had drastically changed over the last twenty-four hours. Instead of having a delicate truce of amicability, they were now lovers, something Angel—and himself, if he was honest—was unprepared to accept.

Now, still laying on his back in his bed, he barked a mirthless chuckle as he remembered telling himself that getting laid would make him feel better.

"Yeah, right," he murmured into the darkness. His situation was anything but better. If anything, his discomfort and dissatisfaction were a thousand times worse.

He wanted to be angry with her, and he was, but he was far angrier with himself. Did he honestly expect her to react differently to their unexpected union merely because of some downright, mind-blowing sex? From the day he'd arrived, she'd treated him kindly but remained aloof. Why would that change now?

My God, I'm an idiot! he thought bitterly, turning onto his side, punching his pillow into a ball, and planting his head in the middle. *I let her use me and enjoyed it as much as she did!*

At least until she threw him out.

I've got to get away from her.

The thought gave him pause.

Do I really want to run? Now? A part of him leaped at the idea, but the deeper part, though bleeding and sore from Angel's rejection, hesitated. Until his hard side, the one that sounded like his hated uncle's voice, reminded him of her rebuff and his ribs constricted with remembered pain.

He didn't have a choice. If he stayed now, she truly would own him and he couldn't accept that. He would not be her toy, regardless of how much he still wanted her. No matter how different she may be otherwise. Not now that he knew she looked at him not as a man, but as a slave—a breeder to give her pleasure not someone with whom to share her life. Her story about the laws and being afraid for him was just that, a story to keep him quiet and coming back for more. He wouldn't play that game.

Hardening his heart, the way he should have kept it, he began to rebuild the protective battlements he'd lowered just for her. He would run, and not even Angel's soft skin or the haunting scent of lilacs that followed her would stop him this time. As soon as the opportunity arose, he would escape and not look back.

2

BRET BREATHED A SIGH of relief as he and Jake exited Angel's office and closed the door behind them. He'd been avoiding her as much as possible since she'd thrown him out of her bed a week ago, but he still had a job to do, and reporting to her was part of it.

"What was all that about?" Jake asked as he turned and faced Bret.

Stepping away from the door, Bret shrugged but didn't meet his friend's gaze as he headed down the hallway for lunch. "Just the weekly update."

Jake had known him for years, had been there for him through most of the worst parts of Bret's life, and could often read him like a book. But Bret didn't want to discuss his problems with Angel. Not even with Jake. Especially since her increasingly odd behavior—her growing silence, her progressively gloomier disposition, and her unnatural paleness—brought out an uncommonly strong desire in Bret to uncover the truth behind what troubled her and fix it. A feeling he stubbornly fought.

"You didn't need me in there for that," Jake said as he caught up to him. All the odd glances his friend had thrown Bret's way in Angel's office should've told him that Jake would question his motives the minute they left.

Bret shrugged again. "She likes you better." It was a lame excuse, but far better than admitting how much she'd hurt him and why.

"Did you already forget what I told you about making friends?" Jake asked as they entered the dining hall.

Bret gave him an annoyed look. "I've made friends. There's Theo, and Dean, and that kid who works in the kitchen, Carl, and some of the other guys."

"But none of the women."

Bret frowned and headed for a table where some of the friends he'd mentioned already sat. "I've talked with some of them. Theo's woman Peggy is pretty great."

He'd pitched his voice loud enough for Peggy to hear as he passed, and she turned a big smile and twinkling ebony eyes on him. "Well, thank you, Bret."

Taking a seat at the table, Bret grinned at her and winked. "I'm always happy to compliment a pretty woman."

"Hey, now," Theo joked, "go flirt with one of the other pretty women." He wrapped a long arm around Peggy's shoulders. "This one's mine."

The others at the table chuckled at that, but Peggy looked up at her man with such loving adoration it twisted a dagger of lonely disappointment in Bret's gut.

They spent the rest of lunch chatting about the day's work, and Jake seemed to have let his questions go, and Bret silently thanked his good luck for returning, if only briefly.

Autumn was a busy time of year and the next couple of weeks were spent gathering the various crop harvests. A host of kitchen staff and other volunteers canned fruits and vegetables from their flourishing gardens for use over the cold season, while others began preparing for the winter gardens. Amid this bustle, August passed into September without much fanfare as their seasonal work continued.

The next task on Bret's list was to bring in the cattle for winter. They planned to attend an auction in early November and they needed to prepare for the winter calving as well. The barns and new corral they'd started last spring were ready and all of the most experienced riders worked to move the animals from the hills into pastures closer to the homestead.

Shortly after they'd begun the cattle roundup, Bret had a suspicion that several head were missing. Further investigation had proven him right. Upon their return to the house, Bret informed Angel that repairs on the downed fences they'd found were underway and the workers would return after lunch.

"I want to take Dean and Theo out with me when I go to check the adjoining pastures," he said once his report wound down.

"All right, but guards will need to go with you. In case anyone…shows up," Angel replied.

He'd caught the slight hesitation, but, though not crazy about the idea—technically the job only required one or two at the most—Bret didn't argue.

He had wanted to take Jake with him to check on the fences, but when Bret brought up Jake joining the round-up that morning, Jake had declined. He'd claimed he needed to prepare for his upcoming stay with Monica, and then his cryptic allusion to "other duties" had made Bret curious.

"All you have to worry about right now is the new housing construction," he told Jake, "and that's nearly done. They can survive without you for a day or two, and the barracks will still be finished before the weather changes."

"I'm not going, Bret."

"Give me one good reason why you can't come along to help. Is it because Monica will be stopping by and you'll have our room all to yourself for a couple nights?" Bret asked with a crooked grin, probing the way only a long-time-best-friend can.

"No," Jake snapped. "She has as much work as we do right now."

Bret wasn't deterred by Jake's irritable response and, after suffering through several minutes of needling inquiries, Jake had finally revealed his reasons.

"I'm worried about Angel, all right? She's not doing well and her mood's getting worse."

Bret sobered abruptly and refrained from further questions.

After lunch, Bret, Dean, Theo, and Sam—a tall, black-haired, brown-eyed leader among the guards—gathered the things they would need for an overnight stay in the wild before heading out again.

They were in the midst of Indian summer, and the days were warmer than usual for September as the riders came across another long length of downed fence line.

"Why the hell did they cut so many lines?" Dean Williams grumbled aloud late on their second day.

"No reason I can see," Bret replied, wondering the same thing. "Maybe they just wanted to make more work for us."

"Looks like they drove off a few head," Theo commented some yards away.

"Yeah," Bret agreed, seeing the trail heading away from the pasture. "About a week ago from the look of the tracks."

"Maybe they meant to come back for more," Theo said.

Bret shook his head. "Don't think so. Not their normal routine."

Dean pulled off his hat to run his fingers through his dark, sweat-dampened hair. "Might've figured the others would wander off. Head up into the hills where they could pick 'em up later."

"Could be," Bret said. "Lucky for us the animals mostly stayed close by." He sat studying the trail a minute more before he spoke again. "Why don't you two gather the supplies from the line-shed and get started on the repairs. I want to check out the trail and gather any strays."

"Not by yourself, you won't," Sam, who Bret had begun to think of as his own personal watchdog, said. "I'll be coming with you."

"Suit yourself," Bret muttered as he turned his horse to track the missing cattle's route.

The rustlers didn't bother to hide the direction they had traveled. They'd headed west and a little south, straight into the mountains.

"We need to head back," Sam said as Bret stared at the tall, bluish peaks in the distance. "We're getting too close to the edge of Angel's property. I don't know about you, but I don't feel like dealing with the Section Guards today."

Bret glanced at her then returned his gaze to the distant, snow-topped crests. "Yeah, all right," he said, not wanting trouble with the strange guards, either.

Upon their return, they drove the few strays they came across through the gaping hole in the fence line Dean and Theo were working to close, but Bret went through the motions with half a mind. The other half kept turning over the convenient timing of this most recent raid. The schedule to move these animals had been set for next week. This, and the fact the rustlers got away cleanly once again, meant either someone had exceedingly good luck or they knew the ranch's schedule. Someone had to be feeding them information. His thoughts flashed back to the stranger he'd seen slinking around the homestead grounds in the middle of the night last June and then the shadow of a second person that Bret had seen sneaking in Angel's front door a short time later.

Whatever's going on, he told himself, *soon it won't be my problem anymore. I'll be gone, and on my own again.* He felt a little guilty about that. Not the running part, the leaving a mess for Jake part. But Bret couldn't stay, he had to escape. Besides, Bret didn't think they'd be returning anytime soon, especially not after the haul they'd made on this trip.

"Looks like we're going to be out here a while," Bret said, wiping sweat from his forehead with his arm. "I need one of you to ride back to let Angel know we'll be staying out another night and to send some hands out in the morning to help with rounding up strays and fixing the fence." His gaze pointedly settled on Sam.

"Don't look at me," she said. "If you all are out here, so am I."

"I'll go," Theo volunteered. "I don't like leaving Peggy alone too long with the baby coming."

Bret glanced at Sam, but she only shrugged. She knew as well as everyone else that Theo wouldn't go anywhere without Peggy or their future child. Sam's reaction also reinforced Bret's suspicion that her orders were to watch Bret above the other two.

"It'll be dark before you get there," Bret told Theo, "so be careful. I don't want you or your horse to get hurt."

* * *

The workers Bret had requested arrived early the next morning. With the extra help, they quickly finished the repairs, moved the cattle, and returned home before lunch. Unfortunately, being back on the homestead also meant reporting the incident to Angel directly and getting her approval for the next step of his plan.

"I want to check the rest of the pastures for signs of trespass and do a headcount," Bret said when Angel came to the barn to check in with him.

"I'm sure there are others who could do that." The wariness of her tone contradicted the relief Bret had thought he saw on her face when they rode in.

Stop worrying about her moods, he told himself. *It's time to go!*

"Aside from Dean and Jake, no, there isn't," Bret replied. "Dean's been out with me the last two nights and Jake has…his own duties. Looking after the cattle is my responsibility, and I'm the best person to do the job."

Angel glanced at Sam, who was in the stall across the aisle unsaddling her horse. He assumed Angel was looking to get Sam's opinion about his request, or maybe to determine Bret's trustworthiness, he wasn't sure. But Sam merely shrugged and said, "He did a great job out there. He knows what needs to be done."

Angel's stiff stance relaxed and he sensed her resistance fading, but that didn't stop her from voicing a few more minor arguments, all of which Bret easily countered.

Finally, hesitantly, she agreed, but with one last warning. "The Section Guards are not supposed to be on my property, but they sometimes travel the outlying areas despite my objections. We are *always* monitored. If any of them should come across you out there alone, they might think you're trying to escape and hurt you before bringing you back. So, be sure not to ride beyond my property lines."

He nodded his understanding, but, despite Angel's warning, and her trust in him, he intended to take advantage of the opportunity.

* * *

Bret rolled out of bed before sunrise the next morning. Being careful not to wake Jake, he quickly gathered his belongings and began to dress.

Unexpectedly, Jake's voice broke through the gloom. "Getting an early start?"

Bret's heart nearly jumped out of his chest at the sudden sound. He glanced up from his saddlebags and found his friend watching him. The tenseness in his shoulders and around his chest increased. Jake was the last person he'd wanted to talk to this morning.

Sighing, Bret quickly refocusing on checking his provisions. "Yeah," he grumbled, not wanting to say too much to the man who knew him so well.

"Taking an awful lot of stuff for a day or two trip aren't you?" Jake's tone rang with suspicion, and Bret knew Jake had guessed his intentions.

Damn it! So much for keeping Jake in the dark.

Without looking up again, Bret replied, "I like to be prepared."

An uneasy silence fell, and Bret tried to hurry without appearing to do so. The last thing he wanted or had time for was a drawn-out argument with Jake.

"Where will you go?" Jake's abrupt question stopped Bret mid-motion and drew his frowning gaze to his oldest friend.

"What?"

"You're running," Jake said as if he'd known it all along, "and you're not coming back. So, where will you go?"

Bret stared, several excuses and false rebuttals running through his mind, but knowing he'd never fool Jake, Bret's shoulders slumped. "How did you know?"

"We've been friends a long time, Bret, and though you have your secrets, I can read you like a book. You've been hiding something for several weeks."

Uncertain what to say to that, Bret said nothing at all. Instead, he watched his friend from the corner of his eye while he finished his task.

"You've also been avoiding Angel," Jake said, "and she's been doing the same to you. What's up with that?"

Bret stopped as his gaze locked with his friend's pointed stare. He intentionally kept his answer short. "We had a disagreement. It's not a big deal."

"You two do that a lot." Jake sat up and propped his pillows against the headboard and leaned back against them. He crossed his burly arms over his furred chest and observed his friend with a critical eye.

"Yeah," Bret said as he went back to his bags, but he couldn't shake the feeling that Jake knew there was more to his reason for escaping than his aversion to slavery. Then he surprised himself with a question of his own. "What's wrong with her?"

Jake frowned at the concern evident in his question, but Bret couldn't help that. Before he left, a deep part of him wanted to know why Angel was so depressed.

Jake didn't answer right off, only staring at him long enough to make Bret uncomfortable.

Did Angel tell him about the kisses we shared? Bret wasn't sure why that thought bothered him.

"You noticed," Jake said.

"Kind of hard not to. She's been moodier than usual, not her normal independent self at all."

Jake looked away and sighed. Sadness and worry filled his hazel eyes when he turned to Bret once more. "Do you remember the promise you made to me about looking after Angel before you left on the cattle drive last June?"

A jolt of anxiety rocketed through Bret. *Is he going to demand I stay to keep a ridiculous promise that he tricked me into?*

"Yeah, I remember."

"Do you remember why?"

"Something about her being sick, but she was fine. What does that have to do with this?"

"I said she's not well," Jake corrected, "and she's not. The worst of it is just starting, which is why I was hoping you'd grow to like it here."

Bret sighed but said nothing. Why should Angel's moods have

anything to do with him?

"But I see now," Jake said sadly, "your opinion hasn't changed. So, back to my first question. Where will you go?"

Bret stared at him, stunned Jake would let him off the hook so easily. He wanted to tell his friend everything, but how far could he trust Jake?

Still fighting with the strong desire to confide in his friend, he hesitated.

"I'm still your friend, Bret. Whatever your plans, and despite my better judgment, I'll keep your secret."

Bret's heart leaped at that and, knowing Jake wouldn't say that if it wasn't true, he blurted out the news he'd been holding back for weeks. "I know where the rebels are."

"How do you know that?"

Bret grinned as he closed and secured the flaps on his bags. Then he sat on the edge of his bed, brushing off the oddly forceful tone in Jake's voice as long-time mutual interest.

"When Angel and I went riding before her party..." he said and then paused. He couldn't tell Jake the whole story. If he did, he'd have to reveal what had happened to Angel. Bret had given her his word to keep the details of that incident a secret, and his honor required him not to break his promise, no matter what may have happened since.

"I met a guy in the forest," he said, hoping his alteration of the events sounded believable, "when I went to get the horses."

"Where were the horses?" Jake asked and Bret realized he started in the middle.

He explained about the luncheon at the river and where they'd left the horses to graze. Then Bret fabricated a tale about how a strange man had appeared while Bret was alone with the horses.

"The man knew the whereabouts of the base," Bret said, excitement prickling his skin. "He wanted me to come with him, but I didn't want to leave Angel out there alone without a horse."

"Hmm...unusually kind of you." Jake's sarcasm wiggled under Bret's skin.

"What does *that* mean?"

"Just that I know how long you've been looking for the rebels and what joining their ranks means to you. I also know she's not your favorite person. So, why would you pass up such a great opportunity?"

Bret silently cursed himself. He'd given away more than he intended, but he couldn't change it now. He didn't want to anyway.

"I don't hate her, Jake. I just don't like what she did to me." He silently acknowledged the last to be true on several levels as an image of Angel, naked and beautiful, lying open and yielding under his gaze popped into his head. He quickly pushed it away.

"What did she do?"

Jake's suspicious tone raked at Bret, and he replied more harshly than intended. "She made me a slave. I can't forgive that."

"She saved your life, you jackass!" Jake shouted, and then visibly took control of himself. "But then, you've always valued your freedom more than anything else."

"You're angry with me for wanting to leave." It was not a question.

"No, Bret, just disappointed. I had hoped we could make a life here like we once had, but I see I was wrong."

They sat without speaking for several long seconds, the tension between them like a physical barrier pushing them apart.

Bret hated that.

Hated the thought of losing his best friend all over again.

Hated worse the damage another woman had caused to their bond.

"I hope whatever you find out there will finally make you happy, Bret."

He didn't reply immediately, weighing his next words with caution. "Why don't you come with me, Jake? I could tell Angel I need your help and we—"

Jake shook his head and interrupted what remained of Bret's statement. "No," he said in a hard, flat tone, "I have to stay. She needs me, especially now."

"Why now?" Bret asked.

"It doesn't matter," Jake said. "I have other reasons to stay."

"Like what? That pretty little blonde who was here for the party? What was her name?"

"Her name is Monica, and, yes, she's the other reason. I get that you don't understand that, so don't bother with the lecture."

Bret's throat tightened, and his tattered heart felt like lead in his chest.

"What makes you think I don't understand? I know what loneliness feels like, Jake. I also know what a pretty woman can do to your head."

"Or to *better* your life," Jake said and Bret didn't miss the emphasis on the third word. "I can appreciate your experiences with women haven't always been what you hoped for, Bret, but you can't shut yourself off, either."

"I'm not." Bret sounded defensive, even to himself, and when he glanced at Jake's disbelieving face, he couldn't help but laugh. "Okay, maybe a little, but I don't expect you to do the same. If Monica makes you happy, then I'm glad for you. You should stay, but if you change your mind, you know where to find me."

Jake's eyes had widened slightly, but by the end of Bret's comment, he smiled. "And if you change yours, you can come back."

"Right, and what will *she* do to me if I do? I shudder to think of it." Bret lifted his shoulders and shivered dramatically.

Jake ignored his friend's theatrics. "Angel would have to do *something*, but she'd never hurt you. She might have you confined for a while, but she'd never torture you like others would."

"Good to know, Jake, but I'm not coming back."

Another long pause ensued.

Bret wondered if Jake shared his growing fear that their separation would be longer than the last. It had taken five years for them to be reunited. Now, Bret was planning to leave his best friend behind again. Jake had other interests now, and Bret didn't want to fall into the same trap. But, he couldn't help trying one last time. "I still wish you'd come with me."

"I know."

There was nothing else to say.

Bret stood and hefted his bags over his shoulder as he made his way to the outside door. Despite the low light, he could see his friend clearly and understood that Jake didn't want him to go any more than Bret wanted to leave Jake behind. It cheered his heart a little to realize their bond was still so strong.

"Goodbye, Bret," Jake said quietly, "and good luck!"

"Yeah, thanks. You take care of yourself, Jake."

They exchanged unhappy smiles, but no matter how much it hurt to say goodbye, Bret would not pass up this golden opportunity. He would escape, he would be free again, and this time, no one would stop him.

3

BRET SAT ON HIS HORSE, staring across the rolling hills to the distant mountains, the hot mid-September sun beating down on his head and shoulders. He'd spent most of the morning and into the afternoon wandering well within the boundaries of Angel's property, putting off the next leg of his journey. The area he traveled consisted of long, thin ranks of evergreens and wide, open areas with nothing but dry, sandy ground, covered in sagebrush, rocks, and prickly weeds. His neck prickled with unease and he rubbed at the sensation with one hand, feeling horribly exposed passing through the treeless sections. The main body of the forest lay ahead and to the west, and, even though this was the shortest path to his destination, he still had a long way to go.

Technically, he was still on Angel's land, but that didn't stop the nervous sweat from covering his body. Once he left the boundary of her ranch, he'd always be in danger. Jake's warnings and stories had come back to haunt him ever since he rode away from the homestead, but as long as he stood on Angel's property, no one could harm him; he was safe.

The fact that he found himself yearning for safety irked him. Since when did he start playing it safe? Freedom was worth any cost. Even becoming a fugitive was better than living as a slave. At least, that's what he kept telling himself.

He heaved a frustrated sigh and removed his hat. All this indecision was going to cause him trouble later. Using the sleeve of his shirt, he wiped the sweat off his face. He pulled the hat low over his eye again and took up the reins.

Safe, he thought again. Not a word he readily associated with himself, but after all that had happened to him thus far, his apprehension was understandable. Though that didn't make it any easier to accept. Yet, he couldn't deny the other reason for his uncertainty.

Angel was a hurdle he had to get over. She'd gotten into his head and now she wouldn't leave. Something had brought them together the night of her party, and it wasn't just loneliness.

Horniness is more like it, he thought bitterly, but that wasn't entirely true, either. Something special had passed between them when they'd made love. He'd felt it, and he couldn't get it out of his head. He had to get away from her before anything more—anything worse, if that was possible—came from their proximity. Preferably, before his heart led him astray once more.

He reached the border of Angel's property shortly after dark and camped beside a small river, intending to wake early and cross over. Lying in his bedroll listening to the gurgling water, his anxiety returned, keeping him from sleep. He tried going over his planned route into the mountains and how he was going to find the rebel base, but that only heightened his nervousness.

As the darkness deepened, his mind slowly drifted and he thought of the people he'd left behind. Guilt tugged at his heart for those he'd gotten to know—his friends and the kids; one little boy in particular. Bret had promised an eight-year-old named Gavin that nothing would ever happen to him. That he would make sure Gavin was safe, but Bret couldn't do that now. He told himself that Angel would ensure their care, but he couldn't help wondering if he was wrong about that nor could he get Gavin's teary-eyed gaze and terrified voice out of his head. Disappointing the child by breaking his word rankled, especially as he'd never done it before, but at this point, in this world, what other choice did he have?

Bret grumbled to himself, adjusting his blanket and forcing his mind to the next day's plans.

They weren't expecting him back at the Lazy A until late tomorrow afternoon, and he had followed a different route than the one he'd told them he would, so there was plenty of time to flee in the morning. He had nothing to worry about.

He rolled onto his back for the third time, not sure if he actually believed that. Several minutes passed as he lay with his eyes closed, trying to relax and not think, until, eventually, the bubbling of the slow-moving river finally soothed his jagged nerves and lulled him into a restless sleep.

The sun was already up when he woke the next morning. It was unusual for him to sleep so late. Cursing himself and his luck, he quickly rolled out of his blankets, pulled on his boots, and began to gather up his small camp. Once everything was packed and his saddle was secured to the gelding's back, Bret refilled his canteen at the river. Capping and setting it aside, he braced his hands on the bank and dunked his head under the surface. Sitting up a moment later, he released his breath with a groan for the chill of the water. It definitely helped clear the fuzziness lingering around the edges of his thoughts and cooled his already overheated skin, but the cold made his head ache.

Crouching on the riverbank with his arms dangling over his knees and water dribbling down his neck dampening his blue shirt, Bret stared out across the rolling hills to the distinctive, white-tipped mountain in the distance. At a modest pace, he estimated he'd be well into the forested foothills by afternoon.

Suddenly in a hurry to be on his way, he grabbed his canteen and stood.

He stopped cold when he turned around and an electric jolt of fear crackled through his body like lightning.

Not more than thirty feet away, four riders were sitting on their horses watching him. They were strangers, and he assumed they must be the Section Guards he'd heard so much about. Apparently, Angel had been right about them patrolling her property.

Bret's gaze flicked to where his gelding stood waiting for him to mount. Maybe he could make it to Smoke's back and outrun the guards.

He let that idea go. The horse was too far away; the guards would be on him before he could reach the animal. Besides, if he tried and failed, they'd know he'd been planning to escape. It was too late to consider fleeing now. All he could do was try to charm his way out of this. Luckily, he was still on Angel's land, and she'd been the one to send him searching for missing cattle.

He grinned despite the fear chilling his bones as the four women urged their mounts forward. As they approached, he recognized the black eyes and brunette hair of the lead rider. He'd never learned her name, but she was the same woman who had beaten him for trying to escape the Auction Hall before he was sold.

He swallowed mechanically and waited, the sound of his heartbeat thumping in his ears.

"Bret Masters," she said in a saccharine tone, but he knew better than to drop his guard, "what are you doing way out here?" She paused and glanced around. "And all alone, too?"

"Looking for strays," he replied, ignoring the rest of her comments.

She looked him up and down with the cold appraisal used by nearly every woman at the Action Hall. It irritated him no less now than it did when he'd been under their control.

"Oh, really?" she asked, again in the too-sweet voice. She dismounted, followed closely by her three escorts, and they walked deliberately toward him. The three other women stopped about six feet away, but the leader continued forward to circle him slowly.

He stood motionless, the heat from the sun and his internal anxiety caused his body temperature to skyrocket.

"Does Aldridge know you're out here?" the woman asked from behind him.

"Yes," he said and was unexpectedly shoved. He stumbled forward and landed on his hands and knees. Grinding his teeth, he started to rise, but the stranger's hand on his shoulder stopped him.

"Don't stand, *fibber*," she hissed in his ear. "I like you better on your knees."

Trembling with rage at the humiliation, Bret suppressed the urge to respond. He had gotten used to the modicum of control he'd gained in his life and didn't like being at their mercy again. On his own out here with no one to help him, they could torture him for entertainment or simply kill him outright and leave his body for the coyotes. No one would know what had happened.

If he disobeyed her commands, his fate seemed inevitable; he remained on his knees.

"Know what I think?" the woman asked as she paced in front of him.

He didn't reply, but his input apparently wasn't necessary.

"I think you're trying to escape again," the stranger told him and then stopped abruptly and turned toward him. "Am I wrong?"

Bret didn't miss the challenge in her words or the cruelty in her eyes.

"Angel sent me out to look for missing cattle," he said carefully, avoiding the woman's glare. "I'm out here by her instruction."

"This far?" She scoffed. "I doubt it. Aldridge is soft, but she's not stupid." She paused to glare at him again. "I think you found another opportunity to run. You took advantage of it and her plainly misplaced trust in you."

Guilt flared to life in his belly once again, gnawing at him. For some reason, he felt bad about breaking Angel's trust, and, strangely, that eclipsed most of his fear for the precarious position he found himself in.

"Well?" the leaders asked, hovering over him when he made no effort to respond.

"You're wrong," he said, and she rewarded him with an open-handed strike that knocked him to the ground. His cheek burned from the impact and he worked his jaw slightly as he lay in the dirt. He'd obviously misjudged her mood. The power behind that slap revealed her fury.

"You're lying!" she screamed as he rubbed at his face. "Men like you are all the same…conniving liars. Now, tell me the truth! What are you doing way out here?"

"I told you the truth," he said, meeting her gaze. This woman would never believe him, and he refused to give her the satisfaction of knowing she'd caught him twice.

"We'll have to work on that stubborn streak of yours," she said. "You *are* lying. No woman, not even Angel Aldridge, would be foolish enough to send a man out here all alone. Even the most devoted slave might think about never going back, and you are *not* devoted."

He lowered his eyes, concealing his anger.

"Take off your boots," she ordered.

He frowned and looked up again. "What?"

"You heard me, and your socks too."

He paused, trying to determine what she was planning to do. Maybe she planned to repeat the last beating she'd given him or maybe something worse. It didn't really matter at this point; there was no way he could avoid whatever she intended to do. He didn't want to make things worse for himself, so he complied with her orders.

When his feet were bare, she smiled. "Now, remove your shirt. I want you bare-chested too."

He frowned again, but complied, wondering if she would force him to strip naked. When he was sitting in the dirt, wearing nothing but his jeans, he watched silently as one of the guards gathered his belongings and packed them away in his saddlebags, secured his hat to his saddle, and took up the reins.

"Back on your knees," the leader ordered, and Bret did as he was told.

A second guard came to him carrying his lariat in her hand. The woman ordered him to hold his arms out in front of him and then tightly tied his wrists together. She tested the knot with a rough tug that dug into his flesh and made him wince. Satisfied, she handed the other end to the leader.

"What're you going to do with me?" he asked as the leader mounted, the rope attached to his wrists trailing on the ground.

"You'll know soon enough," she told him, taking the slack out of the line. "Now, keep quiet and get on your feet." She jerked on the rope and then gave him another terse order. "Walk."

"You want me to *walk* all the way back to the homestead?" he asked incredulously.

"Yep."

"But it's miles from here, at least give me back my boots."

"No," she said with a quick glance over her shoulder. "If you're going to lie, you're going to be punished."

"But I didn't—"

She cut his protest short, pulling the rope taut and yanking him off his feet. He landed hard on his knees and then sprawled face-first in the dirt.

"Walk!" she barked again, kicking her horse into motion.

Knowing she would happily drag him if he didn't, Bret hustled to his feet. It would take several hours to walk back, if not all day, but Bret suspected this woman had more plans for him. He didn't expect they'd arrive at Angel's house until sometime tomorrow. But those were worries for later. For now, he had to concentrate on staying on his feet.

The sudden thought of how Angel would react to his return and the news of where he'd been popped into his head. He banished it as soon as it appeared. Angel was the last thing he needed to worry about, but he couldn't banish the guilt as easily. She would be upset, but as far as he was concerned, she had no right to be surprised.

4

ANGEL STOOD BAREFOOT on the deck outside her bedroom, still dressed in the white shorts and blue T-shirt she'd worn all day. The sun had set in magnificent pink and purple fashion, with the fluffy white clouds looking like huge balls of cotton dotting the indigo sky. Darkness had long since fallen. A breeze now rustled the trees surrounding her home, and the once warm evening had cooled to an autumn chill.

Even so, Angel remained on the deck, hugging herself and shivering. She should get ready for bed, should already be in bed, but her concern for Bret kept her outside, hoping to catch a glimpse of his return. He should have been back that afternoon and she was worried. This trip would've been the perfect opportunity for him to escape, but she didn't want to jump to conclusions.

Not yet.

The thought that he might not return bothered her more than it should, and she couldn't get the idea that he'd run away out of her head.

I should've gone with him, she thought. Considering what had happened between them and the hurt she'd caused him, she shouldn't have let him out of her sight or should've at least sent a guard along to make sure he didn't stray.

She'd let her guard down the night of her party. Taken everything he had freely offered and loved it all. But when reality struck the next morning and her monumental lapse in judgment crashed into her mind, she'd forced him to leave when he clearly meant to stay.

Her heart ached with the memory of the pain she'd seen in his eyes when he walked out.

Once he left, she had cried for hours as every tiny detail of what had transpired between them the night before played on repeat in her mind. Even now, the memory of how good Bret's touch, his kiss, his everything had felt, stirred her blood, but it also terrified her. Caring too much was dangerous, but the way she reacted made her more than a little ashamed of herself. After all, she'd started the whole mess by telling Bret she wanted him and following that up with a kiss. A hot, bone-melting, forbiddingly-erotic kiss that she'll never forget, no matter how hard she tried.

At the time, she had meant every word and deed. But now, she felt more than guilty for all of it. She had no right to endanger him or to risk all she'd built and everyone else there just because she was overly attracted to him. Nor was it right to give him the impression that there could ever be anything between them, which, she had no doubt, was exactly what he'd been thinking. She hadn't expected Bret would want that, but then, what had she expected? With his background, his anger shouldn't have surprised her. She should've been more shocked by her own behavior and stopped it before making a ridiculous fool of herself.

Not only all that, but the fact that she'd sworn to herself over Michael's grave that she would never get involved with another man.

"Oh, Michael..." She sighed and let the memories of Michael and the first time they met fill her mind.

"Hey!" the stranger said as he jumped back, avoiding her teeth when she'd tried to bite him.

"Leave me!" she shouted, straining at the ropes that bound her to the tall tree behind her. "Don't touch me!"

The underbrush that she'd stomped flat since she'd been left here by a raiding party to die, crackled as she shifted her feet, pulling the rope from one side to the other, trying to get enough slack to push him farther back. The quiet buzz of the rope sawing around the back of the tree was a familiar one, but after all her tugging, the damn thing still held. Even the rain that had fallen the night before only hindered her attempts by soaking her to the skin and chilling her bones. It did nothing to loosen the ropes.

"I'm not going to hurt you," the stranger said gently, his dark blue eyes earnest as he once again eased toward her, while the others who'd arrived with him searched through the carnage in the tall grass. "I want to help you, to make things better."

She stared at him wide-eyed with disbelief. Tears streaked through the grime on her face, but she didn't pay them any mind. Three days she'd slumped beside this tree. Three days of stink and despair. And this guy thought he could make it better?

The scent of decomposition no longer burned her nose, but this stranger wrinkled his, wiped his forearm across it to block the smell, and coughed.

Angel laughed at him, at his discomfort, and his foolish beliefs.

"You can't help," she said coldly. "Nothing will ever make it better."

A smile tugged at the corners of his mouth and she lifted her chin, daring him to tell her different.

"Things can always get better," he said and took another step closer. "You just have to let it happen. I'll show you how, if you'll let me."

She snorted and shook her head. Can't he see the destruction around him? Can't he see what she'd lost? That she didn't want to go on?

Suddenly, she was too tired to fight anymore. Too tired to argue. Too tired to even breathe. Let him do what he wants. They were all dead, anyway.

"Just let me die..." she muttered, slumping against the tree and sliding to her knees.

He crouched beside her. "I can't do that..." the man replied with *so much compassion in his quiet voice, her gritty eyes burned and her vision blurred once more.*

"Michael!" someone shouted from a few yards away. "There's another body here."

The man in front of her looked back over his shoulder. "How many have you found?"

"Three, unless there's more farther out...?"

The man, Michael, turned back to her with such a look of concern in his blue gaze that it wrung a sob from her constricted throat.

She shook her head before he could ask about any others.

"That's all of them," he shouted back to his friend. "Get started." His eyes never left her face. Even when she wasn't looking at him, she could feel his gaze. "Did you know these people?"

The quiet question stabbed into her heart and she dropped her chin. "I couldn't save them..." Her voice was nothing but a hoarse whisper.

Michael leaned forward. "What did you say, honey?" The endearment drove the knife deeper. She didn't know him, but he cared. It was in the sound of his voice and his mournful gaze.

She looked up, questioning him with her eyes before she spoke. "Why do you care?" It wasn't a challenge or an accusation, she truly didn't understand why anyone tried anymore.

"Seems to me that you're worth it," he said with a slow grin that eased some of the tension in her body. She dropped her eyes, unable to take his kindness. She didn't deserve it.

He leaned forward and with the knife he'd pulled from its sheath on his belt, he cut the rope that bound her wrists to the tree. Her arms fell to her sides, but she didn't move.

"It also seems to me that these people deserve a proper burial."

Her head snapped up, her shiny eyes wide, but in wonder this time.

He brushed a few strands of her wild hair from her face and for the first time since she'd laid eyes on him and his friends, she really saw him. With his dark-blond curls, a couple days' scruff on his chin, and dark blue eyes, he was handsome in a youthful, beach-bum kind of way. But older too, as if he'd seen too much to be as naive as she'd dubbed him at first.

His hand came to rest on her shoulder, warm and strong, and she liked the feel of it there.

He nodded toward where his three companions had begun digging in the hard mountain soil. "Were they friends of yours?" He ducked his head to draw her eyes back to his when she looked away. "Your family?"

Tears swelled in her eyes, in her throat, in her chest. She'd thought she had cried them all out by now, but a vast sea of them remained.

"We're going to take care of them," Michael said, rubbing her arm consolingly and nodding toward where his friends worked. "And then, we're going to make sure you're okay too. Get you someplace safe and warm."

Anguish tightened her chest, closing her lungs. She tried to hold it all back, the tidal wave of emotion. She tried not to let this good man see just how broken she was, but when his fingers gently wiped the wetness from her cheeks and met her questioning gaze with empathy and more internal strength than she'd ever known, she lost it.

The trembling started in her hands and knees, but quickly spread to the rest of her body. A heavy lump rolled up from her chest, pushed through the barrier in her throat, and a low keening sob ripped from her lips.

"Oh, honey, come here…"

He pulled her against him and she fell into his arms. Fisting her hands into the back of his shirt, she clung to his solid heat, and held on for dear life.

"It's okay…just let it all out. I got you."

He cradled her against his chest and let her cry, continuing to murmur comforting words until she finally wound down to halting breaths and hiccups.

"Feel any better?" he asked and she nodded. The world was still a cheerless, dreary place, but Michael had brought light into her darkness with the warmth of his smile, his quiet sympathy, and his lighthearted, easy manner.

Michael sat beside her as the other men buried her family. His arm stayed around her shoulders, his warmth a balm for the cold inside her, and his strength slowly gave her the courage to face the world again.

When they left that place of death, he'd held her hand. To this day, Angel didn't know if he did it to keep her calm, to let her know she was safe, or just because she wouldn't let him go. She'd been so terrified, and Michael had been her rock.

In time, after months of healing, loving words, and soft caresses, the evil of the world finally caught up with them. When she'd knelt at his grave to make her vow, she did so not only to avoid a repeat of Michael's fate and her pain, but to ensure she finished what she'd promised—to fight from within all those who had destroyed everything she loved and to make changes for the better.

She sighed, stretching her back and arms before folding them over the deck railing again. She looked up at the willow on the hill and felt the pang of regret.

Keeping those promises had meant everything to her and yet, the night of her party, she'd thrown them all away. That was bad enough, but somehow she also kept confusing the love she still had for Michael with the undeniable attraction she felt for another unbelievably handsome man.

Was she that shallow?

She didn't think so, but, if not, why couldn't she stay away from Bret?

In part, the fault for her lack of restraint should fall on Monica and all her absurd suggestions about healing and letting someone in. Angel knew better than to listen to that, but she'd followed Monica's advice anyway. Now, she was burdened with the consequences of her actions. She just hoped Bret wouldn't suffer for her lack of restraint.

A knock on her bedroom door interrupted her dark musing.

"Come in," she called from the deck, glad for the distraction.

Jake poked his head into the room and she smiled. "Hello, Jake."

"Hi," he replied as he entered and closed the door behind him.

"Come, join me." Angel returned to her place on the deck. Jake followed and for several minutes, they stood silently side by side.

"I'm worried about him, Jake," she confessed, tightening her folded arms, while her eyes skimmed the shadows beyond the walls. "I shouldn't have let him go alone."

"Don't worry about Bret. He can take care of himself."

"I know," she said, turning to face him, "but I'm still concerned someone might've done something to him. He may even be hurt somewhere. Anything could've happened."

"And he could've decided to take an extra day," Jake said and something in his voice made her frown.

Was that fear and hesitation she heard? Was Jake lying for his best friend? Did he suspect—or know—what had happened between herself and Bret?

Too afraid to risk exposing what she'd done, Angel let it go.

"Yes, he might have," she said tiredly. "Maybe he'll be back tomorrow."

"Probably."

Jake put his arm around her and she rested her head comfortably on his shoulder.

"You're shivering," he said.

"It's getting cold."

"I think it's time for you to go to bed. Warm-up and get some sleep, and stop worrying. Bret'll be fine. He always is."

She smiled up at him. "Yeah, you're probably right."

He led her back into the bedroom. Angel slumped on the edge of her bed while Jake closed the French doors and drew the long curtains closed. The lamp she'd previously lit on her nightstand was the only illumination in the room.

"You know, Jake," she said sadly as she slipped beneath the covers, unconcerned that she'd never donned her nightclothes, "there are times I wish things could be the way they used to be between men and women."

"I know, honey," he said gently, worry for her shining in his eyes. "Me too."

"It can't be that way anymore."

"No, but we can still try. We don't have to let them take *everything* from us."

She nodded, knowing he referred to women like Darla. Then she frowned. "Do you see me as one of *them*, Jake?"

He paused in tucking the blankets around her to meet her gaze. Again she saw fear and doubt in his eyes and another knot of worry twisted around her heart. Blinking sleepily, she waited for his response, afraid of what he might say.

"No, Angel," he said and his face softened. "You're nothing like them."

"Thank you," she whispered, and tears unexpectedly burned in her eyes. She hid them quickly by turning on her side. She didn't want to explain her strange question or the wetness in her eyes. Thankfully, Jake didn't ask.

"Get some sleep," he said. "Everything'll seem better in the morning."

"Yeah, I know." Though she doubted that would be the case this time.

DOUSING THE LAMP, Jake headed for the door. "Goodnight, Angel."

She mumbled a reply and Jake paused. He hated seeing her deteriorate like this—questioning her role in their lives and talking about the past as if she wanted to slip away into it forever. But he'd known it was inevitable. Though weeks late in coming this time, something painful darkened her moods every autumn. Jake wondered what had held it off for so long. He had hoped that maybe something finally changed. That something unexpected, something bright and powerful had come along to break the dreadful spell. Maybe it wouldn't be as bad this year. Maybe her previous thoughts of death wouldn't assail her as they always had in the past. He could only hope.

Looking back at her, he could just make out her huddled form under the covers on the big bed. She seemed at peace, but he knew deep inside a battle waged, and it would get drastically worse before it was over.

Bret had picked a lousy time to make his getaway. Now, not only was Jake worried about Angel, but about Bret and his safety as well.

Am I doing the right thing? Jake wondered. If anything happened to Bret, he'd never forgive himself. He had a growing suspicion that Angel wouldn't either. From what he'd seen, lying to her was the fastest way to lose her trust and he'd done that, and more.

What a mess. He shook his head sadly as he pulled the door open and quietly left the room.

5

September 20

ANGEL WOKE LATE the next morning to someone knocking loudly on her door while frantically calling her name. She recognized the voice as belonging to Esther, her house cook.

"Come in, Esther," she called tiredly from the warmth of her bed, knowing no one else but Jake or Michelle would enter her room without her permission. The door flew open instantly and Esther rushed in. Her face looked drawn and worried, and her fingers fidgeted with the hem of her gray cardigan, but she didn't immediately speak.

Esther's obvious anxiety drove all the drowsiness from Angel's groggy mind and alarm drew her immediately upright. "What's wrong?"

"Bret's back," Esther finally blurted out and then paused as if unsure how to continue.

"Is he hurt?"

"It's hard to tell," Esther said slowly. "He's not here yet, but my guess would be yes."

"I don't understand," Angel said, confused by the older woman's disjointed information. "What are you trying to tell me?"

"He's with the Section Guards."

Prickles of fear danced down Angel's spine, and she sat a little taller, suddenly understanding Esther's concern. "What did he do?" Angel mumbled to herself.

"Don't know, but I think you'd better come and see. He may need you."

"I'll be right down," she said as she hurriedly got out of bed. "Will you have Michelle meet me in the dooryard and ask her to send one of the other guards to keep Jake out of trouble?"

"Yes," Esther said, dashing out the door as Angel slipped off the wrinkled clothes she'd slept in. She hurriedly ran a brush through her hair and then pulled it back into a curling ponytail. Without looking, she grabbed the nearest thing from her closet and pulled it over her head. A blue, cotton dress, simple and modest, with a button front, cap sleeves, and a back-tie. There was nothing special about it, just an everyday dress, but she paused as she settled it over her hips, unsure if a dress was the best thing to wear when confronting Darla Cain's agents. A second later, she decided time was more of a factor than her appearance. She quickly located a pair of low-backed, slip-on shoes and stepped into them before rushing downstairs.

Angel found Esther and the kitchen staff clustered on the deck as she came out the front door. Many others congregated in the dooryard, including her head guard Michelle.

The deck crowd followed as Angel headed toward the gate with Michelle at her side. They reached the end of the bunkhouse just in time to see four riders pass through the homestead's open gates. Confused when she couldn't locate Bret among the group, Angel turned a questioning glance to the taller woman beside her. Michelle simply frowned and shook her head slightly. She didn't see Bret either.

Angel watched the riders advance, chest tight, her heart in her throat, when Jake, who'd exited one of the barns and was much closer, started toward the riders alone. He glanced at her and she shook her head. She didn't know what was going on just yet, and she didn't want him in the middle of it.

Jake took her warning and paused no less than ten yards from the visitors. Anyone who didn't know him would think him calm, but his powerful stance and the severe frown that wrinkled his brow disclosed to Angel the extent of his fear and agitation. A few seconds later, one of Angel's guards hurried to his side as Jake turned a worried frown Angel's way. A similar look from the guard beside him followed, increasing the heavy weight of dread already bowing Angel's shoulders. She'd intended to make the Section Guards come to her, but the look on Jake's face so alarmed her that she started forward again with Michelle right beside her.

The riders were still some distance from her when Angel finally caught a glimpse of Bret. He staggered along behind the leader's horse, his hands tied in front of him, the taut line gripped firmly in the leader's hands. Shirtless and covered in dirt and what looked like blood, his jeans were torn at the knees, and several other places too, and his boots appeared to be missing. Angel's breath caught in her throat, paralyzed by stunned horror when Bret stumbled and sprawled forward. The woman leading him didn't halt, she didn't even look back, just held tightly to the rope wrapped securely around the pommel of her saddle and kept riding, dragging Bret over the rough ground.

"Stop!" Angel yelled as she hurried toward them, waving toward the guard beside Jake, who was much closer, to intervene. Instead, Jake hurried forward and reached them a minute or so before Angel and Michelle.

"Let go of that bridle or I'll beat you myself!" Angel overheard the Section Guard threaten Jake.

"Oh, no, you won't," Angel said as she reached up and jerked the rope out of the other woman's hands. The guard had been tugging on it, hindering Bret's efforts to stand. Which, Angel suspected, was what the woman had intended—to hurt and humiliate him as much as possible. "What the hell do you think you're doing?" Her tone was vehement.

"You should keep better track of your slaves, Aldridge," the woman on the horse said, seemingly undisturbed by Angel's anger. She jerked her thumb in Bret's direction. "We caught this one on the edge of your land, preparing to head into the hills…" she gave a short description of the location. "Did you forget he's already tried to escape once?"

"No, I didn't," Angel hissed.

Out of the corner of her eye, Angel saw Bret stagger to his feet, then stand tall and motionless, trying to catch his breath. She looked him over, taking in the long, dark bruise on his right cheek and the stream of blood oozing from a gash in his scalp. The blood covered the right side of his face and dribbled down his neck to his chest. Several other signs that they had beaten him further were evident, but she didn't take the time to catalog them all. She met his gaze briefly and read what she had feared to find in his green eyes.

He'd tried to run! And now he dared to stare her down with a lazy smirk that said he didn't care what she thought or how she felt.

Angel was suddenly so angry with him, she couldn't react. Then she wanted to scream that he was an arrogant, selfish idiot but held it in. Anything she had to say to him had to wait until they were alone. Instead, she turned her fury on a no-less-deserving target.

"He had some excuse, but I knew better," the Section Guard leader said, but she stopped when Angel turned livid sapphire eyes on her.

"What did you know?" she asked in a low, menacing voice.

"That he was lying, of course."

"Whether he was or not," Angel said, "you had no right to touch him, let alone *beat him* without my permission. And what if he'd been telling the truth?" Angel began coiling the rope, gripping it tightly in her hands to keep from dragging the other woman from her saddle.

"Looking for cattle? Way out there?" the leader asked incredulously. "Come on, Angel, I'm not stupid."

"Guess again," Angel said, glaring darkly at the woman, who scowled at the slur. "A lot of my cattle have gone missing in the last year and they've started disappearing again. I sent him out there to check the fences and to look for strays."

The guard's superior expression slowly changed to doubt.

"So," Angel went on, "next time, mind your own damn business and stay the hell off my land! I've warned you people about that before. I will file another complaint and, this time, I'll require recompense for your actions."

"Whether you want to believe it or not, he was planning to run," the leader said, not willing to allow that point to be ignored. "You may have sent him out there looking for cattle, but we both know he had other plans, and you should punish him for it."

Angel glared up at the other woman until she squirmed. Heat and fury pulsed through Angel's veins, but whether because of the woman's callous actions or Bret's, she wasn't sure. She felt the eyes of every member of her ranch drilling into her back, wondering what she would do. She should do something if the accusations were true—and they were, the look in Bret's eyes told her that—but she wasn't about to let them beat him again.

"Don't tell me my business," she said quietly, then raised her voice. "As for punishment," she glanced over at Bret, her eyes sliding over him from head to toe, and then back to the woman on the horse, "*if* it was deserved, I think you've done more than enough for both of us. Now, get out of here before I have you thrown out!" She turned to her guards. "Be sure to get his horse and clothing back and make sure they leave immediately. If anything is missing, note it so I can add it to my complaint."

"Yes, ma'am," Michelle and her assistant, Sam—a tall, black-haired woman, the opposite of Michelle's pale beauty—replied with matching grim smiles. Angel held her breath as they turned to the Section Guards. A formidable-looking Michelle waved a hand toward the open gates behind them and said, "After you, ladies."

6

Angel watched the riders start out the gates, then turned her eyes on Bret. She hid the hurt squeezing her heart as she ran her angry gaze over him before she started for the house. Using the rope to lead Bret back, Angel was both relieved and surprised that he complied without resistance.

Part of her was furious that Bret would try to run, but then again, she should've known he would. He'd never made a secret about his desire for freedom or the fact that he'd intended to run. After what had transpired between them, it made sense that he would want to escape even more. Still, his selfishness could harm every person living on the ranch, not just Angel.

She met Jake's gaze as they marched across the dooryard. He blinked once, apparently reading the conflicting emotions on her face, and fell in line to tag along. She knew he wanted to defuse this situation before it exploded, even if he had to take a large portion of the blame himself. Thankfully, he remained silent until they could speak alone.

They finally reached the door leading into the men's apartment at the house and Jake moved to follow them inside. But after Angel unceremoniously forced Bret inside, she turned and blocked the doorway with her body, effectively stopping Jake on the threshold.

"Did you know about this?" she asked Jake, her eyes intent on his face.

"Leave him out of this," Bret said from inside. "He doesn't know anything."

Angel glanced over her shoulder at him. "Why should I believe you? You've already lied to me. I'll deal with you in a minute."

"It's all right, Bret," Jake said.

"Not this time, Jake. You can't smooth this over for him. Wait outside, I'll handle this alone." With that, she closed the door in his face, not allowing him to answer her question or offer further comment. She didn't want to hear that he had deceived her as well.

She took a deep breath before she turned to face Bret. His disheveled state struck her again, tugging at her heart. She couldn't *leave* him like that. Dropping the coiled rope onto the floor, she went to the small bathroom near the kitchen door. She came out a minute later with a wet towel and tossed it at him.

"Clean yourself up," she said coldly and watched as he wiped blood and dirt from his face, chest, and arms as best he could while still being tied. She waited, gathering the rope into her hands again; some of her resentment over his lies diminished as she observed his injuries. His wrists were raw and bloody, and he moved as if his arms pained him. Yet, when he took his time wiping himself clean—his way of telling her that she held no control over him—her irritation returned. When he continued to linger overlong in his task, she swiftly yanked the towel out of his hands and threw it in a heap near the door. Turning back to him, she saw his smirk and her anger returned in full force.

"What the hell were you doing way out there?" she demanded.

"Like you said, looking for cattle."

"That's crap!" she shouted, unconsciously pulling on the rope that bound his wrists. He grimaced slightly but said nothing. "We both know that area has been checked and monitored constantly. You *were* trying to run, weren't you?"

BRET DIDN'T ANSWER, only stared back at her evenly. He didn't owe her anything after the way she'd treated him, and he'd never kept his intention a secret.

"Answer me!" She jerked the rope again, much harder this time, and he collapsed onto his knees with a grunt of pain.

"Damn it!" he growled. "You know that's what I was doing. Do whatever you're going to do to me, but stop jerking me around!" His wrists and arms hurt far more than he'd intended to disclose, but that last tug had been hard. She obviously hadn't realized the amount of force she'd used, but he didn't care about that. He just wanted to get this confrontation over with so he could get away from her.

Angel glanced at his badly chafed wrists and her face softened. "I didn't mean to hurt you," she said quietly with an abortive move forward, but then her hand dropped to her side without touching him. "Why did you do this? I trusted you."

"Now you know better," he scoffed, glancing up with a nasty half-smile.

"Damn it, Bret!" It was her turn to be frustrated. "Why do you try so hard to make me believe you're nothing more than a callous ass?"

"I don't care what you think of me."

She stared at him. "I don't believe you."

"Suit yourself," he said with a shrug, "but if you must know, you're the reason I ran. I wanted to get away from this comfy prison of yours, and as far from you as possible." He saw the hurt in her eyes, but he refused to back down. He wouldn't let her in again.

"If they had caught you off my land they could have done much worse, don't you realize that?"

"It was worth it to be free."

"But now you're beaten and tied, which doesn't sound free to me."

He didn't respond.

"Don't you understand that you've had as much freedom here as you're ever going to get in this world? At least for the time being."

"I don't want your fake freedom."

"Fake, huh?"

"Yeah."

"Someday you should ask Jake what would happen if you'd ended up almost anywhere else."

"Anywhere else would be the same," he said bitterly, "head games and power trips."

"You think that's what I do?" she asked, her voice unsteady. "And what we did together…? That was a game too?"

Her reference to the night they'd shared after her birthday party made his stomach clench. He straightened his spine. *How dare she bring that up!*

"Yes," he said after only the slightest hesitation.

She gazed at him disbelievingly, almost seeming to deflate as some other strange emotion he couldn't quite define burned in her eyes. "I see," she whispered and dropped her gaze. She struggled with something for a moment before she met his stare again. "Maybe it's time you did, too." Her eyes searched the room, not expecting or requiring a response, but Bret was curious what her words meant. Even so, he kept his silence, worried that showing too much interest would lead in directions he wasn't willing to discuss.

She turned back to him, determination clear in her expression. "Stand up," she ordered and gripped his upper arms to urge him upright. She pushed him back several steps toward the rear of the room where his bed waited in the corner. When his thighs butted up against the mattress, she released him and tossed the rope she still held over his shoulder onto the bed. Then, with an order for him not to move, she quickly crawled onto the bed. He heard her shuffle around behind him, but was too tired to investigate.

"Angel, what are you doing?"

"You just stay right there," she told him. "You'll find out soon enough."

The nearly identical repeat of the Section Guard leader's words before she almost literally dragged him back here sent a shiver up his spine. Maybe he'd finally pushed Angel too far. After all, he knew she saw him as nothing more than a slave. Except for the biased opinion of others, he had no reason to think she wouldn't hurt him. How many of them had spent the night with her? Maybe Jake, but he was too close to see the games she could play. No one else had their heart ripped out and stomped on or were used and heartlessly tossed aside as she'd done with him. Bret actually preferred spending the night in the company of honest hatred as he had last night. He'd gotten little sleep and a number of bumps and bruises while his arms hung from a tree limb by the rope tied to his wrist, freezing and trying to catch short naps between their bouts of abuse. He hated them as much in return, but at least their attitude was sincere. Angel's approach was more subtle, but in his estimation, cut deeper and hurt far longer.

Back on her feet, Angel stood in front of him, placed her hands on his chest, and shoved him, hard. He came off his feet and landed on his back, bouncing on the bed. She didn't give him any time to collect himself. The moment his back touched the blanket, she heaved on the rope. His arms jerked painfully over his head, and the rope dragged him a foot over the blanket until his knuckles struck the headboard and were pulled under it. He groaned in protest at the stabbing ache that shot through his already tender shoulders, but Angel ignored him. Instead, she concentrated on something to do with the rope above his head. He tugged at his bonds and found his hands tied fast to the headboard. He tried harder, but all he succeeded in doing was rattling the bed against the wall and digging the rope more painfully into his already raw flesh. He couldn't lower his arms! He tried to push himself into a sitting position, but there was no slack in the rope. She had tied him down! He tried to roll over, intending to get to his knees, but she stopped him with a less-than-gentle hand on his chest.

"Stay where you are," she said in a far harsher tone than she'd ever used with him. He stared at her in stunned disbelief, afraid of her for the first time since he'd met her.

"WHAT THE HELL ARE YOU DOING?" Just a touch of panic infused his question, mildly surprised that anger over her actions hadn't consumed him…yet.

She looked down at him with a slight smile as she traced her finger and gaze over his bare chest. "Fake freedom," she murmured.

"What?"

"You called living here fake freedom." She rested her hand purposely on his thigh. He felt the slight pressure like a searing brand.

"Yeah, so what?" He struggled to keep the irate edge in his voice. He couldn't let her know how much her simple touch still affected him.

"You think it would be the same anywhere else?" she asked as her hand moved toward the button on his jeans. One slim finger curved inside the waistband, and he swallowed as she lightly slid it back and forth, brushing over his belly, tantalizing his skin.

"Yes!" He couldn't quite keep the breathlessness out of his voice.

"You have no idea what kind of games some women play…" she said quietly, her eyes going soft as she met his stunned gaze, "women who are very different from me. You seem to want a sampling. Well, I'll do my best to accommodate you."

He swallowed involuntarily again as the button on his jeans popped open and the zipper started downward. He lifted his knees and held them slightly apart to give her less to work with. "Angel?" he asked, unsure of exactly what he wanted to say. He let it hang and tested his restraints once again. The bed shook, but he remained securely tied.

"What?" she said, her eyes wide with faux innocence. "Isn't this what you expected?"

He said nothing, but his mind raced. This was new, and he wondered where she would take it. Despite the minor discomfort she'd caused, her action had turned him on more than just a little, and he wanted to see where it would lead. But deep down, he was terrified of what he would reveal if she pressed him, though he wasn't completely conscious of what it was himself.

Conversely, a part of him wanted to fight harder, to push her away. But his uncertainty of her behavior and his own mixed-up feelings—as well as his desire not to encourage further abuse to his person—kept him from doing that as well. Though she'd never raised a hand in physical violence against him—aside from their argument in the barn, which strangely, he didn't count—she'd never acted like this or tied him down either. Combined, it was enough for him to jerk at the ropes repeatedly, but he didn't try to thrust her away.

It suddenly occurred to him, that if anyone else had done this to him, he'd be furious; but, at the moment, he was too distracted by Angel and her touch to ponder the implications of why that wasn't his reaction with her.

She pulled open his fly and flattened the edges of the stiff material with her hands, setting his already rapidly beating pulse to pounding. She traced the thin line of paler flesh exposed above his boxer-briefs and smiled when he flinched at her light touch, then she glanced at his bent knees.

"Put your legs down, Bret," she instructed, but he merely stared back at her with suspicious eyes.

She smiled at him and got to her feet to walk across the room.

"Where are you going?" he asked, more than a little apprehensive.

She paused to glance at him over her shoulder, a mischievous look in her eyes. "What's wrong," she asked in a saccharine-sweet voice that sounded nothing like her and grated his nerves, "miss me already?"

He mentally rolled his eyes.

"No," he replied more coolly than he felt and laced his next words with heavy cynicism, "just wondering if you're planning to torture me now or later." She looked away, but a moment later, she peered back and gave him a wink.

"Well, now, of course," she said in that same sugary tone that was like nails on a chalkboard.

A cold shiver tickled Bret's spine as he gaped at her in disbelief. She'd never openly threatened him with torture before. Would she do it? A minute ago, he would have said no, but now…? He wasn't so sure. Jake had adamantly assured him that Angel would never have him beaten, but what did that mean? There were several other ways she could cause him pain, any one of which would leave him far worse off than he was now.

Angel turned away and stopped near the outside door to rifle through the assorted horse tack hanging from the hooks on the wall. He watched her every move, curiosity, fear, and his body's amatory response getting the better of him, but she blocked his limited view of her actions with her small frame. She pulled something off one of the hooks and returned to the bed. When she was halfway back, Bret could see a lead rope in her hands. He'd brought it to the house to fix the dangling clasp, but he hadn't gotten around to repairing it yet.

She stopped at the end of his bed, tugging on the metal fastener, not looking in his direction. A moment later, the clasp came free in her hand. She glanced at him with a small, secretive smile, and he was riveted. She knelt on the floor and began doing something below Bret's field of vision. She dropped the heavy clasp with a loud clang on the wood floor and Bret jumped involuntarily at the sudden, sharp sound.

"What're you going to do to me?" He hadn't meant to ask the question, but it slipped out. Her comments about torture apparently disturbed him more than he'd thought.

She stopped what she was doing and looked up at him, a strange light in her cerulean eyes. "What do you think I'm going to do?"

When he didn't immediately respond, she tilted her head as she regarded him.

"Seriously, Bret, what do you think I would do to a man who lied to me and endangered the people I care about, including himself?"

"I don't know," he said, disregarding her claim to care about him. He didn't believe it before and he wouldn't believe now. "At this point...anything."

"Just what every other woman would do, right?" she asked with a mixture of derision and hurt.

"Yeah." It was an anxious sigh.

"Of course, what else would I do?"

He frowned. Though he'd accused her of being capable of violence, until this moment, he hadn't truly believed it, and it was a shock. He'd only said those things to be cruel, to push her buttons, to put and keep distance between them, but it appeared he'd finally gone too far.

She finished what she was doing below the bed and stood, setting one end of the rope on the mattress. She glanced around the room again as if trying to locate something, before her eyes settled on his face once more. She looked him over again, lingering on his feet and bent knees then slowly drifted back up. Her gaze turned intense, capturing his, and curiosity pricked him again.

His eyes widened as she lifted her hands and began to unbutton the short line of buttons on the front of her dress, her gaze never wavering from his.

Bret blinked in surprise. This was not at all what he'd been expecting.

EVER SINCE SHE'D DECIDED to teach him a lesson, Angel had silently hoped she wasn't going too far. His comment about their night together after her party had cut deep and struck a nerve she didn't want to examine too closely, but that wasn't the main reason for her actions. She knew she was risking ever gaining his trust, but kindness wasn't working, and she had to discourage him from attempting to escape again. If she didn't make her point exceptionally clear to him, and if he didn't accept it, he may not be as lucky as he was today the next time he did something stupid.

She smiled at the confusion on his face, glad to have him off balance. He was clearly intrigued, and she wanted to keep his attention diverted from her real objective as long as she could. So far, it seemed to be working. His eyes kept shifting from her hands, to her body, to her face, and back again, all while she continued to smile suggestively into his wary green eyes.

The fifth button on her dress came loose, and she reached around behind her to work the clasps of her bra. He knew what she was doing, she could read it on his face, but he didn't know why, which was exactly what she wanted. She knew that the open front of her dress revealed a vast expanse of her bosom and arching her back put it more prominently on display. She was a little surprised that he was so befuddled by her performance, but he seemed to have lost some of the caution she'd seen in his eyes only a minute before, which was, again, the reaction she had hoped to engender.

When she finally got the hooks unfastened, she slipped one arm through the sleeve and bra strap and back again. Under his intense scrutiny, she repeated the motion with the other arm. A moment later, she reached inside her open bodice, grabbed her bra, and, in a quick motion, tossed it at his face. Luckily, her aim was true and the item landed on his head, stinging his eyes, and marring his vision. He was preoccupied long enough with getting it off and blinking away the burning sensation the garment had caused when it raked his naked eyes for her to wrap the rope around his legs and hurriedly tie it into a snare. Even as he became aware of what she'd done, she was pulling the loop tight and, as it constricted, his legs were forcibly drawn together. He struggled against her hold, but she had deftly pushed the knot between his wiggling feet before she jerked on the other end of the rope. He attempted to pull his legs away, but it was too late. All he succeeded in doing was settling the trap around his bare ankles. It tightened around the leg of the bed frame and stretched him diagonally over the double mattress. She crouched to tie off the line and then stood to admire her handiwork.

Even though all of this was foreign to her and she had no extra strength to draw on any longer, she was amazed that she had succeeded in tying him down so easily. She had no doubt he'd allowed her to do some of it by not struggling harder at the beginning and she was curious about that, but now wasn't the time to investigate.

She hadn't been at all sure how to accomplish this part of her hasty idea, but she had simply asked herself, *How would Darla do this?* Then she tempered that into something she would actually do. She didn't want to hurt him after all, just scare him as he'd done to her, in an attempt to make him understand. Endeavoring to think like Darla or any of her ilk, however, was akin to trying to think like a spider—how to capture my prey. It also made Angel uncomfortable and again she prayed this crazy plan would work.

Now, for the next step.

8

ANGEL'S GAZE RAN OVER Bret's long body stretched across his mattress, and she smiled when their gazes met once more. The impish expression on her face started a heatwave over his skin and prickled the hair on the back of his neck.

What the hell is she doing?

Licking her lips, she lifted the skirt of her blue cotton dress and climbed onto the bed, her eyes locked on his face. While her movements were simple, there was nothing simple about them. Her body swayed, sinuous and erotic, as she crawled along his body, the suggestion in her eyes putting images of her naked beneath him in his head. The heat inside him tripled and, unable to stop himself, his gaze dropped to inspect the view inside her open bodice.

When she finally came to a halt, her legs straddled his knees and she smiled even more suggestively. Slowly, she leaned forward and, sliding her hands over his thighs, she tugged at his jeans until they slipped off his hips. Exposed from his belly to his thighs—except for his snug-fitting undershorts—he could feel every soft inch of her body as she crawled along his until she was propped over him on her hands and knees.

Breathing hard and fast, he stared up at her, unable to look away.

Her lilac scent engulfed him and the soft warmth of her limbs against his bare skin made him all too aware of her as a woman he desired, rather than one he wanted to hate.

Still holding his gaze, she bent at the hips and knees until she was sitting on his lap, her body intimately nestled against his rapidly hardening erection. Separated by nothing more than the thin layers of cotton underwear, every hot inch of her caressed the pulsing hot length of him, and he trembled at the sensation. He'd thought her hand on his thigh had burned him, but it was nothing compared to this. This contact was like a physical blow as heat permeated his skin and his blood seemed to boil in his veins. God, how he wanted to sink into her body's soft heat. To feel her press into him, her heart slamming against her ribs, matching the wild rhythm of his own, while they got lost in each other just like they had the night of her party.

Damn it! Despite everything, he still wanted her. He tried to cast off the spell she'd woven over him but just couldn't shake it. His body wanted hers, his wounded heart begged to try again, but that would be a waste of time. He wanted love *and* trust; she wanted a toy.

She smiled, a naughty, suggestive grin, no doubt detecting his physical reaction. Sitting where she was, it would've been impossible to miss.

No use trying to hide it now.

"What are you doing?" he rasped, overly conscious of the unsteadiness in his voice.

"I should think that was obvious" she replied as she lowered her head the last few inches to kiss him. Her lips were soft and warm and so damn enticing he nearly betrayed himself. Instead, he lay rigid and unmoving while she plied his unresponsive lips with her own. When he refused to answer her invitation, her tongue slid out to slip seductively across his mouth. That slow, beguiling brush of her tongue was nearly his undoing. The tight clench of his jaw was all that kept him from capturing her mouth and giving her everything she demanded. Fortunately, for his self-control and his pride, she paused. Inches from his face, she stared down at him, that little mischievous smile once again curving her lips.

"You're not interested?" she asked, teasing him just as he had done to her that night in the barn months ago.

"Not like this," he said, gently tugging at the rope that bound his wrists. "Untie me, and we'll see."

She chuckled and shifted her hips forward and back in his lap. That small motion drew a stunned gasp from Bret as the resulting friction between their bodies sent a shockwave through him. She kept up the gentle torture until the powerful need to sheath himself in the warm softness she ground against him was overpowering. His hips bucked upward and her resulting grin made him grind his teeth.

"That's not what your body's telling me," she said in a low, sultry voice, mocking him with his words from that same night in the barn.

He nearly groaned in relief when the movement of her hips abruptly ceased. Then she kissed his cheek, along his jaw, and nibbled at his neck. He closed his eyes and tried not to moan. She was making him crazy, and he knew if she kept at it, she would prove him the liar she accused him of being earlier.

"You know," he breathed roughly through clenched teeth, his head back and eyes closed, as she traced lazy circles around his navel with her tongue, "by doing this, you're just making my point for me." He glanced downward.

"Am I?" She peeked up at him through her thick lashes, her bright eyes smiling at him as she continued lower.

"Yes..." It was a breathy whisper as his hips involuntarily lifted in response to the erotic stroking of her mouth. She pulled away from him, grinning evilly, and wiggled down his legs until she was sitting on his knees. Her hands once again slid tantalizingly up his thighs to his hips and he watched with bated breath for what she would do next.

Part of him wanted her to finish what she'd started, but he knew what that would make him. She would *own* him in more ways than just on paper. The thought terrified him, but he was incapable of stopping her and, despite that and the fact she was toying with him, he still wasn't sure he wanted to stop her now. He wanted her, had desired her from the beginning, and now that he'd had her once, his appetite for her had only increased. So much so, that he was internally bargaining with himself to accept what she was doing to him.

She's only doing what you want her to do, he told himself, but his pride would not accept that.

She's playing with you, you idiot! You can't give in to that! If you do, you'll never be free.

He held his breath as her hands looped inside the waistband of his shorts. Slowly, they slithered down over his hips, exposing the curling mass of wiry, black pubic hair and sliding over his backside. The elastic caught on the end of his hardened shaft and she tugged the material, trying to dislodge it.

He had to stop this. Now. Otherwise, despite his will and stubborn pride, he would soon be begging her to ride him. He closed his eyes and concentrated on anything else.

"Stop this, Angel," he said hoarsely, pressing his tailbone into the mattress to anchor his shorts beneath his body before they could slip off. "Stop… Stop it!"

Her hands, still knotted in his shorts, ceased trying to remove them. Her forehead dropped onto his thighs and she inhaled deeply, as if relieved. When she lifted her head, he met her twinkling gaze, but her somber expression confused him.

What is she up to now?

Releasing his underwear, she crawled back up his body until she hovered over him once more, and he couldn't suppress a groan when she sat back, straddling his hips once again. Anger burned in his chest and he fought the need to jerk at the ropes. She grinned, but he wasn't going to give her the satisfaction of seeing him lose his temper.

"What makes you think," she began in a condescending tone, "that I would do anything simply because you *asked*?"

He froze in place as a shot of fear churned to life in his gut. This was not the woman he knew and that worried him, but he kept it locked away and said nothing.

"If I am just like all the rest, as you say," she continued, "like Darla or Carrie or any of their friends. Do you really think I'd stop just because a slave demanded that I do so? Even if he begged?"

He hadn't expected that, and he didn't know how to answer it. Not that he didn't know the answer—those women would *not* have stopped. They would've done whatever they wanted no matter what he said. But that didn't concern him right now. What he wanted to know was what *Angel* had planned to accomplish by tying him down, stripping him nearly naked, and teasing his body to attention?

He frowned at the answer that popped into his mind.

"So, you're going to fuck me?" he asked crudely. "*That's* my punishment for trying to escape?"

She laughed at him.

"Not much of a punishment," she said, "but interesting." She giggled and then sobered abruptly. "No, Bret," she sounded tired, "what I'm saying is *they* would *not* have stopped...I did."

"And that makes you different? Right. Try again. You tied me down. You played with me, treated me like a thing. A toy. A slave! You're no different than they are. Do you plan to beat me afterward too?"

Her eyes narrowed. "If I wanted to beat you, Bret, if I was anything like them, I would've had you stripped and tied out there." She nodded toward the dooryard where the majority of the homestead's population had gathered to watch the parade that had dragged him back here. "I'd have had you beaten in front of everyone as an example and to humiliate you even more."

"Instead, you tied me to a bed in private," he sneered. "You know, if you wanted to fuck me again, all you had to do was tell me. The ropes weren't necessary."

"If I was like them," she went on, ignoring his blatant taunt, "I wouldn't have done it myself. I wouldn't have sullied my hands. I'd have ordered someone else to tie you down and made sure everyone knew what was happening to you." She glared hard into his eyes, driving her point home. "Only after you were securely tied would I have come to you. If I had wanted to, I would have raped you by now without all the foreplay and left you here, most likely for days. And then, if I desired to do so, I'd come back, again and again, to do *whatever I wanted* until I tired of you or until all of the dozen or so of my friends had tired of your services or of making you scream in pain.

Then you'd be chained up in a cell somewhere and forgotten until I decided you were useful again."

He had known life as a slave was terrible in other homes, but he found it hard to believe what she was telling him. *She's trying to scare me with lies,* he thought and narrowed his eyes, irritated by the tactic. But then a small voice from the back of his mind piped, *But what if she's telling the truth? What if there were places worse than the Auction Hall?*

The fact that a tiny part of him wanted to believe her pissed him off even more.

She returned his scowl with one of her own. "But none of those things have happened to you."

He heard the word she didn't say—*Yet.* Those things haven't happened to him yet. *Now she's threatening me?*

"What do you want from me?" he asked.

"What do *I* want?"

"Yes."

"I want you to listen," she said. "To *really* hear me when I tell you, you can't keep doing this. You can't try to escape. You won't be as lucky again. And you can't keep questioning my authority in front of the others. You can say whatever you like when we're alone, argue as much as you want, but only in private. Otherwise, someday you're going to say or do the wrong thing in front of the wrong person and they will demand I punish you. And I may not be able to protect you. I won't have a choice. I don't want to do that. I don't want to hurt you, Bret. I never have."

"A little late for that," he said scornfully and wanted to bite his tongue off for saying it out loud.

She closed her eyes and sadly said, "I know I hurt you that night."

Stifling a groan, he mentally cursed himself. His big mouth had brought up the one incident he didn't want to discuss. But now that he had, he couldn't help tweaking her with the truth. "The night was fine. It was the next morning that was rather chilly." Every word was as sharp as a well-honed knife.

"I'm sorry," she said, opening her eyes again, "but it was a mistake.

It shouldn't have happened."

"Right," he said, his voice filled with scorn, "because you're *afraid for me*."

"Yes, I am."

"I can take care of myself," he nearly shouted. "I don't need you to do it for me. I don't need you to do *anything* for me!"

"Really?" she asked and lowered her lips until they hovered inches from his own. Her lilac scent filled his senses, swirling through his brain, and despite himself, he got lost in the deep sapphire of her eyes. Her lips parted and, suddenly unable to resist, he lifted his head to capture her waiting mouth. She didn't back away but returned his kiss with as much heat as she had in the past, despite her claims about mistakes and enemies.

That alone should've had him pulling away and mocking her for her lies, but he didn't. What he had meant as a meaningless exchange filled with nothing more than lust, soon became an overwhelming need for more. The air around them felt charged, the electricity bouncing between them, through them, drawing them closer while pushing everything else away. He was no longer an unwilling slave and she wasn't his Mistress. They were two people drawn inexplicably together, each needing everything the other could give.

He'd intended to turn the tables on her game, but her response and the strength of their attraction surprised and pleased him far too much to turn away. He'd planned to make her regret her reckless acts, but the passion between them flared out of control and he couldn't make himself stop.

Angel's hands slid up over his sides and her unbound breasts swelled against his chest. Her arms wrapped him and pulled him closer, clinging to him like life itself, as if she'd never let him go.

He didn't *want* her to let go. He wanted to hold her, wanted to feel every part of her again and again, but he was still tied. The thought of begging her to release him so they could explore this more fully flitted through his mind, but then she pulled back to stare down at him, her pretty eyes wide and shaken. Her breasts lifted with every deep inhalation through her parted lips and the amorous flush of her cheeks darkened as he watched. Something stirred in his chest, something like hope, but he squashed it. She rejected him once, why should he continue to hope? Instead, he chose to bait her with a provocative insinuation.

"If that was part of the game," he said with a suggestive smile, "then I'd like to play some more."

He'd only meant to tease her a little, test the waters so to speak, to see where he stood. But when her eyes narrowed into furious slits, he got his answer and immediately regretted the comment. He opened his mouth to smooth over his error, but words halted in his throat when she slapped him.

Every muscle in his body tensed as his head dropped back to the mattress, eyes closed, sucking air through clenched teeth. The burning brand on his cheek was nothing compared to the pressure building in his chest.

"I'm sorry," she murmured. "I didn't mean to do that."

When his eyes opened, he saw the regret on her face—eyes wide in disbelief, fingers pressed to her mouth in shock—but at this point, he didn't care.

"Why?" The word dripped with scorn. "That was more like it. Way to keep the game going. Much better." He paused and then nastily added, "And you thought you were different."

"Damn it, Bret," she said, dropping her hands to his chest and frowning, clearly upset and frustrated, "I am not like them! Why won't you see that?"

"Because there isn't enough difference to acknowledge. You use men. You used *me*, just like the others did." But he knew that wasn't entirely true. She had used him, but she'd never hurt or humiliated him the way they had at the Auction Hall. She'd injured his pride, which was bad enough, but he'd felt her wheedling her way inside him again with that kiss, and he could not allow that to happen. Anger rolled through him for the first time since she'd tied him to the bed and he suddenly didn't care if she was telling him the truth or not. "I tried to escape, and I will try again, so punish me however you want. Just get it over with!"

"And *I* can make things much worse for you. Don't try to win this, Bret. You *will* lose."

"And one day, I'll return the favor."

"Until then," she said sarcastically, "you'll have to get used to living here and obeying the rules." They glared at each other as resentment hung in the air between them. "You asked what your punishment is, I'll tell you. You don't want *comfy freedom*," she hissed, "well, you don't have it anymore." She grabbed her bra from where it rested beside his shoulder and sat up abruptly. She moved away from him, then turned to glower at him once again from her perch on the edge of his bed. "You no longer have the run of anything or the freedom of movement granted to everyone else here. You're not allowed outside the perimeter walls for any reason without my consent and not without a guard that I approve. Only when I feel I can trust you again, which, believe me, will take a *long* time and a *lot* of convincing, and only then will you be given your freedom again. Until then, you are the prisoner that you keep complaining of already being."

She turned away from him and began pulling her dress off her shoulders. Bret was momentarily struck dumb as she disrobed. He watched rapt as the satiny skin of her trim back and shoulders was revealed before she rapidly put her bra back on. His stupid heart fluttered and sped up when he caught the barest hint of one pale breast before the undergarment was in place. Then, just as quickly, she tucked her arms back into her dress and began fastening the buttons. It all took no more than a minute, but it had seemed like a very long time to him.

Disappointment welled inside him. Cursing himself for a fool, he swallowed hard and concentrated on picking up their argument.

"What about the ranch and the cattle?" he asked as she stood, her sudden movement getting his brain working again. "Who's going to monitor them? And calving is coming up; who's going to take care of that?"

"Calving will be inside the walls, so no issue there. As for the rest, you'll still direct the work, Bret," she said calmly, "and while Jake is here, he can take care of the fields, and when he's not, Dean can. They both know enough to cover for you and what they don't know they can ask you."

"That's going to make things real sloppy," he warned.

She shrugged. "We'll manage."

"You can't keep me here," he tried again.

She glared at him furiously. "Oh, yes, I can. Get used to it, Bret, because if I have to confine you to this one room, I will. For however long it takes."

"For what?"

"For you to see reason," she snapped. "I don't want you hurt again and if you keep on the way you have, that's what's going to happen."

"Afraid you'll lose your new favorite toy?"

She sighed and shook her head. "Why are you doing this?"

"Why are you?"

"Because I don't want to see you dead." She sighed again. "They will hurt you, Bret, far worse than before if you keep doing what you've been doing. I wasn't lying to you. Being with me makes you a target and you already are one. For Darla at least, if not her friends too. There's no reason to make it worse."

"Makes no difference to me," he breathed as he shifted his gaze to the ceiling, refusing to meet her eyes.

YOU'RE JUST TRYING *to make a point,* Angel had repeatedly reminded herself as she'd caressed his chest with her mouth. She'd had trouble staying detached throughout this little charade. His skin was so hot, and he had felt so good. The smell and taste of him had been wonderful, intoxicating, everything she'd missed since the morning after her party.

But that's not what this is about! She had scolded herself more than once. Yet she enjoyed being close to him again, liked the way his muscles tensed, how his chest heaved, and how the rapid pounding of his heart beneath her lips echoed her own. But she'd been increasingly afraid her performance was going to backfire on her, and it nearly did.

But her impromptu plan had almost worked. At least, it seemed as if he was coming around, but then she'd kissed him…or he kissed her. Either way, everything nearly blew up in her face.

Until he ordered her to stop, she'd begun to wonder if he even wanted her to. She'd hurt him with her rejection, but she hadn't thought he'd be so reckless with his own well-being as to try to escape. Then again, he thought she was lying to him. She suspected he kept insisting she was like the others to bait her, to cause an argument, to push her away as Jake said he often did. But knowing that didn't keep his callous comments from hurting.

She hadn't meant to slap him, didn't even really know why she had, but it had brought them both back to reality. Even if a part of her had been disappointed to leave the warm, erotic fantasy that had been building between them while they kissed.

Now, staring back at him, trussed up, more than half-naked, and stretched out over his bed, he looked like he always did—every woman's fantasy. Unbelievably handsome and so damn appealing her body had already responded. Her skin felt hot, her nipples hard and achy, and little tremors of need fluttered in her belly. But this whole thing hadn't been about desire. It had been about convincing this stubborn man that he was better off with her than risking his life trying to escape.

She inhaled deeply and sighed, feeling bone-weary all of a sudden. He looked tired too, and they were getting nowhere. He wouldn't believe her, and it was time to try something else.

"That's your choice, Bret," she said in response to his assertion that it didn't matter who claimed to own him. She turned on her heel, intending to leave.

"Where are you going?" he asked.

"Away," she replied without meeting his gaze.

"Aren't you going to untie me?"

She wondered if the insecurity she heard in his question had anything to do with someone else knowing what she'd done to him. She paused, then looked over her shoulder.

"No," she said before she headed for the door.

"Wait!"

"For what," she asked, turning angrily as her voice rose. "For you to lie to me again? It's time you learned who runs this place, Bret, and in case you need it spelled out, it's not you."

"You can't leave me like this." His eyes darted around the room, to the drape-covered window, then to the doorway before meeting her gaze again. "At least untie me."

Her eyes drifted over the splendor of his long, hard body, and knew he was right. In time, he'd be able to break out of those bonds, but it would take a while, and he would probably injure himself further in the process. She didn't want to leave him helpless and hurt. Her heart clenched at the thought. She'd be as bad as Darla if she did that.

"It's a slipknot," she told him. "The end is by your hands. You could've untied yourself whenever you wanted." She couldn't help one more little dig at his expense though. "I suggest you hurry. I'm sure Jake will be in here as soon as I leave. You might want to…adjust your clothes before he comes in." She smiled when he froze, glanced down at himself, and then back to her. Anger turned his eyes silver-green and a muscle ticked in his jaw as his long fingers found the end of the rope and pulled. He'd unravel the knot soon enough.

"Remember what I said, Bret," she reminded him as she placed her hand on the doorknob. "Stay within the walls."

"I heard you," he said, glaring at her as he tugged on the rope harder.

"Good," she said and opened the door. Stepping out on the deck, she saw Jake at the end of the walk heading toward her. Not wanting to embarrass Bret any further, she closed the door quickly and met Jake before he could reach the door.

"Give him a few minutes, Jake," she said quietly, putting her palm flat against his chest. "Bret wouldn't appreciate you going in right now."

"Is everything all right?" he asked with a frown and Angel quickly explained Bret's new standing in their little community.

"That's going to be messy," Jake told her, and Angel glared at him for using nearly the same words as his friend.

"We'll manage," she repeated and then elaborated on her point. "He can't have the freedom to roam around if he's going to abuse it."

"I didn't say you were wrong," Jake replied. "I just know it's going to make things difficult."

"Well, welcome to life with Bret Masters."

9

ONCE HE'D PULLED the loop free, Bret quickly dislodged the rope from the headboard and sat up. He used his teeth to loosen the knots around his wrists and soon had them unfettered as well. The binding around his legs was also tied with a slipknot. He pulled it loose, and he was free. Still seated on the bed, he gathered up the ropes and hurled them across the room where they landed by the small wood stove near the door.

The severity of Angel's anger surprised him. Even though he'd been captured and forced back here, she should've expected him to run. He'd warned her that he couldn't live as her slave forever and he'd never given any indication that his plans had changed. Why would she have assumed they had?

Maybe she'd been as affected by our night together as I was. He brushed that thought away. It didn't matter. He didn't want to get wrapped up in another drama-fest. He wouldn't allow himself to be trapped again. Besides, she'd made her wishes crystal clear when she kicked him out of her bed.

He got up and adjusted his clothing, then went into the bathroom to clean up a little more. Bret had just turned on the cold water to let it run over his throbbing hands and aching wrists when the door opened and Jake came inside. Bret ignored his friend's entrance, taking the time to splash cool water onto his face and overheated skin. He was inspecting the cut on his head in the mirror when he saw movement off to the side behind him. He turned and found Jake leaning against the doorframe, looking cross and worried.

"I thought you weren't coming back," Jake said as if accusing him of a crime. Detecting Jake's underlying anger, Bret frowned at his friend before he returned his attention to his injured scalp.

"What're you so angry about?" he asked, poking at the cut and wincing.

"You," Jake said as Bret tucked his hands back under the cold water.

"What do you mean, me?"

"I don't know why I ever thought you'd make it, or why I helped you, but I did," Jake said, though Bret couldn't tell if it was concern or annoyance that tinged Jake's voice. "Now look at you."

"I've had worse," Bret said and splashed more water over his head. The coolness felt good against his chafed wrists and burnt skin, but he saw red in the sink. The wound on his scalp must still be leaking blood.

"It sure looks bad," Jake said. "You look like hell. Angel thinks I betrayed her, and I feel like a low-life for lying and letting her worry."

"Worry about what?" Bret asked as he shut off the water and grabbed a towel off the rack.

"You."

"Me?" Bret paused in patting his face dry with the towel to gaze curiously at his friend.

"Yes, you," Jake said and stepped back to allow the younger man to leave the bathroom. "She's not what you think, Bret. She cares about the people here, even you."

"Sure she does," Bret replied cynically as he sat on the edge of his bed. With a corner of the damp towel pressed to his head, he gave his friend a dubious look.

"I know the two of you don't always get along, but she does care."

"How do you know that, Jake?" He checked the towel for blood.

Seeing a small amount, he changed corners and held it to his head again.

"She told me so."

"Really?" Bret scoffed.

"Yes, really."

Bret checked the towel again, and finding no blood on it, turned his attention to his sore, abraded feet.

"I doubt her concern was entirely for me," he said, using the dampness of the towel to clean the debris from his soles and toes.

"I don't understand why you can't see the good in her," Jake said, still sounding annoyed. "She's human, she makes mistakes, but she's a good woman."

Bret chucked the dirty towel onto the one Angel had snatched from him earlier and stood. "None of those are left." He limped to the chest of drawers to pluck out a pair of socks. "Not any with their own penitentiary filled with slaves," he continued, winding the material snugly around his wrists. Aside from asking Angel for medical supplies—which he wasn't about to do—the socks were his best option to stop the bleeding.

"That's not what we are here," Jake told him. "After all you've seen, after what you, no doubt, experienced last night, can't you see that?"

Bret gave his friend a blank stare and Jake shook his head

"She just saved you from being tortured again. Don't you realize that? She knew you lied, but she still protected you!"

"Only to drag me in here and play games with me," Bret replied. "She's not the sweet, innocent angel you paint her to be, Jake."

"And she's not the devil you paint her as either," Jake shot back angrily. "She trusted us and we both let her down, but all you can see is that she got angry. We *hurt* her, but she still risked herself and the rest of us to protect you. Can't you see that?"

"No," Bret said, meeting his friend's gaze. "I see a woman who's worried about herself and her reputation."

"She risked her reputation to save *you*!"

Bret didn't reply.

Jake stared at him for a quiet moment before he spoke and, though Bret knew he was still irritated, he sounded calm. "You're just as much to blame as she is for whatever passed between you in here," Jake told him and hurried on over Bret's heated reply. "I *know* she's a good person. I *know* what she's done, what she's risked, for all of us. I'm just sorry you can't get past your prejudice to see that for yourself."

They glared at each other, neither willing to give an inch, but then Jake dropped his gaze and shook his head sadly. Bret felt the change in his friend's mood as the air in the room turned heavy and Jake's face hardened.

"You can't keep doing this," Jake said slowly. "You can't try to escape again…I won't let you."

Bret dropped his hands into his lap and raised his brows. "You won't *let* me?"

"No," Jake said firmly, "I won't. I won't help you, I won't lie for you, and I won't let you out of the promise you made to me. I will hold you to your word."

"What are you talking about?" Bret asked, though he knew exactly what his friend hinted at.

"You gave me your word to look after her when I'm not around."

"That was just for the cattle drive."

"*Any*time I'm not around," Jake corrected. "You agreed."

"You knew I was going to run," Bret said, narrowing his eyes and raising his voice. "You knew I only made that agreement to keep the peace, that it was only until I had an opportunity to escape. You can't expect to hold me to that now."

"I can, and I do expect you to keep it."

Bret tilted his head. "Why are you doing this?"

"Because I'm leaving soon and she needs someone to look out for her," Jake told him. "I want someone I can trust to take over for me while I'm gone."

"And you think you can trust *me* with her?"

"I know I can," Jake said with a half-grin. "You gave me your word."

Bret stared at his friend in disbelief. He was trapped and they both knew it. He wouldn't break his word to Jake, but if he'd known the man was going to demand this, he would've never agreed to Jake's entreaty all those months ago.

Arguments swirled through his brain. *There has to be a way out of this,* he told himself. Even as his mind railed against the constraints of his long-held beliefs, he knew he'd never find an excuse good enough to break his word. He had agreed without qualifying the specifications of the request, and now he was stuck.

"She's not going to let me do anything for a long time, Jake," he said, attempting to sway his friend's thinking. "What makes you think she'll let me help her if she needs it? Whatever *it* might be."

"Because you're as stubborn as she is." Jake smiled knowingly. "More so even, and you won't let her order you to do one thing when you think you should be doing something else."

Bret sighed at Jake's description, knowing it was accurate. "What exactly is she going to need help with?"

"It's different every time," Jake told him, "but you'll know when it comes up."

"I don't want to do this, Jake." Bret let his frustration bleed into his voice.

"Too bad."

Bret lifted his gaze to study his friend, but all he read on Jake's face was determination.

"This time it's about what I need," Jake continued. "And I need to know she's safe. After all she's done for us, it's the least I can do. And after what she just saved you from, it's the least you can do too. Besides, you owe me."

"I believe you owe me a favor or two as well."

"You gave me your word, Bret. What I owe you doesn't negate that. Besides, keeping your last secret should've already made up for those."

Bret looked away and shook his head. There wasn't going to be a way out of this.

What is Jake so afraid of? he wondered, but he thought he knew.

Angel was starting to show signs of severe depression. Bret had suffered from it himself when he was younger, and sometimes he could still feel it darkening his life.

"I'm not asking, Bret," Jake said, interrupting his thoughts.

"I'm well aware of that, Jake." His tone said he didn't like it much either.

"Good. She protected you, now it's your turn." There was a long moment of silence where they glowered at each other and then Jake got to his feet, grabbed his jacket, and headed for the door. "I need to talk to Dean and Daniel about the change of duties. I'll see you later."

Bret stared at the door Jake had exited through, his mind replaying what had just happened. He didn't want to be Angel's keeper. Being close to her was the last thing he wanted. It would kick up the riot of emotions he always felt around her. An affliction she didn't appear to suffer, despite the longing looks she always cast his way when she thought he wouldn't notice. Unfortunately, he knew those lustful looks had nothing more promising behind them than alleviating a physical need, and, as he'd told himself before, he wouldn't be her purchased stud. Being around Angel was dangerous for the lonely side of him that wanted to be loved for himself so badly, but he had no escape this time. He'd given Jake his word without stipulating its limits and now he had no choice.

Jake was partially right; Angel *had* protected him, but he also knew if she hadn't, she and her home would've come under some heavy scrutiny. His escape attempt had been too easy. He'd reached the border of her property without being seen and her peers would assume he'd had help in obtaining it. She suspected Jake had assisted him in one way or another, and Bret believed that suspicion had been the key factor in her defense of Bret.

"Sure she helped me," he muttered, "but she did it for you, Jake. Not me."

Friendship

1

BRET SAUNTERED THROUGH THE EMPTY DOORYARD on his way to the new calving barn. Stars filled the velvety black sky and the three-quarter moon illuminated the path and the white buildings before him with a silvery glow. In the week since the Section Guards dragged him back to Angel's home, he'd made a it habit to check on the animals one last time each night after dinner. Bret liked the time alone. The calm and quiet appealed to him—the silent acceptance of the animals and the earthy scent of hay, mud, and cows. There was something comforting about it, a familiarity that brought back happy memories and better times.

Tonight, as normal, everyone else had either settled down in their rooms or were finishing their evening meal when Bret stepped into the barn. Occasionally during these short trips, he would take extra time to muck out a stall or two, just to work out the tension in his body, but not tonight. This evening he was only there to check on the one baby, her mom, and the other two pregnant cows before heading to bed.

The little calf came right to him as he entered the stall. He smiled down into her big brown eyes and ran a gloved hand over her boney head. "Hey, little girl, how're you doing tonight?"

She nuzzled his hand, bumped against his leg, then tottered back to her mother to finish feeding.

Ever since his forced return and Angel's order to remain within the homestead walls, his and Jake's responsibilities on the ranch had switched. With Dean Williams as back up, Jake and the other cowhands rode out every morning, falling into the work with practiced ease. Bret, on the other hand, felt clumsy and inefficient in his new duties. Aside from the cattle and their care—which were still an enjoyable part of his job—his new tasks at the homestead were another issue.

God, he thought as he grabbed an armful of hay from the bales beneath the thin work table in the hall, *give me a cattle ranch and a bunch of rowdy cowboys any day.*

But instead, he was saddled with a pack of non-ranchers and their kids.

He quickly filled the other two cows' feed bin then returned to the stall with the calf. Happy to find the calf nuzzling her mother's swollen udder, he smiled and tossed more hay into mama's bin, then dusted himself off as the list of his new duties still ran through his mind.

When he wasn't checking on things that needed to be ordered, repaired, or replaced, refereeing personal disputes, or dealing with the cattle, the maintenance of all the buildings on the ranch—including the completion of the new housing they'd started earlier that spring—still needed his attention. Jake's knowledge of construction kept that last project on track, but it felt to Bret as if so many others were spiraling out of his control.

The minute details of running the homestead were tedious and a bit outside his area of expertise. Acquiring essentials the ranch didn't already provide or dividing their surpluses to barter at the local market in town were things he could handle. Overseeing the sale of their excess hay and alfalfa stock to other ranchers Angel had found or purchasing metal stock for the resident blacksmith and farrier to make or repair tools and shoes for the horses were closer to things he knew. But looking into cotton thread and cloth for making or repairing clothes and other household items, or consulting with Esther about replacing the old hens and when to send out hunters to replenish their ever diminishing food supply, and what to do with the hides they acquired in the process weren't things he'd ever had to worry about on the ranch he'd run before the war. And when the children's teacher cornered him in the dining hall to talk about books, pencils, and more paper for their classroom, he'd had to ask Jake where to start—since his friend had been doing the job for the last two years.

He hadn't realized an organized school existed on the ranch, but that teacher had set him straight on that when he mentioned as much.

"Of course, we have a school," she'd said, sounding appalled and looking at Bret as if he was some kind of Neanderthal. "We're not savages, Mr. Masters. The children here will know how to read and write, perform mathematics, and know exactly what our world was like before everything fell apart. The girls *and* boys will learn everything we can teach them, but we need supplies."

The revelation that boys would learn right alongside the girls had surprised him, but then—and he hated to silently admit—the equality on Angel's ranch seemed to be far more prevalent than anywhere he'd seen since before the wars.

With a resigned sigh, he pulled off a glove to run his fingers through his short-cropped hair. He'd had no idea Jake's responsibilities were so vast and tedious until he took them over. Still, Bret was determined to perform his new duties to the best of his ability—if for no other reason than to prove that he could.

However, that didn't mean he liked being stuck at the homestead while Jake and the others roamed the range. Daily, Bret fought the powerful urge to ride out with his friends despite Angel's orders, because he knew where that would lead. And even if he *had* kind of liked being at her sexual mercy, so to speak, he wasn't ready to repeat the hog-tying she'd put him through the last time he tried to leave. For now, he remained a prisoner inside the homestead walls, stuck training the greenhorns of the ranch in calving care, milking, mucking stalls, repairing tack, feeding and watering—a huge chore on its own—and other assorted jobs for all the animals on the ranch.

At least the kids listen, mostly anyway, he thought, pulling his glove back on and gently patting the brown and white hide of the cow while she munched on the fresh hay he'd given her. The children of the ranch seemed to take to Bret and were anxious to learn whatever he would teach them. They understood far more than their parents wanted them to know about the fractured society outside the walls of their home, and the boys and girls alike wanted to be useful in maintaining their reasonably safe refuge. Bret was more than willing to share whatever the parents would allow him to, but he limited his teaching to the ranch duties and kept his personal opinions to himself as much as possible.

"Maybe this is a good thing," Bret murmured to the cow as she continued to eat happily. "The kids argue less than their parents *or* the cowhands."

He chuckled to himself, but cut it short when he heard the front doors squeak open and several sets of footsteps shuffle inside. The barns were all wired for electricity, so the building was well lit, but he could hear the creak of several lantern handles as people moved down the central aisle. Wondering who would be out wandering around at this time of night, Bret gave the cow and calf one last affectionate pat and exited the stall.

Stepping into the wide hall and closing the stall behind him, he turned to a crowd of people rapidly surrounding him. Sensing the tension in the air, his muscles tightened as every face glared at him angrily, their hostility rolling over him like a heatwave. Some he recognized, such as the blacksmith and farrier, Hugh Blocker—a giant of a man with a wide, granite-carved face and a quick-fire temper that Bret had learned to avoid whenever possible. He thought two or three women near the back of the crowd might be guards, but he wasn't sure and didn't have time to verify it anyway. His instincts told him this was a fight and, preparing for the battle, he straightened his shoulders.

"Howdy," Bret said as he pushed the brim of his black hat back on his head.

Not one of the stern faces wavered.

Bret inhaled slowly, then rolled his shoulders inside his brown farm-jacket, hooked his thumbs in the front pockets of his jeans, and grinned. "What's up?"

"We've come to make sure you don't try to destroy us again," a blonde woman in the front row told him and the others nodded their agreement. He didn't know her name, but he had seen her with some of the children and at the blacksmith's shop beside the barn. She was handsome rather than pretty, thin, and very tall. Her honey-blonde hair was straight, yet its warm color was quite appealing, but her gray-green eyes—probably her best feature—were cold as she gazed intently at Bret.

"And how did I do this before?" Bret asked with a confused frown.

"You tried to escape."

"Ah," he said with a nod. It seemed Angel wasn't the only one angry enough to confront him about his failed getaway.

"Your actions could've destroyed everything we've built here," the woman said heatedly. "We want to make sure you won't do it again."

"And how do you plan to accomplish that?" he asked with a cocky half-grin, eyeing each face in turn.

"We want your word that you won't try it again," the blonde drew his attention once more. "We'll accept that if you give it."

"Well," he said with a derisive chuckle and a shake of his head, "I'm afraid I can't give that to you."

A displeased murmur broke out among the group, but the blonde spoke up. "You'd risk all our lives for your own selfish needs?"

"Look," he said slowly, unwilling to discuss his needs with these relative strangers, "y'all can do and believe whatever you like, but I can't live as a slave."

"That's not what we are," a woman from the back of the crowd stated. "Not here, not on Angel's ranch." Several of the others nodded once again.

"You may not be," Bret said, "but I am. I can't accept that."

"Why?" the blonde asked. "You prefer the starvation and insecurity of the wild to the relative comfort and safety here?"

"I prefer freedom over slavery," Bret replied.

"You won't change your opinion on that, will you?" she asked almost regretfully.

"No."

"Then you give us no alternative..."

Bret frowned again. "To what?"

"There are other ways to make sure you can't run again," she threatened.

"And what exactly are those?" Bret asked, narrowing his eyes and dropping his hands to his sides.

"We break your legs," Hugh Blocker said simply from a step behind the blonde.

A conflicting rumble swept through the others. Apparently, not all of them approved that course of action.

Bret's heart sped up as his gaze swept over the huge, older man in the red flannel shirt, assessing Hugh's bulk before returning to the challenging glare of his dark brown eyes. The big man's thick lips were pulled back in a gap-toothed grin that split his face. A thin scar crinkled his cheek from the corner of his mouth to just above his left ear where it disappeared beneath his black knit hat. Bret could handle an attack from any of them, but the big man worried him. If it was just the two of them, Bret might've had a chance, and while he wouldn't bet on it, he wouldn't count himself out either. But with all the others present, Bret was in serious trouble.

"I don't recommend you try that," Bret replied coolly to Hugh's threat, his fingers knotting into fists at his sides.

"We don't want to." The blonde stepped aside, giving Hugh a clear path to his intended victim. Bret stood his ground, but didn't take his eyes off the giant. "You're not giving us a choice," the woman said. "We won't let you threaten our families."

A man rushed toward Bret, distracting him from the blacksmith. He easily shoved the man away, but that short diversion was enough for Hugh to attack. He struck Bret across his already bruised cheek with a ham-sized fist, catching the bone near the younger man's eye. The blow was as hard as Bret had expected it would be; hard enough to spin him into the stall door behind him. Hanging over the door, Bret gripped the top as he shook the ringing from his head. Sensing the big man's approach for a second attack from behind, Bret shoved himself away from the stall door and lifted an elbow in a high arc, aiming for the other man's mouth. He connected, drawing blood, but only succeeded in shifting the big man's objective. Hugh's intention had been to subdue Bret with a powerful bear hug and take him to the ground if needed. But Bret's sudden movement changed that. Instead, one of Hugh's thick arms snaked around Bret's neck, dragging his back against the giant's barrel chest. Bret reached back and attempted to gouge at the other man's eyes, but Hugh reached up and crushed Bret's still raw wrist in a meaty fist before cruelly yanking the younger man's arm behind his back. Bret repeatedly slammed his free elbow into Hugh's ribs, inciting a chorus of grunts from the larger man.

"Someone get his other arm," Hugh shouted as he spun to face the crowd. An instant later, Bret's free arm was twisted harshly and pulled back around Hugh's large bulk.

Bret still had weapons in his legs, but there were too many of them.

"Grab his legs too," Hugh ordered and several others swiftly swarmed forward to comply.

"No!" Bret tried using Blocker's bulk as an anchor to kick a few of them back as they came at him, but eventually they managed to secure his legs too.

Bret struggled doggedly against the arms that held him, but he found no weakness in their grasp.

"Go ahead, pretty boy," the blacksmith hissed in his ear as the man's arm constricted painfully around Bret's throat, "fight me." He chuckled. "I'll enjoy hurting you."

His ability to draw a breath grew more difficult and Bret attempted to free himself one last time as black specks floated through his vision. The bigger man held Bret—bent backward over his twisted arm and secured tightly against Hugh's enormous frame—while the others immobilized his legs. Bret's eyes darted over the crowd, hoping in vain to find an unexpected ally among the group. Some of them looked unhappy with this turn of events, but no one moved to stop it.

"Find something to use on his legs," Hugh ordered. Several things happened while the mob searched for a weapon and Bret continued to fight against the giant. The tall worktable where the hay bales sat was dragged into the aisle and Bret's right leg was draped and held down over its rough surface. Bret's opposite thigh was wedged painfully against the table's edge as two men used their grip on his ankle and combined weight to stretch him out.

"Wait!" a female shouted above the racket of other voices and the shuffling search. Hope burgeoned in Bret's chest as two of the women he'd thought were guards earlier stepped forward. Relief swept through him, but then he remembered both of them had been there from the beginning.

They pushed their way forward and were joined by a third guard with dark-blonde hair and delicate features. "We came to talk to him," the smaller of the two dark-haired women said, "not cripple him."

"Talking wasn't doing any good," Hugh said, his breath hissing through his teeth.

Am I actually wearing this mountain of a man down? Bret wondered. Optimism lifted his heart again, but then Hugh tightened his hold and Bret's air cut back a little more.

"Now it's time for stronger measures," Hugh continued. "If you don't have the stomach for it, leave."

"We can't let you do this," the light-haired guard said, but the three were quickly pushed back and buried in the surrounding crowd, crushing Bret's potential rescue.

At that moment, another woman stepped forward with a thick, four-foot wooden dowel in her hand. It appeared to be a handle for one of the tools used to clean out the stalls. Slightly plump and pretty, her mouse-brown hair was pulled back and tied behind her head, but her black eyes sparkled. Bret suddenly recalled her name. Gloria, Miles and Gavin's mother, two of the boys he'd chopped wood with every day this week. He'd spoken to her briefly the day before and she'd seemed sweet and kind, a great mother. She'd been grateful for the time and instruction he'd given her children, but she wouldn't even look at him now. She hesitated, but when Hugh shouted for her to get it over with, she lifted her weapon to batter his leg.

"Gloria," Bret rasped through the harsh constriction of the big man's merciless hold, "don't do this—"

She hesitated, but the rest of what he would have said was cut short by Hugh's arm jerking him backward, wrenching a strangled croak from Bret.

Hugh shook his prisoner like a wild animal. "Shut up!"

Gloria stared at Bret's grimacing face as if for the first time. He saw her eyes drop to the healing bruise on his cheek, then down to the thick arm wrapped around Bret's neck, and over the rest of his long body. She had been there that morning when the Section Guards dragged him back to the homestead. She'd seen the cuts and bruises he'd suffered at their hands and she seemed to be considering all that as she stood stock-still staring.

The boys had told him that their father had died from illness a year ago and now, they seemed to have attached themselves to Bret. He remembered the odd expression that painted her face the other day as she watched him work with her sons. She had to have seen the adoring looks they'd bestowed on him and Bret wondered if that was her reason for being here now. Could it be because she wanted him to be the father her children had lost? He wouldn't mind that so much, but what if she wanted more from him than he would give. Or was it more than that? After all, if her boys took to him so quickly, how long before they followed his example as well? He remembered how she'd smiled at her boys laughter as Bret patiently instructed them in their chores and wondered if she'd considered what her young sons' reactions would be to her participation in maiming him.

That thought must have crossed her mind, because her hazel eyes went wide in alarm and her upraised arm, along with the weapon she held, dropped to her side.

"Do it!" Hugh yelled. "Or do you want him to be the reason you lose your children?"

Gloria shook her head. "No," she said softly and dropped the rod on the floor, stepping back from them all. A murmur of discontent ran through the crowd, but those who knew this was wrong were unsure how to disarm the situation.

One of the unfamiliar men, caught up in the viciousness of mob-mentality, snatched up the dropped pole and without preamble, brought it down with all his strength across Bret's outstretched thigh. Head arched backward, Bret's body surged against his captor as he bellowed in agony, but Hugh cut his cry short by tightening his crushing hold around Bret's throat. Despite the intense pain throbbing through his thigh, Bret knew the bone was unbroken.

"Hold him," Hugh shouted at the men holding Bret's leg. Then Hugh took a step back, dragging his hostage back with him. Bret felt their hold on his ankle lessen and, recognizing his opportunity, heaved against their grasp. Instantly, his air was cut off and someone slammed a fist into his belly, taking his wind. Choking, Bret forgot about kicking out of their hold and fought to breathe instead.

Sensing his victim's weakness, Hugh took one more backward step and then stopped. Strong hands held Bret in place from his ankle to his knee, with his thigh suspended over the table's edge. With no support below it, a hard enough blow would definitely fracture the bone. A chill raced down his spine and Bret redoubled his efforts to escape Hugh's hold.

"Do it!" Hugh urged the unknown man once more.

The man didn't seem to care if Bret had been injured, didn't seem to acknowledge Hugh's shouted encouragement, only concentrated on the business at hand.

"Your desire for freedom could break our families apart," the new man murmured. "I'm here to make sure mine will be safe from your selfishness and I intend to see it through." He lifted the pole for a second time, clearly ready to finish the job.

Bret's breath halted and he squeezed his eyes closed in expectation of the pain.

But then a new voice suddenly cut through the ruckus. "What's going on in here?"

2

IN AN INSTANT, all noise ceased and every eye in the barn turned toward the voice that had shouted above the din. The head guard, Michelle Smithmore, stood near the barn's front doors. Taller than some of the men, fit, and leanly muscular, Michelle could rival any of them and everyone there knew it. To Bret, however, it appeared a few of his attackers still wanted to finish what they'd started, apparently unconcerned about the repercussions.

But Michelle was not a woman to take lightly and they all knew that too.

Tilting her head, the light danced over her shoulder-length, red-gold hair as Michelle arched a questioning eyebrow when no one replied to her question. Her pale blue eyes were hard as granite as she closely considered the scene before her.

"I asked a question," she said in a voice that demanded a response.

No one seemed in a hurry to explain what they had been up to, but the tall blonde who'd first spoken to Bret showed her strength by stepping forward. "We wanted to talk to him," she said.

"This doesn't look like talking," Michelle replied, once again surveying the crowd.

"We hit an impasse," the woman said.

"And what was the topic?"

"We wanted to convince him not to try to escape again."

Michelle furrowed her brow. "And when he refused to agree, you decided to take it upon yourselves to *beat* him?" Her cold eyes dared the other woman to deny it, and the blonde backed down without further comment.

Michelle's shoulders seemed to sag slightly as if disappointed by their actions tonight, but an instant later, her back straightened and her gaze settled on Bret. He struggled against the hands that imprisoned him while imploring her with his eyes and trying to speak.

"Stop…him…" Bret choked out, his gaze slashing toward the man in front of him before looking back at her. He saw her eyes zero in on the short, brown-haired man who stood with his back to her. He was partially hidden by several others who had moved to block him and the long weapon in his hand from her view. Her eyes widened in seeming recognition and her lips parted as if her breath had caught in her throat.

"Ray," Michelle called softly and the man beside Bret twitched. "Ray, put that pole down." When he didn't immediately comply, she stepped forward. "Put it down! Don't make me take it from you."

Bret breathed a sigh of relief when the man lowered the pole. One of the others took it from his hand and tossed it aside. Ray was then quickly shuffled into the crowd by the others.

"Now," Michelle said to the crowd in general, "the rest of you, release him."

Glances passed back and forth between them, but eventually, all the hands restraining Bret dropped, except for Hugh's. The big man increased his hold as Bret lowered his injured leg and tried to pull away. As soon as Hugh's arm cut off his airway, Bret ceased his struggles for release and fought to breathe instead.

"I said, let him go, Hugh," Michelle repeated.

"No," the blacksmith hissed. "He's going to ruin everything! He should've been punished, not promoted."

"Let. Him. Breathe!"

About to lose consciousness altogether, Bret heard Michelle's order as if from far away as his legs sagged and his vision slowly faded.

In the next heartbeat, the constricting arm around his neck eased and he could finally gulp in air.

"You think his new duties are a promotion?" Michelle asked, and Bret thought he heard incredulity in her tone but his brain was a little too foggy from lack of oxygen to be sure.

"What would you call it?" Hugh ground out. "He shouldn't have been given a position of power over the rest of us."

An odd look passed over Michelle's stern face, and Bret's stomach tightened, suddenly worried that she agreed with Hugh.

"Power?" Michelle laughed, dispelling Bret's fears. "Do *you* want to do the job? Do any of you want it?" She paused and perused the faces of the crowd, but many of them turned from her gaze. "At least two of you have attempted it before and couldn't do it. The only one who's succeeded at the job for any length of time is Jake, and he only volunteered when no one else would. It's not an easy job, Hugh, and not one this man," she indicated Bret with a wave of her hand, "is particularly comfortable with, in case you hadn't noticed, but he's trying. It's not power, it's work."

"Still, he should be punished for what he tried to do."

She cocked her head, her expression pensive. "And you thought that was your responsibility?"

"It needed doing," Hugh shot right back.

"Punishments are dictated by Angel, not you." Michelle's tone held a dire warning that Bret understood. She would back up Angel's orders whether she agreed with them or not. "As I've made clear to you before," Michelle continued, "it's not your place to harm the other residents, whether they deserve it or not."

"Miss Aldridge didn't do enough to keep him from trying again. He told us as much," Hugh argued, tightening his hold again and shaking Bret when he tried to break away. "He deserves more!"

"Bret!" Michelle shouted. "Stop struggling!" He met her eyes, anger and fear surging within, but he did as she said, though his free hand continued to grip the big arm around his neck.

"And, Hugh! Let. Him. *Breathe*!"

The blacksmith loosened his grasp but did not let go.

"He deserves far more," Hugh repeated.

"What do you want, Hugh?" Michelle walked toward where they stood, casually clasping her hands behind her back in a non-hostile posture. Bret had seen her use her size and height to intimidate, but Hugh was a little too big for that to work. "Do you think he should be whipped? Is that it?"

The big man said nothing, just stared back at her with livid brown eyes, but Bret could feel his answer in the tightening of Hugh's body.

"That *is* it," Michelle said, clearly shocked, as she approached the two men. The crowd parted for her with the soft sound of shuffling feet and she stopped before them, gazing up at the giant with disbelieving eyes.

"He *will* run again," Hugh said with conviction, "and then the council will send their guards to split us up. We won't see those we love again."

In his position, with his head held forcibly against Hugh's shoulder, Bret could see the big man's attention drift to the thin blonde woman who'd first spoken before jerking it back to Michelle.

"So, you think we should string him up," Michelle said, still clutching her hands behind her back as she rocked on her heels, her voice cold and her blue eyes boring into Hugh's, "and let the whip rip the flesh from his back. Tear at his skin until it hangs in tatters, peeling away down to muscle and tendon and bone. Until blood bubbles and rolls off him like a river; until he screams and begs for mercy. Until he passes out or dies from the pain and loss of blood. Is that what you want?"

Would they do that? Bret shuddered at her graphic description, then felt Hugh's angry stare turn on him. Clenching his jaw, Bret mentally cursed himself for giving away his fear.

"I would've thought with everything you've experienced, Hugh, you'd've had enough of scenes like that," Michelle said slowly and his eyes turned back to her.

Bret wondered about that statement. Did that mean Hugh had been flogged like that? *It would explain a lot if he had.*

"Do you really want to make a man suffer so much agony, just for wanting his freedom?" Michelle's tone was softer this time.

The blacksmith's belated reply was just above a whisper, barely loud enough to hear. "No."

Bret's breath halted, waiting.

"Then let him go," Michelle said. "His punishment has been decided and there's nothing more to it…unless you push this and bring problems down on yourself."

Hugh silently debated for what seemed like forever to Bret. Fear that the man would refuse wound around his chest, constricting his airway even more. Suddenly the arm around Bret's neck disappeared and he was standing on his own—well, swaying might be a better description. Bret's legs trembled as they took his full weight, and he only stayed upright by mere force of will. That is until Hugh shoved him. Bret's injured leg flared with pain and collapsed beneath him. Landing hard on his knees with a grunt and, toppling to his side, he slid across the hay-littered concrete floor and skidded to a halt a foot from a wooden stall door.

A hand touched his shoulder and, grasping the wrist tightly, he jerked it away. He looked up, wary of another attack, and his muscles eased slightly when he saw Michelle crouched beside him. Concern filled her pale gaze, and she flinched from his grip on her arm.

A wave of guilt flooded his chest and his jaw clenched at the absurd emotion. He had every reason to be angry and cautious, but no matter what he told himself, the feeling remained. Dropping his chin to his chest, Bret closed his eyes with a sigh and released her. He scooted back and propped himself against the stall door.

"Are you all right?" she asked softly once he'd come to rest.

He glanced at her, then toward the crowd and back. Nodding, Bret closed his eyes again, taking stock of his injuries. His throat ached a little and his thigh hurt like hell, throbbing with sharp bolts of pain shooting up and down his leg, but otherwise, he was all right. Even so, he wasn't about to admit any weakness while the mob that had attacked him was still so close.

"Stay here," she said with a dubious look for his affirmative response, and then stood to face the crowd milling nearby. She looked them over, and Bret was glad not to be the recipient of that cold, assessing stare.

Hugh Blocker stood close to the tall blonde; his huge fists jammed into his jeans pockets. At least he had the decency to look abashed when Bret glanced at him. Most of the others had the same expression in differing magnitudes.

"You all should be grateful that you didn't do more harm to him," she said in a hard voice. "I know you intended to."

A soft shuffling echoed inside the barn as many of the group averted their eyes and shifted uncomfortably.

"As it appears, he's none *too*," she emphasized the word significantly, "worse for wear. So, I see no reason to take this further."

A hushed silence followed and Bret frowned. Did she intend to let their attack slide? With his back against the stall door, his injured leg stretched out along the floor, and his arm draped over the other bent knee, he eyed Michelle and the mob equally. He wanted to challenge her decision, to shout that they'd tried to cripple him, but she didn't give him a chance to speak or the crowd time to celebrate their good fortune.

"But, I'll remember each of you, and if anything unpleasant should happen to this man again," she pointed at Bret, "anything at all, I will hold all of *you* responsible, whether you had anything to do with it or not." She waited a moment to let that sink in. "Do you all understand what I'm saying?"

They answered in a quiet though disgruntled murmur of assent.

"Good," she said. "Now, those of you who answer to me," she glowered at the three guards, who, Bret noticed, had been cowering near the back of the crowd, "I expect to see you in the office before breakfast tomorrow morning. We'll discuss your participation in this disgraceful exercise then.

"As for the rest of you," her stony gaze raked over them, "if you lived anywhere else, you'd very likely have taken this man's place at the whipping post for your actions here tonight." She paused. "Now, get out of here and go home! I don't want to see any of you again until morning."

The crowd quickly headed for the door. Not one of them would meet Bret's angry glare as they weaved a wide path around the injured man on the floor.

When they were gone, Bret used the stall door to pull himself up. He groaned when he put weight on his injured leg, but forced himself to stand, intending to hobble back to his room.

Michelle's hand on his arm stopped him.

"Stay a moment, Bret," she said as the last of the group passed through the barn doors.

"Why?" he asked suspiciously.

"Because we need to talk."

He frowned but didn't speak further as he slowly lowered himself back to the floor. Preparing for the lecture he was sure would come, he crossed his arms over his chest and gave the head guard his best stubborn, disgruntled scowl. He had a thing or two to say as well and, with the pain shooting through his leg, he was just angry enough to not care how he said it.

3

"ARE YOU HURT BADLY?" Michelle asked, appearing troubled by his clumsy movement.

"It could be worse," he said, leaning back against the stall door and wincing as he straightened out his leg once more.

"Can you walk?"

A sour chuckle escaped the tightness in his chest. "Not easily."

"Is it broken?"

"I don't think so. Badly bruised, I'd say. Nothing a little ice won't help."

Michelle frowned, obviously debating in her head.

"Is there something else you wanted?" he prompted, gently rubbing his thigh.

She tilted her head and her face settled into a concentrated frown as she crouched beside him. "Yes, there is. I want to know if you're going to hold a grudge."

"Over this?" he asked, hiding the achy hurt of rejection with sarcasm. "Now, *why* would I do that?"

"They have a right to be upset with you," she told him. "Most of them have families, and even if Angel was able to convince the governing council that none of them had helped you and they were allowed to stay, the law that restricts the Section Guards from entering our homestead and poking their noses in everyone's business would no longer be in effect."

"Yeah," he murmured. "Why's that?" Confusion and anger sharpened his voice, but Michelle didn't seem to notice.

"Because you'd escaped." When Bret merely stared back at her, Michelle elaborated, "The law states that the home of an escaped slave must be monitored closely, and anyone who helped him is to be punished as an example. If Darla and her sidekick, Carrie Simpson, had their way, once the Section Guards arrived to *monitor and investigate*," Michelle's last three words were filled with derision, "they'd find any excuse to never leave. And that would've changed *everything*."

Michelle's explanation dropped another lead weight into Bret's belly. He had known there would've been a search for him and an inquiry at the ranch, but he hadn't known the rest. Still, Michelle seemed more concerned about that possible inconvenience than the reality of what had just happened. "And that makes attacking me forgivable?"

She shook her head. "I didn't say that."

"Yes, you did," Bret growled, the hurt and anger squeezing his chest, "when you let them walk away without any consequences for what they did."

Michelle heaved a sigh but met his eyes evenly. "I'll ask you the same question I asked Hugh: What do you want? Would confining them to their rooms for a week have been enough? We don't have cells here, so it wouldn't have been much of a punishment. Maybe we could have denied them food too. Should we have flogged them all? Or perhaps just the ones who'd held you? Or maybe just Hugh? What do you want me to do?"

He frowned at her, thinking furiously. He wouldn't wish flogging on his worst enemy, but he still thought she should've done *something*. Confinement might have been acceptable, but she was right, it wasn't much of a deterrent, and he didn't want to be responsible for anyone going hungry either.

Unable to think of anything more appropriate, he shook his head. Then another thought occurred to him and he turned his stunned gaze to the tall woman beside him. "You agree with them!"

"Yes," she said, and Bret blinked, surprised at her open admittal. "I was worried that something like this would happen, and I did think Angel should've done more. But, after seeing how uncomfortable you've been over the last few days, I think she may have known how to deal with you better than any of us could've guessed."

She smiled to take some of the sting out of her words, but Bret still bristled. Did this woman know what Angel had done to him? Did Angel tell her guards how she'd humiliated him to placate them and exact some small measure of revenge for her own irritation? It didn't seem like something she would do, but he wouldn't have believed she'd tie him to a bed and threaten him either.

"So, why didn't you let them finish?" he asked.

"Like I said, it's Angel's decision. Right or wrong, I work for her. Besides, we need you to be able to work. Life here has been much more prosperous and stable since you arrived. I don't want that to change, and neither do any of the others...not really."

"I think Hugh Blocker and the little guy with the big stick would disagree with you on that one," he said, sarcasm still edging his words as he carefully rubbed his injured leg.

"Ray was just afraid, probably made that way by what the others told him. He wouldn't normally react with violence and Hugh..." She looked away briefly then shook her head and met Bret's gaze. "Hugh comes from a much different atmosphere. He's only been here about a year and he's still getting used to our ways."

"So, instead of their Mistress doing the dirty work, where he came from the slaves did it for her?" He sounded bitter and felt it too.

"They were expected to police themselves," Michelle said. "If they didn't, they all would suffer. It was easier to punish one than torture or starve all of them. Some would even volunteer to save the others the trouble. It was no way to live, and while it doesn't excuse what he did, it does explain his thinking."

Bret didn't respond, only hung his head with a sigh.

"You have a right to be angry too," Michelle said and he lifted his head to gaze at her in surprise. "But you need to accept that their actions were a direct result of your disregard for their welfare."

"I didn't want anything to happen to them," he said, gazing at the small sprigs of yellow-green hay stuck to his black jeans. "I just don't want to live as a slave."

"Do you plan to run again?"

He laughed, a hard, bitter sound. "And if I say, yes? What are you going to do to me then?"

"Nothing," she replied and narrowed her eyes. "We're already watching you closely. There isn't much chance you'd succeed if you tried again. I'm merely asking if you've learned anything from this experience."

"And what was I supposed to learn?" he sneered, and though he tried, he couldn't hide the hurt in his voice. "That all those people I've been working so hard to support hate me?"

"They don't hate you, Bret. They're afraid of you. Of what you may do that'll hurt them."

Bret stared at her, wanting to argue her point but knew she was right. He hadn't thought about it that way.

"They accepted you," she continued after a short pause, "were glad to have you and all the knowledge you brought, we all were, but..." she stopped again, and then hurried on, "but you ruined that when you risked their families and the safety of the ranch by trying to escape. If you try again, especially if you somehow regain their goodwill, you'll only make things worse for yourself. With them, and the rest of us too."

Bret's shoulders slumped a little more and he sighed. From the beginning, he'd never intended to stay here, but somehow, for one reason or another, he'd felt compelled to remain. Those reasons hadn't had anything to do with the other members of the ranch, at least not at first. But they'd grown on him, and now he had more to consider.

"So, how long do you think it'll be before they try again?" he asked, pushing his uncomfortable thoughts aside.

"I doubt they will, not now. At least, not for a long while," Michelle replied. "I was serious about holding them responsible, and they know it."

"And what about the guards? Those who were here and the others too. What about them?"

"Those three who participated in this will be punished," she said, a steely edge to her voice. "They won't dare harm you again. The rest will be reminded of their duties."

He looked away, considering her words and his next statement. Then he straightened his spine and faced her again. "Those three guards, they tried to stop the others. And they would've if they hadn't been outnumbered."

She frowned, tilting her head as if studying him. "That must have been hard for you to say."

Heat crept up his neck, but he only shrugged.

"Thank you for telling me," Michelle said quietly. "I'll have to amend my plans for them."

He nodded and the silence between them lengthened. Outside, the fall winds whistled under the eaves, and inside, Bret heard the faint shuffling of the animals in their stalls.

"You do realize things are different here, don't you?"

He frowned again and turned at the sound of Michelle's soft voice. "How do you mean?"

"The guards," she replied. "We're more like security guards than prison guards; just glorified ranch hands mostly. This is our home, not a penitentiary. We don't run regular patrols or man the gate and walls at night like most places do. Angel prefers to give people the benefit of the doubt before treating them like criminals...or worse. There are a few other landowners who feel the same, but many don't. That's part of the reason why the people here want to stay so badly. Can you understand that?"

He gazed at her for a long moment and then nodded.

"Good," Michelle said as she stood. "Now, do you think you can walk back?"

"I don't know," he said with a sigh.

The barn door suddenly swinging open drew their attention. Bret's muscles tensed in anticipation of another attack, but the only person to come through the door was Gloria. She looked shamefaced and nervous as she approached. Tightly gripping a lantern in one hand, she kept flashing furtive glances in their direction.

"Gloria," Michelle said, and the other woman jumped visibly, "I told you to go home. What are you doing back here?"

"I didn't see either of you head toward the house," Gloria said in an anxious voice. "I was afraid he was hurt worse than we thought." She glanced at Bret before straightening her shoulders and meeting Michelle's hard gaze. "I came to help him if he needs it."

Michelle stared a moment, then turned a questioning glance to Bret. He shrugged, unsure what to make of the woman's offer either.

Michelle faced Gloria once more. "What do you think you can do for him?"

"I can…help you get him back to his room. He's too big for just one of us if he can't walk on his own."

Michelle chuckled and looked at Bret. "She's right. Shall we get you up and see how much help you're going to need?"

"Yeah, all right," he muttered and let them help him to his feet. Once standing, he took a slow, experimental step and pain shot through his injured leg, nearly dropping him to the floor again. He slumped against the stall door, waiting for the pain to subside.

"Can you make it?" Michelle asked, and he grimaced. He could make it to the house on his own, but the journey would be slow and arduous.

He looked up and found the concern he'd heard in Michelle's voice reflected in her face. He gave her an apologetic grin. "I think some assistance would be wise."

With that, the women stepped forward and, draping his arms over their shoulders, they turned toward the door. Gloria had handed him the lantern, and he held it over her shoulder, careful to keep it from burning her as they walked.

"You're going to need an excuse," Michelle murmured as they stepped into the windy, cloud-shadowed night. Gloria stabilized him for a moment while Michelle shut off the lights and secured the barn door.

"An excuse?" Gloria asked as Michelle returned to them.

"Yes," she replied as Bret settled his arm over her shoulders again, "to explain the injury."

"Oh," Gloria muttered, sounding a little confused as to why the head guard would want to hide the truth.

"I already thought of that," Bret said and groaned as he put a little too much weight on his leg.

"What did you come up with?" Michelle asked.

Between grunts and grimaces, Bret laid out the story he'd come up with.

"Can cows actually kick that high?" Gloria asked curiously, visually measuring the length of Bret's legs.

"Not if I'm standing," Bret replied with a crooked smile, having seen Gloria's inspection, "but if I was kneeling or crouched next to one for some reason they could."

"Why would you be doing that?" Gloria, being part of the kitchen staff, couldn't understand wanting to be that close to the big, clumsy animals.

"A number of reasons," Bret told her. "I was going to go with checking on a pregnant cow since that's mostly what I've been doing lately."

"Should be believable enough," Michelle said. "As long as no one looks at the bruise."

"I think I can keep that under wraps," Bret joked. He fully intended to wrap it after icing it tonight anyway. Jake was the only other person who might see it, and Bret was sure he could convince him it was nothing serious.

"Bret?" Gloria asked after struggling along in silence.

"Hmm?"

"Why are you so willing to hide what we did to you?"

He glanced at her, surprised. *Good question*, he thought dryly, but he'd had a little time to think about that too. He could feel Michelle's eyes on him and wasn't surprised to meet her gaze when he glanced in her direction. He read the warning in the look she gave him, but he'd already made up his mind not to recount tonight's activities to anyone else.

"Well," he said slowly, gingerly putting pressure on his sore limb, "I guess I can understand why y'all were upset with me, and I think Michelle was right... I don't see why anyone else needs to know."

"But we intended to cripple you," Gloria said, stopping to stare up at him in disbelief. "How can you be so willing to hide that?"

He glanced down at her shining black eyes and smiled reassuringly. "I'm not going to forget any time soon, believe me, but there were a few who tried to help me and one who refused to go through with what the others had planned. I wouldn't want them to suffer the same penalty as the others." His smile broadened, letting her know that he included her in the former. Shyly, she returned his grin and her cheeks flushed, from embarrassment for her involvement in the attack or because of his attention, Bret couldn't tell.

They started walking again.

Upon reaching the house, they helped him up the deck steps and to his apartment door. Michelle turned the knob and pushed it open to find Jake sitting on his bed in jeans and a T-shirt, his legs stretched out and his stocking feet crossed at the ankles. He looked up from the book in his hands, and in the light of the single lamp burning on his nightstand, Bret saw his friend's expression change from surprised to curious to concerned in rapid succession.

"What the hell happened to you?" Jake asked as he set his book aside.

"I tussled with a cow and lost," Bret said and then launched into his story as the women helped him to his bed while Jake got up to shut the door.

"You're not usually that clumsy," Jake murmured as he lit the lamp on Bret's nightstand. Bret caught Jake's suspicious glance and hoped Jake had missed the bruise Bret felt on his cheekbone.

Once the women had helped Bret ease down onto the mattress, he pushed himself back a little and hissed at the stabbing pain that lanced through his thigh.

Eyeing his leg, Michelle pointed at it and asked, "May I?"

"I-I don't..." Bret stuttered warily.

"I'll try not to hurt you," she said. "It looks swollen. I just want to see how bad it is."

He hesitated a moment longer before he gave in. "All right."

She placed her hand on his knee and began testing the muscle, moving slowly upward. At about mid-thigh, Bret grunted and straightened up and she pulled back immediately.

"You're going to need ice and meds for that," she told him, stepping back, "and rest too. I think you should stay in bed tomorrow."

"I've got work to do tomorrow," he said, more annoyed than he should be at her suggestion as he leaned forward to pull off his farm jacket. The truth was that he didn't want to sit by himself most of the day with nothing but his thoughts for company. He knew where that would lead and he didn't want to spend the day dwelling on Angel.

"Still," she said gravely, "you should stay off it as much as possible. Someone should take a better look at it too."

Bret frowned. He didn't want them playing doctor with him.

Jake gave Bret a knowing look. "I'll take care of that."

"Good," Michelle said, the corners of her mouth curling upward slightly, clearly catching on to Bret's discomfort. "Gloria, can you get an ice pack from the freezer, if there is one?"

"Yes, I'll get it," she said cheerily and started for the door.

"I'll see about getting some meds to help with the pain and swelling," Michelle said and cocked her head as Bret tossed his coat toward the desk chair across the room.

"What happened to your wrists?" Michelle asked as Bret's jacket slid along the floor and under the chair.

Bret glanced at the blood on his gray shirtsleeve and pulled it back. He peeked at Jake—who looked completely unconvinced—and thought of a quick lie. "I think I scraped them on the wall when I fell."

Michelle also glanced at Jake and then nodded as if suddenly remembering their story. "I'll see about those meds," she said and hurried from the room.

Jake frowned at the door, then turned his scowl on Bret. "You don't expect me to buy all that crap, do you?"

"Just leave it, Jake," Bret said with a sigh. "Help me with my boots, would you?"

Without a word, Jake carefully removed Bret's boots and helped him to remove his jeans. Bret pulled the blankets back before he sat down again and once Jake tossed his jeans away, Bret pushed himself farther back on the mattress.

Jake crouched and took one look at the long, dark bruise spreading horizontally over Bret's mid-thigh and suspicion darkened his hazel eyes. Bret grunted as Jake tested the discolored area.

"This is not from a cow," Jake said, turning a glare on Bret. "Someone hit you with something."

"It doesn't matter," Bret said tiredly. "It's over and I'll live. Don't make more out of it than that." Bret clenched his jaw and could see his friend didn't want to let it go.

"Will they try it again?" Jake asked.

"I don't know," Bret said with a sigh. "I don't think so. Either way, I'd prefer to keep it between us."

"You mean you don't want me to tell Angel."

"Exactly."

Jake's lips thinned in annoyance and he shook his head. "What if they *do* decide to try again? You may not be this lucky next time."

"I don't think they'll try again, Jake. Michelle knows who they are and she made it very clear what would happen to them if they did. I'd rather not make matters worse by stirring them up some more."

Jake stared for a moment as if stunned, but then he nodded. "All right, but can you at least tell me why?"

Bret frowned, unsure he wanted to reveal that much but then decided it didn't matter. "Because I tried to escape."

"I was afraid it might be that," Jake muttered, and then, to Bret's relief, he changed the subject. "That's a deep bruise." Jake stood. "You need to take it easy for the next few days." He went to the closet as he spoke and returned with some pillows.

"I will," Bret replied as he pulled his flannel shirt off over his head and tossed it on top of his discarded jeans, leaving his white undershirt in place, "but I'm not going to sit in here all day. There are things I can do without aggravating this overmuch," he pointed at his leg, "and that's what I'm going to do."

"That's not taking it easy," Jake scolded as he carefully lifted Bret's leg and stuffed the pillows under it. When he finished, Jake pulled the covers over Bret's legs.

"It's the best I can do," Bret replied once he was settled. To his relief, Jake let the topic go and, instead, chatted about the cattle and the progress of the roundup until Michelle and Gloria returned.

Gloria brought the ice pack wrapped in a kitchen towel. She paused a moment when she saw Bret sitting under a blanket, clearly having shed his jeans. Her eyes went wide and she swallowed hard before she finally stepped forward and handed the ice pack to Bret. He smiled warmly at her, knowing the reason for the crimson in her cheeks. He was used to women responding to him that way.

"Thank you, Gloria," he said softly, hiding his amusement as he pulled the ice pack under the blankets and gently placed it on his thigh. She nodded solemnly in response, and Bret sobered immediately.

He understood their position and might even forgive them all in time, but Gloria was different. He found he wanted to forgive her in particular. Maybe because she'd refused to hurt him or maybe because he was so fond of her boys—he could relate to the pain of losing a father at a young age. Either way, it would still be a while before the resentment faded, but it was a start.

Looking over at Jake who stood beside the desk, Gloria moved a little closer to the bed and leaned forward. "Let me know if you need anything," she quickly whispered with an earnest yet hopeful nod of her head. "I'd like to make up for my participation in what we did to you."

Bret glanced at Jake, who tactfully turned away and became busy with something on the other side of the room.

"You already have, Gloria," Bret said quietly. "Just take care of your boys and don't worry about me. I'll be fine." Just then, Michelle entered, interrupting anything more Gloria may have said.

The head guard faltered just inside the door, then smiled, recovering far more quickly than Gloria had to Bret's state of undress.

Seeing there was nothing left for her to do, Gloria said her goodbyes and left through the front door.

Michelle handed two pills from Angel's medical supplies to Bret, followed by an elastic wrap-bandage, then set a glass of water on his nightstand with a stern admonition to stay in bed. Jake had crossed the room as Gloria left and upon reaching them, Michelle pulled a small bottle of anti-inflammatories and some gauze to wrap Bret's bleeding wrists from her pockets and handed them to Jake.

"Two every four to six hours as needed," she relayed the directions for the meds as she headed for the kitchen entry. "Try to keep him out of trouble." She indicated Bret with a nod of her head and left the room without further comment.

"I'll try," Jake said to the closed door, "but I've never been all that successful at it." He winked at Bret, who rolled his eyes dramatically as he reached for the glass of water.

Jake chuckled good-naturedly. "Get some rest, Bret." He set the medicine bottle on Bret's nightstand and went back to bed and his book, leaving Bret to his thoughts.

How would the others respond to him tomorrow? Would they believe his story? Would those who'd attacked him treat him differently now? Would they find other ways to show their displeasure? And what about Angel? Would she believe him or demand he tell her the truth? What would she do when he refused? Would he see anger or hurt in her eyes? Then he wondered why the thought of her being upset bothered him at all. After what she'd done to him—after playing with him the way she had—her comfort should be the last thing he cared about. The problem was, he did care, and that scared him more than all the rest.

4

September 24

BRET HOBBLED INTO THE DINING HALL under his own power the next morning. The pain in his thigh was intense but manageable, and he didn't want anyone to think they'd kept him from his duties. When Jake offered to accompany him, Bret insisted on going alone, partly due to his pride and partly because he didn't want to imply weakness—at least as far as facing those who'd hurt him were concerned. He was injured, but he was not afraid.

His show of masculine bravado, however, did not impress his friends overmuch. Theo, Dean, and a few of the other riders he worked with regularly had been concerned for their friend when they saw him limp up to their table.

"Good God, Bret," Dean drawled, his blue-green eyes wide, "what did you do to yourself?"

When Bret relayed his story, however, they'd laughed openly at his misfortune.

"Oh, no," Theo had chuckled merrily, "those lady cows are picky about the cowboy they let under their skirts." That got a huge laugh from Bret's friends, and when he smiled humbly and slowly eased himself into a chair, carefully swinging his injured leg under the table, the jokes at his expense only got worse. He had expected their ribbing and took it in stride, but the embarrassment burned up his neck nonetheless. Still, it was a small price to pay for keeping the peace and avoiding another episode like the one the night before. Once seated, he shared a look with Jake, who gave Bret a half-grin and a shake of his head, clearly not feeling one bit sorry for his friend.

They were nearly finished eating—and thankfully, the jokes at Bret's expense had long since died down—when Angel stopped by the table with a half-nibbled piece of toast. Bret took one look at her face and felt a rush of anxiousness flood his body like ice water in his veins.

She looked terrible! Her black hair was pulled severely back from her very pale face, and its usual shine seemed dull and lifeless as it hung drearily down her back. Everything about her appeared haggard from the unusual droop of her shoulders to the dark, bluish-purple circles that shadowed her haunted-looking eyes.

From lack of sleep or something else?

She seemed thinner than Bret remembered, but that might just be his imagination. He wondered what caused such a drastic change in her appearance. He glanced at Jake and saw his worry mirrored on his friend's face. An instant passed and Jake met Bret's stare but shook his head ever so slightly when he saw Bret's concern.

"How are the cattle doing?" Angel asked as she stood beside their table.

"Good," Bret said, fighting the urge to find out what ailed her. "We should have them all rounded up from the hills in a couple of weeks, and then we can concentrate on the calving."

The discussion quickly turned to the auction in town coming up in early November, and Bret was in the middle of explaining the number of animals he estimated they could take to the sale when he noticed Angel frowning at him.

"What?" he asked, wondering if he'd said something wrong.

"What happened to your face?"

Confused, Bret stared, then remembered the new bruise around his eye and blundered into his story. "I...had an accident," he stammered, knowing he sounded less than convincing.

"Yeah," Dean sniggered, "he forgot to warm his hands before getting familiar with his favorite cow." A chorus of stifled giggles erupted around the table. Bret turned a narrowed gaze on his friends before he glanced back at Angel, who looked less than amused as she eyed Bret askance.

"It's not a big deal," he said with a half-grin, hoping to deter any more questions.

"Your wrists are still bleeding?" she asked, staring at his hands. Bret followed her gaze and found a thin strip of the gauze he'd wrapped around his raw wrists the night before peeked out from under the edge of his shirt's blue- and black-plaid cuff. The partially healed wounds left by the rope the Section Guards used to haul him back to the homestead four days ago had been ripped open in last night's struggle. He'd meant to cut the bandages off this morning before leaving his room but had forgotten all about them.

He lifted his eyes to her face and fumbled for an excuse. "I...sc-scraped them...on the...the barn wall last night too."

"And your eye?" she asked, referring to his new shiner. "Did you scrape that on the wall too?"

"Hit the wall," he corrected.

"Were you drunk?"

A loud snickering broke out around the table again and he tossed a quick "*Shut up*" glare at his friends. When he turned back to Angel, he found her still watching him closely.

"No," he replied, a little offended, "I was not drunk."

"Then what made you so clumsy? That's not like you."

Jake cleared his throat and gave Bret a significant look, but Bret already knew Angel was suspicious.

"I was checking one of the cows who's close to dropping her calf," he explained. "She took exception and kicked me. I scraped my wrists and hit my head when I fell."

A chorus of grunts and coughing rounded the table once again.

He ignored them this time.

"I see," she said evenly as she sat in the recently vacated seat beside Bret, setting her toast on the table. "And where did she kick you?"

He cringed inwardly. He'd been hoping she wouldn't ask him that. "In the thigh."

She looked down and reached out with slightly trembling fingers to touch his right thigh. "This one?"

He jumped at the discomfort her gentle touch caused, and not only because of his injury. It was the first time she'd touched him since she'd tied him to his bed, and despite everything, his body came alive.

"It's pretty badly swollen," she said peering up at him and pulling her hand away. "Did you wrap it?"

"Yes," he said, trying to ignore the warmth her hand had left on his leg. "Michelle also gave me some anti-inflammatories."

"I have some liniment that will help with the pain and swelling too," she said as she stood, leaving the toast she'd taken for breakfast behind. "I'll send it down later. You should be more careful." She held his gaze a moment longer, a frown darkening her pale face before she turned and left them.

Bret heard the soft rumble of voices as Angel left the hall. He glanced around and saw many of the faces from the crowd in the barn with their heads together whispering. He also locked eyes with Hugh Blocker, who glared at him from three tables away. Reminding himself that he didn't want to rile any of them up again, he gave the blacksmith a cocky but friendly smile and then turned back to his friends as if completely unafraid. Not for anything would he reveal the anxiety that knotted his insides. Not only for himself, he realized, but for Angel too.

* * *

After dinner that night, while Bret rubbed the liniment Angel had left in their room into his sore muscles, he finally had a chance to ask his friend if Angel was sick.

"I don't think so," Jake replied as he pulled off his boots and threw them toward the front door. "Sad is more likely."

"About what?" Bret almost groaned and silently cursed himself. He hadn't meant to ask that question, but it was out now, so he went with it. "What does she have to be that upset about?"

Jake shook his head as he sat on the edge of his bed. "I don't know the whole story…"

Bret got the impression that wasn't the whole truth, but he also knew Jake wouldn't say more.

"She doesn't like to talk about it, but from the little I've been able to glean from Monica, Angel lost someone close to her."

"Who hasn't?" Bret scoffed.

"I'm sure there's more to it than that," Jake said stiffly, "but that would be her story to tell."

"I just meant—" Bret started to explain his insensitive comment, but Jake didn't let him finish.

"I know what you meant," he growled, then softened. "People react to loss differently. Some bounce back while others don't. Whatever it was, it was horrible enough to still affect her years later. That's why I asked you to look out for her when I can't. I assume you'll be keeping your word?"

Sensing his friend's irritation—and ashamed of himself without really understanding why—Bret just nodded and said nothing more.

* * *

Three days passed without Bret seeing Angel again. Her absences at meals made him curious, but he assumed she was busy and taking them when she could.

His leg had improved, though he still limped slightly, and he was back to working a full day around the homestead.

About an hour after breakfast, he was out in the calving barn showing Gloria's two boys, Miles and Gavin, how to bottle-feed one of the calves whose mother had died giving birth two days before. Before his assault, Bret would've already grafted the calf onto a nursing cow from their dairy stock, but that required attention that he hadn't been able to provide while he was laid up. Instead, he'd explained the important details of why and how to bottle-feed the calf, and the new workers had done well with the task. Now that he was back on his feet, however, he'd wasted no time in arranging for the mother and new baby to get acquainted later today. But the calf still needed to eat in the meantime.

The boys had shown an interest in learning about the cattle, especially the calves. With Gloria's approval, the boys had joined him in the barn that morning to watch in rapt fascination as Bret milked one of the dairy cows and poured the warm, white liquid into a bottle. Now, Bret crouched on his heels in the calving barn, the knee of his still tender leg resting against the floor, while he held the calf against his chest. He was instructing the earnestly attentive boys on the proper way to hold the bottle for the animal when Gavin's excited greeting clued him in to Michelle's presence behind him.

"Hi Miss Michelle!" the young boy nearly shouted, beaming happily from his spot next to his brother. "Mr. Bret is showing Miles and me how to feed the baby cows."

The calf started with the boy's excited shout, but Bret calmed her easily and offered the bottle once more.

"I see that, Gavin." Michelle laughed. "Are you boys having fun?" Both children looked up and nodded eagerly.

Bret had turned slightly to greet her, curious as to why she was there. "Hi, Michelle."

"Bret," she said, the smile sliding away, "may I speak with you a moment? Alone?"

"Sure," he said after a slight hesitation. He turned back to the boys and drilled them on the rules for dealing with the calf and her feeding. Once satisfied that they and the calf would be safe, he joined Michelle outside the stall. He shifted over to where he could still see his three charges and then asked the question he'd been holding in. "Is something wrong?"

"Yeah," she murmured. "I don't know if you've noticed, but Angel hasn't been doing too well."

"Yeah, I noticed," he said, keeping his tone carefully neutral. "What happened?"

"Nothing happened, exactly," she told him, but he could see she was anxious and not telling him everything, "she just hasn't been eating. Esther just told me this morning. I tried to get Angel to eat some breakfast, but she just got angry and threw me out of her room…along with the food. Made quite a mess of it too."

"How long has that been going on?" he asked, thinking back on the morning after his assault and the half-eaten toast Angel had left behind.

"Esther says the last time she ate much of anything was Saturday at breakfast. Angel's been hiding in her room ever since."

"That was four days ago!" he said, shocked. *No wonder she looked so thin the last time I saw her.*

"Believe me, I know." Michelle wrung her hands, obviously concerned. "Esther tried sending Carl up with some food on Sunday when Angel didn't come down, but she wouldn't eat. He tried again that evening with the same result, but Carl is still leery of her. So, when he was unsuccessful, Esther went herself. She tried Monday and Tuesday, but she had no luck either. This morning she asked me to try, with similar, if messier, results."

"What makes you think she'll react any differently with me?"

"I don't necessarily," Michelle said, giving him a commiserating smile. "Normally, I would ask Jake, but he's not here and he told me if something like this came up that I should talk to you."

Bret grunted a short, humorless laugh. "Of course, he did."

"Is something wrong?"

"No, nothing's wrong," Bret said and glanced at the children still feeding the calf. "Let me finish with the boys and I'll see what I can do."

* * *

Rain pounded down in sheets as Bret made his way back to the house. The torrent had started as he walked the boys home from the barns, and now, water poured off the back of his hat like a river as he mounted the main house's front steps. Once he'd cleaned the mud off his boots on the boot brush near the deck rail, he pulled off his slicker and hung it on a hook by the door.

Fall has finally arrived, he thought with a sardonic grin as he pulled off his hat and shook it free of the remaining water and then pushed open the front door.

He set his hat on the table beside the entryway then went to the kitchen, where he found the cook waiting for him. Esther looked relieved, and her first comment made it a certainty. "Oh, Bret," she said anxiously, "I am so glad to see you."

"Hello, Esther," he replied. "Is the food ready?"

"Yes," she answered and pointed to a silver tray with a domed cover sitting on the counter across the room. "Michelle told me you were coming. I made up the eggs and toast and juice, just like you asked."

"Good," he said and crossed the kitchen, "thanks, Esther."

The cook nodded, though she still looked worried as Bret picked up the tray. His hands felt a little shaky and his heart thumped heavily in his chest as he tried to mentally prepare himself to once again see the woman who'd ripped open his heart. Being alone with Angel wasn't something he wanted to deal with, not yet, but he couldn't ignore her refusal to eat—though he didn't want to think about why that was—and waiting for Jake to return from the fields tonight would take too long. He didn't want to see Jake's disappointment or listen to his lengthy reminder about Bret's promise to look out for Angel either.

"Be gentle with her, Bret," Esther said as he turned to hurry from the kitchen. "She's…fragile right now."

Bret frowned. "Do you know what's going on with her, Esther?"

"All I know is that around this time every year, she needs…someone to care for her," Esther said carefully. "Not that she asks for it, mind you. It's just that Jake's usually here to keep an eye on her and set her straight, but he's not here now. I'm glad you are though. She can bully the rest of us when she's like this, but she can't with someone who'll stand up to her."

Bret's eyebrows shot up in astonishment. "She…*bullies* you?"

"Sort of," Esther said. "Oh, she doesn't get violent or anything like that, at least not toward us. We've heard shouting and clanging and banging at times with Jake—like what happened with Michelle this morning—but he won't let her get away with the tactics that work on the rest of us."

"Like what?"

"The shouting mostly," Esther said. "She doesn't mean any harm, she's just hurting and we do what we can to help."

"Why?" he asked, trying to decide if he was asking why they tried so hard to help or why Angel was hurting.

Esther chose for him. "She's a good person, Bret, and important to all of us."

He nodded. "So, what am I walking into up there?"

"She'll be angry and obstinate," the cook said. "Don't let her chase you out."

Nodding again, he grinned and said in a voice more cheery than he felt, "Well, into the fire I go, then."

5

ANGEL FELT WORSE than miserable as she lay in bed staring up at the canopy above her, trying not to think. She'd been awake for hours after clawing her way out of another nightmare, unable to close her eyes again. The familiar, unstoppable pattern made her question every choice she'd ever made, and kept her trapped in an endless loop of sadness and fear.

For days now, she'd been hiding in her bedroom, trying to get her growing despair under some measure of control with predictably little success.

Another set of tears wet her eyelashes and trickled from the edge of her eyes. Her hands knotted into the sheets in frustration. She couldn't face anyone like this!

A crucible of guilt and regret had boiled over inside her, heavier and hotter than ever. The feeling pouring through her like molten lead, spreading, growing heavier, crushing her—becoming a mountain too insurmountable to overcome. She couldn't take what lay in that darkness, couldn't face it again.

I am such a coward!

At first, she'd thought the blissfulness of sleep would award some relief from the torment inside her. The nightmares disabused her of that notion a week ago when they started up again—like they do every year—after she'd hoped and prayed they wouldn't return. Even worse, those horrific images from almost seven years ago had become an amalgamation of past and present that confused her and tore at her heart, until she felt more shattered at waking than when she'd fallen asleep.

After a few nights of that, she'd been terrified to close her eyes.

When she couldn't fight sleep any longer and her eyelids slid closed, she'd kept seeing Michael die over and over. She could smell the blood, feel the chill of the cold wind, see his blond hair matted with rain and sweat, and his dark blue eyes glazed over in death.

Every time, her heart shattered all over again.

"No," she told herself. "Don't think of him like that." She didn't want to remember how he'd looked that day. She wanted to remember him smiling, his blue eyes shining with affection. Her mind dug into the well of memories to drag out a happy moment and, even knowing how it would eventually end, she dived in.

"You're beautiful, Angel," Michael said reverently as he brushed the back of his fingers along her bare shoulder. She lay on her belly in bed with a pillow beneath her chest and she hugged it a little tighter, her heart swelling at his tender words. She looked over at the man beside her. Laying on his side, his head resting on his bent arm, his eyes were cobalt-blue pools of male appreciation as they roamed over her naked back.

Holed up for days in the little, one-room cabin they'd found months ago, they'd been sharing body warmth, slow kisses, and so much more. She couldn't remember being so close to someone who wasn't family, but over the long months of their acquaintance, Michael had become her family, her other half. Her partner and lover, protector and confidant. So when they decided to take a break from hiking through the forest looking for signs of raiding parties or anyone in need, they'd snuck away from their friends to spend some time together.

"You're exaggerating, as usual," she said, in denial of his compliment. "I'm just the plain, old girl-next-door. Nothing special

about me."

"Oh," he said, rising to her implied challenge, "you are wrong about that, my dear, Miss Aldridge. You…" He propped himself on his elbow to slide the pad of one finger slowly along her naked spine from the back of her neck to her butt. His soft touch raised all the little hairs on her body at once. "To me, you are gorgeous and I won't listen to any disagreement on the matter." The sheet slid off her hips as his finger traveled downward, and she'd shivered expectantly. But instead of beginning another round of lovemaking, he startled her with a playful smack to her ass.

"Hey!" Reaching down, she jerked the sheet up and flopped onto her side, tucking the pillow beneath her head. With an impish giggle, she slapped his chest. "That's no way to get what you want, mister."

"Oh, really?"

"Yes, really." She turned away in feigned aloofness, but Michael wasn't having any of that.

He reached out, curled a strong arm around her waist, and pulled her flush against him. Kissing her soft and slow, he nibbled her lips until she opened for him, then dived inside to plunder her mouth. She loved it, meeting his bold advance with a brave assault, using both her mouth and body, wiggling against him.

He growled in his throat, his arms tightened, and she could feel his racing heart beat in time with hers. Heat pulsed deep inside her as she wrapped her arms around his neck and pulled him closer.

He broke the connection with a soft chuckle and met her eyes, slightly breathless and his face flushed. His expression turned sober.

"Let's stay here," he said in a serious yet hopeful tone. "Stay and forget about the rest of the world. Just you," he kissed her again, "and me."

The sensual excitement that had been building inside her evaporated in an instant. Her smile fell into a frown and she shook her head. "We can't avoid the rest of the world. You know that as well as I do."

"We can try," he said with a little smile. "I'm willing to…if you are…"

More tears blurred her vision and escaped from her gritty eyes. If she'd listened back then, he wouldn't have died. Michael would've never been alone in the forest that night, would've never been captured, tortured, murdered.

A sob broke from her lips and she jerked a handful of sheets up to her mouth. Squeezing her eyelids shut, she shook her head in denial. She would've done anything to take his place, to save him, but she'd been too late.

Now, fear of a broken heart was only part of her problem.

Lately, like last night, a different man appeared in her nightmares. A man with black hair and green eyes and a too-handsome face she knew all too well—Bret.

The pure agony of seeing Bret's lifeless body in her dreams was as gut-wrenching as watching Michael's passing all over again, and she couldn't bear it! Pounding her fists against the mattress, she flipped onto her side and howled her aggravation into a pillow.

How could Bret Masters intrude on such a horrid and sacred memory? And how could *she* allow herself to think of anyone but Michael?

How could she touch, kiss, and hold another man after what she'd done?

Hadn't she learned her lesson?

She curled her body around one of her pillows and buried her face in its softness. "I don't want to live like this anymore," she cried into the lilac-scented pillow cover and guilt twisted her heart.

What can you do about it? the darkness inside her asked. *You can't just walk away, not after all you've put into this place. And definitely not after all your promises—to Michael, your family, yourself...*

No, she couldn't. Could she?

She owed the people here more than that. Right?

And then there was Bret Masters. Why did she keep dreaming that he would come to the same bloody end as the man she had once loved? Bret wasn't Michael; he wasn't even close. He may be a perfect example of masculine beauty, but the man had no loyalty, honesty, or trust in him. He was too self-absorbed, too callous to see beyond his own desires and that made him not only dangerous, but useless to her as anything more than a foreman for the ranch. Luckily, he excelled at the job. They'd been more prosperous under his care so far this year than they had over any two years in the past. Still, she couldn't ignore his obsession with his freedom or her lapse in discretion with him. Bret would only use her to achieve his goal. He'd done it before with that guard at the Auction Hall, and Angel refused to be his next victim.

If it's that easy, that little voice spoke up again, *then why can't you stop thinking about him?*

Groaning again, she rolled onto her back, the bedsheets twisting around her while her thoughts kept right on spinning.

Why couldn't she stop their night together?

Were her nightmares tormenting her because of her inability to get Bret out of her head?

Making love to him had been…wonderful. She'd actually thought they had made a connection. But that was ridiculous, even if it was the first time in…well, forever that she'd felt anything other than anger, fear, or empty loneliness. Maybe, if she'd slept with some other man sooner, her reaction to Bret would've been different. But then, he affected her even when he wasn't around.

No one else did that. Ever.

She'd been avoiding him, not wanting him too close for fear she'd fall apart.

Seeing him at breakfast last weekend with new bruises on his face and serious swelling in his leg had twisted her belly into intricate knots. That he was lying about how he'd been injured was obvious, and she wanted to know who'd hurt him, but she refused to allow herself to be lured back in, especially now. She needed all her energy just to take her next breath and sometimes—like today, despite her best efforts—her sorrow seemed to suffocate her. That's why she'd stifled her questions about his injuries, feigned mild indifference, and left the room. What more could she do and still keep her word to fight the society she hated?

The thought of joining Michael, no matter how morbid, was more than a little appealing, but she had yet to have the courage to do anything about it. With the anniversary of his death closing in, she felt as if he called to her. She wanted to go, but something held her back. Something more than her instinctual desire to live, and she suspected it had to do with the people she'd brought here.

Despite the actions she'd taken to ensure their well-being, she was less than positive they would be safe from women like Darla and her friends if Angel wasn't around. If anything went wrong...

She blinked back the burn in her eyes. Could she accept their fate if she followed the cold voice beckoning her from the grave?

Sighing resignedly, she shook her head. If she did that, she would be as selfish as she'd accused Bret of being. How could she leave, knowing Darla wanted him? He would *loathe* being Darla's plaything and would fight her at every turn. Darla wouldn't put up with his stubbornness for long, and Angel had no doubt the experience would eventually kill him...one way or another.

And I'm back to Bret again, she thought with a disparaging groan. She turned onto her side once more and pulled the pillow close against her chest.

She would not think about him anymore!

"Yeah, right!" she grumbled as she rolled onto her back yet again.

A knock at her door made her jump. *Why won't they leave me alone?*

Feigning sleep, Angel tossed the blankets over her head and didn't answer, knowing no one but Jake would come in without her consent. He was out with the cattle and she knew Michelle wouldn't try to confront her again so soon. Which meant, whoever it was would eventually go away and leave her to her misery.

Apparently, her displeasure didn't faze this visitor though, because a heartbeat later, the knob turned, and the door swung open.

6

WHOEVER HAD INVADED her space didn't speak or move once the door banged shut, and she knew why. The chilly room was darker than it should have been for that time of the morning because she'd drawn all the curtains, and no fire crackled in the fireplace. Not that she had noticed. The cold darkness within her seemed to consume everything.

Trepidation and irritation made her heart stutter, and she quickly wiped her tear-streaked face with her blanket. She didn't want anyone to see her like this.

"Who's there?" Angel called from beneath the bedcovers, her tone petulant and guarded.

"Get up, Angel," a man said as he set what sounded like a serving tray on the dresser, then crossed to the first set of French doors and threw open the curtains.

Angel groaned at the sound of his voice. She'd know him in any darkness anywhere, and he was the last person she wanted to see.

She listened as he paused to light the oil lamp on her nightstand, then he marched around her bed to yank open the other set of curtains, and her self-loathing simmered into displeasure. *Of all the people living here, why Bret?*

"What are *you* doing in here?" she asked testily, still buried beneath her bedding.

"Getting you up," he said as he jerked the blankets back and headed around her bed again.

Angel blinked at the brightness from the lamp and uncovered windows and pulled the blankets back over her head. "I don't want to get up."

She hated the whiny note in her voice.

Clearly unmoved, Bret set the tray he'd collected from the dresser on her bedside table and then jerked the covers off her again. "Too bad," he said. "It's time to eat. Get up!"

She reached for the blankets once more, but he sat on them before she could drag them over herself. He gripped the covers and held them in place against the mattress. The heat of his arm where it pressed into her side sent tingles shooting through her, waking parts of her she wished would stay dormant.

"If you pull those back over your head again, Angel," he warned, "I'll strip them off the bed."

Thankfully, she was wearing her favorite flannel pajamas so she was decent, but that didn't keep her annoyance from kicking up a notch—not only at his conceit but because of that tingling sensation as well.

"You have no business being up here," she said. "Get out!"

"You made it my business when you gave Jake my job and stopped taking care of yourself," he replied, still gazing down at her with intense green eyes and a calmness that infuriated her.

"What the hell do you care!" she shouted, irritation jumping to anger in an instant. She knew her hair was a tangled mess around her head and her eyes were red-rimmed and puffy, but at the moment, she didn't care about her appearance or if he knew she'd been crying.

Bret frowned, but his voice remained even. "Never said I did. But did you think no one would notice when you stopped eating?"

"I don't care!"

"You should care," he said, releasing the blankets and standing in a swift, smooth motion. "All the people here depend on you. You brought them here. You owe them at least that much."

Heat flashed over her skin and she fisted the fitted sheet below her. He'd used almost the exact words she'd told herself about the same thing.

The reminder cooled her anger, if only slightly.

"I told you, I don't care," she said, a little subdued.

He tilted his head and his frown deepened, but he didn't say a word. His eyes said it all, and she cursed herself for letting him know he'd struck a nerve.

Impatience returned to her voice. "Just leave."

His lips pressed into a flat, stubborn line. "No. Now sit up so I can bring you the tray."

She glowered at him as he rose from his seat beside her, her brief calm vanished. "No. You. Get. *Out!*"

"Angel," he said, turning back to the bed and crossing his arms over his broad chest, "if you don't sit up, I'll be forced to make you sit up. Is that what you want?"

Eyes widening at this new intimidation, she was too shocked to speak. He looked so big and strong and perfectly capable of doing exactly what he'd threatened. Then her anger resurfaced and her eyes narrowed. She might be weak from her long fast, but she was angry enough to make things difficult for him.

"Just you try it!" she taunted, not entirely believing he would.

He eyed her while she sat tense, gripping the bedcovers in tight fists against her chest. "All right." His arms dropped to his sides and he sighed like a man shouldering a heavy burden. "If you want a fight, I'll give you one, but I warn you… I'll give as good as I get."

Angel stared as he crawled onto the bed, though a little clumsily. *His leg must still bother him.*

Suddenly she flashed back to this same man, making that same movement, only minus all his clothes and with a steamy gleam in his smoky green eyes.

Mouth instantly dry and her traitorous body heating in excitement, she recalled the last thing she wanted right now was Bret Masters' hands on her. Her insides clenched at the erotic images that replayed in her head. She could almost feel the warmth of his strong, lean fingers caressing her body…

Oh, no! She bolted upright.

"Fine!" The word shot out of her mouth like a granite projectile. "I'm up, just stay away from me."

He sat back on his heels, frowning at her unexpected compliance. "I'm not going to hurt you, Angel," he said, misinterpreting her fear.

"Whatever," she dismissed him as she looked away, feeling heat in her face and a slight tremor in her body. He was already too close. She couldn't let him any nearer.

Already on the verge of falling apart, if he touched her or showed her any kindness now, it would push her over the edge and she didn't want to lose control in front of Bret Masters. Not again. If she lost it now, Angel was afraid she'd tell him everything and she couldn't fight him if he knew what really ailed her. He could use her pain against her, and she was determined never to give him that much power over her.

Movement on the bed and pillows being plumped behind her caused Angel to swing around. Bret was even closer than before. So close she could feel his body heat, smell his musky scent mixed with hay and leather. Closing her eyes, she breathed him in, relishing him and this moment. Unconsciously, her body leaned toward his and their shoulders brushed. Her eyelids snapped open and she jerked away, pulling the covers with her and glaring at him. "What are you doing?"

"Trying to make you more comfortable." He sat back and grinned his arrogant I-know-all-your-secret grin.

"I'm not going to eat anything," she said. "I already told Michelle this morning that I'm not hungry."

"Yeah," he said, scooting off the bed to stand beside it, "I heard how you told her."

"You should take her example," Angel said, trying to cover her embarrassment over the tirade with Michelle earlier, "and leave before I get really angry."

"What're you going to do, Angel?" he said, his voice light and teasing. "You won't even get out of bed."

"You're a *slave*," she said, knowing the word would annoy him.

She hoped it would make him leave too. "I am your Mistress. You must obey me."

His grin turned cruel, but after taunting him, she deserved it.

"I am my own master," he said coldly, "and if you make me prove that, I will."

"By doing what?" she asked, her voice rising once more. "Running away again?"

"Maybe," he said and she heard the note of menace laced into the one word. Then he crawled onto the mattress and she froze.

Fear of him getting too close, of her body's reaction, and her chaotic emotions all crashed into her at once and she yanked the sheets up to her chest like a shield.

"Or," he continued, not more than a foot away, "maybe I'll show you why you're so afraid of me."

She sat up a little straighter. "I'm not afraid of you," she said, proud that no sign of her nervousness showed.

"Yes, you are."

"Don't be absurd," she said dismissively.

"There's nothing absurd about it," he said, leaning a little closer.

Instinctively, she backed away from him.

His lips curved up smugly. "You're afraid of my touch."

Heat burned up her neck, but she refused to look away. "You are very conceited, you know that?"

He laughed. "And you're a liar."

"I am *not* lying."

"Yes, you are," he said, still too close for her quaking nerves. "You're afraid I'll touch you and that you'll remember how much you liked it."

That wasn't quite right—although it wasn't quite wrong either—but he was still too close to the truth for comfort.

Straightening her spine again, she shot back, "My God, you're arrogant!"

He lifted a hand toward her face, plainly intending to brush the backs of his fingers against her cheek, but he stopped just short, his green gaze challenging her. "Shall we test my theory?"

With wide eyes, she watched his hand approach, then they narrowed and she jerked back before she could stop herself. "Stay the hell away from me!"

He laughed once more and dropped his hand to the bed. They both knew he'd made his point.

"Eat," he said, pushing away from the mattress and standing, "and I'll leave. But believe this if nothing else…if you don't eat on your own, I will hold you down and force-feed you."

He had to know she'd fight him if he tried to follow through with that threat. She suspected in her weakened state he would prevail, though it wouldn't be easy.

Picking up the tray, he set it in her lap and then stepped back. The smell of eggs and toast made her mouth water and her stomach queasy. Turning away, she blinked repeatedly at the burn threatening to bring on more tears.

Anger beat them off.

Meeting his stare with a glare of her own, several long seconds ticked by before he sighed and moved as if to follow through with his threat.

Angel decided that making him wait had proven her point. Now was the time to bend, but only a little. Slowly, with her eyes never leaving his, she picked up the fork and began to eat.

Her stomach rebelled at first, and she struggled to keep the food down, but she managed.

Bret standing sentry beside the bed until she finished kept her anger at a simmering boil, and she glared at him as he deftly plucked the fork from her fingers.

"Good girl," he teased, grinning as he quickly removed the tray to set it aside.

Her glower was her only reply.

"There'll be a little more for lunch," he said.

When what he'd done suddenly occurred to her, she thought her teeth might crack with how hard she clenched them together. He'd purposely requested small portions of easily digestible food because she hadn't eaten for several days—looking out for her, despite her prickliness, and risking her wrath to make sure she was okay.

Her heart softened a little. His concern touched her, but she couldn't afford to drop her guard or give an inch—for his sake as much as her own.

"What are you doing now?" she asked when he crossed over to the fireplace and slid open the glass doors. "You said you'd leave if I ate."

"I will," he said, collecting the tinder needed to rebuild a fire in the cold hearth, "as soon as I get a fire going and enough time has passed that I know you've digested some of it."

"You bastard!" she hissed.

His spine stiffened into an iron rod and, even though his back was to her, she saw his jaw tighten.

Why would that particular slur bother him so much?

He shook off whatever had caused him to pause and crouched beside the open hearth.

"I don't want you in here," Angel said. "Why can't you understand that?"

"Oh, I understand just fine," he said, not bothering to face her, as his sarcasm bit back. "I just don't care."

She was silent for a long time, watching him, memorizing the color of his hair, the shape of his broad back and shoulders, the easy way he moved as he stacked the kindling and logs in the hearth.

Strangely, when they weren't arguing and she wasn't fighting to keep her emotions in check, Angel actually felt better with him in the room. She couldn't explain why. She hated that she felt that way, but it was true nonetheless. She sighed and lay on her side. Pulling pillows under her head and against her chest, she watched him build a fire.

When the flames licked hungrily at the new logs, Bret stood and went to sit in the wingback chair that sat nearby. He stretched out his long legs and crossed booted feet at the ankles.

Watching him, letting her mind drift, it hit her that she not only felt safe but so terribly aware of him as a man that her body ached with it.

Why? What was it about him that always seemed to make her melt?

Taking in his straight nose and chiseled lips, his lean, whisker-shadowed cheeks and strong chin, she knew why she couldn't stop looking at him. He was the epitome of the perfect female fantasy, and the beauty didn't end with his face. He was muscular and lean in all the right places, tall and powerful, and she knew from personal experience how extremely tender and exciting his touch could be. Remembering how his hands had moved over her flesh, something hot and quivery tightened deep inside her.

Forcing a deep breath into her lungs, she swallowed the lump in her throat and reminded herself that she couldn't have him, could not *trust* him. He didn't want her anyway, so why was she even thinking about this?

How could he be so casually indifferent when she was such a mess every time he came around? Granted, she was in chaos at the moment—not much of which had anything to do with him—but he had definitely added to her burden.

Damn him! she silently seethed. *I will not melt!*

BRET FELT HER EYES on him again, just as he had felt them on his back while he'd built the fire. Only then, it had felt like a sharp blade sliding along his spine. He'd ignored her despite the prickly tingle of anticipated attack, thankful he'd removed the food tray and its utensils. A few minutes later, she'd huffed and laid back down, arranging the pillows and blankets around her, and some of the tension in his shoulders eased.

He'd taken his time building up the fire before he slouched into the wing-backed chair on the far side of the bed. Stretching out, he watched the flames and waited silently for the room to begin to warm up. Now, that same prickly sense of doom rose the hair on the back of his neck.

He glanced toward the bed—from where that troubling feeling emanated—to find Angel lying on her side, cuddled up with one of her pillows, while her sleepy gaze regarded him closely. She didn't say anything, but her eyes didn't seem to be as angry as they had been and he read something there that intrigued him. His body warmed and the longing inside him ached a little more. It hurt to see her in such obvious distress. Part of him wanted to take her in his arms again, protect her, help her heal, banish whatever cursed her now.

His mind rebelled. *What? Why on Earth would you want that?* She had used him and thrown him aside, given him hope only to rip his heart out. And now she resorted to reminding him that he was a slave and calling him names—one that struck a little too close to home. He shouldn't care how she felt, shouldn't care if she harmed herself, starved herself, or anything else.

The problem was…he did care.

He stared into her pretty blue eyes and wished things were different. Cursing himself for a fool, he abruptly stood and crossed the room. Feeling her eyes still on him, Bret picked up the tray with a rattle of dishes.

What he'd read in her gaze had stabbed him as surely as any knife. There'd been longing in her eyes—fear and anger too—and something else he couldn't quite define. If he didn't leave immediately, he'd be tempted to discover *all* the secrets she hid behind those blue pools. He turned toward her and found the angry challenge had returned to her face. He ignored it—but regretted it too—as he headed toward the door.

"See you at lunch," he said with a mocking little grin and gave her a short bow from the threshold. Her expression warned him not to return, which, he told himself, was exactly the reason he would.

"You'd better not," she said, her voice low and dangerous.

"You can count on it." He winked at her and flashed his most charming smile at the fury he read in her eyes, then dashed out the door before she could find something to throw at him.

* * *

Bret spent the next several hours getting things set up for grafting the orphaned calf with the cow and training some of the other hands on the process. The possibility of the cow rejecting the calf would mean a lot more work for them. But if she didn't, the calf would have a much better chance at life, and they'd all have a little extra time.

Unfortunately, training people who've had little experience with cattle was frustrating, to say the least, but the more experienced ranch hands were all helping with the roundup and the thousand and one other things that needed doing on a spread like this one.

Despite their lack of skill, Bret didn't understand why so many of the greenhorns hadn't been required to work more closely with the animals in the past. But then, he'd updated many of their practices over the last several months. Angel hadn't been exaggerating when she told him they'd learned mostly by books and guesswork. Jake had been a big help, but his knowledge about actually running a cattle ranch was limited. What Jake did know, he'd learned from Bret, and Bret could only imagine what it had been like before Jake arrived. No wonder they'd only managed to barely break even most years.

Later that afternoon, Bret collected another tray from Esther and carried Angel's lunch up to her room. He had hoped not to have a repeat of the battle from breakfast, but she hadn't given up the fight.

Maybe he lost his temper because he'd already expended his patience in training ignorant—if not fearful—newbies on how to deal with the grafting process, or because his injury was paining him a little more than normal, or maybe he was just tired. Whatever the reason, after she'd screamed at him to leave for the umpteenth time that day, he'd finally had enough.

"You want me to go?" he shouted at her from beside the bed, his body tilted slightly forward and his fists balled up at his sides.

"Yes!" she shouted from her seat under the covers in the middle of the bed. She still wore the white flannel pajamas with the lamb embroidered on the left chest. And with her black hair a wild tumble around her shoulders and her eyes shooting blue sparks, she appeared mad enough to cause him harm. Back rigid as she leaned toward him, she clutched the blankets in tight little fists and glared up at him with red-rimmed eyes. She looked livid, tired, and vulnerable. The vision twisted his insides, but, like so many other things today, he ignored it.

"Then eat!" he bellowed.

The tray of food sat undisturbed in her lap. Thankfully, she chose not to fling it across the room as she'd threatened, but only after he supplied a few threats of his own. It was a good thing she'd believed him when he said he would turn her over his knee if she tried it. He would have if she'd forced him to, but he really wasn't feeling up to a physical battle, nor was wrestling around with her on the bed the best idea either.

He pointed at the untouched tray. "The sooner you eat, the sooner I'll leave!"

That had finally done it. She ate the chicken salad sandwich and homemade chips that Esther had prepared for her and scowled at him with so much heat he should've combusted in his boots. She swallowed the food more easily than at breakfast, but he suspected she valiantly struggled through any difficulties in silent fury simply to get rid of him.

Just like at breakfast, he stayed to make sure she didn't rush to the bathroom to undo his hard-won battle and spent his time building up the fire once again. As soon as she finished, he took the tray from her and set it aside, while calmly explaining that he'd bring her dinner as well.

She laid on her side, her eyes shooting daggers at him for several long seconds before she turned over and settled in for more sleep.

Just as he had that morning, Bret wondered what was eating at her. No matter how much she annoyed him, he didn't like seeing her like this. But she'd already rejected him once, and he wasn't about to open that door again. Still, seeing her in pain worried his mind and made his gut ache. Knowing he could do nothing to help made it worse. With Angel, all he seemed to do was make things worse, which was a new experience for him. Women usually went out of their way to gain his interest, not shun him. At least he'd been able to get her to eat, if reluctantly. That was something. Right?

He speculated for the hundredth time that day on what had caused her swift spiral into what he could only label as severe depression.

Did his escape attempt trigger her despair?

An ache squeezed his chest and, no matter how hard he tried, he couldn't banish it.

Jake and Esther had both told him Angel fell into this despondency every year, so at least he wasn't the cause. Even though his departure probably hadn't helped, there was no reason to feel guilty for wanting to be free and no reason to feel further obligated to help her either.

Still, the desire to do just that kept him coming back. As he exited her room and ambled toward the stairs, Bret told himself he was only doing it to help Jake and to ensure the security of everyone on the ranch.

And not because he felt a desperate need to make sure Angel survived another year.

7

THE SUN HAD JUST KISSED the horizon when Jake and the other riders returned that evening. After repairing another line of downed fences—damaged by the cattle this time—and then tracking the missing animals over rough terrain in the increasingly wet and windy conditions, Jake decided to head back early and pick things up the next morning. Dinner would be ready in about an hour, which gave them plenty of time to get clean and warm before eating. And Jake intended to take full advantage of the time by doing just that.

He found the room he shared with Bret empty and hadn't seen his friend near the barns when stabling his gelding either. But, despite his nagging concerns about Angel, Jake was too cold and worn out to hunt Bret down for an update.

The shower he'd stepped into had felt wonderful, but a long, hot soak for his sore muscle's sake would've been better. Still, he felt quite restored as he dried off and dressed. The whole process took about thirty minutes, leaving Jake plenty of time to check on Angel himself. He'd missed her at breakfast for the last few days and a bad feeling had been haunting him all day. Depending on what he discovered, he'd be talking with Bret about that along with the cattle update tonight.

A knock at his door startled him as he finished tucking in his blue, button-down shirt. Even more surprising was finding Michelle standing there when he opened the door, and she seemed out of sorts.

A concerned frown creased his brow. "What's wrong?"

"Angel wants to see you," she said, "but I wanted to speak with you first. If you don't mind?"

"Sure." He stepped back to allow her entry and waved a hand at the desk chair as he settled on the edge of Bret's bed. "Have a seat."

Michelle smiled her thanks and then perched on the edge of the chair. Her eyes glanced around the room and she appeared nervous, which, for her, was strange.

"Did you know Angel hasn't been eating?" she asked, getting straight to the point.

"No, I didn't," he said slowly. He had hoped Angel wouldn't go there again this year. "I've had my suspicions though. Do you know for how long?"

"Esther says since Saturday morning, but I think it's been longer than that."

"And no one noticed?"

"Everyone had noticed she wasn't in the dining hall, but most just assumed she ate elsewhere. Esther told me this morning and I tried to talk to Angel, but it didn't go well."

"Did you tell Bret?"

"Yes," Michelle said and then seemed to brighten a bit. "I talked to him right after I cleaned up the mess. That's the good news."

"She's throwing things again?" Jake almost groaned. If Angel was being that belligerent, things were only going to get worse.

Michelle sighed. "Yep, but better me than Esther or Carl. I tried to be firm, but she knows I won't try to physically force her. She's much stronger than she looks when she's angry, but I'd still be afraid I might hurt her. And, I'd like to keep my job. I didn't want to risk a fight. So, I went to Bret. I figured he could handle her better than I could if it came to forcing her to do anything."

"What did he do?" Jake was more than a little curious about his friend's reaction.

"Well, you'll have to ask him for the details," Michelle replied, "but he got her to eat. Breakfast was relatively quiet, at least more so than I'd thought it would be, but lunch was a shouting match."

"But she ate?"

"Yes."

"Did he use force?"

Michelle shook her head. "I don't think so, just a lot of shouting, like I said."

"Well, that's good news." Jake was more than relieved to hear it. He'd been a little worried that Bret wouldn't handle Angel or the situation well, if at all.

"Yeah..." Michelle sighed and shook her head once more. "She's not happy about it though. I think that's what she wants to talk to you about."

"I kind of expected that as soon as you said he talked to her," Jake said with a grin.

* * *

Barely ten minutes later, Jake knocked on Angel's bedroom door.

"If you are *not* Jake, *go away!*" Angel shouted from inside. He slowly opened the door and peeked around the corner.

"What if it is Jake?" he asked with a silly grin he knew would make her smile.

"Jake! Come in. Come in." She beamed and motioned for him to enter. She almost seemed happy, sitting in the middle of her enormous four-poster bed with a grin splitting her tired-looking face, but he knew better.

He closed the door and went to the wing-backed chair. Pulling it closer to the bed, he sat and met her gaze. His heart constricted painfully, but he wasn't surprised by how pale and thin she looked, not to mention her unkempt appearance. He'd seen it all before but that didn't make it any easier to witness.

"Michelle said you wanted to see me," he started, and then went on the offensive. "She also said you stopped eating again."

Angel pouted. "*She* should stop being such a tattletale."

"She's worried about you."

"Yeah, yeah," Angel said, waving a dismissive hand at him, "spare me the lecture, Jake. I've had about as much of that as I'm going to take today."

"All right," he said and wondered what Bret had said to her. "What did you want to talk about then?"

"Masters."

Jake didn't miss the nasty tone or the significance of the singular use of Bret's surname. Jake had never heard her do that before, not with anyone on the ranch. Even the man who'd attacked her a few years ago—the one that Jake had nearly beaten to death before Angel stopped him—had still just been Toby. Bret must have really hit a nerve. "What about him?"

"I want you to find someone else to take over whatever duties he has around the house," she said quickly, but her eyes darted furtively to and from his as she spoke. She was nervous, though she hid it well, but Jake understood her motives.

She had to know he was going to ask why, but he suspected she had a reasonably good excuse. He also knew she could just order him to do as she asked, but *she* had to know that he would refuse that too—if he thought he should. She'd given him that right and others a long time ago, and he'd learned he could trust her word not to punish him for it. He'd also learned that she would only be pushed so far and, right now, she was obviously in no mood to argue. Unfortunately, he was going to do just that.

"No," he said, his face straight and gaze firm as shocked disbelief filled her eyes. He rarely flat-out refused her, usually choosing to discuss it with her first, but they no longer had that luxury. He would be gone in a few months, but only if he knew she'd be safe without him around.

"Why not?" It was unlike her to whine, and he had to fight the smile that wanted to curve his lips.

"Because, aside from me, he's the only one here who'll stand up to you," he said evenly, "at least, the only one I'd trust."

"How can you trust him?" she nearly squeaked with the fury that flared up in an instant, and he knew what was coming next. "Oh, that's right. You lied to me too…*for him!*"

They had never actually talked about Bret's escape attempt or why Jake had kept his friend's secret, but he knew denying his involvement would be a mistake. "Yes, I did and I'm sorry about that."

She glared at him for a long moment, but when she spoke, her voice held a dire warning. "Get rid of him, Jake…or I will."

Wow, he thought, *Bret really pissed her off.*

"No, you won't," he told her with more confidence than he felt.

"I won't?" she asked too sweetly, but her gaze drilled into his.

"I *know* you won't." Her eyes narrowed, but he hurried on before she could speak, "You won't get rid of him because you need him."

He was a little surprised by her reaction. She seemed startled, in a frightened sort of way that he couldn't explain. Bret might argue with her, he might threaten or restrain her, but he would not harm her. Jake was positive about that, but now wasn't the time to explore her reaction.

"You won't sell him because this place is finally starting to come together and that's because of Bret. I don't know how you've managed to maintain this place or where the wealth you obviously have comes from, but I do know it wasn't from the ranch, not the majority of it anyway. With him here, the place has started to become what you've hoped for all this time. You won't jeopardize that."

"He's been here almost a year…" she said softly, almost as if he'd rebuked her. "Surely you and the others know enough to do the work without him."

"Not even close," he told her. "Bret's been doing this work for most of his life, Angel. You'd be hard-pressed to find that kind of experience now. If another man's out there, he's already taken and his owner isn't about to part with him. The rest are lost, hiding, or dead. I can't do what Bret can, none of us could. If we could've, we would've done it long before now. Getting rid of Bret would risk this place and I think you know it."

She frowned even more furiously, licked her lips, and looked away.

She does know it. He didn't know why that surprised him.

"Besides," he said with a small smile, "you don't sell your people once they're here."

"Shut up," she said, but without heat. "Someone else can do the job, Jake. It doesn't have to be him."

"No, I don't think so," he said and she gave him a dark look, but he didn't allow her time to retort. "There are plenty of people here who'd gladly help you, Angel," he chose his words carefully, "but not one of them will stand up to you, and they definitely won't defy you when you're like this."

"And why not? You and your *buddy* don't have any difficulty with it."

He didn't miss her sarcasm.

"If you'll remember," he told her, his tone and expression gentle, "it took me a while to believe you weren't like Darla. It wasn't until I realized how much you expected and *needed* me to do it that I started telling you no." He paused to let her consider that before he spoke again. "The others you've brought here have come from similar experiences to mine—from a life of fear that was hammered into them. They know the punishments that used to be a part of their lives don't happen here, but they're still afraid. Even the guards worry about losing their place. None of them want to risk what they have here, which is why they won't stand up to you." He leaned forward, resting his elbows on his knees. "But Bret will...not just because he doesn't understand what's out there, but because he'd do it anyway."

She sighed, silently staring at the floor. Her shoulders slumped and Jake knew she'd surrendered the argument, but he needed to clarify some things.

"Why are you so upset with him?" Jake asked, nervous about her answer. Just because he was sure Bret wouldn't harm her didn't mean the man wouldn't say something insensitive.

"He doesn't listen," she said quietly, not meeting his gaze.

"You've known that for some time. What's different now?"

"I don't want him here."

"Why?"

She didn't respond and she wouldn't look at him. She flopped back on the bed with a sigh and stared at the ceiling. "I just…don't."

"Did he try to hurt you?"

"No."

Jake breathed a silent sigh of relief for being right about that much—not that he'd thought he was wrong.

"Did he say something?"

"He's always saying something," she complained. "He's bossy."

Jake laughed. "So are you."

She turned on her side to give him such an exaggerated glare it was comical and he laughed again. This was closer to the Angel he knew.

He wondered how long her pain-filled mourning would last this time.

"I'm just so tired, Jake," she said a moment later, "and he pushes too much." She was still lying on her side, her knees bent, her head cushioned on one curled arm, and the other arm wrapped around a pillow, hugging it to her chest.

"I know," he told her and his worry for her returned. She looked tired and sad, and so defenseless that it made his heart ache. He knew a little more about her past than he'd told Bret, but he'd given Monica his word not to let on until Angel told him her secrets herself. He still felt a little guilty that he'd forced Monica's hand in that, but back then, he wouldn't have left Monica's side without her reluctant confession.

Angel sighed but said nothing more as her eyes seemed to drift into another time and place.

"Angel? Honey?" Jake called softly and her gaze focused on him again. She looked at him with so much trust it scared him. What would she do when he was gone? "Have you tried doing what Bret asks you to do, maybe before he asks it, and without a fight?"

"Of course not," she said with a small, mischievous smile. "If I did, I wouldn't get to see him get mad."

Jake chuckled. "But then he gets to see you get mad too."

"True," she agreed.

"Try it and see what happens. You do feel better now that you're eating again, don't you?"

"Yeah, I guess."

"Angel," he said gently as he got up to sit next to her on the bed. He took her hand and squeezed it with an encouraging smile. "I know you're hurting now, but it will get better. I promise."

"I know," she said and returned his smile. "Thanks."

"Anytime." He patted her hand and stood. "It should be almost time to eat," he said good-naturedly. "Bret'll probably be here soon." He grinned openly when she moaned and rolled onto her back, throwing the pillow over her face in dramatic fashion.

"Oh…don't remind me."

* * *

Bret brought her dinner about thirty minutes later. Sitting up in bed, hands clasped patiently in her lap as if waiting for him, he appeared surprised when he first walked in. But then he frowned and eyed her askance, clearly suspicious.

"Good evening, Angel," he said.

"Hello, Bret," she replied with a tight smile as he set the tray in front of her.

As he released the tray, his body seemed to tense as if preparing for an attack. Angel almost giggled as he quickly stepped back.

"Thank you, Bret," she said, then began eating without another word. Angel could feel his eyes on her, his wariness and confusion at her sudden compliance an almost physical touch. A tiny pang of guilt for his unease made her look up. "You are going to eat, aren't you?"

A frown marred his brow and suspicion laced his reply, "Yeah..."

She smiled. "Good." And she began to eat again.

"Are you okay?" he asked.

Once again, she lifted her gaze to his and lied. "Yes, I'm perfectly fine. Just hungry, as I'm sure you are. Please, sit. Eat."

He stared into her eyes for a long beat that had her heart thumping in her chest and then shrugged. Glancing back at her once as he strolled to the dresser where he'd left his plate, he shook his head, gathered the plate and his utensils, and crossed the room to sit in the wing-backed chair.

They ate in silence.

When Angel finished, she set her utensils down and leaned back onto the pillows piled behind her to observe him as he finished off the last of his meal. She was still angry but too tired and heart-sore to fight with him. Jake was right. If she didn't want to be around Bret, the easiest and quickest way to get rid of him was to do what he asked—as far as taking care of herself went.

With his meal completed, Bret looked up to see if she was still eating and caught her staring. She held his gaze, but then dropped her eyes to the empty plate in her lap. She pushed the serving dish away to let him know she was done and didn't look up again. From the corner of her eye, however, she saw him frown and study her as if looking for a weapon before he stood, set his dishes on top of hers, and picked up the tray. He set it on the dresser and then crossed the room to stoke the nearly dead coals in the fireplace.

Kneeling at the hearth, he encouraged the tiny flicker of flames into a rolling pyre and then tossed a couple more logs on top to keep it burning through the night. She watched him through the whole process, amused that her meek obedience and lengthy silence seemed to unnerve him. But he also seemed determined not to give himself away.

Once the fire was burning strongly, he stood and turned toward the bed. He tucked his thumbs into his rear pockets and, though it looked casual, she recognized it as a nervous yet unconscious gesture.

"Do you need anything else before I go?" he asked.

"No, thank you," she said quietly, staring back at him with a shy half-smile.

"Okay." He turned away awkwardly, crossed to the dresser for the tray, and then headed for the door. He swung it open and stepped through, then glanced back at her.

She was still watching him.

"Goodnight, Angel," he said.

"Goodnight, Bret."

Something in her reply made him frown. She tilted her head and smiled. She didn't want to fight, she just wanted him to leave. Thankfully, he simply nodded and then walked away before she did something stupid, like ask him to stay.

"WHAT THE HELL did you say to her?" Bret asked Jake when they were alone in their lamp-lit room later that night. Once he left Angel, Bret had completed his evening rounds of the barns, despite the ache in his still-healing leg, and then returned to their apartment. Jake was already in bed, a book on his chest as Bret stripped off his undershirt and dropped it onto the floor, atop the flannel he'd just removed.

Jake's gaze was sharp when he set the book aside. "Nothing special," he replied as he rolled to his side and propped his head on his hand. "Why? What happened?"

Bret sat on his bed to pull off his boots. "Nothing. She ate and I left. Nothing happened at all." He stood to remove his jeans, remembering that tender smile she'd given him right before he left. The same smile that stopped his breath, made his heart pound, and brought back every moment of their sensual night together that he'd been trying so hard to forget. He'd had to fight the temptation to stay and the memory now made his body uncomfortably warm.

Jake's lips twitched and Bret's hackles stood up. *What's he up to?*

"What's wrong with that?" Jake asked, though his innocent tone made Bret's bullshit meter peak into the red.

Shaking his head, Bret shucked his jeans and tossed them onto the pile with the rest of his clothes, then snatched back his blankets and sat down again. He knew Jake was teasing him and didn't want to encourage it.

"There's nothing wrong with it," Bret said with a shrug. "It was actually kind of...nice." He winced inwardly and cursed himself for making the last word sound almost pleased.

"Then what's the problem?"

"It was damn creepy," Bret said with a dramatic twitch of his shoulders. He still felt the sharp, knife-like tickle of her eyes on his back and the sensation of an imminent attack.

Jake chuckled at his description and Bret flashed a challenging glare at his friend. "Have you ever known her *not* to have something to say? It felt…unnatural."

Jake laughed again, making Bret wonder if Angel had made comments about him as well. *Probably better if I don't ask.*

"Maybe she's just tired of arguing," Jake said. "She's not exactly at her best right now."

Yeah, and why is *that?* Bret wanted to ask but didn't.

"Yeah, maybe…" he murmured instead, pushing his long legs under the covers and pulling the blankets up to his chest. He hoped Jake was right. He didn't relish the idea that she was planning something unpleasant, especially if she was saving it just for him.

"You're doing good with her, you know," Jake said as Bret arranged his pillows.

"By making her eat?" Bret glanced at his friend and raised an incredulous brow. When Jake nodded, he went back to shifting his pillows. "I shouldn't have to do that. I don't have time for it. Not if she wants this place to be profitable, and not with all the duties she's piled on since—" He stopped short and glanced swiftly at Jake, hoping he would let the topic of Bret's escape attempt slide by without comment. When his friend said nothing, Bret continued, "I was already behind before this started, and it'll only get worse with me spending so much time with her." That was only part of it, but he wasn't about to tell Jake that every time he was in Angel's company, he feared losing himself in her eyes. That he longed to touch her and have her respond in kind. That thinking about her soft skin often kept him awake at night. He couldn't tell Jake any of that because Bret worried it would somehow ruin their friendship, that Jake wouldn't approve and would accuse him of trying to seduce her into giving Bret his freedom. But mostly he couldn't tell Jake any of those things because Bret wouldn't admit to all of them, not even to himself.

"I'll be happy to help with that," Jake said and Bret almost sighed with relief. "I'll have a few of the other hands take over some of your less necessary duties. That should free up your schedule and not cause any issues with the work."

"That's not what I meant, Jake," Bret said annoyed, and he wondered if his friend was being purposely obtuse.

"I know," Jake replied, turning onto his back and picking up his book again, "but right now you can't leave the homestead and I'm needed in the fields. That leaves you to deal with everything else here that I'd normally do myself. Even when the roundup is done, that's not going to change, and you're going to need to figure it out."

"Yeah, yeah," Bret sighed and fell back into bed. A moment later, he turned onto his side and met Jake's inquiring gaze. "Why do you do all of this for her?" Bret had been avoiding that question for some time, afraid of the answer, and he hated to ask it now, but it didn't feel as if he had a choice.

"I don't do anything anyone else here wouldn't do," Jake replied simply.

Bret wondered if his friend was avoiding his question, but now that he'd asked it, Bret had to know. "Yeah, sure, but why do *you* do it?"

Jake's gaze drifted to the ceiling as he sighed and Bret got the impression that his friend didn't want to discuss all the reasons why, not yet anyway, not unless he had to reveal them. Did he think Bret would condemn him?

"Because," Jake said after a long pause, "she saved my life." He didn't say anything more and Bret knew that was all he was going to get.

Jake picked up his book again and Bret understood a dismissal when he saw one. He didn't begrudge Jake's silence, though he had several more questions. His friend obviously didn't want to talk about it further and, knowing Darla Cain had once owned him, Bret could guess the other man's reasons.

Bret leaned over and blew out the lamp on his nightstand, then lay on his back for some time. He owed Angel for rescuing his best friend from a horrible life—a life of slavery that Bret blamed himself for, and one that he could never have saved Jake from himself. He just wished he knew more about the details and whether Jake had connected with Angel beyond the friendship he claimed. That question stayed with Bret a long time, and he was still mulling it over when Jake finally blew out his lamp for the night, leaving Bret alone with his uncomfortable thoughts and the emotions he didn't want to feel but couldn't banish.

8

BY LATE AFTERNOON THE NEXT DAY, rain had thoroughly drenched everything in sight. Bret had been listening to its rhythmic beat for a couple of hours while he sat at the desk in his room, pouring over tally sheets and yearly projections, when a knock at the door disturbed him.

"Hi, Nick," Bret greeted one of the less experienced but more enthusiastic teen workers on the ranch. "What can I do for you?"

"I think there's something wrong with one of the pregnant cows," Nick said worriedly.

"Why do you say that?" Bret asked as he grabbed his farm jacket from the peg on the wall and shrugged into it.

"Well, she keeps kicking at her belly and seems really uncomfortable."

Bret nodded, sure of the cause, but followed Nick outside to verify it.

As they hurried through the rain, headed for the long fenced-in area near the barns, Bret's mind drifted to his experiences with Angel earlier that day. She'd responded with the same timid attitude to Bret's arrival at both breakfast and lunch, unsettling him, but she ate without argument and when he'd returned to the kitchen with her empty plates, he had counted that as a win. He still did.

The rest of his day had passed in much the same way as had the last four. He kept reminding himself that it would take time to become accustomed to handling the work, the questions, and the demands—not to mention feeling completely comfortable with them. Back on the ranch he'd managed before the wars, all he'd had to deal with was the cattle's daily maintenance, care, and profitability as well as some repairs, the other hands, and reporting to the owner. His duties now were similar, just not quite the same. There were far more people living on this ranch for one thing and, like the young man he now followed, not all of them were ranchers, which meant Bret was expected to resolve far more social issues and suffer a lot of interruptions.

True to his comments the night before, Jake had assigned some of Bret's less pressing duties to other members of the ranch that morning. They would report to Bret, and then he would decide what to do next. Everything came together rather smoothly, but he still felt a bit overwhelmed.

But this—troubleshooting the uneasiness of a pregnant cow—was something he felt confident doing, though the actual work to ease her discomfort may not be so easy.

As they reached the new fenced-off enclosure near the barns, Nick pointed out the worrisome bovine. She had wandered away from the long, narrow shelter they'd built for inclement weather and found a secluded spot on the far side of the field. After slogging through the thick mud, Bret examined the heifer and found his assumptions were correct—she was in labor. The fact that she'd separated from the other animals and her belly kicking were sure signs she was ready to drop. What Bret saw on closer examination told him they needed to get her inside quickly. Annoyed that no one had noticed her advanced state sooner, Bret barked instructions on how he and Nick would get the mother-to-be into the calving barn.

They had made it just over halfway to the barn when she stopped abruptly. Bret ran his hand over her belly, feeling her muscles tighten.

"We need to hurry," he told Nick. "Her contractions are close."

"Does that mean the calf is coming now?" Nick asked, his dark brown eyes wide with fear and anticipation.

"Not just yet, but very soon," Bret said. "We've got to get her out of the mud."

"Can't she just have it here?"

Bret nodded. "Yeah, she could, but the bacteria and other nasty things in the mud can be deadly to newborns. I'd rather not risk it."

Bret did his best to sound confident, though he worried they wouldn't get the heifer moving again.

Pushing and pulling, coaxing and pleading, Bret and Nick spent the better part of a half-hour attempting to get the young female to move. Eventually, after a lot of slipping, sliding, and falling on the part of the two men, they finally managed to get the animal into the barn.

Once inside, Bret directed two of the more experienced workers to clean the remaining mud off the heifer and get her settled in an empty pen where they could monitor her progress. If anything went wrong, one of them could hunt him down.

Bret breathed a sigh of relief when that was done and looked over at Nick. The young man was as muddy and soaked as Bret, but he grinned as he tried to shake some of the clingy substance from his gloved hands.

"She'll be all right now. Right?" the young man asked Bret.

"Yeah," he replied, looking down at his own dirty clothes, "she should be fine, but *we* need to get washed up. You head on home for the night and warm up. It's nearly dinner time anyway," Bret said. "We can't afford anyone getting sick." He hooked a thumb in the direction of the heifer's stall as they started for the doors. "There's going to be a lot more of those and we're going to need everyone working."

"Yes, sir," Nick said and Bret grinned, slapping the young man's muddy back as the two of them left the barn.

Any other work would have to wait because he still had to deal with Angel and to do that, he'd need to get cleaned up too.

* * *

It was a good deal later than he'd planned by the time Bret finished washing up. Thankfully, the kitchen was as warm as his shower had been when he walked into the bustle of workers.

"Bad day?" Esther queried gently as he picked up the serving tray she'd prepared.

"Muddy day," he replied with a bland smile and headed for the stairs.

She eyed him critically and then grinned. "Well," she said with a hint of teasing, "you look none the worse for wear."

Bret gave her a wink and a gracious smile before he exited the kitchen and headed upstairs with Angel's dinner.

Waiting for him again, Angel was as well-behaved and silent as she'd been for their last two meals. But something felt different to Bret. Her eyes were red-rimmed and puffy—they hadn't been so bad at lunch—and she seemed far more sullen than earlier. He'd thought that her agreeable attitude had meant the end of her depression, but from these signs, that was not the case.

They ate quietly, Angel on the bed and Bret in the chair, ignoring each other.

When they were both finished, Bret once again stoked the fire and asked her if she needed anything else.

She looked at him sadly for a long moment, her eyes seeming to plead with him, though he didn't understand what she wanted. She appeared to be about to speak and he waited anxiously, but she didn't say a thing. Instead, she dropped her gaze and shook her head before she lay back, closed her eyes, and turned on her side, all without a single word. He stood at the end of the bed gazing down at her for some time, but she didn't move.

Should he ask what's wrong?

He doubted she would reply and his hard side kept demanding, *Why do you care?*

He glanced up at the new addition to her enormous bed. Sometime after lunch, a canopy had been added to the top of her four-poster bed. It had a flat, thick-fabric roof and heavy cloth curtains, which, when expanded along a thin iron bar stretching from post to post, would enclose the bed. A very old practice to conserve heat in the winter, Bret suspected every bed on the ranch would soon have a similar device to improve warmth and comfort during the snowy winter nights. With the fire going and the curtains over the two sets of French doors securely closed, Angel's room was relatively warm.

He glanced at Angel's small form curled beneath the blankets and once again felt a pang of unease. She hadn't moved and by the steady movement of her chest, he guessed she was asleep. Part of him wanted to wake her and try to discover what ailed her, but he knew that would get him nowhere. Besides, what and how much was he actually willing to do?

He didn't have an answer for that either.

With nothing left to do for her, but still feeling torn and wanting to do something, Bret picked up the tray from the dresser where he'd left it and quietly left the room.

Nearly three hours later, Bret returned from the calving barn where he'd stayed after his nightly tour to oversee the birthing of their most recent calf. The heifer and her calf had been cleaned up nicely and hadn't needed any assistance from them, but Bret waited to be sure and took the opportunity to teach some of his new team the basics about calving and the animals' health. Once he felt certain the new calf would be in good hands, he'd headed back to the house.

Thanks to the slicker he'd remembered to don earlier, Bret was less wet than the last time he'd ventured out into the storm. Yet the rain pounding on the roof was an audible sign of the power of the inclement weather and despite the slicker, rain had dampened his shirt collar, jacket, and jeans. A little chilled, he'd left his wet slicker on a hook near the door and shook off his damp hat before going inside.

Jake was still up when Bret entered their room and, though he'd been anxious to discuss concerns about Angel with his friend, Bret wasn't sure how to start. He set his hat near the heat of the woodstove, opened his jacket, and grabbed a log to add to the low burning flames.

"Sounds like the rain is really coming down," Jake commented as Bret fed the fire.

"Yeah," he mumbled as he stood. He pulled the desk chair over by the stove where he sat and held his hands toward the growing warmth, hoping to drive away the chill.

"You were out there longer than normal," Jake said. "Anything wrong?"

"The heifer dropped," Bret told him. "Took her a little while, but she did well for her first calf."

"Good," Jake replied, but cocked his head, apparently sensing Bret's unease. "So, what's bugging you then?"

Bret shook his head and sighed, once again reminded of how well Jake could read his moods. "Angel's bugging me."

"What else is new?" Jake asked.

"It's not that," Bret said. "There's something wrong with her."

"Yeah..." Jake elongated the word as if confused, "we've known that."

"Yes, but..." Bret sighed again, unsure how to convey what he'd felt emanating from her earlier.

"But what?"

Bret explained her odd behavior while Jake listened and nodded. Then he tried to explain the change he'd sensed in her tonight.

"It's like she'd given up. Like she wasn't even there," Bret said, knowing that wasn't quite right either. "She'd been crying again too. Sobbing I'd say from the look of her. She looked so...sad...and vulnerable, and... I... She... I...don't know what to do."

"If you're worried about it," Jake said, the concern in his eyes belying the calm in his voice, "you should check on her."

Bret groaned. "Can...can you do it? She likes you better."

Jake chuckled and shook his head. "She doesn't like anyone at the moment. Besides, it's your job now."

Bret shifted on the chair and sighed. He hadn't really wanted Jake to take over for him. Yet...

"Yeah," Bret mumbled, "I suppose it is." He slowly stood, his sore leg complaining some, and headed for the kitchen entry. "Don't wait up." A slow grin tipped his lips up, even though the thought of going upstairs turned his feet to lead.

"Just make sure she's safe," Jake replied, and something in his voice made Bret think it would be a long night.

9

AFTER A QUICK KNOCK, Bret entered Angel's room and the hair on the back of his neck stirred. Something was very wrong. The room was cold, far colder than it should have been. He glanced at the hearth—where a fire should've still been burning strong—and found it close to dying. All that remained was a hint of red among the charred embers. The logs had shifted apart and, without the fuel, the flames had perished.

Another round of trepidation shot through him as he peered swiftly around the room.

The lamp on the nightstand was lit and its soft, golden glow illuminated the bed where the curtains had been pushed aside to reveal empty sheets. Finding nothing in either the closet or bathroom, Bret returned to the main room, searching for a clue. Items that hadn't been there earlier lay strewn around the room. A blue terry cloth robe rested on the end of the bed, an assortment of books sat in heaps on one side of the room near the closet, and a small box sat on its side with its contents of letters and pictures spilled onto the rug next to the bed.

Of Angel, there was no sign. Then the curtains covering the closest set of French doors moved.

That might explain a few things, he thought. The outside door was open.

The room was silent, except for the heavy rain drubbing the roof and tapping loudly at the windowed doors, and he was suddenly worried that he'd find Angel on the deck. Hoping he was wrong, he crossed the room to check, but something on the floor distracted him. He stopped and glanced down at several old photos lying at his feet. Crouching, he picked up the two on top that had caught his eye.

Three male faces filled the first one—two very young boys and an older man who could be their father. Bret saw a resemblance between the two boys, but it was harder to detect a similarity with the man. His dark blue eyes and light brown hair were not a match for the boys' black hair and vividly blue eyes—eyes that reminded Bret of Angel. The picture had been taken with their faces mostly in frame, making the background hard to define beyond them being outside; they were close and smiling happily. Bret wondered about the significance of the photo. Would he get an answer if he confronted Angel about it?

Doubtful, he thought.

A young man in his mid-twenties or thereabouts, with dark blond hair that curled around his ears, filled the other photo Bret had picked up. Like the two boys in the previous picture, this man also had remarkably vibrant blue eyes, only much darker, almost cobalt blue, and he also smiled happily at the camera.

Bret suspected that their eyes—the two boys in particular—had grabbed his attention. He wondered if the blue-eyed man was related to the boys or the other man in the first photo. Holding them side by side, he couldn't determine either way. He was still considering when a cold draft swirl past him, disturbing the other items still strewn on the floor by the box. Bret frowned, staring at the two time-worn photos. He had questions, but he also had more important things to worry about than to speculate why Angel had them, and it was none of his business anyway. Quickly, he picked up all the items still on the rug and placed them inside the box. He pushed it out of the way, then stood to check the deck for Angel.

The edge of the heavy curtain felt wet when he jerked it back and he wondered how long the door had been ajar. A gust of wind blew the door wide open and a blast of cold rain hit Bret in the face so hard, he had to turn away, but it didn't stop him.

He stepped onto the deck and into the night, blinking in the rain, his eyes slowly becoming accustomed to the darkness. The only illumination came from the doorway behind him, and when he could make out shapes—the edge of the deck railing, a deck chair, and a small table—he finally located the object of his search.

Angel sat near the far side of the deck, her legs folded against her chest with her arms tightly wrapped around them. She slowly rocked, back and forth, and if Bret wasn't mistaken, she was crying, her chin resting on her knees as she gazed out over the hills. She looked so small and defenseless sitting there alone. The sight made his chest ache. Right then, all he wanted was to help her, protect her from whatever had driven her out into the elements, to make things right.

"Angel?" he called, but the wind whipped his voice away. He moved closer, using his hand to keep the rain out of his eyes and wishing futilely for the black hat he'd left by the stove in his room. "Angel!" He stood right beside her, but again, she didn't respond, didn't even acknowledge his presence, though she had to see him. Her whole concentration seemed to be aimed at something out beyond the walls. He couldn't see anything in the dark, but all that lay in that direction were hills and trees and wilderness.

He squinted down at her again.

Soaked to the skin—her normally curly hair lay flattened against her head and down her back—she shivered uncontrollably. The white pajamas she'd been wearing for days, though not exactly transparent, were so wet their clinginess left nothing to the imagination. Her feet were bare and her lips looked a little blue.

He mumbled a curse and without thinking, he touched her shoulder and her arm came up to slap him away.

Her head swiveled toward him and she glowered at him with red-rimmed eyes. "Don't touch me!"

When he pulled back and made no further moves toward her, she turned back to the darkness, ignoring him again.

Surprised but undeterred, Bret crouched beside her, being careful not to touch her, and tilted his head so he could look into her face. It was slightly shadowed, but he could just make out her features. She was crying and her lips were trembling while she rocked rhythmically back and forth.

"Angel," he shouted over the storm, "you can't stay out here. You're freezing. Come back inside."

She didn't speak, merely shook her head.

"Please, Angel," he tried again, "you're going to get sick. Don't make me force you to go in." The look she turned on him was cold as death, but there was a hint of immense sorrow in the depths of her eyes.

"Leave me alone," she said, glaring at him for all she was worth.

"I can't do that," he told her. "Not until you come back inside and get warmed up."

"No," she said without looking his way. "You. Go. Away."

"This is stupid," he mumbled, more to himself than to her. She was drenched and he was starting to be himself. They both needed to get out of the weather.

Angel heard his murmur but only briefly slanted her eyes in his direction.

Cold, wet, and at the end of his patience, Bret took hold of her arm and stood, lifting her as he did so. He wasn't going to let her sit out here and freeze. Too many people depended on her for their survival, including him. Her reaction, however, took him by surprise.

She whirled, jerked her arm free from his hand, and struck him across the face as hard as her trembling body would allow. The blow knocked him back a step. A heartbeat later, his jaw clenched and his lips compressed angrily.

A smile of satisfaction curled her pretty lips when he met her gaze again.

Bret's face stung from the blow. He wouldn't hit her, but he wasn't about to let her get away with it either. Slowly, he straightened. "That's the third time you've done that," he said ominously. "*Don't* do it again."

"Or what?" she challenged, apparently too lost in her fury of the moment to care that she'd struck him without reason.

"Or you'll regret it," he warned. "Now, get in*side*!"

"No!"

"Angel," he said, his soft tone a contradiction to the threat implied in his tense, looming body, his face inches from hers, "if you don't get back inside, right now, I'm going to throw you over my shoulder and carry you back in."

"I don't want you to touch me!"

"Too bad," he ground out and took a step toward her.

"I'll fight you if you try," she cautioned.

"You're too weak to put up much of one and I won't be surprised again. So, fight me if you want to, but I'll win and you know it."

"Why can't you just go away?" She was still furious, but the question held a forlorn quality that made his chest feel heavy and tight.

"I'm not leaving you out here," he said. "Either you walk in or I carry you. Which is it going to be?"

"Neither!"

He growled a curse and reached for her. She tried to step away, but he was too quick. In an instant, he blocked the blows she aimed at his head, grabbed her by the arms, and tossed her over his shoulder. She hung there, stunned, while he wrapped one arm around her thighs and the other across her hips, then turned for the door.

"Put me down, damn you!" she screamed, overcoming her sudden shock and drumming her small fists against his back, kicking wildly trying to free herself from his hold.

"I'll be happy to," he said, "once we're back inside."

She swore at him, damning him and his lineage, running a string of curses together he'd never have expected to hear from her—she hadn't seemed the type. She kept at it until they were back inside, and by then, she was screeching at the top of her lungs.

He would have laughed if he wasn't so angry. What the hell was she trying to accomplish besides attempting to annoy and injure him? At the moment, she was doing a good job of both, but he saw no other reason for her sudden belligerent behavior. Even though she fought him like a lioness, it didn't feel like a planned attack, like she wanted to harm him. It felt like desperation.

Once inside, he went to the bed and flipped her over his shoulder so she lay cradled in his arms. She glowered up at him and her hand lifted as if to slap him once more, but he didn't give her the chance. Bret tossed her—sodden clothes and all—onto the center of the mattress. Occupied with loudly spewing curses and fighting the tangle of bed linens and pillows that had kicked up around her when she landed, Bret left her to close the door and pull the soggy curtain over it. He turned back to the bed just in time.

"Stay on the bed, Angel," he said menacingly as she wiggled to the edge as if to climb off the other side.

"And if I d-don't?" she dared him with a glare, still shouting and shivering.

"If you don't," he said in a soft voice that threatened rather than cajoled, "you'll force me to tie you to it." He deliberately stalked around the end of the bed like a cat after its prey. "Then again," he grinned, "I'd greatly enjoy repaying you for that favor." He might even kiss her too, just as she had when she tied him to his bed. Only, the point he meant to make would be far different.

She chose caution rather than battle and scooted back onto the bed.

"Good choice," he mumbled with a lopsided grin, watching her move back to the center of the mattress. No longer needing to round to the other side of the bed, he changed directions without missing a beat and crossed to the fireplace. Shifting his shoulders and stretching as he walked, he attempted to ease the ache from the pounding she'd just given him, but he didn't let her see his discomfort. He crouched in front of the cold hearth—favoring his sore leg slightly—to rebuild the fire, but as he arranged the tinder in the hearth, someone knocked on the bedroom door.

Bret glanced at the door then back at Angel, who's evil grin made the hair on the back of his neck stand on end. She obviously thought someone had come to rescue her from his gentle care. Considering how much noise she'd made, he wouldn't be surprised if someone had. The question was, what would they do about it?

"Stay there," he grumbled at Angel as he stood and went to the door.

The residents who occupied the other four upstairs bedrooms—Esther, Michelle, a lead guard named Sam, and the head housekeeper Jane—stood in the hallway, frowning at him.

"Is everything all right?" Michelle asked, taking a quick look past Bret's broad shoulders. Her eyes widened slightly seeing Angel sitting on her bed, sopping wet and fuming.

"M-make him leave, Michelle," Angel commanded, ruining her tone only slightly by her cold-induced stutter.

Michelle turned her gaze back to Bret, one eyebrow lifted curiously.

"She was out on the deck," he explained, "in the rain. She's cold and combative. She didn't want to come in, so I carried her in. She didn't like it very much. That's what all the yelling was about."

"Where's Jake?" Esther asked, none of them seeming to heed Angel's shouted directive. "He's usually the one who deals with her when she's like this."

"It's my job now," Bret said carefully, unsure how they would respond. He didn't want to remind them that his escape attempt had made it his duty to look after Angel, not Jake's.

"Oh, dear," Esther said sympathetically, "I don't envy you."

Bret's mouth twitched up at the corners, but that was as much of a hint to his thoughts as he allowed.

"Did she...*hit* you?" Sam asked as if shocked to see the red handprint he could feel emblazoned on his face.

He automatically lifted a hand to his cheek and grinned ruefully. "Yeah, she did."

"You didn't hit her, did you?" Michelle asked.

He frowned. "Of course not!"

"I didn't mean to offend," she said with a half-smile. "It's my job."

Bret nodded.

"G-get him o-out of here!" Angel shouted again. "Why are you all just standing there?"

"I'll gladly leave as soon as you get warmed up," he told her over his shoulder, his hard tone conveying his annoyance, "and I'm not going until you are."

He turned back to the four silent women in the doorway. He tilted his head and raised a questioning eyebrow, waiting for one of them to make him go.

"Good luck with that," Michelle told him with an empathetic grin and then turned to go back to her room.

"Yes, good luck," Esther said, then raised her voice. "You do what this young man says, Angel. He'll take good care of you." She gave Bret's arm a consoling pat, then the remaining three women disappeared down the unlit hall.

He shut the door and faced Angel.

On her hands and knees as if waiting for something to happen, she stared incredulously from her place on the bed. Slowly, she sat back on her heels, her eyes still wide with astonishment. Evidently, she had expected them to force him out.

Bret wasn't any less dumbfounded. He wasn't sure why they didn't at least *ask* him to leave, but after dealing with her like this, he wasn't surprised that they wanted nothing to do with her in this state.

"Looks like you're stuck with me," he said, a self-satisfied grin on his face as he crossed to the hearth.

She said nothing as he poked at the ashes.

Once he had the flames licking at the tinder, Bret added two logs from the newly stacked pile nearby. The fire picked up and he crouched there awhile to drive away the damp chill as the blaze quickly warmed the cold room.

He felt Angel's eyes on him again. The whole time he'd tended the fire, the tingling sensation of her sharp gaze boring into his back had never ceased. He listened for any sound behind him, but heard nothing, and breathed a sigh of relief.

He stood and returned to the bed, glad to see her still on the covers. She glared at him for all she was worth as if blaming him for her guards' mutiny.

If looks could kill, he thought, *I'd be dead and burned to a crisp.*

He glared at her from the end of the bed. Even with the burning heat in her gaze, she was still shivering, and with good reason. In the golden lamplight, he could make out her features far more clearly. Her eyes blazed as her teeth chattered through her blue-tinted lips and tiny waterfalls cascaded from the loose tendrils of her hair to dampen her even more. Breathing heavily, her chest rose and fell beneath her skin-clinging shirt, though whether because of cold or rage he couldn't tell, but he rather liked the display. It didn't matter, though, she *was* cold—whether she cared to admit it or not—and it was his job to warm her up.

"You need to get into something dry," he said. "Where do you keep your night clothes?"

"N-none of your d-damn business," she snapped through chattering teeth, blue-fire sparking in her eyes.

"I'll find something whether you tell me or not," he told her, pulling off his sodden farm jacket, "but you might not like it." He laid the coat out near the fire and sat on the wing-backed chair to remove his boots, setting them beside his jacket. Unbuttoning his green-checked flannel, he turned back to her and grinned.

Her eyes widened as understanding finally registered. "I am *n-not* wearing your c-clothes!"

"Then tell me where to find yours," he said as he pulled his shirttail free of his jeans. He could just rummage through her drawers to find what he wanted, but it would take too long. Besides, this was more fun. If she was intent on making this difficult for him, then he saw no reason not to reply in kind. Still, he didn't understand why she had so much disregard for herself.

Her cerulean eyes narrowed into dangerous slits, but he was prepared to fight her as long as needed to get her warmed up again.

"N-no. You n-need to get out!" she stutter-shouted in response.

"Suit yourself," he said as he crawled onto the bed. In minutes, he had her stripped, her wet clothes thrown haphazardly toward the fire, and his shirt pulled up her arms, her small fist inflicting a few new bruises in the process.

Once his shirt hung from her shoulders, he pulled her struggling body against his and pinned her back to his chest, her wet hair soaking his cotton T-shirt while he held her wrists together in front of her, nestled between her breasts. Holding her was more difficult than he'd anticipated. If her strength hadn't been affected by her long fast, he doubted he would've been able to handle her as easily.

She shrieked up a storm through the whole process, repeatedly demanding that he leave. When she suddenly slumped in his hold and went quiet, a prickle of unease danced along his spine. Was she playing him or did he inadvertently hurt her?

"Angel?" He spoke just above her ear and felt a shudder pass through her. "Are you all right?"

"Go away," she whispered, but there was no heat in it. "I want to be alone."

"How long were you outside?"

She frowned over her shoulder before she looked away again. "I don't know."

"When did you go out there?"

She shrugged. "Sometime after dinner…I think."

"That was hours ago. Weren't you cold?"

She shook her head, and he wondered if she'd been too lost in thought to feel the cold. He'd seen that happen with his mother. She had gotten lost in memories of his father and the past. Was Angel's problem similar?

Did he really want to know?

He rubbed her arms gently. "Are you warming up now?"

She hesitated, but then nodded as if she didn't want to admit it.

Bret turned her toward him. She didn't struggle or speak, only glared at him once they faced each other again.

"Are you all right?" he asked again, holding her in place with his hands. Her lips no longer appeared blue, but she was still shivering.

"I'm fine!" she spat, some of her fight returning. "I was fine *before* you showed up! I don't need your help!"

Bret's eyes dropped to the distracting display of soft curves teasing him through the open shirt front. Goosebumps covered her pale skin and her nipples poked prominently into the soft fabric. He sighed, then released her arms and started buttoning it closed.

"You're cold," he said.

She looked away. "I'm fine."

When he finished with the buttons, she sat stiffly as he rolled up the sleeves.

"We need to get you warmed up," he said, glancing behind him for her terry cloth robe. He leaned back to grab it and used its absorbent fabric to wick the wet from her soaked hair.

"Please leave," she begged as he worked the rain from her long tresses.

"All in good time," he replied and she seemed to slump a little more.

Once he finished with her hair, he ran the robe over his own wet head and then tossed it aside. Crawling off the bed, he pulled the heavy curtains closed on either side of her bed, leaving the end open so the warmth of the fire could be captured inside the cloth alcove.

He stood at the end of the bed and gazed at her. She wouldn't meet his eyes and she was crying again. A low sob escaped her lips that wrenched at his insides in unpleasant ways, but he refused to be manipulated—if that was what she was doing.

"Get under the blankets, Angel," he directed.

"No." She hiccupped. "Get out of here!"

"Not until I know you're warmed up." He waited, but she made no move to get under the blankets.

Bret sighed and climbed back onto the bed. She flinched away from him as he approached, but offered only a mild struggle as he gathered her against him and dragged her into position. Laying her back, he lifted her damp hair away from her neck to fan over the pillow, then pulled the thick, lavender sheet over her shivering form as she curled onto her side and closed her eyes.

The two blankets she'd been sitting on were wet from her soaked clothes and dripping hair. Glancing at her shivering back, he shook his head and got off the bed. He yanked the damp blankets from the mattress and dropped them onto the floor at the end of the bed. Thinking to find extra linens, he went to the closet where he located two dry blankets and then went into her adjoining bathroom to grab a towel. A moment later, he returned and snatched back the closest bed curtain to throw the dry covers over her before drawing the heavy comforter over her as well. Carefully, he climbed onto the bed again, lifted her head to spread the towel on the pillow, set her head on top, and wrapped the ends around her hair. It wasn't ideal, but it would have to do. *At least she didn't fight me this time.*

When he was done, he closed the bed curtains and stood watching her from the end of the bed again.

He could see she was still shivering fiercely beneath the blankets and sighed in frustration. She was too chilled to warm up on her own and he knew what he had to do to change that. He didn't let himself think about it too long. Instead, he quickly removed his damp T-shirt and jeans, lay them next to his jacket by the fire, and crawled onto the mattress once more. He slipped under the covers next to her quaking form, reached out to the sniffling, hiccupping Angel, and drew her toward him. She squirmed in token protest, but quickly settled against his side, her head resting on his shoulder, while his arm slipped around her waist.

"Please, let me go," Angel begged, her voice and body quaking with the power of her emotions and the cold. "Please…"

"I can't do that," he said, his free hand smoothing the loose tendrils of her still damp hair. "But I can make sure you're warm and safe."

Her whole body tensed then convulsed with a sob, and suddenly she was weeping heavy, heart-wrenching sobs. "W-Why did y-you have to be…k-kind?" she mumbled, barely understandable.

"What?" he asked, after deciphering her word.

"Why c-couldn't you just be s-smug and…and arrogant? Why c-couldn't you be m-mean?"

"I don't want to hurt you, Angel," he said, giving her a little hug and smoothing her hair from her face. "I want to help you."

"I don't w-want y-you…" she dragged in a quivering breath and something squeezed his chest, but then she finished her statement, "…h-here."

His heart lurched and started beating again. For a moment, he'd thought she would leave that last word unsaid. "I know," he replied without lessening his hold in the slightest. *Get ahold of yourself,* he told himself in silent warning.

As she wept in his arms, he whispered to her, letting her know she was safe by his comforting words and the strength of his body. He was perfectly willing to do both, but the nearness of her soft little body was driving him crazy. Her cold-hardened nipples drilled into his chest and side, one of her silky thighs had slid over both of his, and her free hand lay on his neck. It was too close to a lover's embrace, though he knew it wasn't. At least, it didn't seem purposeful, and he didn't mind, not really, but he was quickly starting to regret climbing under the sheets with her. He should have left the flannel sheet over her when he slid in beside her, but he hadn't been thinking about that. He'd just been concerned with getting her warm.

Well, he thought, resigned, *with the heat she's building inside me, she'll be toasty in no time.*

A hint of lilac filled his brain and brought with it memories of their night together that he would rather not churn up. That scent, coupled with the sensual turn of his thoughts and his body's impossible-to-ignore response, was enough to make him grind his teeth.

He wanted her! As badly as he ever had before, and his body was making that an unmistakable fact. *I should jump out of this bed and go back to my own.*

But she was still cold and he didn't want to leave until he knew she would be all right. Still, as overly aware of her as he was, he had little chance of actually sleeping. Lying next to her, with his mind spinning and his body growing harder by the minute, he would suffer in silence until he could escape this torment of his own making.

She was in some kind of emotional agony, and he would never take advantage of that. Yet, he couldn't ignore the fact that a supple, womanly body was draped over his side.

His jaw clenched as another kind of heat swept through his body. Someone had hurt her terribly and the pain of that trauma still lived inside her. He could understand that, even commiserate with her about it, but he didn't understand why he wanted to help. There was nothing he could do. It made him feel helpless, which infuriated him more. He didn't know what had driven her out into the cold, wet night or why she reacted to him so viciously, but he knew what she needed and it wasn't an ardent lover. She needed warmth and to feel safe, and that was exactly what he would give her.

Why? something inside him asked. *Why do you have to give her anything?*

The answer came swiftly.

Because I care about her. He cared if she was hurt, or cold, or afraid and the knowledge terrified him. Lying there, still as stone, listening to her diminishing sobs, Bret realized he was in trouble. He wanted, no, needed to protect her, felt obliged to ensure her safety, to ease her sadness and fear.

He stifled a frustrated groan. *I shouldn't even be in her bed! What the hell?*

Angel hadn't wanted anything more from Bret than to use him for physical pleasure. He didn't want that, had already suffered through the pain that had caused. Amy had used him in the same way, but Amy had led him to believe she cared about him. Angel had made it clear from the beginning that she didn't. She'd made him a slave, and he should've known better than to trust her.

But she had hooked him. He hated it, but there was no other explanation. He cared about her, wanted to take care of her, and worse than that, he wanted the same from her.

A sudden urge to get up and run before it was too late—if it wasn't already—hit him hard. But he couldn't. She needed him... *Well, she needs someone,* he thought. Jake wasn't around as much as he used to be, and Bret still felt bound by the promise he'd made to look out for her. So he smoothed her hair, whispered soft words of comfort, and held her securely, waiting for her tears to subside.

Several minutes later, Angel's sobs finally calmed to a hiccupping, trembling stillness. She seemed a little chilled, but she'd warmed while curled up next to him. Shivering more from the aftermath of emotion now than from the cold, her body slowly relaxed against him. A few minutes later, she seemed to be dozing, and seeing a chance to escape, Bret slowly began to shift his body out from under hers. He had just pulled free of her arms and the covers when he felt her grip his hand.

"Wait," she whispered and her eyes opened to look up at him. "I'm still cold. Stay with me…"

Bret stared at her in awe. *After all the fuss she made about me leaving,* now *she wants me to stay?* It would serve her right if he ignored this request the way he'd ignored so much the last two days, but one look into her sad blue eyes and he couldn't make himself leave.

"Please…?" she murmured at his hesitation. "I won't fight anymore. I don't want anything. I'm just…cold."

He sighed and crawled back beneath the covers. His arm went around her and she cuddled against him, her fingers combing through the dusting of hair on his chest before it came to rest on his left peck. There was nothing sensuous about the movement, but it left a trail of fire on his skin and her warm breath sent flames shooting through him.

Calm down! he ordered his body, but her leg slipped over his bruised thigh and pushed the sensations to new heights, moving higher until her knee nestled just below his groin. Breath halted, hoping she didn't lift her knee any higher, he almost released it with a groan when she moved again, getting comfortable. He didn't think she realized what she was doing, but he was hard as a rock. If she didn't stop wiggling soon, he'd have to excuse himself or risk another morning like the last one when they'd woken up together. He wanted to stay, but this was torture.

As her leg slid back down his thigh, her knee brushed over his injury at just the right angle to cause a sharp stab of pain. He jumped and gasped at the sudden jolt, his free hand reaching for his leg.

She pulled back slightly, her wide eyes staring up at his face. "Are you all right?" she asked, lowering her gaze and reaching down to touch his thigh. He captured her fingers, pressed them back to his chest, and took a deep breath.

"I'm fine," he told her on the exhale, and tightening his hold while giving her fingers a little squeeze, he let her know it was true.

"I didn't mean to hurt you," she murmured.

"I know," he whispered, meeting her worried expression. "Don't worry about it. Just go to sleep."

"Will you stay?"

"I'm here, aren't I?"

"I mean…after I fall asleep?"

"Do you want me to?"

"You're so warm," she murmured sleepily, her lips brushing his skin and her body snuggling against his.

He gritted his teeth. "I'll stay if that's what you want."

"Yes," she murmured, drifting off, her body relaxing. "Please, stay…"

"All right, Angel. Go to sleep. I'll stay."

She snuggled even closer. "Thank you…"

You're a fool, he berated himself. *She screams at you all day, slaps you silly, and you comply like a good little slave the minute she wants you to stay! What's* wrong *with you?*

He cared too much, that's what was wrong. But she didn't need to know that. He may still want her badly, but he didn't *need* her. Not yet.

And he meant to keep it that way.

10

BRET WOKE BEFORE THE SUN the next morning, feeling less than rested and slightly confused. He blinked at the canopy above him. This was not his room, not his bed, and thanks to the number of blankets he'd mostly kicked off during the night, he'd slept terribly. Then another, more serious problem registered, bringing the events of the night before to the forefront of his sleep-fogged mind.

Angel—the main reason for his restless night—was curled against his side with his now numb arm wrapped around her shoulders. One of her bare legs had draped over his thighs and her hand still rested on his chest. Asleep, with her head pillowed on his shoulder, tucked neatly against his neck, she snored ever so softly.

His heart thudded a slow, heavy beat and the sudden need to flee struck him. He flexed his fingers, trying to get circulation back into his hand while searching for a way to untangle himself without waking her.

He had to get out of this bed. She felt too good to stay much longer. His body was far too aware of the woman beside him, waking thoughts and urges he didn't want to feel, especially not with her.

Still, he'd never been this enticed by a woman before, which was another reason he needed to get away from her. He had himself under control for now, but lying there much longer, with her lilac scent tantalizing his senses and her warm body tempting him, was not a good idea. He was proud that he had the strength to ignore her for this long. After all, it couldn't possibly get worse. Right?

She murmured in her sleep, nestling more securely against him, her softness grinding all along his side, and he moaned in frustration as his body responded.

As much as he enjoyed feeling a woman's every curve and hollow in excruciating detail, this couldn't go on. Having her this close had been bad enough, but now, he had a new problem hacking away at his restraint. The shirt he'd forced her into last night had ridden up around her middle while they slept and the warm nest of curls at the apex of her legs now rested hot and naked over the thin cotton underwear on his hip. It seemed to be the center of the heat washing over him, radiating in ever-increasing waves of intensity the longer he lay there and melting his restraint into a slow, yet inevitable surrender.

To combat it, he reminded himself of the last time they had awoken together. He'd been so hopeful for something better in his life and then she'd rejected him. Her cold dismissal still hurt like an open wound, and he had no interest in having his heart ripped apart again. Unfortunately, his heartache didn't keep his body from wanting her, her closeness testing the limits of his self-control.

He had to get out of there before he did something he'd regret.

Slowly, he shifted out from under her and, pulling the nearest bed curtain back, he rolled off the mattress. Angel curled up under the covers, still asleep but no longer snoring. He gazed down at her sleeping face and was struck again by how much she affected him. Her beauty made him ache and her kindness, when she showed it, made him want to accept whatever she would give him, but his pride wouldn't allow that. To her, he was nothing more than one of her slaves, to use and discard as she chose. He wouldn't do that to himself and he wouldn't let her do it to him again either, not if he could help it.

Bret went to the fireplace and checked to make sure his wet clothes had thoroughly dried. Not that it would have mattered; he'd have to put them on anyway. Luckily, the fire had dried them enough before it burned down. He pulled on his white T-shirt and then spent a few minutes building up the fire again to drive the chill from the room. Once yellow-orange flames licked at the logs, he stood and finished dressing.

ANGEL WAS SO WARM. She felt safe, happy, and she couldn't remember how long it had been since she'd felt either of those things. She wiggled a little more closely to the solid heat next to her and sighed with pleasure.

Sitting in an open meadow of tall grass and wild daisies, she looked up at a deep blue sky and felt the hot sun kiss her skin. She smiled, completely content.

A man sat beside her with his arm around her waist. She nestled against his side, her head on his shoulder and her hand resting on his steely thigh. She glanced up at his vivid blue eyes and her smile widened. Her heart surged with joy at seeing him again. But slowly, he faded into a different man who looked down at her with an intense green gaze. He wasn't smiling, but his eyes held a promise that made her heart speed up and her stomach do excited flip-flops.

This is Bret, she thought dreamily, still smiling. He rewarded her unvarnished adoration with his most dazzling grin. Tingles danced across her skin in anticipation of his kiss, and as his head lowered toward her, so much happiness filled her chest that she thought she might burst.

But before their lips could meet, her perfect little world turned cold. The sky turned cloudy, the wind blew, and the green grass and colorful flowers died out, crumpled, and flew away with the breeze. Nothing remained but dead sward and weeds. It was so cold in this dark place. She looked around for the solid warmth that had been there moments ago, but he had disappeared as well.

Frantically, her eyes searched the dead meadow, trying to locate the man—either one of them—and found Michael at one edge of the clearing with a smile on his lips. Something made her look to the opposite side of the meadow and there she found Bret, unsmiling and gloomy. Her heart leaped at the sight of him, and then she remembered Michael. Why didn't her heart leap for Michael? She had loved him so much, why didn't she feel excited to see him? She looked back in Michael's direction, but he was no longer there. She scanned the area, but he was gone. She turned back to Bret and found him watching her. He smiled sadly and then walked away, vanishing into the sickly trees that surrounded the clearing.

Panic welled up within her. No! No! I can't lose him too!

* * *

On the bed, Angel tossed one way and then the other, reaching out for the warmth that had been there through the night, but all she found was the cooling sheets.

"Bret…?" Angel called out groggily, anxiety edging her voice. "Bret, where…?"

"I'm here, just getting dressed," he said, stepping to the end of the bed as he fastened his jeans. He looked so damn handsome. Even with his short hair messed up, his clothes all wrinkled, and the dark shadow of whiskers on his cheeks, he still made her heart speed up just by looking at him.

"Oh," she mumbled, feeling absurdly abashed. There was no reason she should be embarrassed; after all, he hadn't been privy to her dreams. Though telling herself that didn't stop the heat from creeping into her cheeks. Her eyes dropped and she suddenly didn't know what to say.

"Everything all right?" he asked, apparently noticing her odd behavior.

"Yes," she replied but didn't look up, afraid of sparking the desire that always seemed to assail her when looking at him. The temptation to ogle him in his muscle-hugging T-shirt and the well-fitting black jeans that hung enticingly off his lean hips was almost undeniable.

"Are you feeling better this morning?"

She cringed and then shrugged. "I guess."

"Good," he said as he began to gather her clothes off the floor. He dropped the bundle near the door. "I'll let the housekeeper know you have laundry."

Angel responded with a simple nod of her head, but she could feel his eyes studying her. She couldn't hear the rain pounding on the roof anymore, but guessed the weather outside was still wet and cold. Did he think she'd run out to the deck again the minute he left? Considering her actions last night, he probably did.

"Are you sure you're feeling all right?" he asked again. "You warm enough? Hungry?"

"Yes, yes, and yes," she mumbled, still avoiding his gaze.

"Okay," he said, dragging out the word as he went back to the fire to collect the rest of his things.

She looked up when he bent to retrieve his jacket from the floor. They needed to talk about last night, about her terrible behavior, and why. The why was the hard part. She couldn't tell him everything—no one knew the whole truth—but she had to say something. At the very least, she needed to apologize.

"I'm sorry," she said softly, barely able to speak, and for some reason, when he looked at her, he seemed to see into her soul, to read her dreams, and know her secrets. She bit her lip and her limbs began to shake, but she didn't look away.

BRET TOSSED HIS JACKET onto the arm of the wing-backed chair and met her gaze. He had known something was wrong—something beyond her crazy actions the night before, though that had been bad enough—he just wasn't certain he wanted to know what it was or how to get it out of her if he did. He still wasn't sure, but something about her this morning seemed odd and made him curious. He frowned and cocked his head. "Sorry for what?"

"For…" She paused, her anxious gaze drifting away and then back to where he stood. She looked petrified, her eyes wide, her body trembling, but then she seemed to take control of herself, and words began to spill out of her in a rapid jumble. "I can't always control how I feel, Bret," she said, her eyes beseeching him to understand. "Sometimes I'm not even sure what I feel or what to do about it. I just act on instinct and I can't stop. It just hurts so much, and I…I…" She seemed to choke on her words.

"It's okay," he interrupted, taking pity on her obvious pain. "Don't worry about it."

"But…I…" She stared at him as a tear slid down her cheek.

Seeing that, he winced inwardly and leaned a shoulder against one of the posts at the end of the bed, tucking his thumbs into his front pockets. "Really, Angel, you don't have to explain."

"I'm trying to apologize."

"I know," he said and his lips curved into a teasing grin, "but you still haven't said what for."

She hesitated and then started to speak, her words low and halting as she dropped her gaze. "For making things difficult for you yesterday and…and last night. For…hitting you." She looked up again, her eyes pleading with him to believe her. "I didn't want to. I…I just…did." She paused for a moment and then hurried on. "I know you were only trying to help. I just…I just… just…" She seemed to choke on her words and he could see tears threatening again.

Damn it, don't cry!

"Like I said," he told her, needing to alleviate the fear and anguish he'd read in her eyes, "don't worry about it. It's okay."

Her eyes swung back to him. He smiled again before he turned to pick up his boots and then sat in the wing-backed chair to pull them on. He heard the bed curtain move and had the feeling she wanted to say more, but he wasn't sure he wanted to stick around to hear it. She was wrapping him up again, just by looking at him.

He had to get out of that room.

With his boots firmly on, he stood, grabbed his coat off the arm of the chair, and headed for the door. "I'll bring your breakfast up in an hour or so."

"Bret?" she called and he halted.

He looked over his shoulder, raising his eyebrows. "Yes?"

She swallowed nervously and took a deep breath. "Thank you," she said as her eyes implored him once more, as if desperately afraid of being left alone.

"What for this time?"

Her face flushed the loveliest shade of pink he'd ever seen, obviously embarrassed by something, though he had no idea what.

"For putting up with me," she said in a shaky voice that started strong but slowly got quieter as she spoke. "For taking care of me." She dropped her eyes a moment and then met his once more. "For staying with me. I know you didn't want to. So, thank you... For all of it."

He almost laughed. *I didn't want to stay? Yeah, right. You just keep believing that and we'll both be better off.*

He gazed into her big, azure eyes and felt himself wanting to crawl back into the bed. *I have got to get out of here!*

He swung his jacket over his head and shrugged into it, settling the quilted lining over his shoulders and zipping the front closed. He did it to force his eyes away from her, to give himself time to think and collect his thoughts and tamp down the need pounding in his veins. The problem was that it didn't help. He still wanted to crawl back into bed with her.

He tucked his thumbs in his pockets again and met her gaze with a tender smile. "No worries," he said. He'd meant to stop there, but something in him added one more word. "Anytime..."

Goddamn it! Why did I say that out loud?

He saw something in her eyes that made his chest tighten and then he turned away. "I'll see you in an hour or two," he said, reaching for the doorknob. Without a backward glance, he opened the door and hurried out, before he could change his mind.

11

SEVERAL DAYS LATER, Bret was once again in the calving barn cleaning up a newborn calf who had presented backward. Knowing the dangers of breech birth, Bret had gotten the calf out quickly, but the animal wasn't breathing. Working fast, he cleaned the nostrils, cleared the mouth of fluid, and was trying to initiate a sneeze reflex by tickling the calf's nose with a piece of hay when a shrill neigh split the air followed by a thunderous bang and shouting. A prickle of apprehension straightened Bret's spine and his head whipped around in alarm. Something was wrong in the horse barn. Jake and Dean were both working the fields today, which meant Bret was the only experienced horseman there. He glanced down at the unmoving calf. The newborn was his priority, but that high pitched bray indicated a horse either in distress or about to attack.

He looked at Nick, who'd been assisting him with the birth, and nodded his head in the direction of the other barn. "I can't leave right now. Go check on that and let me know what's going on."

"Yes, sir," the teen replied and followed the other workers who'd already dashed out to investigate the noise.

A few seconds later, the calf's respiratory center finally kicked in. She sneezed and started to breathe on her own. Bret sighed in relief and smiled as he released the calf, watching as she struggled up to her shaky legs. He always loved it when he could save one.

More banging came from the horse barn, the noises growing in volume and intensity. Happy for the calf but anxious for the other animal in distress, Bret left the new mother to care for her hungry calf and exited the stall. He removed his soiled gloves and jacket on his way to the door and had just tossed them onto a hay bale when an enraged stallion's bellow gave him pause. He knew instantly it had to be Ebony and warning signals went off in his head.

That's not like him.

With his heart hammering in his chest, Bret ran for the door and outside, picturing several awful scenarios as he went. Headed straight for the horse barn, he met Nick and Mary Danby, one of the guards who doubled as a cowhand, hurrying toward him.

Nick's face had turned pale as a sheet as if whatever he'd seen had terrified him, and Bret's anxiety shot up a few more notches.

"What's going on?" he asked as he reached them and they all hastened toward the horse barn, the small crowd gathered outside, and the stallion's braying that seemed to get louder by the second.

"Sandy was helping the blacksmith shoe Ebony and then the horse just freaked out," Mary told him in a breathy rush. "He kicked Hugh out of the stall, but Sandy's still in there, and Ebony won't let anyone in or out."

Bret didn't recognize the name Sandy, but he'd met Hugh Blocker the blacksmith and his hard right-cross. He also remembered that Hugh had wanted to break his legs that night they'd ambushed Bret in the barn. But Bret wouldn't let that interfere with doing his job. "Is Hugh all right?"

"He's breathing, and he may have some cracked ribs," she replied, "but he hit his head when he fell. He's out cold."

"And the woman?"

"She's hurt, but I don't know how bad."

"Is she conscious?"

"She was when I came looking for you."

"Odd behavior for Ebony," Bret mused, thinking over all the things

175

that could have upset the stallion. "What set him off?"

"Don't know," Mary told him as they reached the small crowd. "We were just moving some other horses in from the pasture for shoeing. There shouldn't have been anything to upset him like this."

Bret yanked open the barn door to find a few more people standing inside and another round of earsplitting banging.

"Any mares in that group?" Bret asked once the booming sound had diminished.

Mary tilted her head in confusion. "Yes. Two."

"Either of them in heat? It's not too late for that." He pulled the door closed behind them and then winced at Ebony's next shriek and the rapid boom, boom, boom of steel-shod hooves slamming against the barn walls.

"I have no idea," Mary said, raising her voice above the din. "How do I tell?"

"Worry about it later," Bret said as he hurried past the people inside, concerned the animal would injure himself if his tirade went on much longer. "Just get them both out of here and away from the barn. The far paddock would be best."

Mary and Nick, who'd been close by listening, rushed to do as he bid while Bret approached Ebony's stall. No one spoke and Bret was thankful none of the onlookers asked any questions. He needed all his concentration to deal with the dangerous animal.

Normally, Ebony was headstrong—he was a stallion after all—but he didn't rampage like this. Something had to have set him off. His belly tightened with apprehension. *I hope I'm right about the mares.* If he was, Ebony should calm down once they're gone.

As Bret reached the stall, the big horse reared, kicked the door, and snorted as if ready to do battle with any challenger, his long black tail twitching hard and fast. Bret peeked inside and saw the woman Mary mentioned. Sandy had crouched into the far corner, her body curled into a tight ball, appearing to cradle her left arm.

Bret met the gray-green eyes of the tall blonde woman who'd been the first to confront him the night they attacked him. She looked terrified and seeing Bret there, her shoulders slumped as if his presence didn't comfort her in the least. He knew what she must be thinking, it was written plainly on her face, but he wasn't the kind of man to seek revenge, at least not this way, not when an animal or others could be hurt, and not on a woman. Especially since she and the rest of his attackers had only been trying to protect themselves and their loved ones.

"Just stay where you are," Bret said, trying to console Sandy as Mary led the first mare out of her stall, while Nick, still looking scared witless, followed with the other. "We'll get you out of there as soon as we can."

Ebony landed a hard, kick high on the stall door, throwing splinters in all directions and Bret jumped back to avoid the flying hooves, right into the path of the second agitated mare. His sudden movement startled her and she snorted then attempted to rear up. Luckily, Nick held her bridle tight and she stayed on the ground, but the cranky mare tried to take a bite out of Bret in her frustration. She only just missed his arm as he jerked himself out of the way.

"Get her out of here," Bret growled.

Just then Dean Williams came rushing through the barn doors. "What's goin' on?"

"You got any horse treats?" Bret asked, stepping up to the stall once more.

"Just an apple."

"Give it to me," Bret said, holding out his hand and watching the stallion as he paced his stall, huffing and snorting.

Dean handed him the fruit.

"Get me a lead, would you?" Bret asked the other man who quickly went to the tack room to retrieve the rope.

With soft, steady words Bret spoke to Ebony, letting the animal know everything was all right. By the time Dean returned with the lead, the stallion had quieted considerably.

"Thanks," Bret said as he took the short rope from Dean and draped it over his neck. He also saw Mary kneeling to check on Hugh in the stall across the aisle.

Bret's gaze met Dean's. "If he wakes up…"

"I'll keep him quiet," Dean replied, recognizing Bret's concerns.

"And away from Ebby's stall," Bret said, nodding toward where Hugh lay. The last thing he needed was to have Hugh's anxiety upsetting the horse again.

Dean nodded. "You got it."

Bret grinned his thanks and turned his attention back to the stallion. He spoke quietly, comforting the horse, but his words were for Dean and the frightened woman inside. "As soon as I get Ebby out of there, you take care of *her*." He tilted his head to indicate Sandy.

"Will do," Dean replied in the same low tone Bret had used.

A frightened, angry horse could cause a lot of damage and Bret was grateful to have the aid of another experienced horseman. Dean's assistance lessened Bret's worries about a worst-case scenario significantly—one where the stallion injured himself, Bret, someone else, or all of the above. Still, anxious sweat beaded his brow and every muscle felt tight, ready to spring at any moment. Using the back of his arm, Bret wiped away the perspiration and then tugged his black hat back into place, focusing on the horse.

Ebony's ears twitched, and he snorted periodically, but his tail had ceased its angry switching and now sat flat against his rump. The heavy muscles in the stallion's shoulders trembled as his hooves shifted over the hay-strewn floor, but his eyes looked less wild. The animal was still clearly unsettled, but Bret's calm eased Ebony's agitation.

Keeping his voice soothing, Bret met Sandy's wide, pain-filled eyes and tried to reassure her, "Don't make any noise or sudden movements. I'll have you out of there in a few minutes."

Bret reached for the stall latch and pulled it back slowly. The horse didn't start or show any further signs of distress. "Good boy," Bret crooned and then spoke over his shoulder to Dean. "Man the door. If he rushes me, I don't want to get trapped."

"I got it," Dean replied.

Bret pulled open the door and slowly moved inside. The horse's ears twitched, but settled forward, listening to the man's soothing voice.

"Easy, boy," Bret said as he stepped slowly toward the big animal. He lifted his arms toward the stallion and the horse tossed his head but made no further threatening movements. Bret stroked the black's neck, still talking to him quietly. A couple minutes of this gentle attention and Ebony was willing to be friends. He nudged Bret's shoulder with his velvety nose and sniffed at the pocket of Bret's flannel, his lips nibbling at the bulge inside.

"Ah, I see you found the apple," Bret said as the stallion nipped at the treat. "O-oh, no, you don't. Not yet," Bret told him with a chuckle, shifting his body so the pocket and the fruit were out of reach. "You're going to have to wait until we get outside."

Slowly, Bret pulled the lead from around his neck and hooked the clasp to the loop in Ebony's bridle. Still speaking calmly to the stallion, Bret began making his way step-by-step toward the door.

"How about we go outside, Ebby," he murmured. "You can have a treat and run off some of that pent up energy. That girl had you all wound up, huh, boy." He leaned toward the stallion and patted his neck affectionately. "I understand," Bret whispered. "Believe me, I know how you feel."

Dean opened the stall door as Bret made his way toward the exit. As he made his way down the wide aisle, another of the hands gradually opened the barn door to let them outside. Bret continued talking to the horse and smiled when it became clear Ebony was more interested in the apple in Bret's pocket than causing a ruckus.

Mary was at the pasture gate and had swung it open before Bret emerged with the stallion. She closed it behind him as he led Ebony into the near field. A few yards in, he stopped and patted the animal's neck, heaping praise on him for good behavior. Ebony tossed his head and then began searching for the apple once more.

"Okay," Bret laughed, pulling the fruit from his shirt and offering it to the stallion. "I guess you deserve this." He smiled and patted the big animal's neck once more. "You shouldn't let those fillies get under your skin. They'll make you crazy, I know." He unclipped the lead clasp and stepped away, while Ebony happily chewed the apple. When he finished and no other treats were offered, Ebony dashed off to the other side of the field, head and tail held high and proud.

Bret shook his head with a chuckle, relieved that it had gone so well, and turned back to the gate.

A loud cheer and applause erupted from the onlookers as he approached, and several of them patted him on the back as he headed toward the horse barn. Uncomfortable with all the attention, Bret smiled stiffly and kept walking, but their appreciation was nothing compared to the surprise he got just outside the barn door.

Dean stood there with Sandy, who cradled her arm protectively, and Hugh, who seemed to be favoring his left side. All of them observed Bret's approach with varying expressions that he couldn't decipher. Knowing that Hugh still held a grudge for his escape attempt, Bret watched the big man closely.

In the two weeks since Bret's attack, those involved had avoided him, but when nothing else happened, they'd begun to grudgingly accept him once more. Hugh was another story.

A hard man to convince of anything, getting back into his good graces was nearly impossible. Hugh had made it very clear that Bret had endangered not only Hugh's well-being but that of every other person living there. For that, Hugh had refused to forgive the younger man.

Though leery of the blacksmith, Bret refused to be intimidated. Also not being stupid, he made certain to stay out of reach. Hugh, might be injured, but he hit hard, and Bret had no interest in revisiting that battle.

"Thank you," Sandy said a little shakily as Bret approached, and he couldn't tell if her unsteadiness stemmed from her harrowing adventure in the barn or from having to say those words to him.

"No problem," he replied, his eyes on the woman, but not letting Hugh out of his sight. "Are you all right?"

"I think my arm is broken," she said in a tight voice.

Bret empathized, the pain had to be terrible. "I'm sorry to hear that. I'm sure Michelle will have someone take you to the hospital in town to get it checked out."

"Yes, I'm sure," Sandy replied and then hesitated. "I-I…just…"

She heaved in a deep breath and sighed. Then standing a little taller, she met Bret's curious gaze. "I just wanted to thank you before I left. I know you had reason not to help me, but I'm grateful you did."

"No reason for me not to help," Bret said and meant it. "I wouldn't have left anyone in there with Ebby like that. He's usually a sweetheart, but something got him riled."

"Yeah," she replied, "I know, but I appreciate it anyway."

"You're welcome."

Sandy smiled and then turned toward the house, no doubt to seek out that ride to town. Bret watched her go, then looked at the huge man still before him.

Hugh stood, one arm pressed to his ribs and his other hand extended between them, a grim expression on his face. Bret's eyes dropped to the large hand and then back up to Hugh's face, a frown marring his brow.

"What's this?" Bret hadn't meant for the question to sound accusatory, but it did anyway.

"I'd like to offer my thanks as well," Hugh said, still holding out his hand, waiting for Bret to shake it. "She's right. You had reason not to help."

Bret glanced at Dean who simply pursed his lips and lifted his eyebrows as if to say "Well, are ya just gonna stand there?"

Hugh stood patiently, still holding his hand out like an olive branch, waiting. Bret hesitated only a moment before he took the big man's hand and, though he was still guarded, he tried to smile. "Like I said, no problem."

Hugh's grip tightened and, though not hurtful, it instantly put Bret on guard. The big man's eyes bored into Bret's and his expression was serious. The scar on his left cheek stood out more than normal with that look on his wide face.

"If you ever need anything," Hugh said, "anything at all, you just let me know."

Taken aback, Bret eyed the blacksmith warily, not sure what to make of his comment.

"I mean it, Masters," Hugh told him, "anything at all. I'm your man." He released Bret's hand, dropped his arm to his side, and hurried after Sandy. When he reached her, he placed his broad hand on the small of her back and escorted her to the house.

Bret turned his amazed gaze to Dean.

"Looks like you made a new friend," Dean quipped. Thanks to the ranch's unavoidable gossip, Dean, like most of the workers, knew about the animosity between Hugh and Bret.

"What the hell was all that?" Bret asked, astonished.

"You didn't know?"

"Know what?"

Dean nodded his head toward the departing couple. "Hugh's been in love with Sandy since almost the minute he arrived. I'm surprised you didn't notice. Everyone else has."

Bret's eyes swung to the retreating couple in wonder, then shrugged. "Been busy I guess."

"Yeah," Dean chuckled, "I guess."

Bret gave him a dirty look, but without malice. "Get back to work," he said sharply and Dean laughed again.

"Yes, sir, you're the boss."

"Then get to it already," Bret said, but couldn't help a small smile. Dean was teasing him with the honorific. They were friends, and the man knew Bret didn't expect him to call him "sir."

Dean gave him a very badly executed salute, made worse by his cocky grin, then spun on his heel and marched back to his horse.

Bret shook his head, chuckling again as he ambled back to the calving barn. He wanted to check on the calf he'd just helped into the world and to pick up his soiled gear. He planned to return to the house to drop them off, grab his other jacket, and another pair of gloves.

As he neared the barn, Bret sensed something, like a sharp blade tickling his spine. Someone was watching him. Expecting an attack, Bret spun around, tense and ready to fight if necessary.

No one was there, but the feeling didn't cease. He searched the area, but it wasn't until his eyes glanced toward the house that he saw Angel standing on her deck, arms wrapped around her middle, gazing toward him. He hadn't seen her since he delivered her breakfast that morning. She'd been as amenable then as she had been for the last several days, and he'd tried once more to convince her to take her meals with everyone downstairs. She had refused, which meant he'd be spending more time alone with her.

Part of him had liked the idea, but because of all the mixed emotions being around her always stirred up, the greater part him, the harder part, dreaded it.

Now, his reaction to her, even from this distance, was no exception. Just seeing her, he felt a familiar tug inside him, urging him to go to her. Heat suffused his body. His fingers, that had clenched into fists when he'd expected attack, uncurled while everything else felt tense and ready. His skin tightened, sensitive to everything around him, especially her, and made him very aware of his body's response.

Still dressed in her shiny, white robe that seemed to glow in the intermittent, afternoon sunlight, she looked like a warning beacon in a storm. One that he didn't want to heed. Somewhere, as if from far away, his mind screamed for him to walk away. Not to stand and gawk as her pale garment shifted around her legs with the slight breeze and her dark curls fluttered around her shoulders, instantly reminding him of the softness of her skin and the silkiness of her hair on his calloused hands. But he couldn't move. She didn't move either, and he wondered how long she'd been standing there—for the whole show or just the last bit? Then he decided it didn't matter.

Finally, he lifted a hand in a friendly wave, wondering once more what had happened to make her shut herself off from everything and everyone—and again, his instinct to protect her from that hurt and every other threat rushed to the surface.

Dangerous, his mind murmured, though the words were weak. *Too dangerous. Get away!* The battle inside him waged briefly, but then those tender feelings were locked safely away and his hand dropped to his side.

Angel returned his gesture and then—to his relief and regret—she went back inside without another look.

Her strange behavior a few nights before—screaming at him to leave and then begging him to stay—still disturbed him. He didn't like seeing her so downhearted and wished he understood what was behind the pain she suffered.

Damn it, man, will you never learn? that dark part of him asked, but he couldn't help it. He kept reminding himself that without her every person there would end up back where they had come from and for most, that was not a pleasant thought. Bret had no desire to return to the Auction Hall, but he didn't enjoy being played with either.

Whatever Angel's game, he wouldn't let her suck him in.

He'd keep his promise to Jake, but he would do it on his terms.

The Visitor

1

AFTER BREAKFAST AND A WEEK after the incident in the barn, Jake and Bret were settled on the couch in the main house's living room. The rest of the ranch hands had dispersed to complete their morning chores, while the two men had discussed the upcoming cattle sale and their plan to move the herd overland to the sales lot in town.

"Damn," Bret mumbled, shaking his head as he looked over the old map.

Jake lifted a questioning gaze. "What? Something wrong?"

Bret glanced at him and shrugged. "No, I just don't like the idea of being so close to this damn place." He tapped a finger on the map over where the Auction Hall had been marked, not far from the cattle sales lot.

Jake chuckled. "Yeah, I know what you mean."

The old clock on the mantel ticked through several seconds while each man shifted, uncomfortable with their thoughts.

"It's not like we have a choice, though," Bret said breaking the somber tension. "We've got to sell to buy and we need to bring in some young stock."

"Nope, no choice, but at least Angel and her guards will be there to make sure no one bothers us."

"I'm not sure that's a plus, Jake."

"You'd rather head into that den of man-haters alone?"

Bret laughed, then sobered and shook his head. "No, I wouldn't. I'd rather it wasn't an issue at all."

Jake grinned and nodded.

A few minutes later, they were gathering their things, preparing to leave for their day's work, when they heard a commotion outside. Glancing out the big picture window, they saw visitors pull up to the front of the house. Leading the small procession was an attractive woman with long, blonde hair that hung in waves around her shoulders. She was pretty, but there was a sharpness to her features that lessened her beauty and a domineering manner when speaking with her subordinates that irritated Bret.

The woman was accompanied by five female guards on horseback and a sixth who drove a wagon that carried two, very large male slaves, each of whom would rival Hugh Blocker in size and strength.

"They're not chained," Bret muttered as if in shock.

Jake swore viciously and Bret glanced at him, surprised by the vehemence of his friend's reaction.

"You know them?" Bret asked, nodding toward the group outside the window.

"Yeah," Jake said in a low voice. "Unfortunately, I know the one in the lead…though I wish I didn't."

"Who is she?"

"Carrie Simpson," Jake said, gathering the papers he'd been going over with Bret. "She's one of Darla's minions and head of the Section Guards. She shows up about the same time every year for an annual inspection, or so she says. More like trying to take advantage of Angel if you asked me."

The last sentence was a murmur that Bret barely heard.

"What do you mean?"

Jake paused, looking both nervous and harassed. "Nothing," he said as he rushed to gather his things. "Look, I don't have time to explain.

I've got to let Angel know she's here before Carrie comes inside. You should go."

"Why? If there's a problem, I can help you."

"If you stay, there *will* be a problem," Jake said, heading for the foyer and the stairs, leaving the papers on a side table to be collected later.

"What the hell does *that* mean?" Bret asked, moving to follow his friend.

"It means, I know her and you don't," Jake snapped, but the footsteps on the deck told them both it was too late. He fixed Bret with a hard look. "Just keep your distance, Bret, and keep quiet. I'll do the talking. Don't let her upset you, she'll try to—"

The front door opened behind him and Jake cut his warning short as he turned to greet the woman who was entering the foyer.

Taking Jake's warning to stay back, Bret retreated into the living room and cocked his head, wondering what it was about this woman that had Jake so edgy. Then again, she seemed to think she could do whatever she wanted, including entering someone else's home without knocking first.

"Hello, Miss Simpson," Jake said, standing beside the newel-post at the bottom of the stairs.

Bret leaned against the archway leading from the foyer into the living room. Crossing his arms over his chest, he watched the scene before him closely, especially the way Jake made sure to keep the slight woman's attention on him. It was as if his friend wanted to keep her from noticing Bret, and he suspected he knew why. Bret was well aware of how most women reacted to him, as was Jake, and considering Bret's temper of late, it wasn't hard to guess that Jake was concerned for his welfare. So far, the woman hadn't noticed him, and Bret was content to leave it that way.

"If you'll have your guards wait outside and have a seat in the living room, I'll let Angel know you're here."

Bret stared at the woman, wondering if she had noticed the forced pleasantness of Jake's voice or the strained grin on his face. She didn't seem to as she looked Jake over with that slow, full-body perusal that always angered Bret. But somehow, Jake remained where he was with that pleasant-looking grimace on his face.

"Still acting above your place, Jake?" she asked with an edge to her voice that set the hair on the back of Bret's neck on edge.

"Just doing my job," Jake replied.

Surprised at Jake's calm, not to mention his politeness in the face of her blatant hostility, Bret watched in aggravated fascination. The comment hadn't been directed at him, but it annoyed him nonetheless.

"Must I constantly remind you that you're a *slave*, Jake?" Carrie said, sounding as if she was scolding a disobedient teen. "You don't have a job. You do as you're told."

"I was *told*," Jake's emphasis on the last word was not missed by anyone in the room, "no one was allowed to disturb Angel but me."

Bret's eyebrows rose at his friend's outright lie. It was true only Jake, Michelle, and Bret would enter her room without permission as it pertained to her current health, but Angel never forbade anyone to come to her room.

"She won't mind if I do," Carrie said as she attempted to pass Jake, but Jake blocked her path and moved back onto the first step.

"Yes, she will," he said as he started up the stairs. "I'll let her know you're here. Please have a seat and I'm sure she'll be right down." He'd reached the top of the stairs and headed down the hall. He didn't even flinch when Carrie flung curses at his back, and Bret found himself hoping Jake would hurry back with Angel. He had a sinking feeling they were going to need her.

* * *

Anxiety nipped at Jake's heels as he hurried up to Angel's door. He didn't like leaving Bret alone with Carrie, but there had been no choice. He would not let that nasty woman invade Angel's refuge, especially not in her weakened, distracted state.

He knocked on Angel's bedroom door, but there was no response. Sighing, he turned the knob and peeked into the dimly lit room. The soft click of the grandfather clock beside the door was the only sound as he crossed to the bed where Angel slept. He hated to wake her, especially knowing how little she'd been sleeping lately, but she'd want to know Carrie was waiting downstairs. "Angel?" he called, shaking her shoulder. "Angel, wake up."

"Hmm...?" Her eyes blinked open then focused on Jake. "Oh, Jake, what is it?"

"Sorry to wake you, but..." he said slowly. He knew how much she dreaded these visits and he hated to bring her the bad news.

Angel frowned and sat up, clearly picking up on his anxiety. "What's wrong?"

"Carrie Simpson's here to see you."

Angel groaned as she flopped back onto her fluffy pillows and threw the blanket over her head. "I don't want to see her."

"All right. I'll send her away."

"No, Jake, don't. I'll talk to her," she said, sitting up. "She won't believe you and she'll just cause trouble."

"Are you sure? I can have Michelle take care of it."

"Yes, I'm sure," Angel replied and swung her legs over the edge of the bed. "She'll only come back at a worse time. Just let me get dressed."

"Sure," he said, turning to go back downstairs. "I'll tell her you're on your way down."

"No," she said as she crossed to her walk-in closet. "I'd rather you waited for me. I'm still not feeling well and I don't want you to go down alone. We both know how she feels about you."

"I won't be alone," he told her. "Bret's waiting for me."

She peeked around the closet door, her eyes wide with concern. "He's down there with her alone?"

"He knows to keep his temper in check."

She ducked back into the closet. "And you think he'll be able to with *her*?" she asked dubiously, her voice muffled by the shirt she pulled over her head. "You know she has a talent for getting under people's skin. One look at him and that's exactly what she'll try to do."

"I know, but I didn't have a choice." This time he did sound apologetic. "Would you rather I'd let her up here on her own?"

"No!" Angel nearly shouted from the closet. "God, no! It's not your fault, Jake." She hurriedly finished dressing and came out to run a comb through her knotted hair. "I'm a little surprised she didn't try to hurt you for stopping her though. I know how much she dislikes you."

"I'm sure she would've tried if I'd given her the opportunity..." Jake replied, "and the feeling is mutual."

"I know. You did the right thing, just keep it that way, please. And tell Bret to do the same."

"You know I will," he reassured her, knowing the last thing Angel wanted to do was go down and face Carrie. He also knew Carrie's arrival was not a coincidence. Somehow, she always knew when Angel was at her weakest, and each year Carrie showed up at the most inopportune time to nag Angel about purchasing or borrowing one or another of the men on the ranch. This time would be no different. Jake had a sinking suspicion that her visit this year was for one breeder in particular.

He prayed he was wrong.

CARRIE GRUMBLED ANOTHER CURSE under her breath as that stubborn and infuriating Jake Nichols disappeared down the upstairs hall. He'd always thought he was better than the slave he was. Carrie had enjoyed more than a few opportunities to disabuse him of that notion when Darla had owned him. A cruel smile tipped her lips as she remembered how she'd made him scream and beg.

"Go out and take care of the horses," she said to her guards, who'd been standing by the door as if unsure what to do.

She turned as the entry door closed behind them, intent on awaiting her hostess' appearance in the more comfortable confines of her living room. She stopped instantly when she noticed the tall man leaning against the doorframe.

Oh my, she thought, sure of his identity though she'd never met him. *He's more attractive than I thought he'd be.*

Looking like the cowboy he was in his blue-plaid flannel, blue jeans, and boots, he was enough to take a woman's breath away. She took in his long legs, his muscular arms and shoulders, and his too-handsome face. She couldn't remember seeing a more attractive breeder. This had to be the one she'd heard so much about. But seeing him in person put every account she'd been given to shame. He was everything Darla had told her and more, right down to the striking green of his eyes.

The smug curve of his well-shaped lips said he knew the effect his appearance had on women, but he didn't know her.

Time to see if his attitude is as bad as Darla said. The more she learned, the easier it would be to provoke him into action. Thanks to the council's most recent law, that action would give Carrie the right to punish him herself and take him from Angel, if only for a given time. Darla wanted him for herself, but now that Carrie had seen him, her incentive to procure him for her mentor had changed into a far more personal endeavor.

"Hello," she said with a soft smile. "I haven't seen you here before."

He merely stood there with his arms crossed, leaning against the entry, looking down at her with that infuriating grin.

"You must be Bret Masters," she continued with a secretive smile of her own. "I've heard about you."

He arched an eyebrow. "All bad, I hope."

"No, not at all." She moved toward him. She read no fear or insecurity in his eyes. At that moment, she knew the stories from the Auction Hall touting his strength of will were true. He would have to be broken, but there was plenty of time for that after she succeeded in her task. For now, she concentrated on testing his limits. "I've heard some good things," she crooned as she stood in front of him. "Some things were very good." She reached up and traced her finger along his jaw before running it down his chest.

Bret continued to lean against the doorframe, ignoring her advances, but Carrie was undeterred. She pressed her hand flat against his belly, admiring the taut, chiseled muscle she felt beneath his flannel shirt and ignored the frown that marred his brow. She stepped around him, allowing her hand to slide across his hip and drop deliberately over his buttocks. She liked the firmness of the carved muscle beneath his jeans. She noted his surprised jerk, small though it was, and smiled. She let her hand linger for a moment before she reversed direction and stepped around to face him again. She left her hand resting on his hip as she looked up into the masculine beauty of his face. The irate look in his silver-green eyes startled her, but his next words shocked her more.

"Didn't anyone ever teach you that it's polite to ask a man if he wants to be fondled before you do it?" She heard the irritation in his voice and a thrill of power shot through her. The game she played was dangerous but worth it.

"That's the best thing about our new society," she said with a slow grin. "I don't have to ask."

"Here, with me, you do." His voice was low and dangerous, and it sent a thrill of excitement dancing along her spine. She smiled as her stomach fluttered in anticipation of having him at her mercy.

"You know, Bret," she said as if speaking to a wayward child, "you are quite nice to look at, but your manners leave a lot to be desired."

He laughed bitterly. "*My* manners? Lady, you're the one who didn't ask!"

"Does that mean you'd be willing if I had?"

"I didn't say that," he said with a nasty smile.

Carrie heard a door open upstairs and knew her time was limited. Looking up into his silver-green glare, she decided to push him, hard. She stepped closer, her hand moving down his flank as she grinned up at him.

"Tell me something," she said as her palm slid down his hip and then up his inner thigh, speaking quickly as her hand found its target between his legs, "are you as good with *this*," she squeezed him roughly, "as you are to look at?" She smiled as he stiffened, straightened away from the wall, and pulled back from her in one quick movement, his arm coming down harshly to knock her hand away.

"*Get your hands off me!*" he shouted, clearly upset by her deliberate attempt to hurt him.

He was going to be so much fun to play with.

"Come on, Bret," she cajoled, hearing footsteps at the top of the stairs, "are you afraid you won't be able to satisfy me?"

"You little…" Bret began, taking a threatening step in her direction, but he must have heard someone coming and hesitated.

Carrie grinned a challenge at him, daring him to come after her, to do something. She could tell he was sorely tempted and an exciting buoyancy filled her chest. *Just a little more and I'll have him all to myself…*

"What's going on down here?"

Carrie nearly growled in frustration. "Come on," Carrie said softly to Bret, ignoring the question from above. "Let's see what kind of man you really are…"

Only a few feet separated them, but Bret Masters' was a big man and he seemed to loom over her. More excitement bubbled up inside her. *I might even get to have him tonight. Then I can do what Darla never got the chance to do.*

"STOP!" ANGEL SHOUTED from the stairway as she rapidly descended to the foyer, making a quick motion for Jake to remain on the stairs while she moved to block Bret's slow advance.

Bret towered over her as she planted the palms of both her hands firmly against his chest and looked up at his angry face. He halted, but his jaw was set, his arms at his sides, his hands opening and closing as he glowered at the blonde woman behind her. He was all bulging muscle and bristling fury and if he wanted to get by Angel in that instant, she would not be able to stop him.

"Bret?" she whispered, not wanting Carrie to overhear. "Bret, please don't do this."

Slowly, his gaze shifted to meet hers and the rage she read in those silver-green depths frightened her.

"Why?" His voice was hoarse as his gaze returned to his attacker. "She tried to—" He stopped, suddenly uncertain of himself. His eyes dropped to Angel's and she saw the first glint of anxiety as understanding began to take root. He took a deep breath and tried to compose himself. A moment later, he mimicked her soft tone. "Why?"

"Because it's not worth what she'd do to you." Angel spoke quietly so as only Bret could hear her words, hoping that her calm voice would help subdue his anger.

He stared down at her for the longest time without moving. He seemed perplexed and his frown deepened. But a moment later, his lips pulled upward slightly.

Angel returned his smile, lost in his tender regard, glad that she'd reached him. Then Carrie broke the spell.

"Let him go, Angel," she said, seemingly eager to face off with a man more than twice her size. "I'll teach him to respect his betters."

Bret's head snapped up at the sound of her voice and he stepped forward, forcing Angel back a step. Suddenly, Jake was behind her, lending his strength to hers.

"Bret, don't…" Jake began, but Carrie grabbed him by the arm and shoved him bodily across the room. He slammed head-first into the solid front door with a loud thunk.

"Stay out of my way!" Carrie screeched as Jake collided with the door and slumped to the floor.

It had been surreal for Angel to watch a big man like Jake be handled so easily by such a lean woman.

"Jake!" Bret and Angel said together before both turned on Carrie.

"You're going to pay for that," Bret threatened, attempting to bypass Angel to reach the other woman.

"No!" Angel commanded as she saw Jake slowly get to his feet, rubbing his shoulder, flexing and rolling it experimentally. She breathed a sigh of relief before her attention was once again focused on Bret. "No, Bret," she stated more calmly than she felt, "I won't let you if you try."

"You won't be able to stop me," Bret threatened, his voice barely above a whisper.

"Don't bet on it." She matched his glare, daring him to try. She could see him considering it when Jake suddenly appeared beside him, well out of Carrie's reach.

Jake's presence was enough to calm Bret down. "All right."

"Good," Angel said, touching his arm in an unconscious gesture of relief. Harming Jake was a sure way to cause Bret to attack.

"Come on, Angel," Carrie grumbled from behind her, and Angel felt the muscles in Bret's arm turn rock-hard under her hand.

"Shut up, Carrie!" she ordered, glancing worriedly at Bret's face.

"Let him go," Carrie baited, still several steps behind Angel. "It's time someone taught him some manners."

Angel felt the sudden burst of anger like a physical blow. She began to shake, her blood raced, and her heart pounded—all from the effects of the torrent of adrenaline flooding her system.

She'd had enough of this.

"What the hell is that supposed to mean?" she hissed as she turned to face the blonde.

"I'm not afraid of him. You seem to be. So, I'll do you the favor," Carrie told her as Angel dared a backward glance at Bret.

"Whether I am or not is none of your business, Carrie," she told the woman with cold malice. "But you, on the other hand," she brought her gaze back to Carrie, "should be."

"Why? He's just a man."

"Yes," Angel replied, "one who could easily match your strength."

Even though she couldn't see his reaction, Angel felt Bret's surprise. She only hoped he didn't read too much into it. Carrie's adrenaline was flowing and hysterical-strength gave her an edge, yet the outcome of a battle between them wasn't set. Unfortunately, the aftermath would harm him no matter who won.

"That's not possible," Carrie told her, her brown eyes flashing a warning.

"Oh, yes, it is," Angel said. She had intimate knowledge of just how strong Bret Masters was and that he knew how to use it. "You know as well as I do that even with our increased strength, size can play a huge factor. You might be able to stand for a while, but you won't win. Not when the fight is fair."

Carrie bristled at the reminder, clearly annoyed that Angel would state it so bluntly in front of her slaves.

"Do you have no sense of self-preservation?" Carrie hissed. Angel knew her beliefs—that men without fear of the women who controlled them would try to overpower their owners and that would be a disaster for their one-sided society. "You don't know that he'll—"

"Shut up, Carrie!" Angel said once again, silencing the other woman, though she wondered how long it would last this time. "Wait for me in the living room and behave yourself until I come for you."

Carrie hesitated and Angel suppressed an angry growl. Carrie had almost had Bret where she wanted him, and obviously, she didn't want to let him go, but Angel wouldn't let that happen. Unfortunately, now Carrie also had a better idea of how to rile him in the future.

"Now!" Angel shouted when the other woman didn't move.

Carrie jumped at the harsh sound of Angel's voice and without another word, she crossed into the living room.

"Jake," Angel said with a calm she didn't feel and a meaningful look for him to stay clear of the other woman, "would you please accompany Carrie until I return?"

"I don't want *him* around me," Carrie said from the other room.

"You'll wait for me to get back, Carrie," Angel said, "and you *will not touch him*. Do you understand?"

Carrie glared, but a moment later, she gave a brief nod and said no more.

Jake smiled bleakly, and then, rubbing his sore shoulder, he went to stand at the opposite side of the room.

When they had gone, Angel turned to Bret. "I'd like to speak with you in the other room for a moment."

"After you," he said as he gestured courteously with his arm and bowed.

Angel ignored his flamboyant mockery and proceeded down the hallway without another word, though she felt a little queasy at the thought of being alone with him. Still, she had to warn him and she needed to do it quietly. She didn't want to annoy Carrie. It would cause too many other problems with the conniving woman, and Angel didn't feel up to that. Not that she felt confident in dealing with Bret either, but at least he might listen. Carrie would not.

She heard his boots thump on the hardwood floor behind her and was suddenly self-conscious, feeling his eyes on her. Was this a mistake? Was leaving Jake alone with one of his past tormentors also a mistake? Was anything she did the 'right thing' anymore? She didn't know. All she could do now was follow through and hope it all worked out the way she had planned.

2

ANGEL WAVED BRET into the apartment he shared with Jake while she paused to ask Esther to send someone to locate Michelle. She wanted to make sure a woman who wouldn't be intimidated by Carrie's domineering personality took over for Jake until Angel returned. The last thing she needed right now was an unchaperoned Carrie Simpson wandering around the ranch.

"What did you want to speak to me about?" Bret asked once she'd entered his room and closed the door, though he didn't seem overly interested in her reply. She turned to face him and was startled to find him only a few steps away.

"While Carrie is here," she said in an authoritative air, though his nearness unnerved her, "I want you to stay away from her."

"Why?" he asked with a wry smile. "Are you worried I'll like her better?"

"Hardly," Angel replied dryly. "And why would I care if you did?"

"I don't know," he said, his mouth curling up at the corners and his eyebrows arched upward. "Why do you? Are you…jealous, perhaps?"

"Of what exactly?"

"Of losing me to another woman."

"Who? Carrie?" Angel gave a disbelieving laugh. "Believe me,

Bret, you wouldn't like her. She plays too many games."

"And you don't?"

Angel sighed. "We've already been through this."

"Yes," Bret said, taking a step toward her, "and as I recall, you lost."

His reference to their night together after her party made her chest tighten.

"That was a mistake," Angel said, shifting her eyes to the ground and stepping back. "It should've never happened."

"Why not?" Bret asked with an amused smile as she retreated from his advance.

"Because…" she said, backing into the wall behind her. Her eyes flashed to his, realizing she could go no further while he continued to advance.

"Because why?" he asked, seeming to enjoy her unease.

Did he think that was the only power he had over her?

"Didn't you enjoy our night together?" he asked softly. "You seemed to… I know I did."

"That's not the point, Bret." Her hands automatically came up to press against his chest, but the innocent contact sent shivers up her spine.

"Sure it is," he said, bracing his right hand against the wall, blocking her attempt to step around him. "Either you enjoyed it or you didn't."

"I didn't," she affirmed and tried to slide to the other side, but the desk was in the way. He caged her between his arms and quickly repositioned himself in front of her.

"You're a liar," he said as her eyes slowly locked with his.

She could feel the warmth of his breath against her face and it was all she could do to keep from shivering with dread. Or was it something else?

"It's not nice to lie, Angel. Especially about that."

She knew she should push him away, but all she could do was stare up at him, her heart hammering in her chest, deafening her ears to all else but the sound of his voice. His heart beat wildly beneath her fingers and the desire to feel the heat of his body against hers was almost overwhelming.

"I'm sorry," she whispered, "but it was wrong."

"Why?" he asked with a bitter edge to his voice. "Because I'm not good enough for you or because there's...someone else?"

She frowned. *Did he really believe that?*

"There's nothing and no one," she told him, looking away only for her eyes to be drawn back to his face. "Not you, not anyone."

His lips tightened and his eyes narrowed warily.

"You're wrong, Angel," he said, leaning toward her. "There's me." His lips brushed against her hair, her temple. "I'm right here."

"Please, Bret." Suddenly she wanted to pull him in close, to hold him and kiss him again, craved it so much that her whole body trembled with her need for him.

"Yes, angel eyes," he said cupping her chin in his hand.

She tried to think of something to sway him from the course he seemed determined to follow, but she couldn't form the words. She wanted him to kiss her, but she also didn't. She stared up into his jade-colored eyes, darkened now to nearly emerald, unable to look away as wave after wave of desire crashed through her, pounding against her last defense until it began to crumble into ruin.

"Please, Bret," she repeated her plea, but this time it was no more than a whisper.

"Please what?" he asked. "Please hold me?" His right arm encircled her waist while he shifted the weight of his body to hold her firmly against the wall. She hardly noticed his subtle movements as she stood entranced by the deep green of his eyes.

"Please kiss me, Bret?" he asked even as his lips lowered to her unconsciously waiting mouth.

She'd forgotten how much she needed his kisses, how dangerous it was to be so close to him until the fire of his possessive lips claimed hers. His tongue slipped into her mouth, invading, conquering, and she surrendered. She forgot everything—the problems with the home and the cattle, with Carrie and Jake down the hall, Bret's escape attempt, and even her vows were clouded into oblivion.

All she could do was feel. Feel the rough texture of his unshaven face as his cheeks rubbed against hers. Feel the corded muscles of his encircling arms trapping her against the breadth of his chest. Feel the solid strength of his shoulders as her hands slowly slid around his neck. Feel the hard sturdiness of his masculine body weighing heavily against hers and loving every single sensation. His scent was intoxicating, drugging her senses, yet exciting every atom of her being. And the heat of him was like a blanket of safety that blocked out the world around them.

He wanted her. She could feel his need for her along her belly, setting her body on fire. Her blood seemed to boil as it pumped through her, her bones melting with the heat, and she trembled, her legs going weak at the knees. Much more of this and she'd be a puddle of desire at his feet.

I already am.

Right then, she wanted more than anything to repeat their actions from the night of her birthday, and if he'd taken her to his bed at that moment, she'd have been hard-pressed to stop. She wanted him too, desperately, and it didn't matter if it was right or wrong.

She hugged him closer, returning his kiss with every ounce of her being, letting his fire consume her. Then reality abruptly intruded into her passion-dazed mind in the form of Carrie's shrill voice. It resounded through the walls all the way from the living room, dousing the heat searing through Angel, and she froze. Her once warm, lithe body went as rigid as ice.

"Bret," she whispered as she touched his face, "please, don't do this. Not here, not now."

"Would you rather wait and do it somewhere else?" he asked, his voice rough and slightly out of breath.

"No," she said, turning away as a piercing ache stabbed her deep inside. "I told you, it's wrong. It'd just be another mistake."

"Why?"

"Because," she said, "I...I don't...love you." He pulled back, surprise on his face, and she took the opportunity to put some distance between them while ignoring the hurt she read in his expression. "I could never...love you."

"Never is a long time," he murmured and she saw disappointment in his eyes.

"Yes, it is," she said, wanting to apologize, to explain as she moved to the door, but it would be another mistake. She paused with her hand on the knob and then looked over at his intense green eyes.

"Please be careful around Carrie, Bret," she said. "She could be...dangerous for you."

He arched a doubtful eyebrow. "Dangerous?"

"Yes," Angel said and then sighed heavily when his expression didn't change. "She has a way of abusing her status as a guest. Not that she was ever invited in the first place, but that isn't the point. She exploits the law to acquire what she wants, including people. You'd be an easy target, and one she wants, I'm sure. So, be careful around her."

A smug smile curved his chiseled lips. "Well, thank you, Angel. Does that mean you find me," he raised his eyebrows suggestively, "*desirable*?"

"It doesn't matter if I do or not. She will, so please, Bret, stay away from her." He seemed surprised by the sincerity in her plea, and she hoped he didn't read more into what she'd said, even if there was more.

"All right, Angel," he agreed. "I'll do my best to stay out of her way."

"Thank you," she said. One less thing for her to worry about.

"You're welcome." Something in his voice made her look up as he rested his forearm against the wall. She was expecting sarcasm or worse, but he merely smiled. She tentatively returned the gesture, then opened the door and headed for the living room.

AS SOON AS THE DOOR CLOSED, Bret released the breath he hadn't known he was holding. He placed both forearms against the wall and rested his forehead on the cool surface as he leaned into it, trying to think of anything else but how Angel had felt in his arms. He had no idea why he'd pursued her, why he'd kissed her. Maybe it was because she'd just looked so damn tempting, but he was paying for it now. He wanted her, so badly he ached!

What was it about her that made him lose his mind every time she was close? To forget all his vows to avoid her? He couldn't remember ever being this idiotic about one woman, especially one who repeatedly refused him. Amy was the only one who'd come close. Amy had fooled him so completely, but she'd also seduced him—not that she had to try very hard. By the time he'd met Amy and she had made it plain that she wanted him, he'd been more than willing to follow along. Even Jake's warnings had little influence, at least not until she betrayed them both.

Angel was a new kind of trap.

She appealed to him on so many levels beyond what Amy had touched. She was physically attractive, though shorter and curvier than the women who usually interested him, but her lack of stature didn't matter. With Angel, he wanted all of her, not just her body. Everything about her had been imprinted on his mind, ruminating over each one in turn. Like how he enjoyed her company and liked that she could hold her own against him—whether in a conversation or a disagreement. He liked that she wouldn't back down if she felt strongly about something, no matter what he said or did. He liked her long, silky hair and loved how it seemed to be infused with that lilac scent that followed her— even when it drove him mad with desire. He could still smell it now on his clothes and in the air all around him. It made his pulse quicken just thinking about it…about her. He loved how she looked up at him with those big, brilliant, sapphire eyes and how he got lost in their depths every time he met them. He loved her low, naturally sultry voice and how she could goad him to anger or passion with just the tone she used. He loved the softness of her skin, the round fullness of her breasts, and the curve of her backside. He loved the taste of her, the sure-fire brand of her kisses, and how she melted in his arms. He loved—

"No," he murmured, his eyes popping open as he abruptly pushed himself away from the wall. His hands braced against it, he stared at the plain white surface in stunned disbelief of the words that had just crossed his mind.

No, no, no, he thought desperately. *I am* not *in love with her! I'm just hot for her, that's all!* He knew that last was true, but even if he couldn't remember having better sex with anyone else…well, ever, that didn't mean anything. The fact that—except for that one magnificent night—she'd never encouraged him, never reacted to him the way most women did, had made her a challenge, nothing more. That explained why other women no longer appealed to him. She had piqued his interest and he wanted to explore her passions to their limit. He knew there was an ocean of emotion below the surface, but she held herself apart while she mourned an old sorrow, unwilling to allow any other soul to bear its weight.

Why did that bother him so much?

He pushed away from the wall and began to pace the room.

She was attracted to him, the signs were unmistakable. She'd said there was nothing more, that she wasn't in love with him, that she could never love him. Those words had gutted him, but he didn't understand why. He wasn't in love with her, didn't want to be either, so why should it matter if she felt the same?

Despite all that, he couldn't help but wonder if she was in love with someone else. Jake maybe, like so many had speculated, including Bret himself? They were awfully friendly, but as long as Bret had known Jake, the man had never been a two-timer and he knew how Jake felt about Monica Avery. It was obvious in the way he looked at her and how he spoke about her. Maybe Angel's affections were one-sided. Maybe she was in love with Jake, but he didn't know it.

Maybe it was something else entirely.

"Or maybe I'm just a damn idiot," he mumbled, irritated with his thoughts as he ran his fingers through his short, black hair. He should not have kissed her, of that, he was well aware. Now he was going to be useless for the rest of the day, distracted with his musings, which he was under no illusion would cease simply because he went to work. But, if given the chance, he would do it all again. There was just something about her that he couldn't seem to resist, at least not for long, and he was going to have to learn to guard against it if he intended to remain unscathed.

Now there was another woman—their far more aggressive and apparently dangerous houseguest—he'd have to worry about for who knows how long. He had no problem with Angel's request that he avoid Carrie. He'd already understood the kind of woman Carrie Simpson was and wanted no part of her, but staying away from her could prove difficult if she was as determined as she seemed. Then there was the problem of dealing with her antagonistic attitude should his attempts at evasion prove futile.

"Damn it," he mumbled heatedly. "When will I get a break?" Everywhere he turned it seemed a woman was trying to destroy him. First, there was Angel with her feminine wiles weaving a spell to ensnare him. And then all the others who either wanted something from him he wasn't willing to give or wanted to punish him for some meager transgression. He wasn't sure which he feared the most.

Snatching up his brown farm jacket from the desk chair where it had rested since his return from his early morning rounds, he shrugged into its quilted lining and crossed to the outside door. Snagging his black hat from the hook by the door, he went outside knowing he'd succeeded in nothing by kissing Angel again. Nothing at all except confusing and frustrating himself.

3

ANGEL LEANED HEAVILY against the wall down the shadowed hall from Bret's door. Closing her eyes, she let her head thump back against the plaster and pressed her hands flat over the cool surface, struggling to rein in the torrent of feelings clashing inside her. Bret's unexpected kiss had set her heart to racing and strewn her tattered emotions to the four winds.

She'd let him do it again. She'd let him kiss her! And this time, she'd wanted him to do it. She'd waited for his lips expectantly, holding her breath while her heart hammered in her chest. She couldn't seem to catch her breath and where he'd touched her skin still felt overheated. She took a deep breath and tried to calm down, but he'd left her lost and adrift with that kiss, and in so much more need of what they'd just shared. But the wolves had come to the door and now sat in her living room waiting to pounce. Showing any kind of favoritism toward Bret with Carrie around would be like waving a scarlet cape in front of an angry bull.

Gloomy thoughts about her guest seemed to be the signal for Carrie to begin her normal prima-donna routine. Strident words demeaning Jake echoed down the hall, followed by his quiet response. Angel's shoulders sagged and a sigh spilled from her lips. It was time to confront Carrie and lay down the rules. *Again.* They'd gone through them so many times, the other woman should've been able to recite them in her sleep, but she never seemed to remember. Or maybe she didn't bother to follow them because she didn't care. Carrie's harassment of Bret in the foyer wasn't an uncommon performance, and Angel had to wonder if her visit this year was for one purpose—to acquire Bret Masters by antagonizing him into doing something rash, like lashing out verbally or, God forbid, physically. If she succeeded, that stupid law they passed last summer would allow Carrie to take him and there'd be very little Angel could do to stop it. Just the thought of Bret in the hands of that woman made her so furious and anxious her palms began to sweat.

The front door opened and Angel pressed her shoulders into the wall. Michelle's barely civil greeting for their guest reached Angel's ears and she sighed in both relief and frustration. Michelle disliked Carrie almost as much as Angel did, but the head guard was far better at remaining detached than Angel was on her best day.

Knowing she couldn't hide out in the hallway much longer, Angel pushed away from the wall, steeling herself for the upcoming confrontation, even though she didn't feel up to the task.

Earlier that morning, Angel had awakened from another terrible nightmare. Just like all the others, it had left her sweating and gasping for breath, her chest on fire with heart-wrenching agony. Finding sleep again had been impossible. Lying awake through long, dark hours, she'd tried to tell herself it was just a dream; it wasn't real. That the scene had already played out long ago and she'd lived through it. She *had* survived. Unfortunately, none of it was comforting, anymore. Everything seemed gray and bleak, monotonous and so utterly pointless, making it increasingly difficult to recollect why she had built this ranch or what had driven her to do so in the first place. Weighed down by pain, and fear, and responsibility, choking on it, feeling she had no recourse, deepened the darkness that tormented her. The emotions this time of year dredged up inside her always led to the inevitable desire to let it all go. Not that she needed additional encouragement to feel that way, the dreams just made everything worse—overwhelming. Daydreams of getting away from all of it assailed her too often, she found herself wanting to run away from everything that seemed to be dragging her into deeper darkness and despair. But that argument just went in circles and always ended with one man—Bret Masters.

Standing in the dim hallway, she knew where her comfort lay, what she truly wanted, but instead of lightening her burdens, it just made them heavier. She wanted to escape it all—the home and its responsibilities; the crazy-stupid laws and the fear for the people in her care; the pain and the loss, and the unrelenting knowledge of her guilt for it all. She wanted to escape everything—except the tender embrace of Bret Masters' strong arms.

Dropping her chin to her chest, Angel's hands fisted at her sides and she groaned quietly. She hadn't tried harder to get away from Bret because she'd wanted to find out if kissing him was as wonderful as she'd remembered. If the feel of his mouth and hands and body would wipe away everything as they had before. She was both pleased and distressed to discover that it was better than she had remembered. In his arms, she could forget and, for a few minutes, find a kind of happiness that had eluded her for years. Yet, all of that was only one part of her problem. Was what she felt with Bret due to the real man himself or to the one she'd built in her mind while listening to Jake's stories?

Now he was here, invading her mind and dreams, awakening feelings she'd thought long dead...until he kissed her, making her want to feel them again and to forget everything she'd taken such care to build. Worse, she wanted to let him in, to share her burdens and take on his, but she couldn't do that. She couldn't risk anything real to grow between them.

Pulling herself together, Angel straightened her shoulders and stepped into the light on her way to the living room and her guest. Whether she felt up to it or not, she had to face Carrie and deal with the situation her presence represented.

Jake stood below the archway that led into the living room from the foyer, looking nervous and irritated as Angel entered. He gave her a tight-lipped smile that she returned before focusing on the rest of the room. In the center, Michelle faced their blonde visitor who, sat tensely on the edge of the sofa. Michelle's arms were crossed over her chest and the look on her face said she'd reached the end of her patience and was barely holding back. Opposite her, Carrie stared pointedly at the far wall, ignoring everyone, apparently in a snit.

"Thank you, Jake," Angel said, touching his arm and hoping to keep Carrie from starting a tirade. "You may go now. You too, Michelle, and my apologies to both of you for interrupting your work."

Jake wasted no time in beating a hasty retreat, but Michelle stood her ground, giving Angel a look of commiseration.

Holding back another sigh, Angel sat in the large black chair beside the couch and smiled blandly at each of them.

Michelle nodded at Angel's controlled expression. "I'll be in the kitchen when you need me." She knew the drill. Angel would chat with their unwanted guest and then turn her over to Michelle for the tour of the homestead Carrie would undoubtedly insist on taking right away. As their uninvited visitor often said whenever anyone complained, it was Carrie's duty to inspect the home and all its inhabitants to ensure everyone's safety and security. No slave rebellions on her watch, not that one would start on Angel's property—the people here knew what it was like living outside these walls.

"I was beginning to think you were going to leave me in here with *him* all day," Carrie complained once the others had left the room.

"You know I wouldn't do that," Angel said genially, ignoring her growing headache.

"Well," Carrie said, giving Angel a sidelong glance, "all right then. It's just been a long morning already, and I was not expecting to have to be in *his* company."

Angel stifled the instant anger that heated her skin. "My apologies." It galled Angel to say those words.

"Yes, well, don't worry about it," Carrie said. "No harm done…this time."

Angel nodded and didn't rise to the bait.

"On the other hand," Carrie said with a suggestive smile, "who's the new slave with the attitude?"

Angel groaned inwardly. At least the woman got straight to the point. "Why?"

"Just wondering. He has bad manners, but he's quite attractive."

"I guess so," Angel said. The last thing she wanted was to discuss Bret with this woman.

Carrie scoffed, "You guess? Are you blind?"

Angel's jaw tightened, but her visitor didn't seem to notice.

"Angel, that man is gorgeous!" Carrie tilted her head. "I don't suppose you'd consider lending him to me for a while? Or even selling him?"

Angel sighed. "You know my policy on that." They'd had this conversation several times, but Carrie never failed to ask as if it would change.

"Would you make an exception?" Carrie asked and Angel had to struggle not to roll her eyes. "I mean, I'd be very appreciative of just a little of his time and attention. I'd have him back in a week."

"No."

"Why do you have to be so strict about that?" Carried asked in a whining voice that grated on Angel's headache. "You have all these handsome men at your disposal, all breeders too, and you don't use a single one for yourself...or has that changed?"

"No."

"Come on, Angel," Carrie cajoled, "I'll give you a good price for him. I'd even trade three, or four, or possibly more of mine for him. Most would jump at an offer like that."

"No!" Angel's voice held a note of finality. "No one who lives here is for sale. I do not *lend*," she made the word sound like a curse, "them out, nor do I allow my guests to pressure them into anything they do not want. You know all this, Carrie, so why do you ask?"

"What if he wants it?" Carrie asked, disregarding Angel's last comment.

Angel sighed again. "That's entirely up to him, as you already know."

"Well," Carrie said slowly, "we'll just have to see about that."

"Carrie," Angel warned, "you leave him alone. I don't want you bothering any of my people this visit. You caused a lot of problems last time and I don't want a repeat performance."

"I'll be no bother at all," Carrie replied, getting to her feet and heading for the door. "I'll just ask him, that's all."

Like you just did? Angel thought but said nothing.

"Will I be staying in the same room?" Carrie asked from the foyer.

"How long are you planning to stay this time?"

"I'm not sure," Carrie told her, "a week or so."

"I'm afraid you'll have to wrap it up more quickly," Angel replied. "I haven't been feeling well, and we are quite busy at the moment. I can only spare a day or two, and the rest of my people won't have time to wait on you. You'll be on your own with Michelle most of the time."

"Too bad," Carrie said with a practiced pout. "I was looking forward to a lengthy review, but I understand. I'll do my best to stay out of your way."

Angel had to struggle to keep from rolling her eyes, noting that Carrie did say she'd wrap things up more quickly. "I'd appreciate it," Angel replied, but she doubted Carrie would avoid causing problems.

As the manager of the Section Guards, Carrie was not required to run inspections herself. Yet every year she showed up at Angel's house, looking for some weakness that could be exploited. Angel had no doubt that Darla was behind the yearly visits, and she didn't find it coincidental that Carrie always showed up when Angel was feeling her worst. Someone was supplying them with information. They had a spy hidden somewhere among the people on her ranch.

"So," Carrie elongated the word, drawing Angel's attention from all the unfortunate possibilities that Carrie's presence brought with her, "the same room then?"

"Yes, the same room upstairs." Angel got to her feet and followed Carrie into the foyer. "But the rules are the same. Stay away from the men's quarters and the men. I don't want any problems. I won't take it kindly if you cause issues for me or them."

"Whatever you say, Angel," Carrie replied, but Angel doubted she heard the warning.

"I'll have my slaves take my things upstairs," Carrie added, opening the front door and instructing the two large men to do just that. Angel didn't miss their downcast eyes and the anxious trembling of their hands—signs of the fear drug, though she suspected it was a low dosage due to their position in Carrie's entourage. When she finished ordering the men around, Carrie turned to Angel again, waving a hand toward her slaves. "As soon as they are done, I think I'll take a little nap before my first tour."

That was a surprise. The woman usually wanted to get started right away.

"Oh, and my people?" Carrie asked as an obvious afterthought. "Is there a place for them? One of the men will stay with me, *of course,* but the others and my guards will also need a place to stay."

"The rules apply to all of them as well," Angel cautioned. "If they can abide by my rules, *all of them*, then something can be arranged."

"They'll behave," Carrie said as she headed for the stairs, presumably to take her nap.

"I'll have Michelle assign them a room. We are a little crowded at the moment so they may have to share, but I'm sure we can arrange something."

"That'll be fine, thank you," Carrie said. "I should be ready for my first tour of the grounds in a couple of hours."

"I'll let Michelle know to check with you in two hours. I won't see you until dinner."

"Whatever you say, Angel," Carrie said again as she topped the stairs, clearly dismissing her hostess.

Angel seethed as she watched the other woman walk down the hall.

"Whatever you say, Angel," she mimicked in a low, singsong voice. *Damn woman!*

Angel went to the kitchen to inform Michelle of her new duties and Carrie's plans before she headed for the barn. She wanted to catch up with Jake before he left for his chores and ask him to pass on the warning about their unwanted guest to all the other men: *Carrie*

Simpson is dangerous. Stay away.

SEVERAL HOURS LATER, Jake returned from the evening feeding. On his way to the house, he saw Angel standing on her back deck staring off toward the ancient willow tree on the hill, idly stroking Grayling—the big, gray cat that had taken to sleeping on Bret's bed whenever he could. She looked sad and withdrawn, and he felt the familiar inclination to shelter her from whatever tormented her. She'd spent most of her time alone lately—except for her meals with Bret, or Jake when Bret wasn't available—but Carrie's arrival would change that. Angel always felt obligated to ensure Carrie didn't bother anyone during her visit, which Jake considered a wise notion.

Riding through the homestead gates, Jake shook his head, frustrated by the hated woman's presence and the situation. Carrie—and the problems she caused—was one thing, but more ailed Angel than she would say. Even after three years, he still had no idea how to help her, and soon he wouldn't be around to help anymore. Bret was living up to his promise to look after her, but Jake worried it wouldn't be enough. He was afraid a time would come when Angel needed Jake and he wouldn't be there.

Damn it, I just want to move back to Monica's! His horse tossed his head, pulling at the reins, and Jake relaxed his tense fingers.

Bret's not-so-secret desire to escape plagued him as much as Angel's severe mood swings. Fear for both of his friends compelled Jake to stay, at least until spring when Angel's spirit would brighten again. He'd already tried to convince Bret to stay, but whether he did or not was up to him. Though if he didn't, Jake would be hard-pressed to choose between the woman he loved and the little sister he'd adopted.

Jake steered his horse toward the barn, anxious to get the animal settled and himself inside for dinner. He dismounted outside the barn door, murmuring soft words to his horse, then he fell silent. *Am I hearing voices now?*

Tilting his head, he paused to listen and recognized Carrie's voice coming from somewhere inside the barn. Stifling an aggravated groan, Jake slowly entered the unlit structure through the open doors. No one else was around, but he could just see Carrie as her voice echoed from the shadows at the back of the barn.

"I *really am* impressed, you know," she said to someone outside Jake's field of vision.

"I'm glad," a man replied, and Jake couldn't mistake the sarcasm or the sound of Bret's voice. A moment later, he saw his friend exit one of the rear stalls carrying a large, flat shovel.

Seeing them together shot bolts of wariness and fear ricocheting inside his chest. Carrie must have somehow arranged this opportunity to corner Bret alone. Thankfully, Bret had enough sense to humor her, but from the tone of his voice, his patience wouldn't last much longer. Jake needed to separate them before Carrie antagonized Bret into doing something she'd make sure he would regret.

"Come on, Bret," Carrie crooned as she took hold of his arm and pulled him toward her. "I know you want it and, unlike Angel, I'd be happy to give you the pleasure."

"Yeah?" Bret asked, his derision only slightly masked. "What's the catch?"

"No catch," Carrie said, stepping closer to run her hands over his chest. "Just you and me and a really good time." Carrie was a pretty woman and could be persuasive when she wanted to be. Jake only hoped Bret saw the sweet and sexy act for what it was—an act.

"I don't think so," Bret said after a short pause. He reached up to remove her hands from his chest, but she snatched them back.

"What's wrong with you?" she demanded. "Don't you like women?"

Jake could only see the back of Carrie's head, but he clearly saw Bret's face as he glared at her. The tension in Bret's shoulders and the frown darkening his brow encouraged Jake to intercede before anything got out of hand.

"That's not—" Bret growled in a dangerously low tone, but Jake didn't let him finish.

"Hey, Bret?" he called as if he'd just entered.

Seemingly glad for the intrusion, Bret stepped around Carrie, dismissing her, and marched down the aisle toward his friend, his back ramrod straight and his shoulders stiff.

"What's up?" Bret asked, rubbing the jaw of Jake's mount affectionately.

Jake stared. He should have thought of an excuse to call on his friend before he spoke. Quickly thinking of something lame, he stumbled through a reply.

"One of the guards said that Angel wants to see you." He shifted his feet as his eyes swung between the horse and Bret's face, hoping his friend wouldn't hear the lie.

"What does she want?" Bret asked, irritation plain in his tone.

"I don't know…she didn't say," Jake replied. "Just told me to send you up to the house. Angel hasn't been looking too good lately."

"Yeah." Bret sighed and leaned forward, lowering his voice to keep Carrie from overhearing. "Can't you take care of it?" he asked quietly. "I'm not up to dealing with another aggravating woman."

Jake laughed softly. "Not my job anymore, buddy," he said quietly. With a commiserating slap on his friend's shoulder, Jake led his horse farther into the barn, using the animal as an obstacle between Bret and the approaching Carrie.

"Great. Thanks," Bret replied as he headed for the door, ignoring Carrie's presence.

She's not going to like that, Jake thought as he watched his friend leave.

He shouted over his shoulder at Bret's retreating back, "Any time!"

"What the hell was all that about?" Carrie asked, a clear threat in her eyes. "Are you trying to interfere again, Jake?"

"No," Jake answered and warned himself to be wary of her tricks.

She poked a finger against his chest. "Then what do you think you're doing?"

"Just delivering a message."

Carrie jammed her small fists on her lean hips and stared at him, clearly disbelieving him. But, aside from asking Angel—and Jake felt certain Carrie wasn't about to do that—she had no way to prove he was lying.

"You never did know when to stay out of the way, Jake."

"I just do what I'm told," he replied.

She glared at him to see if he was mocking her with her own admonitions from earlier that day, and Jake carefully maintained a perfectly innocent expression.

"Well, that may be so, but you listen good," she said softly, a threat in every word as she prodded him in the chest with one finger, "really good, because this is the last time I'm going to say it. Stay *out* of my way! The next time you interfere, Jake, I'll break your arm and you'll be thankful if I stop with only one. Do you understand?"

"Yes," Jake said, his face expressionless.

"Good!" Carrie stepped around him and his horse, heading for the door. "Just don't forget," she threw over her shoulder. "You know how much I would *hate* to hurt you again."

Anger percolated in his veins and heated to a slow simmer as she walked away. As if he could forget all the torment she and Darla Cain had put him through. After all that, he could happily wring their vicious and manipulative necks and not feel the least bit guilty. He'd be doing the world a favor. The only problem was, if he lived through the torture the authorities would put him through, he would eventually follow them in death—and it would be a long, painful time.

"That's all in the past," he muttered to himself as he led his horse into a stall and began to remove his saddle. He had Monica to consider now, Angel and Bret too. If it was just him, Jake would've taken care of Carrie the moment she arrived after he'd come to live here three years ago, but by then it was already too late. He loved Monica and didn't want to risk her *or* Angel—who had helped him when he really needed it.

He ran the brush over his horse's flank and shook his head. Thinking about his misfortunes now did no good. The past was over. He would never go back to the cruelty those women had dished out daily, and he felt confident he'd just saved Bret from a similar fate.

4

CARRIE SIMPSON SAT on hay bales in Angel's horse barn—just yards from where she'd cornered Bret Masters earlier that day—and brushed a twig from her white sweater. The task complete, she folded her hands in her lap, shrugged her shoulders, and sighed, anxious for her guest to arrive. She glanced at the low-burning lantern sitting nearby and wondered if she shouldn't turn it down a little. She wanted to illuminate a small portion of the barn but not so much as to be noticed outside.

No moon graced the sky on this chilly October night, and she was glad she'd brought the thin wool blanket that covered her legs. Despite the coolness, she'd dressed for the occasion in a blue denim skirt and sandals. Her wavy blonde hair hung loose around her shoulders and an expectant grin pulled at her lips.

She hated having to meet in the barn. Though the horses had all been turned out for the night, the smell of hay and manure made her nauseous. But it was necessary for her plans and the best place to conduct this clandestine meeting. The barn allowed her the privacy she needed to complete the second half of the task she'd assigned to herself tonight. Still, she looked forward to the warm, clean-smelling bed that awaited her return.

To ensure privacy and security, one of her huge personal guards hid somewhere outside. The second of the large men stood patiently beside the door, his eyes carefully averted, but ready to fulfill her smallest whim. Just a tool to be used when needed and ignored the rest of the time, she barely noticed his hulking presence. Regrettably, she didn't trust the man she was waiting for—despite the influence she held over him—which made the large guard's attendance at this meeting a necessity.

Her spy had been living in Angel's home for some time now. Unfortunately, getting information from him had proved more difficult than she'd anticipated. They'd only met twice before and both times had been rushed.

During their last encounter, she'd gotten the distinct impression that he had lost some of his fear of her and his concern for the brother he'd left in her care.

Seemingly well-trained and obedient, she suspected the brother still harbored a stubborn streak as deep and wide as her spy's. He'd gotten better at hiding it since his punishments could no longer be diverted by his overprotective big brother. She'd accepted his apparent submissiveness, though, and would continue to until he proved otherwise.

Her reluctant spy was a different story. She sighed and shook her head.

Boy, as she'd come to call her slave-spy—mostly because he detested the nickname—had always been difficult. Due to a failed uprising in another home out of state, Boy had been one part of two slave groups she'd purchased a little over two years ago. At first, he'd constantly questioned her, opposed her authority, and, though he'd tried to make it appear submissive, she knew what he was doing.

Despite their rebellious attitudes, this group's troublesome pride—Boy's included—didn't last long. Her quick and often arbitrary punishment had corrected most of his and the other slaves' stubbornness. But, even though Boy had become far more malleable, she knew he hadn't been broken. It wasn't until she discovered his hidden secret—a younger brother who was just as headstrong, but far less cautious—that she'd been truly able to control him. Using the younger brother's continued welfare against Boy had finally bent him to her will.

She smiled at the thought, but a frown quickly replaced it.

Boy had been away from her authority for far too long and his arrogance had returned. She intended to steal it from him again tonight. Then she planned to thoroughly enjoy the other part of him she'd missed since his sale to Aldridge.

She smiled again and adjusted the blanket in her lap. She enjoyed men, enjoyed hurting and humiliating them, forcing them to meet her demands unconditionally. She used to think she was strange, perverted even, for the thoughts she had about men or the excitement she experienced while hurting them, but meeting Darla had changed that. Under Darla Cain's tutelage, Carrie had come to realize it was natural to want control, to expect obedience, and to punish those who displeased her. She'd become quite good at it. So much so, that when Darla became too busy to keep up with the demand, other women sent their slaves to Carrie for training instead.

Some men were far easier to break than others. Her last failure, and the only one who still breathed, lived here with Angel Aldridge. She'd purchased him from Darla when another woman became interested in the brutish slave who'd lost his mind. Carrie didn't know the particulars, but she knew it was one of the many reasons Darla disliked Angel so intensely. Of the four men Carrie had failed with over the years, he was the only one who'd nearly succeeded in attacking her directly.

She shrugged her shoulders and adjusted her seat on the hay bale. Part of her was still a little afraid of him and for that, she hated him with a passion she found hard to contain, whether in his presence or not.

Stop it! she told herself sternly, shifting again and straightening her sweater. *You'll have time to deal with that later.* For now, she had a more pleasant meeting with Boy to consider.

It didn't matter that Boy and his brother were both adults, Boy would do anything to protect his younger brother, and she planned to use his weakness tonight. She would keep him off guard and hurt him as much as she dared just to remind him of his position. His body would remind him of her displeasure for days and, hopefully, it would stick in his mind far longer. She smiled hungrily at the possibilities.

A slight sound came from the door and Carrie noticed her giant guard tense, prepared to defend her. She was unconcerned. It could only be Boy finally coming to meet her. Who else would it be at three in the morning? He was late and she would remind him of how unacceptable his tardiness was in a moment. For now, she watched as the door slid open and the tall, lean man she waited for stepped inside. He quietly closed the door and then turned to face her.

She could just make out his handsomely carved features, and his light-colored eyes, shadowed by the black cowboy hat he wore, seemed to glow in the dim light. He had on the same black farm jacket he'd worn earlier, what looked like a dark blue shirt, blue jeans, and boots. He looked like what he was—a cowhand—but looks could be deceiving. She knew from personal experience that under his clothing was a chiseled, muscular body that would make a woman's mouth water in appreciation. A tightening gripped her deep inside as she sorted through her memories of him. She was anxious to get started, but first things first...

"You're late," she said firmly and frowned when he shrugged. She pressed her lips together as heat built around her neck.

He glanced at the huge man to his right, and then back to her.

"One of the other hands was prowling around," he explained, pushing his hands into his coat pockets. "I couldn't leave until he went to sleep." He paused, glancing to his side. "Was it necessary to bring *him* along?" Boy tilted his head toward her guard.

Yep, he definitely needs a reminder, Carrie thought.

"Come here, Boy," she commanded, completely ignoring his question. She almost grinned at the annoyance that tightened his jaw.

"My name is—" he started and her spine straightened.

He's correcting *her!*

"I know your name!" she said harshly. "You belong to me and you'll *answer* to *whatever* I call you. Your name is Boy!"

He nodded and lowered his eyes the way an obedient slave should.

Good, she thought, *but a little late and not enough.*

"Now, come here, Boy," she said in a hard, clipped tone.

Taking off his hat and setting it aside, he did as she ordered. He stopped about four feet in front of her, awaiting her next command. She knew he found her expectations of him hard to accept. He'd had far more freedom living here than he'd known in years, but he had to remember the consequences if he forgot how to act.

Carrie studied him for a long minute. She'd missed training him, missed his body. Some of her other slaves were as attractive, but this one she'd always enjoyed taming—she liked the challenge he represented. She'd been more than a little irked that she'd had to part with him for this mission, especially since he wasn't fully broken yet, but when they succeeded in pulling Angel down, she would get him back. And a few other new toys too.

"Kneel," she ordered, unwilling to allow him the advantage of towering over her. And she wanted to test his attitude. It was the first step in what she had planned for him.

Far too reluctantly, he went to his knees but kept his eyes lowered. She added one more black mark for his reluctance on the tally she'd started the minute he walked through the door.

She didn't bother to keep track of what he did right.

"Now, tell me what has been happening here," she said.

He inhaled a long, deep breath and released it slowly.

Carrie's hands, tucked beneath the blanket, tightened into fists at his delay.

"I need to know my brother is all right," he said, and she had the satisfaction of hearing the desperation in his voice.

He'd made it seem meek and submissive, but Carrie knew it was a threat.

She was going to have to hurt him more than she'd thought.

"Please," he said, risking a peek at her face, "is he alive? Is he well? It's been a long time and—"

"Yes," she said. "Your brother is fine. Though, your hesitancy in obeying me makes me reconsider his condition." A little threat of her own.

He shook with a slight tremor and his head dropped a fraction lower as he exhaled sharply.

She smiled.

"No need for that," he murmured apologetically. "Thank you."

The tightness in her chest and the heat of her anger faded as he began to disclose everything he'd seen or heard on Angel's ranch over the last several months.

One of the reasons Carrie had purchased Boy was because he had ranching experience, which made him the perfect spy to pass on detailed intelligence about Angel's operation, even if he wasn't a major part of its management. Carrie had planned the whole thing with Darla Cain, and now it was paying off. He was their eyes and ears inside Angel's fortress—when they could reach him for information, that is. Getting close to him was more difficult than getting him inside in the first place.

Carrie asked questions about the cattle, the harvest, what had changed, what was the same, and he explained all the changes Bret had made and how they had improved the prosperity of the ranch. Carrie was interested in everything Boy had to say about the ranch, but she was equally intrigued by Bret Masters and questioned Boy meticulously about each detail.

"So, he has previous ranch management experience," Carrie mused aloud. "That explains why Aldridge wanted him so badly. And you say he's friends with Jake Nichols?" Her pointed gaze fell on Boy once more and he flinched as if he could feel it boring into him.

"Yes," he answered.

"When did that start?"

"Before the wars. From what I understand, long before. They were separated by a raid that captured Jake. Bret got away."

"Hmm..." Carrie mused, crossing her arms and frowning in thought. "Are they close?"

"Yeah, I'd say so."

Carrie tapped her index finger against her lips, still thinking. Then a grin curled her pretty mouth. "That's good to know."

BOY FELT A WAVE OF COMPASSION for Bret. If this woman was interested in him, then Bret Masters was in deep trouble. He wished there was a way he could warn the man. Bret had been nothing but friendly with him, but there wasn't anything Boy could do. He couldn't reveal what he knew about Carrie or her intentions without revealing himself and risking his brother's life. He wouldn't do that, not for anyone. Jake's warning to be leery of this woman had already been passed around and it would have to be enough.

"And Bret has been working closely with Angel for the last several weeks?" Carrie suddenly asked.

"Yes," Boy said, "though I don't know why. He and Jake seemed to have changed roles."

"Huh, she's not quite as stupid as I thought," Carrie mumbled.

Boy knew she didn't expect him to reply.

"Is there anything going on between them?"

He frowned, unsure what she meant. "What? Between who?"

"Angel and Bret. Is there anything going on between them?"

"I-I don't...know," Boy stammered, and, forgetting himself, he lifted his eyes to meet hers directly. "They argue sometimes, but I haven't heard of anything else."

Carrie glared at him and the moment he realized his mistake, he dropped his eyes to the ground. "I'm sorry," he mumbled.

Carrie's back straightened and her voice was harsh. "'I'm sorry,' *what?*"

"Mistress," he said, immediately realizing his mistake. "I'm sorry, Mistress." His quick submission made his stomach roil with mortification—he was a thirty-one-year-old man, for God's sake—but the last thing he needed was to give her a reason to be angry with him.

"That's better."

Boy hated the relief that spilled through his gut like an ice-cold drink on a hot, sunny day.

"Now," Carrie went on, "I heard something happened at a big party here a couple of months ago. What was it?"

Boy tensed. He had no idea what she was talking about. *Maybe she meant Angel's birthday party.* He'd been a little too distracted that night to pay much attention to Angel or anyone else. He'd been too preoccupied with a pair of lovely pale blue eyes and long legs that had felt so warm and smooth beneath his hands...

"Well?" Carrie demanded and he jumped.

"I...I'm..." He tried to think of what she could be implying, but nothing came to mind. "I'm not sure what you mean," he finally blurted out, fear of her temper burning in his belly.

Even with his eyes diverted, he discerned the exasperated shake of her head. She was clearly displeased by his lack of observation.

"I heard they danced together," she said, her tone strained and he wondered, not for the first time, how she knew so much about the activities on the ranch. "I heard that something was going on between them."

"They did dance," he said, hoping to curb the irritation in her shrill voice, "but I didn't see or hear anything else. As far as I know it was just a dance, nothing more."

"Just a dance? After she turned every other man down?"

"I don't know about that. I did see her dance with others..."

"What *do* you know, *Boy*?"

Boy cringed. "Just what I've told you," he said desperately, telling himself the urgent tone was intentional as his eyes beseeched hers. "I don't have a lot of interaction with Angel...ah, Miss Aldridge."

Carrie's warning look reminded him not to use Angel's first name and that his eyes should be on the ground at all times. He dropped them hastily. "I know about the workings with the cattle and the harvest, but not much else. I'm sorry, Mistress."

"How about the other slaves?" she asked, ignoring the obvious plea in his apology.

"What about them?" he asked.

"Are any of them willing to speak against her?"

Boy shook his head. "No, no one."

"How about her mental status?"

"Her mental status?" Boy had no clue where she was going with that question.

How the hell would I know about that? It crossed his mind that she may be bouncing between strange questions to keep him off balance. *Well, it's working.*

"I rarely talk to her," he added. "I really wouldn't know much about anything like that."

"What has she been like lately?"

"Been keeping to herself mostly," he said, hoping it was what Carrie wanted to hear. "I heard she wasn't feeling well and hadn't been eating, but apparently, she's better now."

"Doesn't anyone else speak to her?"

"Ah, yeah…"

"Can't you get them to talk to you? Find out what they know."

"The only one she really talks to is Jake. Well, it used to be Jake, but he doesn't say much about their conversations, at least not around me."

Her eyes sharpened on his face. "Who does she talk to now?"

"Bret spends a lot of time with her now."

Carrie nodded as if he'd verified something she'd heard elsewhere. "Have you figured out where her wealth comes from?"

"Other than the proceeds from the ranch, I haven't seen anything else." He'd heard that question before and it didn't faze him this time.

"Keep looking," she said as her eyes drifted over his muscular form. "She's bound to give it away eventually. Your brother's continued good health may depend on it one day."

Boy's chest tightened painfully and he hung his head in defeat. Staying in Carrie Simpson's good graces was all that kept his brother from the torture she'd put Boy through for months before sending him here to spy and lie, turning him into everything he detested. But it didn't matter how he felt about it; he had no choice. "Yes, Mistress."

5

"REMOVE YOUR SHIRT," Carrie said, calm yet eager to remind Boy where his loyalties—and his obedience—should lie. Boy stiffened and his shoulders rolled forward. His obvious fear made Carrie smile. He knew what was coming and begging would gain him nothing—though part of her hoped he would, and he didn't disappoint.

"Please, I told you everything I know," he pleaded. "Please, don't do this!"

Her dark eyes snapped fire and her voice hardened. "Remove. Your. Shirt!"

Boy's shoulders drooped and he did as he was told. Once he'd removed his jacket and shirt, she ordered him to hold his hands out in front of him. When he did, the giant guard came forward with a rope to tightly bind Boy's wrists together. Tugging at the bonds, the guard seemed satisfied as he turned to Carrie for permission to continue. She nodded, her belly dancing with anticipation as the big man tossed the other end of the rope over the barn's crossbeams. He hauled on the rope until most of Boy's weight was supported by his arms; the toes of his boots barely brushed the floor. Carrie's guard tied off the rope and she ordered him to stand aside.

She studied Boy as he hung helplessly from the rope, slightly swaying back and forth. His arms bulged from the stress of carrying his weight, his eyes carefully downcast, his exposed skin dotted with gooseflesh, as much from his fear as the cold. He had filled out quite a bit since coming to live here; though he was still lean, his once desirable physique had only improved with food and hard work.

Carrie liked what she saw.

He could try to harm her somehow, but he wouldn't attempt it. The risk to his brother was far too great, and he was well aware that his brother would pay three times over for anything Boy tried.

"You have been out of my influence for far too long," she said, brushing non-existent dust from the blanket over her lap. "Your attitude needs adjusting. I've been overly lenient with your undisciplined behavior, and I've decided to amend that tonight."

Another grin pulled at her lips when Boy swallowed hard and squeezed his eyes closed. Tilting her head as she eyed him appreciatively, she almost regretted making him keep his eyes down. He had such beautiful eyes, the color of a warm, tropical ocean.

"If you take this quietly and do everything I tell you, without hesitation," she told him, "I won't have to hurt you further, or your brother when I return home. Do you understand?"

Boy swallowed again. "Yes, Mistress."

Carrie sat smugly on the hay bale, comfortable beneath her blanket, excitement for what she was about to have done to him washing through her. Thinking about how Boy's muscles would jump and flex with each blow, how he'd writhe and struggle to remain silent, broadened her licentious grin. She lifted a finger and her giant of a guard moved to stand behind Boy, dutifully allowing the bound man to see the implement of his upcoming torture, and her smile widened when she saw her victim begin to shake.

BOY'S BREATH CAUGHT in his throat as the guard lifted the long-handled riding crop and then smacked it repeatedly across Boy's back with hard, heavy strokes. The first strike, though expected, surprised a loud groaning-gasp from Boy, but he suppressed it. Clenching his jaw tight, he concentrated on making as little noise as possible and hoped his will held out longer than her need to brutalize him.

By the time she signaled for her guard to stop, Boy's head hung limply from his shoulders. His perspiration stung the cruel welts on his back and he had to concentrate to keep from moaning. She'd kept the count low—about twenty lashes if he hadn't missed a few—which was astounding considering how much she liked to cause him pain. Still, he was certain she had plans for more.

Movement spiked his fear. When her hand brushed over his chest, he jumped.

She laughed.

"You have a nice body, Boy," she said.

He stifled another groan, knowing what she had planned.

"Look at me," she commanded.

Slowly, he opened his eyes and tried to focus on her.

"It's generally polite to thank someone when they give you a compliment," she admonished.

"Thank you, Mistress." He did not hesitate to answer, even though mortification seethed inside him. It was part of his punishment, but letting her see that he also wanted to rip her apart for it—for what she would continue to do if he couldn't find a way out—was suicidal. The additional fact that his actions—great or small—would cause pain for his brother helped keep his fury locked away. She had made his brother's fate abundantly clear long before she sold him to Angel, and it was the only reason Boy allowed her to do this to him.

"I'm feeling the need for male attention," she said as she unfastened his belt and jeans. She tugged the denim down his legs and his underwear followed. She straightened and reached out to fondle him roughly. "Are you feeling *up* to it?"

Boy didn't miss her crude attempt at humor but didn't acknowledge it either. The last thing he wanted was to further betray the sweet woman he'd found here by sexually gratifying Carrie Simpson. He didn't want to touch her or allow her to touch him. All he wanted to do with Carrie was wrap his hands around her neck and squeeze until she stopped moving, but he had little choice, and that knowledge shamed him even more.

"Yes, Mistress," he murmured in reply, and saying it made him sick inside.

"Can I trust you to behave yourself if I let you down? Or do I need to have my man deal with you first?"

"No, Mistress," he forced himself to say what she wanted to hear, the same as he'd force himself to obey, "I'll behave."

"Good choice," she said, clearly reveling in her power over him.

The huge guard untied the knot that dropped Boy to his feet, where he stood unsteadily.

"Get out," Carrie said to her guard. "Don't go far, but don't be seen either."

"Yes, Mistress," the giant replied and left through the front door. Once he was gone, she removed the rope from around Boy's wrists.

"Please me well," she whispered as she untied his wrists and caressed his chest, "and I won't have to hurt you again."

He'd been the pawn in this game she played before, and he should have expected it. She'd been visibly annoyed with him at their last meeting, and he should have guessed she'd hurt him for it. He also knew she would find fault with anything he did, though he did as she said anyway.

He had no choice.

Boy mechanically complied with each of her commands, keeping his mind far from what she took from his body. She made him struggle to gratify her, forcing him into impossible positions and expecting him to keep performing normally. She assaulted him when he couldn't move as she wished, or didn't react quickly enough, or simply to encourage him to a more rapid pace. It was uncomfortable and humiliating, but there was nothing he could do about it. He was thankful the riding crop wasn't handy. She'd used it on him before while he'd attempted to please her in the most intimate of ways. Yet, that didn't mean what she did now didn't hurt almost as much.

He did everything she demanded and tried not to think about it or what she would do after.

When she was sated—and he wasn't—she ended their intercourse by shoving him away. Boy was highly frustrated, but he didn't doubt that she'd thoroughly enjoyed herself. But it didn't matter. At least, not as far as harming him further went. She enjoyed hurting and demeaning men, and right now, he was her target.

"Leave them where they are," Carrie ordered when he'd reached to pull up his garments. He released them and stood motionless, shame burning into his core for obeying, and deeper still for knowing he could do nothing else. He waited while she took her time adjusting her clothes, purposely taking longer than necessary to drag out his anxiety.

Just as he'd expected, she tested his submissiveness by forcing him to stand meekly while she tied his hands again. She called her guard back in and had him haul Boy up by his wrists like they had before, only this time Boy's jeans and boxers were lodged around his thighs. She had the guard stand behind Boy and ordered him to use the crop for a second time, on Boy's bare, unmarred flesh. The guard did as ordered, and Boy did his best to keep his pain silent. Again, she surprised him when she stopped the burly man at twenty.

"You can be thankful you performed everything else so well," she told Boy as she sauntered around him, her fingers tracing lazily over his sweat-soaked body. "Otherwise all of this would have been much worse."

Boy shivered with cold and fear, shock and pain. He wanted to scream—at her, at the guard, for help, in frustration, in humiliation, in pain—but he didn't. He replied as he must, "Yes, Mistress."

She laughed as she walked away. "Let him hang one hour," she told her guard over her shoulder, "and then untie him, but let him get dressed and back to his room alone. If anyone should come before the hour is up, stop them or remove him, whichever is more expedient."

"Yes, Mistress," the huge man replied, but Carrie was already gone.

Boy breathed a sigh of relief. At least his physical torment was done for tonight—well, aside from hanging by his already aching wrists and arms. He was going to be extremely sore for several days and sitting in a saddle would be excruciating. His arms and shoulders were going to ache and he hoped his hands still worked in the morning, but he was still alive and in one piece. Another hour of hanging by his wrists and it would be over...until the next time she became annoyed with him.

He sighed.

Though it was unlikely, maybe he could convince the man standing guard to help him. Boy looked over at him, trying to catch his eye, but the giant stared at the far wall as if the naked, beaten man hanging from the rafters didn't exist. Boy tried to speak, but all that came out of his desert-dry throat was a croak. He worked up a tiny amount of moisture and tried again.

"Help me, please," he whispered and the guard met Boy's gaze. "Let me down, please. Help me."

"She told me to beat ya some more if ya tried to convince me to help ya," the giant said dispassionately, his odd accent slurring the words together. "Is that what ya're trying to do?"

A shock of fear thundered through Boy and he shook his head, his wide eyes staring back at the huge man. "N-No," he mumbled. He should have known better than to think one of Carrie's trained brutes would have any pity for him.

"Good," the guard replied, his pale-eyed gaze returning to the far wall. "I'd hate to have to beat ya again."

Boy wasn't sure how to take that. It was the most compassion he'd ever received from one of Carrie's guards and to say it surprised him would be an understatement. The man may not let him go, but he did warn Boy of the consequences. Boy decided it was a good thing as he resigned himself to suffer through the next hour hanging from his wrists. He only hoped it was still dark outside when the guard finally released him and he was allowed to return to his bed.

* * *

Boy hurt everywhere. His hands had long gone numb from the ropes cutting into his wrists, and he wished that the rest of him was numb too. His arms and shoulders ached from the strain of his weight and the welts running from his shoulders to his thighs throbbed painfully. His lungs didn't want to expand fully, and his chest and belly felt as if they were on fire. His head hung forward, eyes closed, and on the edge of unconsciousness, he silently repeated his current mantra: *Not much longer. Not much longer. Not. Much. Longer.*

Unexpectedly, Boy dropped to his feet, but his shaky legs collapsed, and he hit the floor on his hands and knees. The fog that had invaded his brain dwindled. Finally able to take a full breath, he inhaled huge gulps of air. His hands and wrists hurt and were swollen, but he could feel blood beginning to warm them again. The painful prickle of reawakening nerves started at his fingertips; very soon it would encompass both hands, his wrists, and arms too. He flexed his fingers experimentally and winced at the sharp stab of pain. Being able to move them was a good sign, but it *hurt.* He'd been sure hanging by them for an hour would cause damage to his hands, and he was still afraid that might be the case...

Wait... Has it been an hour?

Unable to stand yet, he pushed back onto his heels and shrugged his sore shoulders. He winced as he did, but forced himself to search for Carrie's guard, who he found two feet away gathering up the end of the rope tied to Boy's wrists.

"It hasn't been an hour," Boy said.

The other man glanced at him and without a word, went back to collecting the rope. Reaching the end, he jerked Boy's arms upward and removed the line from his wrists. Boy grunted at the other man's rough treatment, but he didn't try to pull away. He wanted the rope off.

Finally free of his bonds, Boy started the excruciating task of working circulation back into his hands and arms. The guard stood and looked down at him for a long minute. Boy could feel his gaze and it made him uncomfortable. Unable to stand the silent scrutiny any longer, Boy returned the big man's stare.

"It can't have been more than thirty minutes since she left," Boy said.

"She didn't specify when the countdown began," the guard said in a deep, accented voice as he rammed the coiled rope into a canvas bag that he tied closed and slung over his shoulder. "I assumed she meant from when I returned to the barn, which has been an hour."

Boy stared at the giant of a man, astounded by the unforeseen show of mercy. The man had undoubtedly just saved him from grievous, lifelong nerve problems at great risk to himself.

Why? Why would the guard show him any kindness, let alone chance the consequences? Especially since Boy was certain the other man's addition was somewhat…flawed. The guard had to know the penalty would be severe if Carrie discovered what he'd done, but he did it anyway.

Boy didn't know the guard, had never met him before and, even though he'd been merciless when wielding the whip against Boy's flesh, he'd also shown an amazing amount of compassion and courage to release him early. Maybe the guard simply wanted his bed, but Boy wasn't one to look a gift horse in the mouth, and he wasn't about to start now.

The guard turned away and headed for the exit.

"Thank you," Boy called after him in a hoarse voice.

The guard turned and pinned Boy with an icy gaze. He appeared to want to say something but changed his mind. He lowered his chin once in what Boy took as an affirmative reply before he turned and left the barn.

Minutes later, Boy had succeeded in getting to his feet. It took him a couple more to pull his underwear and jeans up over his burning backside. He left the top button of his jeans undone and didn't even bother to buckle his belt. Stiffly, he shrugged into his shirt, sucking air in through his teeth as his back and shoulders screamed. He left the shirt unfastened, hanging loosely from his shoulders as he picked up his jacket with a groan. He grabbed his hat from where he'd left it and, throwing it on his head, he awkwardly stumbled to the barn door, which the other man had thankfully—thoughtfully, perhaps?—left open. His body complained loudly as he struggled to push the heavy wooden door closed. Then, turning for the bunkhouse, he headed back to his room and the softness of his bed.

Carrie would expect to see him up and working in the morning. She'd be watching, waiting for him to make a mistake or some excuse to get out of it, and he didn't know how he was going to hide the pain. Plus, the bunkhouse wasn't exactly private—they had their own tiny rooms, but they shared four bathrooms, plus two showers and bathing rooms. He wouldn't be able to bathe during the day when anyone could see the welts on his back. He'd have to wait for the bruising to dissipate. A heavy sigh escaped his lips. He would have to sneak around for two weeks at least before he could safely use the bathing rooms.

The pain he was in now would be worse in the morning. The last thing he wanted to do is get in the saddle, tie fence wire, or any other of the thousand and one things he may be called on to do tomorrow. The problem was, as long as Carrie was here watching him—and he knew without her saying it that she would be—he would have to. Because, just like everything else she'd ever forced him to do, he had no choice.

6

BOY PULLED THE BLACK COWBOY HAT from his head as he entered the main house and closed the door behind him. The windy morning stormed outside, whistling around the big house and thrashing the foliage, but it was nothing compared to the anxious tempest inside of him. Uncertain about being summoned, Boy hesitated in the foyer, staring down the hall to where Miss Aldridge's office lay.

A short time ago, Michelle had approached him in the barn as he prepared to saddle his horse for the day. Despite his aches and pains—and the guilt that twisted his heart for his unfaithfulness last night—he'd grinned wide at the sight of her and a little tremor of excitement shot through him. She was gorgeous, all long legs and soft skin. Just looking at her made him think of all the things he'd like to do to that sweet, shapely body, or what she would do to his...

He'd been about to say something smart and flirty, but something in her eyes and the stiff way she held her shoulders made him pause.

"Angel would like a word with you up at the house," Michelle had said, her words clipped.

No "hello," or "how are you doing," only a cold, brittle smile. Something was wrong. But when he'd asked, she'd only shrugged and headed back toward the house.

"She'll be in her office," Michelle said over her shoulder.

"I'll be right there." He tossed the saddle he'd been holding over the stall door, but when he'd turned to escort her to the house, Michelle was already gone and there'd been no sign of her when he exited the barn.

Boy's boots seemed to thunder on the hardwood as he strode slowly down the hall of Angel's house. Fear tightened his chest as he stopped outside her office door. Sweat started on his brow and under his arms, and made the welts on his skin burn. He ached everywhere. His arms and shoulders hurt and the flesh on his wrists was raw. His hands, though, worried him. They felt swollen and clumsy, but there was nothing he could do about it. Carrie was around somewhere, waiting and wanting to see him struggle through his pain.

Reaching for the office door, a shiver ran up his spine and he hesitated, his hand hovering inches from the knob. What if Carrie was with Angel behind this door? Or worse, waiting for him alone? Waiting to unleash more humiliation and pain?

No, he shook his head and chastised himself, *Angel's not Carrie. She's not going to hurt me. So stop stressing over nothing!* He sighed and ran his fingers through his wind-tossed hair, steeling himself as he turned the doorknob and went in.

"Please, close the door," Angel said from behind her desk on the other side of the small room.

Relieved not to see Carrie lurking inside, he did as she asked.

Nervousness made him clutch the brim of his hat in both hands as he turned back to the woman who owned him. It was then that he saw Michelle in the corner, half-hidden by the tall bookcase and file cabinets that lined the wall beside the door to his right. Nearly in full view now, he didn't like what he saw. She stood ramrod straight with her arms crossed over her chest. Her usually placid face was a thundercloud of fury and her eyes, beneath her dark frown, looked cold as death.

Boy swallowed as he stepped farther into the room, anxiety a knot around his ribs. He could feel Michelle's obvious fury fill the room with hot, thick tension as he moved slowly toward the chair.

Something was definitely wrong.

Regret for his acts with Carrie the night before burned inside him and for a moment, he feared Michelle's displeasure had to do with that, but it wasn't possible. No one had witnessed the shaming scene.

Dragging his gaze from the once kind and gentle woman he'd come to know and deeply care for, he focused on Angel. With her back straight and brows drawn down sharply, she looked almost as angry as Michelle.

There's no way they could know anything. He tried to swallow again, but his restricted throat wouldn't let him. He could hardly draw a breath as dread gripped him. "You wanted to see me?"

Gazing back at him, Angel sat quietly, hands clasped on her desk. When he'd first entered, Boy had read compassion on her face, but a stony expression had quickly replaced it. She rubbed at her side as if it troubled her and her complexion appeared paler than normal too, but there was definite mistrust in her eyes.

He glanced nervously around the room, heart pounding, mind racing, wondering why he was there.

"Hello Dean," Angel said gently, and he nodded in reply. "Please, sit down." She waved a hand toward the wooden chair in front of her desk.

Dean moved awkwardly as he shuffled across the room to stare down at the ladder-backed chair across from her desk. He paused beside the uncomfortable piece of furniture and sighed.

"I'd rather stand, ma'am," he drawled in his soft southern accent.

"I insist," she replied and nodded toward the chair.

He wanted to argue but thought better of it. He hesitated for a moment, but when he finally lowered his body onto the seat, he stiffened at the pressure and the burn of denim against his tender skin.

Angel frowned and he shied away as heat flooded his cheeks.

Just get through this, he told himself. *Don't let anything show.* He couldn't afford to make her suspicious, and neither could his brother. *You can do this.* He straightened his back and met her intense stare.

ANGEL'S EYES SKIMMED over him and doubt once again nibbled at her resolve. Something about this didn't feel right. Dean Williams was a knowledgeable, eager-to-help cowboy. He'd always been soft-spoken and a little reticent, but quietly friendly. He'd never given her the impression that he would betray them or that he was unhappy living on her ranch. So, all of this not only confused her, but frustrated her as well.

The last thing Angel had expected to see from her deck early this morning was Carrie's guard exiting one of the barns. It had crossed Angel's mind that she might still be stuck in the nightmare that had awakened her, but she knew that wasn't the case. Part of her wished it had been the case when she'd recognized Dean as he ambled out of the same barn a few minutes later. Her first thought was that someone had been hurt, but then why were they the only ones out there, and so early too? And why hadn't she been called?

Then shock chilled her to the bone when her thoughts turned to Carrie and suspicion set in. Those two hulking guards of hers only went where she did, which meant, at some point, Carrie had been in there with him *and* Dean.

That thought had made her heart clench.

Dean had struggled to close the barn door and something about that battle, his slow, awkward gait as he returned to the bunkhouse, and the disheveled state of his clothes—as if he'd dressed in a hellfire hurry—had seemed off.

And now, sitting stiffly across from her, something about him still seemed...wrong somehow, but she had other things to consider.

"Good morning," Angel said. "I'm sorry to disturb your work."

"Not a problem, ma'am," he replied. "Always happy to help."

"I'm glad to hear that," she said, and then hit him with her first question. "Do you like living here?"

His eyes widened and he seemed a bit shaken. "Y-Yeah. I like living here very much."

"Do you wish to continue to live here?"

He paled and swallowed. "Yes, I-I do."

"Then tell me what you were doing last night."

His eyes widened again and his face turned paler than before. "I...I was...s-sleeping," he stammered.

"You were asleep in your bed. All night. Alone. Is that what you're telling me?"

"Y-Yeah."

Disappointment knotted inside her. She had hoped her suspicions about him were wrong, but his lie only solidified them.

"Dean," Angel said softly, but there was steel in her tone, "I need you to tell me the truth."

His eyes looked almost wild as he glanced at Michelle.

Angel could see her head guard without turning her head. She'd never seen the woman as furious as Michelle was right now. She looked as if she wanted to tear Dean apart. Being a trained mixed martial arts fighter, Michelle could probably do it, but Angel knew that wasn't what her friend wanted.

Ever since the morning after her birthday—when she'd happened to be walking outside Michelle's bedroom as it opened suddenly and Dean appeared—Angel had known there was a bond between these two people. He hadn't immediately seen Angel that morning as she stood with her arms crossed, leaning back against the balustrade, grinning. He'd been too focused on the woman behind him. A moment later, Michelle stepped forward and they'd exchanged a gentle kiss— her arm wrapping around his side, her hand caressing his bare chest through his open shirt.

When the kiss had ended, Angel met her head guard's smiling visage with a raised eyebrow. Michelle's playful smile had disappeared. A flush had darkened her cheeks and her hand fell away from Dean like she'd been scalded.

"I'll see you later," she'd said and gave Dean a little nudge out the door. When he turned, his blue-green eyes widened when they met Angel's, but to his credit, he'd recovered quickly.

"Morning, ma'am," he had murmured politely as he calmly headed for the stairs, leaving the two women to talk.

Back then, Angel had been thrilled for her friend's newfound happiness. Now, the pain Angel read on Michelle's stony face broke her heart. Michelle wanted answers, yes, but she wanted them to exonerate Dean. Like Angel, Michelle wanted their suspicions about him to be wrong.

Turning away from Michelle's angry glare, Dean exhaled a long shuddering breath.

"I want the truth, Dean," Angel repeated.

"I don't kn-know what you mean." More red infused his cheekbones, and Angel feared that she and Michelle would be very disappointed by the end of this uncomfortable conversation.

"You're lying to me, Dean," Angel said in a low, dangerous voice. "And I despise liars."

7

DEAN SWALLOWED AND FOUGHT to keep his sudden flare of anxiety from showing as he stared at Angel. He was on thin ice here and he wasn't sure why. He had tried to stick with his story and played dumb, but she'd known it was a lie.

What does she know...and how? His mind buzzed and his gaze darted frantically between the two women like a trapped animal.

"Why were you in the barn with Carrie this morning?" Angel asked.

His whole body went still. His breath suspended and his fingers tightened on the brim of his felt hat. "I don't—"

"I saw you, Dean," Angel interrupted and he flinched. "I know you were there with her and her guards. What I *want* to know is why? No more lies!"

Oh, God, she knew! She saw me? How? His mind was a jumble of questions and then terror shot through him like a lightning bolt. *What if Carrie finds out?*

Carrie had always said she owned Dean, even after she sold him to Angel. He'd never wanted to accept it, but Carrie possessed the one thing that bound him tighter than any chain ever could. She'd proved it time and again—as recently as last night—by the things he'd allowed her to do to him.

Breathing too hard, he tried to slow it down but felt like he was choking. His heart hammered wildly in his chest and a cold sweat broke out all over his body. The welts that covered his back and lower body burned even more, but he couldn't find the will to care.

He glanced at Michelle—silently begging her to understand, to believe he hadn't lied when he'd said he cared about her--and she glared at him in return. He tried to speak, but his throat was suddenly so dry he couldn't force the words out.

"Don't look at me," she said with unconcealed hostility. "I hate liars as much as Angel does."

His shoulders drooped as his eyes flitted between the two women glaring at him angrily. There was no way out of this. He was trapped. He hung his head and squeezed his eyes closed. Everything he'd been through, everything he'd let Carrie do to him, was all for nothing! He had no other option now, and he hoped Angel would take pity on him.

"Please," he pleaded without lifting his head, "don't sell me."

"Then tell me the truth," Angel demanded. "Why did you meet with Carrie?"

He met her gaze with beseeching eyes. The idea of laying his burden at her feet was tempting, but Carrie's threats burned temptation away.

"I…can't," he said, dropping his chin to stare at the floor.

"Why? What are you hiding?"

He sat stiffly, refusing to reply, and wondered, *How the hell am I going to get out of this?*

ANGEL'S FINGERS TINGLED with numbness as she continued to clench them tightly on her desktop. This wasn't working. He was terrified of something, and terrifying him more wasn't going to get him to speak.

"Dean," she said gently, "I don't want to sell you. I want to *help* you, but I can't do that if I don't know what's happening. Talk to me, please!"

He still said nothing, still wouldn't meet her eyes. She studied him as he slowly crushed the brim of his hat in his hands; and she felt like a monster for causing him such distress. Then an idea popped into her head.

"What's she holding over you?" she asked. When his eyes snapped to her face she had her answer and she pressed on. "For a man like you, it must be something very important. A friend you left behind maybe?" She watched him, but there was no reaction. "No, something even more important. Family?"

She saw how he swallowed convulsively and noted the slight twitch of his eyes.

"Yeah," she murmured, eyeing him critically. His gaze furtively met hers and she knew. "It's family. A...brother." A guess, but the right one. Carrie would have no interest in a woman, so it had to be a brother.

His shoulders sagged and his gaze slowly met hers.

"Talk to me," she said again, softer, almost pleading. Assorted emotions filled his expression from fear to determination. She thought he would speak, but then a crushed look crossed his face and he dropped his head again.

"I can't..."

The weight of duty and regret grew heavier in her chest. "Then you leave me no alternative," she said with a calm she didn't feel. "I'll have to sell you to Carrie or one of the others who'll have you."

The sheer terror she saw on his face when he looked up wrenched at her heart and she almost reassured him.

"Please," he murmured, "don't sell me. Not to her, not to anyone else. I don't want to leave."

"I'm sorry, Dean," she said sadly, "but I can't trust you. Unless you can give me a good reason for what you did, I have no choice. I have to protect the rest of the people here."

His eyes darted to Michelle, and Angel could clearly read his feelings for the head guard in his expression. Then hurt suffused his face and Dean dropped his pleading eyes. A tremor rocked him and his big hands twisted the brim of his hat in his lap.

Angel glanced at her head guard. Michelle hadn't moved and her expression hadn't softened. She doubted if the other woman had gotten past his betrayal yet. Angel had considered that there might be more to Dean's story, and now she suspected a great deal more. She just didn't know if she could get him to tell her, or if she really wanted to know.

What if this was Bret? The thought struck her from out of nowhere. Would she be as angry with him as Michelle seemed to be with Dean? Would she be willing to let him go? The answers came immediately: Yes, and no. So why should it be any different for this man? She wouldn't give up Bret, or Jake, or any of the others without a fight, and she wouldn't give Dean up without one either. If not for the talent and skills her home would be losing, then for the feelings she knew Michelle still had for him.

"What's wrong with you?" Angel asked and was surprised to see him jump at the quiet sound of her voice, or maybe it was the question itself.

"Nothing," he said, straightening, but a soft groan gave him away.

"I told you, Dean, no more lies."

His gaze shifted between them again, then dropped back to his lap.

Angel's next question was more specific. "What's wrong with your back?"

"Please, don't do this," he whispered. "Please…"

Angel sat back and her breath paused. He was begging her. Actually begging! She didn't know him very well, but she knew he still had his pride. If he was beseeching her now, he was terrified.

"Please," he said again, barely a whisper this time, "don't do this." His teal eyes locked with hers and she was surprised again to see them shining with unshed tears. His gaze shifted to Michelle and instantly flinched away. Was he afraid of Michelle's response? Or was there something he didn't want her to know? Maybe he'd be more forthcoming if Angel questioned him alone.

"Michelle." Her friend didn't move, almost as if she hadn't heard. "Michelle," Angel called, louder this time, and the other woman turned her unnaturally darkened blue-gray eyes to Angel. "Would you wait in the hallway please?"

Michelle frowned and Angel knew what she was thinking. Angel's safety was part of Michelle's job and leaving her employer alone with a man who they now suspected may be another woman's spy was definitely not safe.

"What if he tries something?" Michelle asked, sounding cold and detached. "What if he gets violent?"

Angel looked at Dean. "Are you going to do anything violent?"

He lifted his eyes, but just barely, and murmured, "No."

"Please, Michelle," she said, turning back to her friend, "wait in the hall. I'll call you when we're done."

Michelle shifted her gaze back to Dean. "You," she said coldly, "look at me." He slowly turned his head and met her gaze. "If you harm her, you will regret it. I promise you."

He shook his head and the devastation on his face twisted Angel's heart.

"I won't hurt her," he said, his eyes still imploring the head guard.

"You'd better not," she replied, ignoring his pleading look. Then, with long, sure strides, Michelle left the room. The door closed a little louder than it should have and Dean cringed.

Despite the pity she felt, Angel didn't give him time to collect himself.

"Take off your shirt, Dean," she said.

He lifted his head so fast it was startling. "No. Please. Don't."

"Don't what?" she asked. "There's obviously something wrong, and I want to know what it is."

He hung his head and shook it again. "You're not going to give up, are you?"

"No, I'm not."

With a resigned sigh, he reluctantly set his now crumpled-brim hat on the floor. Straightening, his uneven breaths rasped in shuddering gasps between his teeth as his unsteady fingers unbuttoned his shirt. Closer scrutiny on Angel's part revealed that his hands also looked too big. His lean-fingers were abnormally swollen, like an old man's hands with early-stage rheumatism, and she caught the briefest glimpse of crimson around his wrists. Seeing that, she was even more determined and suspected what she'd see when he removed his shirt. Hopefully, she was wrong, but then that meant she still had to deal with his possible betrayal.

Bret popped into her mind again. She remembered how his hands had looked when the Section Guards had dragged him back to the house after his attempted escape. They'd been swollen too, but nothing like this.

Dean finished with the buttons and, flinching, carefully pulled the shirttails out of his blue jeans. Finished, or having gone as far as he was willing, Dean sat stiffly in the chair with his shirt hanging open, shivering.

Angel doubted it was from cold.

"Stand up," she said, "and turn around."

He did as she said.

"Show me."

"Please," he whispered once more, "don't do this."

"I'm not going to hurt you, Dean. Now, please, show me," she said softly but firmly.

His shoulders slumped in defeat and she watched in fearful anticipation as he awkwardly pulled the shirt from his broad shoulders. He groaned and then the garment slipped down his arms.

Angel gasped at the raw, swollen red welts that covered him from shoulders to waist. Her body shook as a wave of rage sent adrenaline coursing through her. She knew what Carrie was like, but Angel had never expected the woman to go this far with one of her people and on her ranch too.

"*She* did this to you?" She didn't have to be more specific.

He nodded.

Angel got up with a wince for the growing pain in her side and went around her desk to get a better look at his injuries. Her stomach churned at the sight. *My God, he must be in so much pain!*

She raised a hand to lightly touch one of the wounds and recoiled when he flinched. Her eyes skimmed lower and then worked his shirt down a little further, frowning at the angry red marks that disappeared into the waistband of his jeans.

"How far down does this go?" she asked, glancing up at him, but he kept his eyes closed and she could barely see his profile. His head hung lower, his jaw clenched, and he hunched his shoulders as if deeply shamed, but he didn't reply.

"Dean, how far down does this go?"

"My thighs," he whispered. He didn't move, just stood stiffly, completely defeated.

Angel carefully worked the shirt back up his arms and over his shoulders, then asked him to turn around. He wouldn't meet her gaze, but her heart clenched at the wetness on his cheek. She brushed the tear away and he gasped as his gaze collided with hers. Embarrassed, he quickly ran his hand over his face, and Angel was struck again by the odd look of his hands. She reached out and took one of his into her own, though he tried to pull away.

"Please," she said softly and he ceased fighting her.

His hand *felt* swollen and shook slightly in her grasp. His long fingers looked like fat sausages and the rest was puffy too. She checked his other hand and found it a match for the first. She tugged at his shirt cuff and he started to pull away again.

"Dean, please, hold still," she said and he ceased. Unfastening the buttons on each sleeve, she pushed them up to find exactly what she'd expected—red, inflamed flesh around both wrists. "She tied you up and hung you by your wrists?" She looked at him and he nodded, still avoiding her gaze. She fastened the buttons carefully and turned his hand palm up.

Again, she thought of Bret, thankful that the Section Guard leader had enough concern for Angel's reaction to ensure she didn't damage his hands. Apparently, Carrie had less fear of risking Angel's wrath.

"Do they hurt?" she asked.

"A little," he replied, but Angel thought that was an understatement.

"Can you move them?"

"Yeah, but it hurts more when I do."

Angel sighed and let go of his hand. She looked up at him and waited for him to meet her gaze. "Did she do anything else to you?"

The crumpled look he gave her was a yes, and Angel didn't push him to say it.

"She forced you to have sex with her." It wasn't a question.

He nodded and gasped from the surge of emotion he'd been holding in. She rested a comforting hand on his arm until he was breathing normally again.

"Please, don't tell Michelle," he said, finally meeting her gaze on his own. "She'll hate me more."

"She doesn't hate you, Dean. She's angry because she thinks you lied to her."

"I didn't…" he started, but the look she gave him made him pause. "I didn't lie about how I feel. I just couldn't talk about the rest."

"How long has Carrie been torturing you like this?"

"Seems like forever," he mumbled as he clumsily buttoned his shirt.

"Were you at her home before they sold you to me?"

He nodded and began tucking in his shirt without unfastening his jeans. The pressure on his back made him wince and he gave up.

"You don't have to do that right now," Angel told him, waving a hand at his untucked shirt and then changed the topic. "I want you to see a doctor, and I know where I'm going to send you until she's gone."

"I can't," he said, sounding panicked again. "She expects to see me working. It's part of my…punishment, to work while I hurt. If she finds out you know…that I told you any of this, she'll hurt my brother. I can't risk that. I can't!"

"Is he younger or older?" she asked, though she thought she already knew.

"Younger," he said and she nodded.

"You must be close." She didn't mean for it to be a question.

"We used to be," he said sadly, and once that was out, the rest of his story spilled out too. "He was barely twelve years old when everything started to fall apart. Our mother was killed in the chaos and our father was taken a few years later. We never knew what happened to him, but I think he's dead. He was tough, he wouldn't have broken easy, ya know?"

She nodded and allowed him to share as much as he wanted to.

"My brother doesn't think much of me anymore. He thinks I'm weak. He doesn't understand why I let her...do things to me without fighting back. At least, he didn't the last time I saw him." Dean cleared his throat and went on, "I made an arrangement with Carrie when she figured out my secret...like you did." He gave her a bleak smile. "I'd do anything she wanted, everything she asked without exception or question...if she guaranteed my brother's safety. Her part of the agreement was that he was never to learn of our pact. She'd insisted on that and I didn't have another choice, so I agreed. I think she knew it would tear us apart, and she enjoyed forcing a wedge between us. She'd make me do the most humiliating things where he would see or hear about it, and soon he thought I was worse than the men who willingly worked as her guards."

Staring at the floor, he suddenly glanced at her before his eyes returned to the floor again. He took a deep breath before he started to speak once more. "It actually started before we were sold up here," Dean told her at length as he slowly, carefully sat down again.

Angel leaned back as he spoke, pressing her arm into her side as her hands curled around the top edge of her desk.

"He's reckless, my brother, always has been. Maybe because I was always so careful, but I had to be." She heard the desperation in his voice. "When we were running and hiding from the raiding parties, I had to be careful to keep us both safe.

"One day he wanted to join a rebel raid of a ranch back in Texas. He was seventeen by then, and we were both hungry all the time. I was barely twenty-three, but I'd been taking care of him since he was a kid. I tried to keep him out of that rebel raid, but he wouldn't listen, not that I was surprised. They'd filled his head with a bunch of idiocy and I ended up going with him, just to keep him safe. We got caught. That was almost...eight years ago."

Angel felt a twinge of guilt hearing his story. It was far too similar to another one she knew all too well.

Dean's will have a better ending if I can do anything about it.

Pushing aside her memories and the pain that came with them, she focused on Dean and asked, "How did you end up here?"

"Some of us tried to overthrow our owner in Texas," he told her and then went silent. She met his eyes and realized he was still protecting his brother.

"You mean, your brother was involved with it and you got dragged along with him," she said, starting to see that she and Michelle had both been right about him.

He nodded and sighed. "Yeah, all of us on the ranch were sold after that, even the ones who hadn't had anything to do with what we did. Those of us who were involved were chained up in groups and sold. They weren't exactly gentle, and they made sure to explain what we'd done before the bidding started. I think that was as much to warn the buyers, as to give them another excuse to abuse us."

"You're probably right," she agreed and he gave her an odd look but didn't respond, merely blinked then started speaking again.

"Most of the others we'd lived with went east or south, and I was sure I'd never see my brother again, but somehow, Carrie bought us both. I'd been thankful at first, at least until I realized the kind of woman she was. I managed to keep him away from the worst of what she did…"

Angel smiled ruefully. "You took the blame for anything he did, didn't you?"

Dean's lips quirked and he nodded. "Only because I couldn't stand to see him suffer. I kept remembering the little kid who used to follow me around, mimicking everything I did. It was annoying when we were young, but by the time we ended up with Carrie, I just kept wishing I could get him back. I tried, repeatedly, but the distance between us only got worse. He resented me taking care of him, but I'd been doing it for so long I couldn't do anything else. When Carrie figured it out, that's when it all started."

A slight tremor rolled through him and he took a deep breath, letting it out slowly before continuing, "Carrie called it training, but that's not what it was."

"I know about that," Angel said. "I've seen some of it and heard about more. All of it is sick."

"Yeah, well, that's how she tried to train me, at least until she figured out how to *really* control me. Then she just enjoyed hurting me. She still does…I was one of her favorite targets because she knew the things she did weren't just painful but humiliating for me, and I had to take it or watch her do worse to my brother."

"That sounds like her," Angel said, disgusted.

"Why do you let her stay here if you dislike her so much?" He seemed to suddenly remember who he was talking to and tried to backtrack. "I mean—"

"It's all right, Dean. That's a fair question, though my answer will be unsatisfactory," she said, stretching her aching side gently. Angel had been too distracted all morning to pay much attention to the ache in her belly. Now, the pain had returned with interest.

Dean tilted his head and frowned as she straightened again.

She smiled at his curious look and the concern in his eyes. "I don't let Carrie stay here by choice," she said. "It's a long explanation, but, basically, we're required to submit to yearly inspections and Carrie runs the department that manages the inspectors. She uses it as a pretense to force me to accept her company, just so she can harass my people and report what she finds to Darla Cain.

"But," she said and winced as she rubbed her side again, "it's going to be a much shorter visit than normal this time."

His expression went from calm to alarmed in an instant. "You can't send her away because of me. She can't know I told you *anything*."

"It's not just because of you," she reassured him. "If that was the case, I'd be dragging her off my property right now." She smiled to let him know she wasn't going to do that, though she wanted to.

He returned her grin, but she still read questions in his eyes.

"I told her the day she arrived that she could only stay a couple of days. We're too busy to be dealing with her crap."

He sighed in relief. "That's good to know, but what do we do now? I mean, what do I do? I didn't want to tell her anything, didn't want to do anything with her—and I still don't—but as long as she has my brother, I don't have a choice."

"I was thinking about that," Angel said as she pushed off the desk and walked around it to sit in her chair again. "I'm going to do my best to help your brother. I don't know how yet, but I'm going to get him away from Carrie, even if I have to arrange for him to escape."

"Why would you do that?" he asked, suddenly suspicious. Clearly, he didn't want to jump out of one frying pan into a hotter fire. "You'll be worse off than me if they find out. They'll consider you a traitor."

Like most slaves, Dean knew very little about the governing laws, but he was correct but about that. Helping slaves escape or giving aid to an enemy—whatever or whoever the council deemed an enemy— was considered a traitorous offense and the consequences were staggering. Loss of her place on the council was certain and flogging was not unheard of, but she could also lose her home and become a slave herself. Stealing a slave was also frowned upon but often overlooked if cash was offered and accepted. She didn't think it would come to her having to help him escape, but Dean had suffered enough for the brother he loved. Angel meant to make sure Carrie would never torment him again.

"Dean," she selected each word carefully, "when you came to live here you became one of us. This place and the people in it are the only family I have, and I care about all of them. You are part of that family now and by relation, your brother is part of it too. I don't let *anyone* mess with my family," she said in a low, menacing tone. "I will do what I can, but until then, I'm going to make sure you're safe."

8

AT A LOSS FOR WORDS, Dean stared at the small woman in front of him and realized Carrie had badly misjudged Angel's character. She wasn't stupid or weak, and she'd be a fierce enemy if Carrie and her friends ever riled her enough. He could see that Angel wanted to go after Carrie right now, but she held back. For him. He swallowed the lump in his throat and tried to rein-in the rush of emotion surging through him.

"Thank you," he said in a hoarse whisper, though he knew it wasn't enough.

"No need to thank me," she said with a small wave of her hand. "It's nothing more than I'd do for any of the others. I do, however, have one demand."

Narrowing his eyes warily, he asked, "What's that?"

"You need to tell Michelle your story," Angel said. "All of it."

Relief rushed through him and the stiffness in his shoulders dissipated. How could he have thought she'd demand something else? Then the thought of telling Michelle what Carrie had forced on him made Dean tense again.

"She won't understand," he said. "She already hates me enough to never speak to me again... I-I can't give her more reasons to hate me."

"I told you before, she doesn't hate you. She's just hurt. She cares about you, Dean. She'll be upset when you tell her, but if I wanted to go after Carrie and repay her for what she did to you—and I do—Michelle will want to do more. Show her what Carrie did to you, tell her everything, she'll understand. I know she will."

"I wish I could believe that," he said, feeling wretched to his bones. "The way I feel right now, it would be a huge relief just to have her *believe me.*"

"I'll talk to her," Angel said, but Dean didn't look too convinced. "Don't worry about it too much. I know her, it'll be all right. Right now, I want you to take care of yourself until I can get you to a doctor."

"My back'll be fine," he said. "I've had *a lot* worse. It's my hands I'm worried about. She's tied me before and they've hurt too, but this is the first time she hung me up by my wrists for any length of time. It'd be worse if her guard hadn't let me down early."

Angel's head snapped up and her intent gaze pinned him in place. "Let you down early?"

He explained what Carrie's guard had done.

"Hmm. He whips you for her and then disobeys her? That's odd," Angel mused. "Which one was it?"

The two men were similar in height and stature, but their coloring was completely opposite. Where one was dark-haired, dark-eyed, and dark-skinned, the other was pale, blue-eyed, and very blond.

"The Swede," Dean told her, using the name Carrie had given the big man.

"Hmm, that might be useful someday."

"I don't understand why he did it," Dean said. "None of her male guards have ever acted that way—they're too afraid of her or too much like her. I doubt his act of kindness will be repeated."

"It's still an interesting bit of information. Either way, I'm grateful for his compassion."

"Why?"

"Because we need you and as bad as your hands look, if he'd let you hang there longer, you probably wouldn't be able to use them.

Nerve damage is not only painful, it's debilitating."

A flush of gratitude warmed his cheeks. He was needed and it sounded like she would let him stay too. "That had crossed my mind, but I still need to get back to work. Carrie will be looking for me."

"You're not going back to work," Angel told him and lifted her hand, palm outward, to stop him from arguing. "Don't worry about Carrie. She won't suspect a thing. I have something in mind."

"What?"

"I've got some things that need to be delivered to a friend. While you're there, I want you to visit the doctor and let him take care of you. He may even have something to ease the pain and swelling. You'll be back tonight and Carrie will never know any different."

Dean had known Angel was kind, had seen it nearly every day since he'd arrived, but he'd never been on the receiving end of it himself. It was a new feeling. Still, he was afraid and less than cooperative about accepting her plan, but after she knocked down his arguments one by one, he finally agreed. Except for one small thing.

"What's that?" she asked.

He hung his head sheepishly, embarrassed by what he must tell her. "I don't think I can ride that far. Not like this. Just sitting in this chair is difficult."

Angel laughed and his lowered head snapped up as heat flamed up his neck.

"I'm sorry, Dean, I'm not laughing at you. It's just that I didn't intend for you to ride a horse there and you won't be going alone."

"Oh," he said. "Okay then, but what about when I get back?"

"What about it?"

"What if Carrie wants to know more, what do I tell her? What if she wants...more?"

"I'll arrange something so you're not alone as long as she's here. As for the rest," Angel said, "tell her the truth. You're a terrible liar."

DEAN CHUCKLED AND ANGEL GRINNED at the sound. His smile made him seem less haunted and very handsome. She could see why

Michelle was attracted to him.

"Besides, if you don't, I'm fairly certain she'll know. I don't think you're the only spy she has here."

"I don't either," he said. "She knows too much."

"Yep, that's what I've been thinking too."

"So you're not afraid of what I'll tell her?"

"There's nothing to hide," she replied. "Plus, there'll be times I may give you things to tell her."

"But if she knows it's not true…"

"Don't worry," she said, shaking her head, "it'll be true enough. She won't have reason to hurt your brother." She frowned suddenly.

"What?" he asked, worry etching his brow.

"There's something else I need to know."

"Okay…" he dragged out the word, visibly nervous again.

"Did you have anything to do with the cattle going missing?" Angel eyed him, assessing every move he made, certain she would know if he lied.

His whole body eased. "No, she just asked for information about what's going on at the ranch or who you're involved with. That sort of thing, not anything like rustling or sabotage."

"Was there anything she asked or you told that might explain why the cattle have gone missing?"

"I don't think so," he said, tilting his head thoughtfully. "No, Carrie was barely interested in their disappearance. I think she would've asked for more details if she'd had anything to do with it."

The tension drained out of Angel and she gave him a slow smile. "That's good. It doesn't answer the question about what happened to them, but I'm glad you had nothing to do with it."

"You believe me?" he asked incredulously. "Just like that? After what I've done?"

"Shouldn't I?" She smiled at the stunned look he gave her. "I believe you because you've told me the truth about everything else. I might have had to drag it out of you, but you had a good reason to be afraid."

Dean sat dumbfounded for a moment, the wind outside whistling under the eaves.

"Thank you," he muttered.

"You're welcome," she said and stood. She waved a hand to indicate his appearance. "Now, finish getting dressed so I can talk to Michelle."

She picked up her books and turned her back. Going to the bookshelf in the corner behind her desk, she took her time putting her things away.

When she faced him again, his shirt was tucked in and his jeans fastened, and she went to the door to open it for him.

In the hallway, Dean held his crumpled hat in both hands and avoided Michelle's angry eyes. Angel shook her head as she stepped into the doorway.

"Dean, why don't you head down to the kitchen and talk to Esther about this afternoon's deliveries."

He nodded, seeming grateful for something to do, and glanced at Michelle's narrowed gaze before he hurried down the hall.

"Michelle?" Angel said and a wave of uncertainty washed over her when she saw the fury still lingering in her friend's blue-gray eyes. She pushed ahead anyway. "Would you come back inside, please?

When they were both seated—Angel in her chair and Michelle sitting with her arms crossed over her chest in the chair Dean had vacated—Angel explained some of Dean's situation and that she would not be sending him away, though she kept her reasons vague. When she finished, Michelle looked doubtful and Angel saw the questions in her head guard's eyes, but she didn't give Michelle a chance to comment. "I want you to take the delivery to Monica's today. Dean will be accompanying you."

"Why?" Michelle asked as her back stiffened a fraction more. "Sam usually does that and I don't want to be stuck with that liar for the day."

"I am making his health and well-being your responsibility, Michelle."

"What!" She jumped to her feet, her eyes wide and heated. "Why me?"

"Because he needs you and *you want* to help him. Don't try to deny it," she said, seeing Michelle's eyebrows squeeze together even more. "And, if that isn't good enough, then because I'm worried about him, and you're the only one I trust to take care of him the way I would. I'm not feeling well and I don't want to leave while Carrie's still here."

"Then tell her to go." Michelle's tone said that option should've been obvious.

Angel smiled tiredly. "I can't do that right now."

Michelle shrugged as she returned to her seat. "You've done it before."

"I have other reasons now, Michelle."

"Like what?"

"Talk to Dean," Angel replied and saw Michelle's shoulders droop. "Give him a chance. If he can convince me to still trust him, don't you think you should find out why?"

"You actually believe she forced information from him?"

"Yes, I do and I think you will too."

"I'm glad you're so sure." Michelle's comment dripped with sarcasm as she crossed her arms again.

"There's more."

Michelle's expression turned questioning, but she didn't speak.

"I want him to stay with you upstairs at night until Carrie's gone."

Michelle's back straightened and her fisted hands slammed onto her thighs. The look in her eyes was dark with instant fury. "You're going too far with that, Angel. I will not invite a liar back into my bed!"

"I didn't say he had to sleep *with* you." Angel released an exasperated sigh. "We have some cots and pads in storage. I'll have one of those put in your room and he can use that, but I don't want him alone at night. If you want, you can kick him back to his room once Carrie is gone."

"You're that worried about him?" Angel heard the change in Michelle's tone.

"Yes. I am."

Michelle glanced at the ground, but she came to her decision quickly. "All right, Angel," she said, dropping her arms and adjusting her seat, "I'll do it. But you'd better be right about this."

"Do you think I'd put you in this situation if I didn't think it would work out right?"

"I don't know about you sometimes," Michelle said resignedly. "I don't always understand *why* you do things."

"Neither do I." Angel smiled and, though she was joking, it was the truth.

Michelle grinned in return and some of the tension left her face. Angel knew then that she'd at least try to give Dean the benefit of the doubt. Angel didn't know if things would work out between them, if their personal relationship would grow into something special, but at least it had a chance.

"Now," Angel said as she stood, wincing at the nagging pain in her side, "I'm going to lie down."

"Are you all right?" Michelle asked with concern. "You're looking awfully pale."

"Just not feeling very good," Angel said as she moved around the desk. "My stomach's been bugging me."

"You're not..." Michelle stopped, uncharacteristically unsure of herself.

Angel tilted her head as she gazed at the other woman. Michelle wanted to know if her depression had gotten the better of her again.

"I'm fine, Michelle," she said as she went to the door. "Just coming down with something is all."

"Is the rest over with?"

"I don't know if it'll ever be over," Angel said more honestly than she should have, but she was too distracted by her side to come up with a believable lie. "Right now, I just want to lie down." She smiled to soften her words, hoping Michelle would let it go. She didn't want to talk about her moods.

Thankfully, Michelle let it go and went to join Dean in the kitchen.

Angel watched her go and said a little prayer that she'd done the right thing. If she had to be alone to fight her battles, at least Michelle had a chance to have what Angel couldn't.

She smiled and headed for the stairs feeling a little sorry for herself, but excited for the possibilities she saw between two people who needed each other more than they realized.

9

BRET EXCHANGED A SURPRISED GLANCE with Jake when Angel entered the dining hall during their afternoon meal. She joined Sam—who'd been tasked with escorting Carrie around the homestead today—and Carrie at a nearby table. Something seemed wrong, not only with that situation, but with Angel as well. She ate nothing and looked paler than normal.

"Where's Michelle?" Bret whispered to his friend across the table. She'd been running interference for the men with Carrie since the unpleasant woman arrived, but now the head guard was nowhere to be seen. He glanced down the table. "Come to think of it, where's Dean?"

Jake shrugged. "Don't know. I haven't seen either of them since early this morning."

"So, is Sam running defense today?"

"Appears so," Jake replied quietly.

"Where's Michelle?" Carrie's too loud voice echoed in the large room.

Bret glanced at Jake, who tilted his head and lifted his brows as if to say, 'I guess we're going to find out.'

"She took one of the cowhands to help deliver some trade goods to a friend," Angel explained. "She'll be back later tonight."

"That must be where Dean went to," Jake murmured and Bret nodded, still eavesdropping on the conversation at the next table.

"You couldn't send someone else?" Carrie asked, her tone indicating her annoyance at being pawned off on yet another subordinate.

"No," Angel said flatly. "I told you we're busy right now, which reminds me... I'd like you to wrap up your inspection. I need my people working on their duties, not answering questions you already know the answers to. You should have plenty of time to finish by tomorrow morning." She stood and Bret noticed she pressed a hand to her right side and winced.

What's that about?

"I'm sorry, but I don't have time to discuss it," Angel said as she turned to leave only minutes after arriving. "Sam will help you with anything you may need."

"But Angel..." Carrie started, but whatever she was going to say dwindled when it became apparent that Angel wasn't going to return.

Carrie pressed her lips together in irritation as she turned back to her lunch, but caught Bret watching. Eyeing him appreciatively, she smiled slowly. He looked away before she made a move toward him and a prickle of trepidation danced over his skin. Danger lived in her smile and a dark promise he didn't want to contemplate.

* * *

Bret brought Angel dinner later that night, but she refused to eat, saying her stomach hurt.

"I think I'll puke if I eat anything," she said, curled up on her side in bed. "Besides, I'm not hungry."

After taking in her pale complexion, Bret pressed his palm against her forehead to check for fever. She shivered slightly at his touch but didn't complain.

"You're a little warm," he said, his brows drawn down in concern. "You may have a fever."

"I just want to sleep," she said as he pulled his hand away. "Tell Jake I'm not trying to be difficult. I just really don't feel well."

Bret nodded but gritted his teeth in annoyance.

"I'll pass it on," he said gruffly. "Anything else you want me to tell him?" He couldn't help the cynical tone, but she didn't seem to notice.

"Just to keep everyone away for a few days," she said, clearly missing his sarcasm. "Oh, and tell Michelle I'd appreciate it if she and Sam deal with Carrie in the morning. The last thing I need is a major issue with her while I'm feeling like this…" She had already started to drift off before she got to the end of her statement and, though she didn't say it, Bret felt her dismissal.

"No problem," he said and then left the room, still irritated that she seemed to have forgotten that, lately, Bret was the one who'd been there every day. Not Jake.

WHILE BRET FINISHED his meal with Angel upstairs, Dean got up from his table and made his way across the dining hall. He longed for his bed in the bunkhouse and looked forward to the moment he could crawl into the clean sheets. It wasn't the softest bed he'd ever had, but the way he felt tonight, it would be a welcome relief. He ached everywhere and sleep was topmost on his agenda. After all, the doctor he'd talked to after reaching Monica Avery's home earlier that day had said Dean would need more rest than normal for the trauma to his body to heal.

Luckily for him, Angel was aware of his ailments. Taking it easy and getting the rest he needed would've been difficult otherwise.

The ride to Monica's had been long, quiet, and tense. Michelle barely spoke to him since their meeting in Angel's office after breakfast. Several times he'd caught her looking at him, a wary expression on her face as they loaded the truck, but she never said anything and refused to meet his gaze.

During the drive, he'd tried to start a conversation, but the icy look she threw his way said he'd be better off if he kept quiet.

Once they had arrived at their destination, they were greeted by a tall, blonde woman who he soon learned to be the owner herself.

Michelle slid out of the truck without a glance or word and

approached Monica, who smiled dazzlingly, but Dean hardly noticed. Michelle handed her two letters while they spoke quietly. Dean exited the truck to start unloading and a minute later, Michelle joined him.

While they carried those boxes from the truck into the house, Monica had opened the topmost letter. Michelle was still inside with her first load and Dean had just grabbed another box from the truck bed when Monica suddenly looked up and eyed him with a frown.

"Stop," she said, extending a hand toward him and he froze. Sweat broke out along his brow as she swiftly approached with a worried look of her own, which confused him. "Put that down." She glanced at the paper in her hand and then back to him.

He frowned, but her eyes had already slipped from his face and down his body to stop on his swollen hands. A soft, pitiful sound escaped her and she reached for him. He didn't try to stop her as she held his palm upright between both of hers, gazing at it. Shaking her head, her concerned hazel gaze met his.

"I'm so sorry," she whispered, though no one was close enough to hear and Dean's tense shoulders relaxed.

"Thanks," he murmured awkwardly, not sure what he was supposed to do and wondering what Michelle would think if she saw Monica holding his hand.

"You shouldn't be doing this," Monica scolded. "I'll have one of my people help Michelle."

"I can do it," he'd replied.

She shook her head. "Not with those hands. Shawn?" she called. A brown-haired man with a mischievous grin came out of the barn with an olive-skinned, older woman right behind him.

"Would you and Rosa come help Michelle with the unloading," Monica asked and then took Dean's arm, leading toward the front of her home.

"What about Michelle?" he asked, glancing over his shoulder, hoping to catch a glimpse of the other woman. He didn't want Michelle angrier with him than she already was.

Monica tilted her head and looked at him sharply. He shifted his feet self-consciously and dropped his eyes—evidence of Carrie's training winning again.

"Rosa," Monica said, "would you also please let Michelle know that I took Dean to see the doctor?"

"Of course," Rosa replied.

Monica turned to Dean with a gentle smile curving her lips. "There. Is that better?"

Feeling a bit silly, he nodded and allowed her to lead him away.

Monica had escorted Dean to a small room in the back corner of her house that had been temporarily converted into a treatment room for the doctor.

"The doctor will be in shortly," she told Dean with another calming smile. "Don't look so worried, Dean. He'll take good care of you."

Despite her words, he'd waited anxiously for the doctor to arrive. He'd pictured a tall, authoritative man, like the ones he used to see in old television doctor shows. Someone competent but not very sociable. Dr. Leroy Hillman turned out to be the exact opposite. He was a short and stocky older man with a ring of salt and pepper hair. Behind his black-rimmed glasses were intelligent and kind soft brown eyes, and he spoke with gentle homey politeness that went a long way in putting most of his patients at ease.

Dean had been terrified that the nerves in his hands were so damaged that they'd never be the same. But the doctor had relieved him of that worry quickly. "The injury to the nerves in your hands is minor," Dr. Hillman said after a physical examination and several questions about how Dean had been hurt. "But you do have severe muscle strain and raw abrasions on your wrists from the ropes. That's why your hands and wrists are so swollen and bruised and hurt like the devil too, I'm sure."

Dean nodded, too relieved to speak.

"All you'll need to heal are some pain meds, icing, and rest," Dr. Hillman said. "As well as avoiding ropes around your wrists for a while."

Dean smiled weakly at the doctor's lame attempt at humor. How was he supposed to do that? There were no restraints of any kind on Angel's ranch and it didn't appear that Carrie had brought any, but it didn't matter. If she got him alone again, she would use whatever was available to tie him and cause more damage. He just had to hope that wouldn't happen. He didn't reveal any of that to the doctor, however; the fewer people who knew his situation, the safer his brother would be.

Dr. Hillman gave him a sheet of paper with directions on it.

"Follow these exercises for rehabilitation," he said. "No strenuous work for at least three to four weeks, and check back with me before going back to work.

"Now," the doctor continued, "take off your shirt and let's have a look at your other injuries.

Dean's startled eyes locked on the doctor's and humiliation heated his face.

Dr. Hillman's expression softened. "Things aren't like they used to be, son. I've heard and seen a lot—some bad, some brutal—so whatever it is, be assured, it won't be new."

He'd hesitated but knew the doctor was right. Lowering his eyes, he stripped off his shirt and lay belly-down across the exam table.

As Dean had expected, the welts on his back and buttocks would heal in time, though it would take about two weeks for the pain and bruising to dissipate. The doctor added some salve for the welts to the pain meds he'd mentioned earlier.

As he headed for the kitchen hallway on his way to the front door, he thought back on his experience with the doctor. The whole appointment had seemed…normal. Aside from the reason for his visit, talking with Dr. Hillman had made it seem as if maybe the world could go back to the way it once was, or at least something close to that.

Shaking his head, he ran his hand through his hair. Hoping for a real-life, for a chance at freedom and love again, was a pipedream. He should have remembered that before letting himself get close to Michelle.

Michelle… She was another problem he didn't know how to fix.

He thought back to the silent ride back home from Monica's. He'd considered speaking to Michelle, asking her to forgive him, but one glance at her frowning profile changed his mind. Michelle had seemed deep in thought as she drove. He hadn't recognized the roads she took—sometimes old, cracked, and broken pavement, sometimes rock and dirt—and quickly realized they weren't headed to Angel's.

Anxiety had dampened his palms and the back of his shirt as they continued their drive. He didn't breathe any easier when they ended up in town. It wasn't the first time he'd been there, and he wondered why their route had been so roundabout, but he didn't ask.

They stopped at a store to purchase a full tank of gasoline and to fill the two, one-hundred-gallon drums that had been strapped in the back of the truck before they left. Michelle told Dean to fill the truck's tank and the drums from the huge, round tank propped several feet in the air next to the building, and then went inside to talk to the owner. It was set up as a gravity pump fitted with a valve to keep track of the amount of fluid released, a long rubber hose, and a nozzle. All Dean had to do was open the valve and watch the numbers turn as he filled the receptacles.

When Michelle returned, they took another overly long drive back home.

Except for the sound of the engine running, the tires grinding over pavement and dirt, and the wind buffeting the windows, most of the trip had been silent, at least until they were nearly home.

"How did your exam go?" Michelle had suddenly asked, never taking her eyes from the uneven road.

He sat up a little straighter and hope flickered in his heart. "Good news. The doctor said there was no nerve damage, but I'll be out of commission for a while." He didn't mention the rest. If she didn't know about the whipping, he wasn't ready to tell her.

"Good," she'd replied, and then everything went quiet between them again.

Dean didn't understand why she had wasted so much time driving around since she obviously didn't enjoy being in his company anymore. Yet, they'd traveled down so many back roads he'd lost count and didn't get back to the house until dinner. When he'd hopped out to help some other men unload the gasoline drums from the back of the truck, Michelle wouldn't let him. Instead, she sent him back to the barracks. Her dismissal had been embarrassing but gave him just enough time to get cleaned up and head down to the dining hall for dinner.

Esther stood at the entry to the kitchen as Dean strolled down the hall and he nodded a greeting.

"How was dinner?" she asked and he grinned.

"Excellent, as always," he replied but didn't stop to chat as he usually would. "I ate so much, I'm gonna have'ta roll outta bed in the mornin'," he joked, patting his flat belly and exaggerating his Texas twang.

"Oh, you..." Esther grinned, swatting at him playfully with a dishtowel. Chuckling, she returned to her kitchen, and Dean continued down the hall, his previous thoughts still plaguing him.

The minute he'd entered the dining hall for dinner, Carrie had skewered him with her eyes. The look was so menacing that his stomach had clenched and he hesitated in the entry. He blinked and then glanced around until he found a table far from where she sat. He tried not to notice her heated regard as he joined Theo and Peggy, Bret, and Jake. The looks she'd given him all through dinner promised trouble and the anxiety it caused had left him feeling less than hungry, but he'd forced himself to eat anyway.

The echo of his boots against the hardwood floor of the hall sounded loud as he left the kitchen and hallway behind him and strolled into the foyer.

His thoughts had returned to Michelle and how he could make up for his mistakes with her when he heard soft footfalls behind him.

It happened so fast, he didn't have time to turn around. One minute he was on his feet, the next, he was on his knees. He hadn't even cried out at the pain that shot through his back, and he didn't pause to do so now.

Scrambling across the floor, he ducked into the living room at the end of the hall. He knew what was coming and he wanted to run, but where would he go?

10

STIFLING A MOAN, Dean pushed up from the floor and turned to face his worst fear. Carrie smiled at him from the entryway, her head tilted slightly, a determined look in her brown eyes. His eyes darted to the only other exit on the far side of the room, but two chairs and a table obstructed his path. It didn't matter anyway—she would block him in before he could reach it. His only option was to face her and hope she wasn't bent on hurting him.

Yeah, right!

"Hello, *Boy*," she said casually as she sauntered into the room, stalking him like a predator after its prey. "It's good to finally catch up with you."

I hate it when she calls me that, Dean thought, but he didn't dare say anything about her nickname for him. The last time he did, she'd had him whipped.

Backing away, unwilling to take his eyes off the unpredictable woman, he came up short against the far wall and winced at the contact.

She grinned. "What, no greeting?"

"Hello, Mistress," he said mechanically, but his mind was racing, wondering if she'd grown reckless—or crazy—enough to play her games with him when most of the ranch's population was just down the hall. He mentally shook his head. Of course, she was. Everyone knew she was unstable, that if pushed too far—or disobeyed at all— she'd become unhinged. He'd once witnessed her nearly murder a man for refusing one of her orders. She'd do whatever she wanted and would expect Dean to take it, silently. There were times she wanted him to scream and times she didn't, and he was supposed to know the difference. Now, would be a time for silence.

She took another slow step and he pushed himself harder into the wall, trying to keep as much space between them as possible, though it did no good. She closed the distance until only inches separated them.

"I'm glad to see you," she said as she began to pull his shirttail out of his jeans.

He wanted to stop her, but fear for what would happen kept him still.

"I was afraid you were avoiding me."

"No, Mistress," he replied, feeling as helpless as he always did when she came for him.

Her fingers unbuttoned his shirt and slipped inside. His whole body tensed, desperately wanting to push her away, to stop her before she hurt him. But, remembering her threats, he simply stood and waited for the inevitable.

"Where did you run off to today?" she asked as her palms slid hungrily over his chest. "You were supposed to be working."

"I was," he said quickly. "I helped M-Miss Smithmoor with a delivery." He was careful to remember her rules, to do everything just how she wanted to keep her happy.

Then maybe all she'll do is humiliate me.

"Hmm," Carrie murmured. Suddenly her hands were gripping his waistband, jerking him forward, intentionally pulling the denim taut over his tender flesh. "Is that all you did with Miss Smithmoor today?"

"Y-Yes, Mistress," he gasped through his teeth as he tried to keep from groaning. The heavy material digging into him and the pressure of being pressed against the wall—not to mention the cold sweat that covered him at her appearance—caused the welts to burn. He should have remembered she was a jealous woman and explained the situation more clearly.

Another rule he'd overlooked.

"Are you sure?"

"Y-Yes!" Gasping, he held his hands flat against the wall, where they quivered with the desire to shove her away while praying she didn't guess at what he held back.

"Good," she said and relief flooded his trembling body. "I wouldn't like that."

"No, Mistress." He swallowed convulsively as she unbuttoned his jeans, but he didn't dare move.

"I have missed you, Boy," she said as her hands slipped inside his shorts, forcing them down over his hips, and he jumped with the intimate contact.

"Yes, M-Mistress."

What else was he supposed to say? It was ridiculous that he was so terrified of her. She was tiny and her guards were nowhere in sight. If he fought her, he'd probably win. He could kill her and his suffering would be over. He wanted to. Oh, how he wanted to! But he couldn't. She'd made dire arrangements for his brother if Dean retaliated. Even if he succeeded, there was no way Angel could do anything fast enough to save his brother. Nor could she stop Carrie from taking Dean if he failed. How long she could hold him before returning him to Angel, he didn't know, but that wouldn't really matter. It was what she would make him watch while she held him that did. After that, physical torture would be meaningless.

"I enjoyed our talk last night," she said as she stroked him and he struggled to stay still. "Though, I think you'd do well with another lesson. You've been far too arrogant as of late."

Dean froze, his breath halted, his eyes automatically searched her face. She watched him, her brown eyes glinting with the promise of pain.

"Please," he implored her, his voice low and shaky, "not again. I still hurt from last night. I've done what you asked. Please, don't hurt me again."

Carrie smiled up at him, but her eyes were cruel; she liked hearing him plead. "Maybe if you beg real pretty like you know how, I won't have to whip you more than once."

Dean choked on a sob and squeezed his eyes closed. She was going to do it again! He couldn't take anymore and still hide it. He couldn't take it again at all! And if she hung him by his wrists tonight, he may not get the full use of his hands back. But what the hell could he do? He was trapped in metaphorical chains, and she held the key.

"I expect to see you in the barn at two tonight," she said harshly as her hand tightened around his genitals, squeezing him to emphasize her threat and he cringed. "Don't be late this time."

He wanted to cry. He wanted to scream. He wanted to kill her.

He nodded. "Yes, Mistress."

"Good," Carrie said satisfied. Releasing him, she stepped away.

He didn't move, was afraid to move. He knew she wouldn't want him to move, so he didn't. Only his chest rose and fell rapidly as he breathed. She crossed the room and then turned to face him again.

"Look at me, Boy," she ordered.

Miserable and afraid, he did as she commanded.

"I expect you to please me well tonight," she said with a salacious smile.

"I'm afraid he's busy tonight."

Carrie jumped and spun around, looking so comical that Dean almost giggled hysterically. But the woman who stepped out from behind the wall made the inappropriate laugh clog his throat.

Michelle strolled in from the foyer and glanced at Dean. Her eyes skimmed over his disheveled state and narrowed with what he read as anger and suspicion when she met his gaze. The knot in his belly tightened painfully. He wanted to explain, to tell her this little scene wasn't what it looked like, but he didn't get the chance.

"What do you mean?" Carrie asked with caution, clearly not wishing to give away her real connection to Dean or her plans for him.

"Exactly what I said." Michelle tilted her head and gave Carrie a knowing smile.

"You should talk to your employer before displeasing a guest,"

Carrie warned and Michelle's smile widened.

"I think you're confusing Angel with someone else. She doesn't play those games and neither do I. Besides," Michelle said, her body relaxed and her expression confident; and to Dean, she looked sexy as hell, "I already spoke with her before dinner." She shifted, straightening until she stood at her full height, towering over Carrie, who stepped back nervously. "This man belongs to me for as long as I want him. Tonight and any other night, any other *time* I choose." Michelle fixed the other woman with a dangerous glare, the threat clear.

Carrie threw a perilous look at Dean that promised to make him suffer for this later. "But—"

"Go ask Angel if you'd like," Michelle said, "but we're not standing around to wait for you. Dean?" She looked directly at him. Anger darkened her blue eyes, but they brightened when they fell on him. Her gaze skimmed over him again and he suddenly remembered his state of undress. Heat crawled up his neck as he quickly pulled his shorts up and his jeans closed. He only halfway zipped them before he hurriedly moved to the buttons on his shirt.

"Don't bother with that," Michelle said, her tone far more gentle than the one she'd used on Carrie. "Just come with me." She waited until he reached the stairs before she turned back to Carrie.

"You're still here?" Michelle's voice was filled with faux sweetness. "I thought you needed to talk to Angel? Oh, that's right," she said as if just remembering something she'd known all along, "she already turned in and doesn't want to be disturbed. Well, I guess you'll have to wait until morning. I'm sure she'll be happy to clear this up for you then. Goodnight." Michelle smiled at the dark look on Carrie's face, and Dean hoped that was all she would do.

Not daring to meet Carrie's irate expression or wait for direction, Dean followed as Michelle started up the stairs. He knew Carrie wanted to call him back, but she wouldn't. That would reveal the hold she had on him. Regardless, he kept his eyes down, but he didn't have to look at her face to know what he'd see.

She would make him scream if she got ahold of him again after this.

He followed Michelle to her room, where she held the door for him to enter and then closed it once he did. Modestly furnished in pastel pinks and greens, Dean glanced around the very feminine room. Michelle's bedroom fit her to a tee, but despite its size and welcoming atmosphere, when the door closed, he suddenly felt trapped again.

Michelle wouldn't hurt him. Would she? He didn't think so, but the detached, irritable way she'd been acting all day worried him. He glanced around and saw a cot set up at the end of her pink-curtained, queen-sized bed. He frowned. Apparently, she wasn't angry enough to let Carrie have him, but she wouldn't allow him in her bed again either.

Wait a minute. That cot was already here. That means she'd intended to bring me to her room tonight before *that scene downstairs. What the hell?*

He looked the question at Michelle, but she didn't smile, didn't blink, only stared back at him.

"Sit down," she said, waving a hand to indicate the brown canvas of the cot or the soft green chair near the fireplace directly opposite. She did not indicate her bed. The cot was closest so he sat there and it squeaked under his weight. His still sore hands curled around the black metal frame, and he stared at the floor, waiting for whatever would happen next.

"Why didn't you tell me?" Michelle asked in a quiet voice.

He lifted his head slowly, reading the accusation in her eyes that he'd heard in her question. Standing in front of him, her long legs braced slightly apart, her arms crossed, she looked bemused, annoyed, and nervous. He wanted to play dumb, to pretend like he didn't know what she was talking about, but he wouldn't do that to her.

"I couldn't." It was a pathetic explanation, but it was the truth.

"Why?" she asked, sounding hurt this time, but then she answered her own question. "Because of your brother?"

He heard the sarcastic, *Yeah, right!* at the end of that.

"Yes." A frustrated sigh escaped him as he dropped his gaze. She didn't believe him and she wouldn't, no matter what he said.

"Did you tell her you were sleeping with me?"

His head snapped up. "No!" He sounded alarmed, even to himself.

Her brows pulled down again. "Why?"

He sucked in a deep breath, trying to think of what to say. How could he explain what Carrie would've done to him? That he didn't want to suffer any more than he had to? That the last thing he wanted to do was make Michelle a target for the other woman's irrational vindictiveness? He dropped his gaze and shook his head. He didn't have a way to explain it that didn't sound outlandish, especially since she didn't trust him anymore.

"Answer me, Dean! Why? Did you miss her that much?"

"No! Hell no!" He lunged off the cot and stood facing her, his back protested his quick movement, but he hardly noticed due to the anxiety pumping through his veins.

Only a few inches shorter than Dean's barefoot six-foot-two, Michelle still seemed to stand nearly eye-to-eye with him. Hurt radiated from her shining blue eyes and misery deepened the lines on her face. He wanted so much just to pull her against him and hold her tight, to tell her how much she meant to him. He could make her believe, make her see the truth, and then she might look at him the way she used to.

He reached out to her but she stepped back, and his hand dropped in defeat.

"Then tell me why!" She nearly sobbed, her eyes swimming in unshed tears. "Why didn't you tell her about us?"

"She didn't ask," he said a little too loudly, "and I didn't offer. I knew what she'd do to me if I told her. *That* I could've handled if I'd had to, but I knew she'd go after you and *that* I couldn't let her do."

A long pause followed his outburst. He shuffled his feet under her gaze as she tilted her head and studied his face.

"What do you think Carrie could do to me?" she asked, clearly confused and leery.

"I don't know," he said, meeting her gaze evenly, "but I sure as hell didn't want to find out!"

Michelle frowned at him and shook her head. "There's nothing she could do to me, Dean."

"I wouldn't be too sure about that," he said and Michelle blinked in surprise. Michelle could handle herself physically, but that's not what he'd meant or what had worried him. He sighed and tried to keep his voice level. "They want to bring down your boss. If they succeed, what do you think Carrie would do to you afterward?"

Michelle's eyes widened with surprise. "How do you know that?"

"It's why they sent me here," he said as he slowly sat back down. "They wanted information, anything they could use against her, against all of you. It wasn't hard to figure out from the questions they asked."

"They? You mean Carrie."

"Yeah, her and Darla Cain, and her followers. Carrie owned me before, so I mostly deal with her."

"That's why she thought she could touch you." Michelle sat down next to him and he looked over at her.

"That sounds like you don't want her to touch me," he said as a little flame of hope surged to life in his heart. He could see she wanted to trust him, but his perceived betrayal held her back. And he couldn't blame her for that.

He took a deep breath and looked into her eyes. If he wanted to keep her, he'd have to bare his soul, and he would, gladly, to convince her that he hadn't lied when he'd said he cared about her. He let it all show on his face—all the mixed-up feelings in his heart, everything he wanted to say but didn't know how—and something flickered in her eyes. Her shoulders drooped and her face softened. He tried a small smile that she returned, and that little flame inside him grew brighter.

"No, I don't want her to touch you," Michelle answered, gently running her hand down his back. He hadn't reacted fast enough to stop her and pulled away with a strangled groan.

"Oh, Dean, I'm sorry," she cried, gripping his biceps. "Did I hurt you?"

He sighed heavily. "No, it wasn't you."

"It was her." The flat statement fell like a barricade dropping between them. "*She* hurt you, didn't she?"

The fierceness of her statement surprised Dean, but it felt good to know that she cared about what happened to him. But then he dropped his chin, realizing he'd have to tell her everything.

"Yeah," he murmured, shame warming his cheeks.

He didn't stop her when she took his hand in hers. He watched her fingers as they lightly traced over his swollen digits, the back of his puffy hand, and over his wrist. He winced when she eased back his sleeve to reveal the raw skin around his wrist.

"She tied you up."

He could feel her looking at him, but he couldn't meet her gaze, afraid to see the hurt and disgust when he told her everything.

"*What else* did she do to you?"

Without looking up, he pulled out of her grasp and shrugged off his shirt. She gasped at the red welts that covered his back, some already bruising darkly, and followed the damage to where it disappeared under his unfastened jeans.

"She whipped you? Naked?" There was fury in her tone.

A little shiver rocked through him as he nodded.

Michelle inhaled deeply. "What else?"

A muscle twitched in his jaw as he clenched his teeth. The moment of truth had finally arrived.

I'm not ready. What if she kicked him out? What if she never spoke to him again? What if she really would hate him as he feared?

He squeezed his eyes closed and took another deep breath.

"What else, Dean?" She had his hand in her lap and used the other to gently turn his chin toward her.

He wouldn't open his eyes.

"Look at me, Dean," she coaxed, brushing her fingers over his tight jaw. "Please."

The plea in her voice did it. His lids lifted and he peered over at her, his head lowered in shame.

"You had sex with her last night."

The statement made his stomach churn and the tears that finally slid down her cheeks made his chest hurt. His hand trembled as he wiped it away with his knuckles, thankful she'd allowed it. Dropping his hand, he gave a hesitant nod in reply and tried to dislodge the lump in his throat.

"I didn't want to do it," he said, his voice rough. "I've never *wanted* to do any of the things she forced on me, but as long as she's holding my brother hostage…I have no choice." He wiped more of her tears away, marveling that she would shed them for him. "I'm sorry, Michelle. You have no idea how sorry I am."

"You have nothing to be sorry for," she said and smiled when his eyes widened. "I can't fault you for what she forced on you, Dean. I'm not like her. I'm not saying I'm okay with any of this, but until we can figure out how to fix it, we'll have to do the best we can."

He stared at her, unable to believe what he'd just heard. "You…you believe me?"

Her soft smile widened. "Yes."

"You don't…" He paused to swallow again. "You don't blame me?"

"No." She brought the hand she'd captured to her lips and kissed his swollen knuckles.

Staring at her in wonder, something broke open inside him, and everything he'd been holding back for so long burst forth in a heart-rending sob. He slid off the cot to his knees and wrapped his arms around her waist, burying his face in her lap while he wept uncontrollably. He hadn't cried in years, not since he'd finally admitted to himself that his father was gone. Back then, he'd been too ashamed to let anyone see him cry, but this was different. He had wronged all the people here, but he'd hurt Michelle the most, and she forgave him. It was the last thing he'd expected. He'd been planning how to avoid Carrie after tonight because he'd been certain Michelle would throw him out and would never help him again. Instead, she'd forgiven him and would shelter him from what he feared. He was relieved and happy and worried all at the same time.

Michelle had solved the most immediate part of his problem. Angel had promised to do what she could to help his brother, which would solve Dean's long-term problem, but what about the time in between? He wanted their help, but he just hoped that his brother didn't have to pay for the reprieve he'd unexpectedly found today.

11

BRET WOKE TO SUNSHINE filtering through the curtains across the room. Turning onto his back to stretch, he groaned when he saw Jake's bed was already empty. Oversleeping was not Bret's habit and knowing Jake, he'd have a day of ribbing from his friend and the other hands too. Kicking off the blankets and pushing the bed curtains out of his way, Bret rolled off the mattress and quickly got dressed.

He headed down to the barns to check on the animals and then hurried back to the house. Breakfast should have started already and his stomach reminded him again of his late start.

Picking stray pieces of hay from his shirtsleeve, he rounded the corner of the bunkhouse and nearly stumbled over his boots when he saw Carrie's two enormous male guards standing outside Angel's front door. As he got closer, he heard shrill shouts coming from inside.

He mounted the front steps, planning to investigate, but the dark-haired half of Carrie's bodyguards stopped him at the top. "You cannot enter."

"I live here," Bret said, but the big man's brown face remained impassive as he shook his head.

"Get out of my way!" someone shouted inside and a thrill of anxiety prickled along Bret's scalp. A quiet male voice responded, but

Bret couldn't hear it clearly. He tried to get a glimpse of what was happening through the partially open door, but he couldn't see around the man in front of him or the other who stood at the opening. His first thought was of Angel, but he quickly pushed that aside—she wouldn't need his help with Carrie. Then his mind turned to Jake and something told him he needed to get inside. Right now.

Bret nodded toward his and Jake's apartment door near the end of the deck. "I'd like to go to my room," he said to the guard.

The big man glanced behind him. His blond partner shrugged and the dark-haired man let him pass.

Bret gave them a nod of thanks and hurried across the deck. The feeling that he was needed intensified- when he thought he caught a glimpse of Jake's dark-blond head near the stairs inside.

He quickened his pace.

Upon entering their apartment, he ran across the room to the inside door and, snatching it open, entered the long hallway near the kitchen.

The voices were clearer as Bret cautiously moved down the hall to the foyer.

"I want to see her!" Carrie shouted. "I have things to discuss with her that can't wait!"

"I'm sorry." Jake's voice reached Bret's ears and—not wanting to cause his friend more trouble, but prepared to interfere—he slowed his brisk pace to a halt.

"Angel doesn't want to be disturbed," Jake continued, his voice calm but strained. "Michelle will help you with whatever you need, but she's in the dining hall. I'll be happy to let her know you need her, but you'll have to wait here or come with me."

Bret recognized the tight sound of anxiety in Jake's voice, and his concern for his friend caused his feet to move again.

Carrie's curse, followed by a loud thump, stopped him and the breath in his throat.

Someone grunted and then groaned loudly, all while Carrie continued her tirade, "I told you what would happen if you got in my way again." A sickening crack filled the air, immediately followed by Jake's pain-filled scream.

Sprinting into the foyer, Bret came to a sliding halt at the scene before him.

Jake lay sprawled on the stairs. His arm had fallen through the spindles, and Carrie had stomped on it, breaking Jake's arm. Her foot rested on the appendage, pressing downward while Jake continued to scream.

Closing the distance in three quick strides, Bret grabbed Carrie's arm and jerked her away. He spun on his heel, dragging her with him, and then bodily shoved her across the room. She hit the doorframe, bounced back into the partially open door, and then fell onto the threshold.

She began shouting something, but Bret had already turned away to help his friend.

"Jake…" he said but saw Jake's pain-filled eyes widen. Sensing someone's approach, Bret glanced over his shoulder, but before he could turn, his arms were seized from behind and he was pulled into the center of the small room. Each of Carrie's two burly guards placed a meaty hand on his shoulders, then savagely twisted his arms backward and forced him onto his knees. They then jerked upward until his arms were nearly perpendicular to his body and, though he struggled, he could not break their hold.

"Let go of me!" he shouted at the two big men who restrained him.

"They will only do as I say," Carrie said from the doorway. She watched Bret's struggle with a dark, narrow-eyed look while she rubbed her face where it had collided with the doorframe. "You will pay for what you just did."

"What *I* did?" Bret said, attempting to give her his nastiest glare, which was difficult from his stooped position on the floor. "You just broke a man's arm for no reason! Was I supposed to let you hurt him more?"

"It was none of your business," Carrie said, "but now you are definitely mine."

Her avid smile sent an icicle of fear down Bret's spine.

"Hurt him," she said to her slaves, "but only a little… I don't want any damage."

The two large men twisted Bret's wrists and forced his arms up higher. Bret moaned as his arms, shoulders, and back flared with instant pain. They pushed until he was bent double, his forehead nearly on the floor, and he cried out. Carrie laughed and fury heated Bret's skin as his helplessness washed over him in a wave of frustration.

"Let me go!" he shouted, but it was hard to sound like a badass while cringing on the floor.

At his wheezing demand, the two larger men twisted his arms farther, and Bret groaned loudly.

"It will do you no good to fight," Carrie said, watching his humiliation with a look of enthusiastic fascination.

Bret forced himself to stop struggling and concentrated on finding a way out of this.

"Let him go, Carrie," Jake said from the stairs, all pretense of meekness gone from his voice. Bret could just see his friend, sitting about a third of the way up the staircase with his back to the wall. He cradled his left arm against his body and frowned at Carrie with anxious eyes. "Hurting Bret will get you nothing."

"Still sticking your nose into my business, Jake?" She sounded astonished and annoyed. "You should learn to keep your mouth shut. You'd be better off." She moved toward the stairs.

"Leave him alone! Your problem's with me!" Bret shouted and surged upward. Agony sliced through his shoulders, but he didn't stop. He may be trapped right now, but he could cause a ruckus that would draw the attention of the other members of the household.

His arms had gone numb and he was having trouble breathing. His heart pounded with anger and fear for Jake and himself. A cold sweat covered his body, but he would not allow her to harm Jake.

"Don't worry, Bret," Carrie crooned, dismissing him as a threat, "I'll deal with you shortly."

"No!" Bret shouted as she stepped toward the stairs. "Deal with me now!"

Angel's comments about the limits to hysterical-strength and Carrie's reaction to them popped into his mind.

"What? Can't you take care of your problems yourself?" he asked.

She paused to glance at him. "I'm about to."

"Doesn't appear so," he said. "Looks to me like you have to force your slaves to do it." He coughed out a derisive chuckle. "It's a wonder they haven't overthrown your control yet. You're nothing without them. Do you think they don't know that?"

Carrie's eyes widened and shifted between her two slaves. Her expression turned uncertain, as if she suddenly wondered if her men would obey her next command.

Footsteps echoed in the hallway behind him and Bret smiled. The other members of the household were finally coming. He desperately hoped it was someone with enough influence to stop this farce.

"Make him scream!" Carrie shouted at the two men holding Bret, clearly annoyed by his show of defiance or maybe to test the compliance of her slaves.

Each man jammed a knee into his back and together, they pulled. He screamed and feared they would tear his arms from their sockets.

"What the *hell* are you doing, Carrie?"

The pressure on his arms didn't decrease, but Bret felt a rush of relief at the sound of Angel's voice.

"Stop that!" she shouted at the two men, but they held him in place, ignoring her command. "Tell them to stop, Carrie. Right now!"

"Back to the first position," Carrie said and Bret was forced back down over his knees, his arms still held tightly.

"What are you doing?" Angel asked angrily. Though he wasn't able to lift his head to see her face, Bret had heard something else in her voice. All he could make out was the bottom of her white pajama pants brushing the top of her feet where she stood on the stairs not far from Jake.

"Your slave attacked me," Carrie said.

"Jake?" Angel said, looking for confirmation.

Jake glanced up at her from his seat on the stairs and a look of concern filled his expression. He opened his mouth as if to speak, but Angel cut him off, "What's wrong with your arm?"

Jake's face darkened as he glanced at his cradled arm and then down at Carrie. "It's broken."

Angel took several steps down the stairs, leaning heavily on the balustrade.

"You broke his arm?" she asked Carrie, and a threat lay in her cold tone.

Bret could just see Angel's face now and what he saw made him pause. *No wonder Jake had looked so worried.*

Her normal, sun-kissed complexion had turned nearly as white as her pajama top, a sheen of perspiration shined from her forehead to her neck, and her cheeks were flushed as if with fever.

Still, fury radiated from her ice-blue eyes, angrier than Bret had ever seen her.

ANGEL STEPPED DOWN and held in a wince of pain. She gripped the handrail with both hands and straightened her spine—she already looked weak enough, no need to make it worse.

"I was coming to see you," Carrie explained as if nothing important had occurred, "and he interfered. I warned him, but he didn't listen."

"I was not..." Angel's words tapered off and this time, she couldn't hold back the wince of pain. She pressed her arm protectively against her right side and leaned against the handrail, taking several shallow breaths, before she started again. "I was not to be disturbed," she finished, uncaring what Carrie wanted so badly. "Your wishes don't supersede mine in my own house! He was doing what he was told and you broke his arm?"

"My apologies," Carrie murmured to Angel, not Jake. "He didn't convey your wishes."

"Right," Angel grumbled at the obvious lie. "Your apologies are meaningless! How are you going to make amends?"

"I'll pay the regular fine for unduly damaging him," Carrie retorted, "as the law requires, nothing more."

"Unduly?" Angel's eyes widened in astonishment. "You broke his arm, Carrie! How is he going to work now?" That wasn't her highest priority, but it was all the other woman would understand.

"I'm sure a doctor will be able to set it and he'll be just fine,"

Carrie replied. "I'll pay for his care as well if you feel it's necessary."

Angel snorted derisively, "Oh, right, because that'll make it *all better.*"

"Accidents do happen, Angel." Carrie's bored, superior tone was infuriating.

"Yes, they do," Angel replied, staring at the hated woman with hard eyes, wishing she could hurt Carrie the way she had hurt Jake and Dean. A moan from Bret broke Angel's threatening gaze and her tone sharpened even more with her next demand. "Tell your men to let mine go!"

Several of the residents had crowded inside the foyer and spilled over into the living room behind where the two men held Bret. Angel glanced at them. Dean and Theo stood side by side in front, looking nervous and worried. Dean's face had gone white and he seemed to want to disappear into the crowd. But the tall, broad, thickly muscled man behind them—who eyed Carrie's guards with a dark appraising look—was in his way.

"We need to discuss his punishment and my provisional ownership," Carrie said with a little too much enthusiasm, drawing Angel's attention once more.

"We aren't talking about anything," Angel said, taking another step onto the floor, though she still gripped the handrail. "Let him go and get out of my house! You're no longer welcome here."

"I have rights!" Carrie shouted and pointed at Bret, her eyes wild as she made her case. "He *attacked* me! He left marks on my arm *and* my face. I'm claiming my rights to him."

"I have rights too," Angel said harshly, then grimaced as pain stabbed into her side. She stifled a groan and wiped at the sweat trickling down her temple. When she looked up, she frowned, confused by what she saw. *It's not real,* she told herself and blinked. When she opened her eyes again, the ghostly image of her long-dead lover was replaced by Carrie's angry visage.

"As you can see," Angel went on after a careful breath, "I'm not feeling well, and I'm not discussing anything with you until I'm feeling better."

"But—"

"No," Angel said. "Tell your men to let him go and get the hell off my property before I have you dragged out of here."

Carrie stared at her astonished. Then a devious smile lit Carrie's face and Angel knew the other woman delighted in Angel's pain and weakness. She was planning something, and that was never a good thing.

"Hugh," Angel said, "come here please."

The big man seemed a bit surprised to be singled out, but he stepped forward between Theo and Dean. "Ma'am?" he asked in his deep baritone.

"Stand between her and those men and don't let her get past you. Do whatever you need to do to keep her out of my way. Do you understand?" Angel didn't bother to lower her voice, wanting everyone to hear her directions for Hugh.

"Yes, ma'am," he said with a crooked grin that crinkled the scar on his cheek.

Carrie bristled and shouted arguments at Angel as Hugh moved toward her with a sinister grin on his face. Carrie retreated, but her angry shouts didn't. "Angel! You can't do this! I have…"

Angel tuned her out, but she did see a possible issue with Hugh and that situation. She glanced around and spotted her head guard.

"Michelle," she said, pointing toward Hugh. "Would you help him, please?" Her head guard moved to Hugh's side and together, they blocked Carrie from view. Michelle made a comment Angel couldn't hear, but from Carrie's shocked outrage, it wasn't flattering.

Dismissing Carrie for the moment, Angel turned to the two men holding Bret. She stepped forward but nearly collapsed as her trembling knees gave way. An arm wrapped around her waist to steady her. When she looked up, she found Dean had rushed forward to catch her. His hand tightened on her hip as he adjusted her weight and she hid the pain his abrupt movements had caused. His sudden appearance was the only reason she stayed on her feet, but it took everything she had not to cry out. She must dissolve this situation before she passed out.

Looking up into Dean's handsome face, she mumbled, "Thank you."

His blue-green eyes looked anxious. "Are you all right, ma'am?" he asked in a whisper as she stood for a moment gripping his arms.

She took a deep breath, trying to think back to his question, forcing herself to concentrate on what she needed to do, and nodded. She peered up at his apprehensive look and did her best to smile reassuringly. "I'm fine," she told him, and then indicated the two men holding Bret. "I want to talk to them."

Dean's expression was dubious, but he nodded and helped her the few feet across the foyer to where Carrie's men stood.

Both of Bret's captors looked ill at ease. Their wide eyes shifted to Carrie, who they couldn't see but could hear shouting at Michelle, and then back to Angel as she approached. Their grip on Bret had lessened with their confusion and they didn't appear to know what to do, though they didn't release him.

Dean stayed with Angel until she stood next to Bret and was looking up at the first man holding him.

"I'm fine, now," she told Dean with a shaky smile, "you can step back."

Dean hesitated a moment, a frown marred his brow. Clearly, he didn't believe her.

"Please, Dean."

He gave her a quick nod and stepped back, but he didn't go far. From the corner of her eye, she caught him exchange a glance with Jake, who nodded in approval of the younger man's protectiveness.

Stifling her frustration with overprotective men, Angel looked up at the closest of Carrie's huge bodyguards.

The soft sounds of Bret's labored breathing and moans of pain increased the fear swirling inside her. She hoped she was right about this. At least one of these men had shown mercy to Dean, so maybe she could convince him to release Bret and the other would follow.

"Please," she said looking up into the blond man's blue-gray eyes, "let him go." Her fingers curled around his thumb as she spoke. Gently, she pulled the appendage back, encouraging him to release his hostage.

His wide, worried eyes glanced toward Carrie arguing with Michelle, but she didn't pay him any notice. His eyes returned to Angel, his fear and insecurity written all over his face. She wondered what Carrie had done to these men to cause them to obey her so completely, but then, she already had a pretty good idea.

"Please," Angel murmured once more, "I don't wish to harm you."

He must have seen something in her eyes because his grip suddenly loosened and he dropped Bret's arm. The second man, taking his cue from his mate, also released his hold when Angel turned her eyes on him. She heard Bret groan as his arms fell to the floor and he started to sit back on his heels, working his shoulders.

"Are you all right, Bret?" she asked.

His eyes were angry when they met hers, but he sounded relieved. "Yeah. A little sore, but fine."

She turned back to the tall blond man. "Thank you," she said with a smile for the two large men. She met the blond's blue-gray eyes evenly, willing him to understand all that she was trying to convey. "Thank you." She paused to reach over to touch Dean's arm and then dropped her hand again. It was a chance, but she was willing to bet that the risk he'd taken to help Dean would keep his mouth shut about Angel's knowledge of Carrie's late-night activities in the barn.

For a moment he only stared, but then he glanced at Dean and his eyes changed. He met Angel's stare and gave the barest of nods. He understood.

She smiled. "You both may go now."

They wasted no time in heading for the door.

"Michelle?" she called as the two men moved away. "Let them pass."

Michelle and Hugh stepped aside as Carrie's two men scurried out the door while their owner watched in disbelief.

Angel hid a smile at Carrie's obvious confusion as she—assisted once again by Dean—went back to the staircase. Dean returned to Theo's side as she gripped the handrail and took two steps up. Lifting a shaky hand to her forehead, she turned to Carrie, silently praying the woman would leave quickly. Angel pressed her hand to her aching side, her knees so weak she wasn't sure how much longer she could stand, and raised her voice once again.

"Michelle," she called, "you have my permission to drag this woman out of my house and off my property. If she resists, do whatever you need to do, with my blessings."

"My pleasure." Michelle turned toward the smaller woman, a truly nasty grin on her face. "Time for you to go," she said, but Carrie wasn't ready to give up just yet.

"We have things to discuss," she shouted at Angel.

"I've already told you," Angel said as she swayed slightly, her death-grip on the balustrade was all that steadied her, "I am not feeling well and you are no longer welcome here."

"I will not let this go," Carrie warned.

"I'm not surprised," Angel said derisively, "but it will have to wait. Michelle, escort her out of here *now*. And there'll be no reprimand if you use a little more enthusiasm than is necessary. Especially if she resists." Michelle nodded before she took Carrie's arm and forcefully hauled her out of the house and down the front steps, while Carrie continued to shout threats and demands that went unheeded. It crossed Angel's mind that her head guard was enjoying the task just a little more than she should have, but she couldn't make herself care.

Angel breathed a sigh of relief and turned to go back upstairs. She'd been having trouble following the whole incident that had just occurred and it had gotten worse. She'd had to concentrate too hard on what was going on, but now that the emergency was over, her mind was slowing, becoming lost and fuzzy as the pain in her side throbbed and grew more fierce.

Still gripping her side, Angel started up the stairs, trying not to grimace with each step.

JAKE WATCHED HER closely, the fear roiling in his belly momentarily overtaking the pain in his arm. Something was wrong.

"Angel?" Jake called. "Are you all right?"

When she didn't respond, he glanced at Bret.

Dean and Theo were helping him to his feet, but his eyes were glued on Angel as she dragged herself up the stairs by the handrail.

Jake's breath hitched when she stopped abruptly and leaned over the railing. "Angel?"

She moaned softly, swayed, and started to fall.

"Angel!" Bret shouted, drawing Jake's attention as he shouldered aside the two men helping him and headed for the stairs.

Confessions

1

B RET CARRIED A NGEL quickly through the open double doors of
the small hospital in town, his cowboy boots drumming loudly against
the polished linoleum as he hurried down the hall with his burden. His
steps slowed as he searched for assistance, but the one-story structure
they'd pulled up to moments before appeared deserted.

At the end of the short, beige-colored hallway, he finally came
across a brown-haired nurse in blue scrubs sitting behind a cubicle-
style desk, shuffling through papers. He hurried forward, worry
quickening his pace once more.

"We need help," he said as he approached.

The nurse's expression changed from bored indifference to alarm
and she practically jumped out of her worn-down office chair. Then
she looked him up and down with a leery frown creasing her brow.

"What are you doing here?" she asked, gesturing to two other
women who had materialized with cudgels in their hands from around
a corner down the hall.

"You can't be in here without an escort or a guard," the nurse told
him, blocking his path as the two other women came up behind him,

while all of them ignored the burden he carried. "Where's your owner?"

Overlooking the nurse classifying him as property, Bret nodded to the small woman bundled in his arms. "This is her."

"Your owner?"

"Yes."

"What happened to her?" The nurse barely glanced at Angel, her mistrusting brown eyes were locked on Bret. "What've you done?"

"She's sick," he said, annoyed by her assumption that Angel's condition was his fault. "She needs a doctor."

"You brought her in on your own?" The question was dubious.

"No," he said and, beginning to lose patience, his tone sharpened. "A guard is coming, along with another man with a broken arm." He gestured with his loaded arms to draw her attention to Angel. "But she's the emergency. Is there somewhere I can lay her down?"

The nurse finally took a good look at Angel and her attitude immediately changed.

"Follow me," she ordered, seeing Angel's pale, sweaty face. She waved the two guards away and rushed to a nearby door. "In here." She held open the door to a small room with an examination table in the middle, two brown, thinly padded chairs next to the door, and a good-sized window. The nurse eyed him warily as Bret conveyed Angel through the opening and then followed him into the room. He laid his burden on the gray, tissue-covered exam table and arranged the small pillow beneath Angel's head. His anxious eyes caressed her ashen face and when her shivering increased, a pang of regret struck him for leaving all the blankets in the truck.

"What's wrong with her?" the nursed asked, elbowing Bret aside. "Has she been sick?"

"Yeah," he answered in a hushed voice, "off and on for the last few days." He shoved his clenched fists into the pockets of his blue jeans and tried to stay out of her way.

"The flu?"

"I don't think so. She complained about a bad stomach ache and nausea last night," he told her. "The fever and sweating were new this morning. She's also favoring her lower right side and burning up with fever."

"What's her name?"

"Angel Aldridge."

"Has she been here before?"

"I don't know."

The nurse gave him a withering look that clearly questioned his intelligence, but she didn't comment one way or the other. She turned back to the patient to begin a quick examination. When she lightly pressed on her patient's belly, Angel groaned and curled up protectively.

Stepping back—the exam apparently complete—the nurse pulled two white blankets from a small closet to cover Angel's shivering form and then turned to fix Bret with a stern stare. "What are you to her?"

"What?" He was confused by the question and the dislike in the nurse's eyes. She already knew Angel owned him, what else did she need to know?

"Are you her breeder?" the woman asked bluntly, and he frowned at the label. "Has she given you rights to make decisions for her?"

"I'm her foreman," he said with a scowl of his own. "We run a cattle ranch. So, yes, I guess she has. Why?"

The nurse ignored his question and gave him a visual once over, from head to toe and back, then pursed her lips as if she were disgusted by something she saw. Maybe she just didn't like men. She plainly didn't believe him and assumed his relationship to Angel was far less than he'd claimed.

"I see," she said disapprovingly. "Stay with her. I'll let the doctor know you're here." She gave Bret a stern look before she left the room.

As soon as she was gone, Bret went to stand beside Angel's bed. He stared down at her white face and used the edge of the blanket to wipe the sweat from her forehead.

During the drive to the hospital, as he'd held her in the back seat of the big truck, he'd been surprised by the amount of heat that emanated from her small body. Her fever hadn't dissipated in the slightest and worry for her weighed on him, tightening his chest and shoulders.

She stirred with a groan and blinked at the bright light of the exam room. She stared up at him, the usual brightness of her blue eyes dimmed by sickness, and then sudden panic widened her gaze.

"You're in the hospital," he told her, tucking a wayward curl behind her ear and placed his hand on her shoulder, attempting to comfort her. The moment he did it, the internal argument he'd waged the whole way to the hospital reared its ugly head.

Why are you trying to console her? the darker side of him asked. *She's the enemy. If she dies, you'll be free.*

Did he want that?

You should run... No one would be the wiser, at least, not until it was too late, and by then it wouldn't matter.

Staring into her fevered eyes, a rush of protectiveness washed over him and he sighed. He couldn't leave her, not until he knew she was safe. "You're going to be all right, Angel. Don't worry."

"Take me home, Bret," she said, reaching for his hand, her expression soft and vulnerable. "Take me home now."

His eyes widened. "The doctor will be here soon," he said, wondering if her fever was worse than he'd thought. "Just relax."

"Bret," she whispered again as she clutched his hand in both of hers. "I don't want to see a doctor. I want to go home. Please, take me home."

His eyebrows lifted. *She's begging?*

Growing increasingly uneasy, he wasn't sure how to respond. Did she really expect him to take her home in her condition? "Do you know what you're saying?"

"Yes," she breathed. "Take me...h-home."

As he stared dumbfounded, he thought he heard movement behind him, but he was so focused on Angel that it barely registered as he shook his head. "I can't do that, Angel. You're sick. If I take you home now, you might die."

"Good! That's what I want. Take me home!" She gripped the front of his shirt, pulling him closer as he leaned over her. Attempting to pull herself upright, her face contorted with pain and she groaned. Her eyes closed for a moment and his hands automatically came up to curl gently around her upper arms, not trying to hold her up or push her away.

He could feel the heat coming off her in waves, sharply contrasting with the trembling of her body. He hesitated again as her eyes fluttered open and her fevered gaze collided with his.

"Please, Bret," she implored as her hands clenched his shirtfront, "I know you hate me. Just do this one thing I ask without fighting me. Please! Take me home. Take me home and you can be free!"

"What do you mean, I can be free?" he asked, his uneasiness growing.

"If I die," she said, confirming Bret's thoughts, "then you'll be free of me and the idea that I own you. You can run...anywhere you want, and I won't stop you."

"You're delirious," he said, unable to believe she was begging him to help her die. "Your fever must be worse than I thought."

"I'm not," she gasped as he tried to untangle her groping fingers from his shirt. "I know what I'm asking. You just don't understand..."

"No, I don't," he said, going still and fighting the anger that swelled in his chest. "Why the hell do you want to die?" His big hands enveloped her small fists, holding them in place.

"It doesn't matter," she said weakly and then hardened her tone. "Just think about what you'd be gaining, Bret. With me gone, you'll have your freedom. That's what you want, isn't it?"

Yes, that's what he wanted, more than anything. *But am I selfish enough to let her die to get it?*

A year ago, maybe. But now...? Not only was he bound by the promise he'd made to Jake, but by the realization that he'd been wrong about her. She was different—part of him didn't want to acknowledge that fact, but it was true. On top of that, he cared about her. He couldn't deny that anymore either, at least not to himself. It was there, insistently tugging at his insides, pulling down his defenses.

How could he let her die? Everyone in the hospital and at the ranch would consider it murder, and he'd never be able to live with himself afterward.

His jaw clenched and a muscle twitched in his cheek, his black eyebrows angled downward, studying her like a difficult puzzle he needed to solve.

"And what about the people on the ranch? What'll happen to us, to them, if you die?"

"They'll be taken care of. I made sure of that," Angel said.

"I don't think—"

She shook her head before he could say more. "Please, Bret," Angel pleaded cajolingly. "I know you want your freedom, and I want mine. Help me! Take me home. Now, please, and I'll give you anything you need, everything I have. Just take me home."

He tried to inhale deeply, but he couldn't get enough air.

I can't do that. I can't let her die. Emotions welled up within him, tightening his throat. The undeniable need to defend her—even from herself—took hold of him and he couldn't ignore it anymore. He was her protector now, and he would keep her safe.

She must have seen something change in his eyes because she bit her lip and shook her head.

"Damn it, Bret," she said, her voice choked with emotion as her hands tugged at his shirt, "I am still your mistress, and I'm ordering you to take me back home!"

She tried to appear stronger—her eyes grew brighter and the grip she had on his shirt increased—but Bret wasn't fooled. She was ill and, right now, he was in charge.

"You're not going anywhere," he told her. Curling his hands around her upper arms again, he gently pushed her shoulders back down to the tissue paper-covered bed.

"No…" she sobbed in defeat.

A soft sound behind him and the room's subtle change in air pressure made Bret turn his head, but no one was there and nothing had changed.

"Yes," he corrected, dismissing the noise as nothing and turning back to Angel to pull the blankets over her again. "You need medical attention, Angel, and you're going to get it, whether you want it or not."

"Bret," Angel pleaded again, "please, let me go…Let me die…" Getting weaker by the moment, her words slurred together as her eyelids drifted closed.

"I'm sorry, darlin', but I can't do that," he said, brushing back her sweat-dampened hair. "The people at the ranch depend on you, they need you, and I won't let you disappoint them." He wasn't sure if he included himself in that description.

Angel groaned and turned her head away with a sob, but she said no more. Angry, defeated tears streamed from her closed eyes and soft moans of despair escaped her lips. A heaviness weighed on his heart at seeing her so distraught, but he wouldn't change his mind. He reached out to her, but she pulled away. She cried out with pain but refused to allow his touch.

"Stay away from me," she hissed. "Don't touch me!"

"All right, Angel," he said and stepped away.

"Get out," she said harshly, but her sheer lack of strength made it a pathetic whisper.

"I'm not going anywhere," he said.

A soft sob escaped her and then she was unconscious again.

2

JAKE DROPPED ONTO A CUSHIONED CHAIR in the small, empty waiting area down the hall from Angel's room. His arm ached inside the plaster cast they'd applied, and he wasn't looking forward to the long weeks he'd have to wear it. The meds they'd given him were taking the edge off the pain, but he had more pressing issues on his mind than his arm.

Angel's will to live had deserted her once again.

Sighing, he shook his head and shifted in the chair. He hadn't meant to eavesdrop on her and Bret, but he was glad he had. The first thing he'd heard were her pleas to be taken home. No doubt she knew how that would turn out, but in her current state of mind, she didn't care.

The first year he'd come to live on Angel's ranch, she'd asked for his help in mitigating the effects of her mood swings. He'd still been afraid of her back then, worried she'd punish him the way Darla Cain had so many times before. By the time she started walking outside at night while still asleep, he'd finally learned that he had nothing to fear. Last year hadn't been too bad, but if what he'd just heard was any indication of her downward spiral, this year would be awful.

The one bright spot in what he'd overheard was Bret.

Jake's heart had thudded painfully upon hearing Angel beg his friend to let her die, but when she offered Bret his freedom, Jake's hopes had sunk with dread. As much as Bret wanted to be free again, how could he turn her down?

But then Bret had surprised him.

He had smiled when Bret refused to give in to her demands. *Maybe he hasn't changed that much after all,* he'd thought as he let the door close quietly and ambled down the hall. After hearing their conversation, his confidence in Bret skyrocketed. He would honor his promise to care for her when Jake was no longer there to watch over them both. At least he wouldn't have to worry about Angel once he moved to Monica's. Bret would be there, and she would be safe.

A few minutes later, Bret strolled into the room, looking tired and weary.

"How is she?" Jake asked as he approached.

With a heavy sigh, Bret took a seat across from his friend. "Not good. Doc says it's her appendix. She said if Angel didn't have it removed immediately, she'd die."

Jake nodded and decided to give Bret a chance to talk about what had happened in the exam room. "Was Angel okay with the surgery?"

Bret glanced out the window and Jake could see the debate going on inside him. Clearly, a part of Bret was disturbed by what had happened with Angel, but another held back. Jake held his breath, waiting, unsure if Bret's reticence was to protect Jake, Angel, or himself. The temptation to take her offer had been there too. Maybe Bret wanted to avoid Jake's disappointment, even though that hadn't entered Jake's mind.

Bret shrugged. "She wasn't conscious to complain. They took her right to surgery." He glanced at his hand and the papers crumpled in his fist. He held them out to Jake, the title on the first one read, *Appendicitis: What to expect.*

"How about you?" Bret asked as Jake reached for the pamphlets. "How's the arm?" He gestured toward the plaster cast on Jake's left arm.

"They said it's a clean break," Jake told him, "nothing more serious than that. It should heal fine. I'll be back to normal in six to eight weeks."

"Good news," Bret said with a tired smile.

"Yeah," Jake murmured as he sat back with the papers Bret had given him.

Bret picked up what looked like a medical journal and started flipping through it, evidently needing a distraction from his thoughts. Jake studied him surreptitiously as Bret fidgeted in his seat, his gaze turned to the window outside, a pensive expression on his face. A frown pulled Jake's eyebrows together as Bret unconsciously rolled and unrolled the journal in his hands before he finally crushed it in his fists. Bret's eyes dropped at the crumpling sound and seemed surprised to find the journal still there, wrinkled beyond repair. He tossed it onto the table next to his chair as he stood and crossed the floor to the three long windows.

Jake read his friend's agitation easily and wondered about it. Did he know that Jake had overheard his conversation with Angel? Or was he just thinking it over, regretting his decision? Either way, Jake decided if Bret didn't bring it up, then neither would he. But he would supply quiet support. Getting to his feet, Jake went to join Bret by the windows to gaze out at the small, well-tended flower garden outside.

A few minutes later, Michelle returned from signing the papers for Angel's procedure. She sat near their empty seats, but when they both glanced at her, she shook her head. She had no news.

They waited, each lost in their thoughts and worries, when Monica Avery bustled into the room, surprising them all. Her hazel eyes looked fraught and her long blonde hair, pulled into a ponytail, swayed against her shoulders as she glanced between them.

"How is she?" she asked, her eyes worried. Jake turned and her gaze widened further when they fell on the cast encasing his forearm. "What happened to you?"

"I'm okay, Monica," he said, putting his good arm around her waist. He led her to a bench across the room where he quickly explained what they knew. Then he asked what she was doing there. "I mean, I'm glad you're here, but how did you know?"

"Sam sent me a message," Monica explained. "She didn't give any details, so I came as fast as I could. There's been no other news?"

"No, not yet," he told her.

She frowned at his tone and tilted her head. "What is it, Jake?" she asked, worry sharpening her tone. "You have that look…"

"What look?"

"The one that says you have something to tell me, but you're afraid it will hurt me."

"Oh, that look," he said, his eyes shying from hers as he ran his good hand nervously over his goatee. He met her gaze again and sighed, giving her a small half-smile.

Her frown deepened. "Out with it, Jake."

He peered across the room to see if their friends were paying them any mind. They weren't, but he lowered his voice anyway as he leaned toward her. "Angel asked Bret to let her die."

"What?" Monica nearly shouted. She glanced across the room to see if her voice had carried and then turned back to Jake, purposefully keeping her voice to a whisper. "Why would she do that?"

"I think you know the answer to that better than I do," Jake said. "Why else would she?"

Monica shook her head sadly. "I thought she was getting better? Your letters said she was responding to Bret."

"She was, but Carrie showed up a couple of days ago and there was a fight—"

"A fight?" Monica interrupted. "Is that what happened to your arm?"

Jake quickly explained what had happened to him and cringed at the fury that burned in Monica's eyes.

"That little bitch!" Monica seethed. "I will make her pay for that!"

"It doesn't matter," Jake said, taking her hands in his to try to calm her. "I'll be fine. It's Bret I'm worried about."

"Why?"

Jake told her the rest of the story, and her eyes widened in amazement. She glanced at the tall man still standing by the windows across the room.

"I'm glad he was there to stop her, but I'm afraid of what it will cost him."

Jake nodded.

"Carrie *will* demand rights to him," she said, her gaze settling on Jake once more.

"She already has."

"Knowing her and Darla, that's what Carrie came for in the first place," Monica said, the accusation making her tone hard. "I've heard rumors that Darla's been in a tizzy ever since Angel *stole* Bret from her at the auction. Those're her words, not mine, by the way. She wants him, and I wouldn't put it past her to use Carrie to get what she wants."

"I wouldn't either," Jake replied.

"What did Angel say or could she say anything?"

"Only that they'll talk about it later. When she's well."

"For his sake, they might want to make that take a good, long while," she said, her gaze focused on Bret's back.

"Yeah," Jake agreed, silently wondering if it was time he shared his experiences at Darla Cain's with his friend so he'd know what to expect and how to act. *It might save him some pain,* Jake thought with a sigh.

* * *

The soft tick of the clock was the only reminder of time slipping by and the oppressive worry that weighed on them all. Well over an hour had passed when the doctor, still in her scrubs, finally entered the small room. They all got up to face her, keenly waiting for what she would tell them.

"How is she, doctor?" Michelle asked as everyone stepped forward.

"She's going to be just fine," the doctor said. "She's in recovery and will be there for an hour or so to make sure there are no major side effects from the anesthesia. Then she'll be taken to her room and you can see her."

"Will she have to stay?" Monica asked.

"A day or two," the doctor replied, "but that's standard practice."

"Can we stay with her?" Bret asked from behind the others and pink colored his cheekbones when everyone glanced at him.

"As long as you don't disturb her or the other patients, I don't see why not."

"Can we see her?" Jake asked and Monica nodded enthusiastically.

"Soon," the doctor said and repeated the information about recovery. "One of the nurses will let you know when she's ready for visitors."

"Thanks, doc," Michelle said and smiled. The others also smiled and looked as relieved as Jake felt

"There is one other issue…" the doctor said slowly.

"Sure," Michelle said with a slight frown. "Is something wrong?"

"I've asked one of the nurses to find you a private room," the doctor said and Jake had a feeling he knew what was coming. "Some of our other patients' families were not…pleased to have men in this waiting room."

"No one said anything," Michelle said, glancing at the others for verification.

"They went to the front desk and complained. I'll admit that it's a bit unusual to see slaves so worried about their Mistress," the doctor said as her eyes drifted to Bret, who looked even more embarrassed than before. "It's because of their obvious concern that I'm offering the private room."

"We didn't mean to cause trouble," Jake said, annoyed that he'd been correct.

The doctor shook her head. "It's no one's fault. Personally, I don't see anything wrong with it, but some people feel men must be kept separate from us. Whatever the cause, it's better for the patients if we keep things peaceful."

Bret grumbled something under his breath, but Jake couldn't make it out. The others either didn't hear or ignored him.

"It's not a problem, doc," Michelle said. "Just tells us where we can go."

They were led to another exam room, almost identical to the first one to wait for news. An hour past and, apparently feeling restless, Bret announced that he was going for a walk.

"I'll go with you," Michelle said as he opened the door. He looked as if he wanted to argue, but she didn't give him a chance. Passing by him, she waited in the hallway for him to join her.

He glanced at Jake, who shrugged. Bret's frown deepened, but then he shook his head and followed Michelle into the hall, closing the door behind him.

"He seems really worried about her," Monica said once the sound of their friends' footsteps dwindled.

"He is."

"How do you know?"

"I just do," Jake replied, but seeing her curious expression, he elaborated. "He's not usually so fidgety and he obviously wants to be here. He wouldn't act that way if he wasn't concerned. I think Angel's demand unnerved him a little."

"About that…" Monica said. "Shouldn't we talk to him about it?"

"No."

"But…"

Jake shook his head. "You need to keep what I told you to yourself."

"Why? Shouldn't we get as much information as we can?"

"I don't know if Bret told Michelle," Jake said, "but he didn't say anything to me, which means he's either protecting Angel or the people at the ranch. Either way, I don't want to push him."

Monica's eyebrows lifted. "Okay, but the fact he's protecting her or whatever is good. Right?" Monica asked. "Doesn't it show he's grown attached?"

"Could be," Jake replied. "He *is* very protective of the people he cares for, but this could also be one of those things he just does. If that's the case, it wouldn't mean anything in particular."

"I see."

"I'm just thinking the fewer people who know about Angel's request—and the less we talk about it—the better."

"Yeah, you're right about that," Monica murmured.

LATE THAT AFTERNOON, they were finally allowed into Angel's room.

Covered by a white blanket and her black hair spread out over the white pillow, Monica thought her friend looked almost peaceful. If it weren't for her pallid face, the IV in her arm, or her unnerving stillness, Monica wouldn't have thought anything was wrong.

"Is she all right?" Monica asked the nurse.

The woman explained Angel was heavily sedated for the pain and to keep her still. "She wasn't a very cooperative patient," she said. "She'll probably sleep through the night, but she might wake for brief periods."

They had waited quietly, but it wasn't until the next day that Angel awakened fully. Her eyelids blinked open in the bright morning light and her brows drew down in confusion.

"Monica?" she said, her voice low and raspy.

"Hello, Angel," Monica replied cheerily. "I'm so glad to see you awake."

"What're you doing here?" Angel's words slurred together slightly and her eyes still looked glassy from the drugs.

"I heard you were sick," Monica explained, taking her friend's hand. "I had to come."

"Oh," Angel replied but seemed disconcerted. When she sluggishly looked up again, she smiled at Jake, standing behind Monica's shoulder. "Hi, Jake."

"Angel," he said with a gentle smile. "I'm glad to see your eyes open."

Her smile broadened slightly, but she seemed uncomfortable, and it slipped away.

"Are you feeling okay?" Monica asked, worry in her gaze.

Angel nodded but didn't say anything else and Monica knew something was wrong, but as usual, Angel kept it to herself.

Angel glanced around the room, giving Michelle a tremulous smile as her eyes drifted closed for a moment. The head guard gave her an encouraging nod. Everything was quiet and seemed tranquil until Angel's slightly unfocused eyes opened and shifted to the back of the room. When her gaze fell on the man standing by the wall, they hardened and her face darkened with anger.

"Get out of here!" she slurred at Bret, her chin lifting and her eyes narrowing. She still seemed somewhat incoherent even as she tried to glare at the man across the room. Her hands balled into fists, clenching the white cotton blanket tightly in her lap as her wild eyes shot blue sparks across the room. "I don't want him in here!"

Monica glanced at Bret. He didn't seem overly surprised by Angel's outburst, almost as if he'd been expecting it, and said nothing in response, only gazed placidly into her fury.

Monica stifled an irritated groan at the challenging arrogance in his calm expression. *He really knows how to push her buttons,* Monica thought and when she turned to Angel, she saw the anger in Angel's unfocused gaze.

Angel opened her mouth as if to berate him, but her eyes flitted over their audience and her mouth snapped shut.

Time to stop this, Monica thought. "Angel, you can't mean that..."

"Yes," Angel said, dragging out the 's,' "I do mean that." She turned her gaze back to Bret. "Get out!"

"What's wrong with you?" Monica asked, and wondered if her friend was confused or hysterical. "Bret saved your life. You should be a little more grateful."

"Fine," Angel replied, glowering awkwardly at Monica's stern expression before swinging her unsteady gaze back to Bret. "*Please,* get out!"

"Angel!" Monica's voice took on a stern quality as she prepared to put her friend in her place.

"It's all right, Monica," Bret interrupted as he headed for the door. "I'll wait in the hall." And just like that, the door swung closed and he was gone.

Angel visibly relaxed against the pillows once Bret was out of the room and Monica marveled at her friend's uncharacteristic fury. Was it because he'd denied her plea to help her die? Or did something else happen between them after Jake snuck out of the room?

Michelle followed Bret. "I should go with him." What she didn't say, but Monica understood, was that she'd make sure there was no trouble. Michelle gave her employer a reassuring smile. "Get better, Angel," she said and then followed Bret into the hall.

Monica glowered at her friend, even as Angel's eyes were drifting closed again. "What was that all about?"

Angel struggled to open her eyes and looked expressionlessly at her friend.

"You're not being fair to Bret," Monica said. "He helped you."

"He doesn't lis-listen," Angel mumbled the slurred words and closed her eyes again. A moment later, she was asleep.

"Stubborn woman," Monica grumbled. "She had no cause to do that."

"Maybe she did," Jake said. "I didn't hear their whole conversation. Maybe something happened after I left."

Monica glanced at him curiously. "Do you really think he did something to deserve that?" Monica asked. "After all the concern you said he showed for her?"

"I don't know. Bret is just as stubborn as Angel can be at her worst. He could have, but even if we asked, I doubt he'd say. It's better to just let it lie."

* * *

Angel woke again that evening and found Jake and Monica sitting vigil beside her bed. Though slightly less groggy than earlier that day, she still felt sleepy and a little confused.

"You're safe," Jake said, reaching over to squeeze her hand as Monica nodded. Their reassurance was helpful, but she still felt despair weighing down her heart.

"We need to talk," Monica said after they'd exchanged some small talk.

Angel groaned at her friend's normal forthrightness. She knew what was coming. "Can we not?"

Monica ignored Angel's comment. "You're going to need a doctor when you get home, to keep an eye on you and your wound." Angel didn't respond, so Monica continued, "Jake and I thought the best course of action would be to make the exchange a few weeks early."

"Jake for the doctor...?" Angel's voice was soft.

"Yes," Monica replied. "It's only a little early, and it will make things easier for Peggy and her pregnancy too."

Angel glanced at Jake but said nothing. She saw hope in his hazel eyes, but she saw worry too. He wasn't concerned with her being angry—she knew that—but for her well-being and her understanding. She closed her eyes, sighed, and nodded. "All right," she said, unable to say no or complain.

"You'll still have help," Jake said and her tired eyes focused on him with a frown. "Bret's going to be there to help take care of everything. You'll be in good hands."

Bret, again. Angel rolled her eyes behind closed lids, then blinked sleepily. She was too exhausted and heart-sore to get angry over how much Bret had failed her. If he hadn't told her friends why she'd been so hostile toward him earlier, then she didn't want to tell them either. It would break their hearts, and she didn't want to see the disappointment in their eyes.

"For how long?" she asked quietly, and both of her friends frowned at her. "How long will Bret stay? How long before he gets angry and tries to run off again? If he doesn't stop, he'll eventually get himself killed, and I don't want to see that. I can't handle that, not again, and not alone." She clamped her mouth shut. The last sentence had been just a murmur, but she hadn't meant to give away so much.

Jake and Monica exchanged a glance that spoke volumes but indicated nothing to Angel, then they turned their compassionate gazes on her. She hated the sympathy she read in their eyes.

"Well," Jake began slowly, "though I believe he meant indefinitely, I can't speak for him. So, I guess you'll just have to ask him yourself."

3

SHORTLY AFTER THEY SPOKE to Angel, Jake left the two women to chat and went looking for Bret. He'd been putting it off, but now that Angel had agreed to his early departure, it was time he explained a few things to his best friend. Jake hated to bring up his past mistakes, especially since they might damage his friendship with Bret forever. Still, considering what had happened with Carrie, he'd be a horrible friend if he didn't warn Bret about what he might be facing. It was time to answer the one question that Jake had never fully explained.

He found Bret in an empty room down the hall. Michelle had arranged for its use when Angel refused to tolerate Bret's presence. It was small and only a few doors down from Angel's room, and close enough that Michelle was comfortable leaving them alone inside. When he met her in the hall, he asked for some time alone with his friend, and she'd agreed.

When he entered the room, Jake found Bret sitting on the wide ledge in front of the window. His back was propped against the wall with one leg flung casually over the ledge, the other bent at the knee. Leaning his head against the window, he stared outside at the fading light, one hand on his thigh, the other dangling over his bent knee. For a singular moment, Bret looked pensive, staring at the fall evening outside. The next breath, Bret turned to him and the thoughtful expression disappeared, replaced with a frown.

"Everything all right?" he asked.

"Yeah, fine," Jake said as he closed the door behind him. He stepped farther into the room, rubbing his damp palms against his jeans. No one would bother them, but nervousness assailed him just the same. He crossed the few steps to one of the two chairs in the room and sat. A frown marred Bret's brow when Jake met his gaze.

"What's wrong?" he asked. "You don't look like everything's fine."

"I wanted to talk to you," Jake said, determined not to get distracted, afraid if he gave in to that temptation, he wouldn't say the things Bret needed to hear.

"Okay," Bret said, dragging the word out as he spun in his seat to face his friend. His legs dangled from the window ledge and he curled his hands around the edge, waiting. Curiosity painted his expression, but his green eyes looked worried as if expecting an argument. "What's up?"

Jake balanced on the edge of his chair, his legs braced apart, elbows on his jean-clad knees, and his hands clasped tightly between them. He bent his head, unable to meet Bret's gaze, and tried to collect his thoughts. Then, shifting uneasily, he began to speak. "Do you remember asking me why I was so willing to do things for Angel? Why I wanted to help her?" He glanced up at Bret's wary expression.

"Yeah," Bret replied slowly.

"Do you remember what I said?"

"You said a lot of things, but what I remember most is that you believe she's a good person and she saved your life."

"Yes," Jake said, "but I never told you how or why."

"No, you didn't," Bret murmured, suddenly appearing as nervous as Jake felt.

Jake dropped his eyes to the floor, his hands unconsciously clenching. He'd thought he was ready to tell this story, but now he wasn't sure how much he could tell. He didn't want to see the disappointment in his best friend's eyes when it all got dragged out into the light. The damage to their friendship would rip his heart open.

Jake took a deep breath, and when he spoke, his voice was quiet and clear.

"I think it's time I explained some of that. You need to know what she risked for me; maybe then what she's done for you won't seem like a singular or self-interested act." He peered at Bret, who inhaled sharply and shifted uneasily on the ledge.

"I've always wondered why you're so devoted to her..." Bret said. "Why you protected her and sided with her against me more often than not."

Jake heard the hurt in Bret's comment and dropped his eyes again.

"To understand all that," Jake continued after another deep breath, "you need to understand what my life was like after Amy had captured and sold me."

"I'm sorry about that," Bret interjected. "I can't tell you how sorry I am...that they took you...instead of me."

Jake shook his head. "I'm not laying blame, Bret. I forgave you a long time ago. You never intended for that to happen. So, let it go and forgive yourself."

Bret's lips compressed unhappily, but he nodded, though Jake suspected it would be some time before Bret actually forgave himself.

"What I'm getting at by telling you this," Jake said, averting his eyes again, "is to give you an idea of what I had to deal with every single day. What they did to me and what they forced me to do so you can understand exactly what Angel did."

"They?" Bret asked gently.

Jake didn't look up. "I say 'they' because there were several women who used me for..." he paused, his head tilting from side to side, determining the best word to use, "...let's say, entertainment. But when I say 'they,' I mostly mean Darla and her friends. Carrie Simpson included."

He gave Bret a meaningful look that promised to explain his warnings about that woman. Then he refocused on the floor.

"Just like at the Auction Hall, one of the first things they did in Darla's home, to make sure we understood we were completely at their mercy, was take away our clothes. They let us wear very little, though most times it was nothing at all. In the fall and winter, many suffered from the cold and damp conditions in the stone cells where they held us. Then there were the others who died, simply because they weren't allowed to cover themselves and weren't adequately cared for when they got sick. Darla and her friends controlled everything we did, and if we didn't follow their rules or direction without hesitation… Well, the whip was a very good motivator." He fell silent remembering the feel of that weapon on his body.

He shivered and saw Bret's similar reaction.

Jake sat staring at nothing for several minutes, struggling within himself. He was thankful for Bret's silence. This wasn't a conversation he could help along, rather something Jake must find his way through. Bret seemed to understand, but apprehension still stretched between them. Jake felt the strain of it in his chest. But he'd come this far, and he had to keep going.

Shaking off the dread that had come over him, Jake cleared his throat and continued. "All the things you'd expect after being sold as a breeder were there. Dozens of women who paid for or were awarded my services, sometimes several times a day. Some of them weren't so bad, others were vicious, and many wanted blood. If I didn't perform as they wanted exactly when they wanted it, they'd complain and have me beaten. Carrie was one of those. Though Darla was much worse and, since she owned me, there was no one she had to answer to for what she did." He paused again and took a deep breath. "That went on for a long while and I was punished a lot, in various painful and humiliating ways. It never got better, only worse, and it didn't take long to be afraid." His eyes met Bret's. "I mean really afraid. More than just the unnatural fear caused by the drug they gave us every day, which was bad enough, but add constant terror to it and you'd only be scratching the surface of that fear. Not just for your life, but for what they'd do to you next if you kept on living."

THE PAIN IN JAKE'S VOICE and on his face made Bret's gut clench. He gripped the ledge until his knuckles turned white, but he didn't notice. He couldn't imagine what they'd done to this strong, capable man to put that tone in his voice, but he feared he was about to find out. He'd known life as a slave was unpleasant, but he was beginning to see that what he'd experienced at the Auction Hall was only the tip of the proverbial iceberg.

Jake shook his head and looked away. "I'm getting ahead of myself." He cleared his throat again and swallowed.

"There were the female guards," Jake went on, "and most of them could be cruel, but what was harder to take were the men."

"Men?" Bret couldn't help it, the statement surprised the question out of him.

"Yes, men," Jake replied with a hard glance at his friend. "There were men who would spy for them. They'd listen to the rumors and pain of others, and then they'd inform Darla exactly what was happening or being said in the open cells. They were on the first level of Darla's slave prison. The solitary cells were tiny and deeper underground, but I didn't learn about them until much later."

Jake shook his head as if to clear it.

"Anyway, some of those men did more than just spy. Some actually worked for their Mistresses and performed their duties freely. Others were transformed into willing slaves...or whatever you'd call it." Jake met his gaze again and Bret knew what he'd say next. "Like those two giants of Carrie's that attacked you."

Bret nodded.

"They were more afraid of disappointing her than anything else, and they would've ripped your arms off if she'd told them to. I don't know why they do it and I only vaguely know what Darla and Carrie put them through to get them to obey so completely, but either those men are cowards who would do anything to ease their own lives, or what happened to them was something terrible that they'll never recover from." He dropped his eyes to the floor and shivered.

Bret couldn't help the prickle of apprehension that danced down his spine.

"The spies were despised by the other slaves," Jake said, a hard edge to his voice, "but there was little we could do to them. They were given special privileges and protected. Attacking one of them meant severe punishment. Once, while I lived there, a slave attacked the man who'd informed on him and nearly killed him. I don't know if it would've been better if he had killed the bastard. Maybe his punishment would've been swifter, easier somehow." Jake's head swung from side to side as if he couldn't believe his own memories. "In any case, he was flogged in front of everyone and then hauled down to the isolation cells. That was more than a year before I left, and I never saw him again."

Jake swallowed and Bret had to remind himself to breathe.

"Most rumors said that if you were taken to the lower cells, you died there. That's what would've happened to me if not for Monica and Angel."

Jake stopped again and Bret could see the anxiety etched into his friend's profile, could feel his tension from across the room.

"About a year after Darla bought me," Jake started again, "I lost my luster, my newness, and they came up with another use for me. The torture they put me through for fun was sick and brutal. There were times, I swear, they just wanted to hear me scream. I won't bore you with those details, except to say it was…extremely unpleasant. Anyway, after a time Darla lost interest in what was done to me and allowed Carrie to use me however she wanted."

Jake shifted in his chair and glanced at Bret once more.

"Carrie was one of the worst. She tried to break me into one of her mindlessly obedient guards. She'd have me beaten for no reason and then expect me to please her in every way imaginable. At first, I did, at least when I could, but then…then she started to do…other things and I couldn't take it anymore. I fought back. I barely got close to Carrie, but if I could've reached her, I would've killed her. Part of me wishes I had, but then I'd probably be dead now, too." He stopped and shook his head, squeezing his eyes shut.

Bret watched his friend struggle with his memories. He was glad Jake hadn't elaborated.

Suddenly, the hard accusations he'd spewed at his friend shortly after he arrived at Angel's ranch—about Jake being brainwashed and questioning his manhood—caused a lump of guilt to constrict Bret's throat and stabbed a jolt of shame through him. Jake's story wasn't even over yet, and Bret understood why his friend hadn't wanted to leave.

"Life after that got much worse," Jake started again, his head still hanging, his eyes on the floor. "Too many bad details to explain, too many painful memories to recount, but I'm sure you'll come close to the truth if you use the darkest parts of your imagination." He stopped for a moment and then laughed mirthlessly. "Carrie wouldn't come near me after that, which was the only good to come out of the whole situation. Instead, I became the favorite target of anyone who wanted to take out their anger, because no one cared what was done to me and they didn't have to worry about repercussions. I spent a lot of time fighting, being punished, and healing, though I was never fully healthy again until I left. My rations were cut and again, no one cared when I complained. They told me to be happy I got anything at all. They said I was lucky to still be in the open cells to complain about it."

Jake paused again and the silence seemed to stretch painfully. Bret wanted to say something, but his mind went blank. So, he said nothing at all and felt like a terrible friend.

"It wasn't long after," Jake said, filling the silence and his voice sounded strained, "that I kept a young girl, who'd been recently enslaved, from being raped by one of those privileged men I told you about. It was her first day there and the guy had her cornered when I came along. She was too small and sick to fight him off, so I did.

"She was grateful and I was punished, though I never regretted it. My food was shorted again, but, apparently, that still wasn't enough to have me imprisoned in the isolation cells. Though I know Carrie asked Darla for it repeatedly. Why I hadn't been imprisoned down there after what happened with Carrie, I don't know. Apparently, Darla still wanted me around, though I have no idea why. She wasn't interested in me anymore, but then Darla may have just enjoyed making Carrie squirm. She wasn't very nice to anyone. It gave her some kind of sick pleasure to hold that type of control over other people. In any case," Jake shrugged, "that's why I was around to stop the bastard before he could hurt the girl.

"She was a sweet kid and she stuck close to me after that. Most of the others stayed away from her and I didn't mind her hanging around. Her name was Anna, and having her around kind of made me feel almost normal, like an uncle or big brother."

The grin that pulled at Jake's lips was bittersweet and Bret's heart ached for his friend. He shifted uneasily. Something terrible was coming, he could sense it.

"After a while," Jake said slowly, "she must have noticed I never had much to eat and started sharing her food with me. I didn't want to take it, I didn't." His eyes pleaded with Bret, but then looked away. Jake took another deep, shuddering breath and when he spoke again, his voice was unsteady. "But I was *hungry* and weak. The small amount of extra food was helpful. I started to feel a little better and it was my turn to be grateful. And that's when…it got…worse…"

He hesitated, and Bret instinctively knew this was what Jake didn't want to share—what he hated and condemned himself for. The one thing he couldn't forget. Bret knew that feeling all too well, and he almost told Jake to stop.

Whatever Jake revealed next had hurt him badly. Bret could see it in the way he hung his head, in the set of his shoulders, and hear it in the slight quiver of his voice. Bret didn't want to hear it, didn't want to see his best friend crumble, but it must be important if Jake wanted to tell him.

Squirming uneasily, with no other way to help his friend except to listen, Bret swallowed his apprehension and kept his mouth shut.

"Darla hosted lavish parties where slaves were the servers and the entertainment, sometimes both at the same time," Jake started again and Bret sensed this was where it would be most difficult—for Jake to say and Bret to hear. "I'd been required to serve at more than a few during the first year. I was sold for nightly services at all of them, but that was early on before they started cutting my food. It was sometime early in my second year there that my role changed. Instead of serving, I was slated as entertainment. I don't know who told Darla or who thought up the sick game they forced on me, but someone talked and we suffered."

Bret wasn't sure who the other part of 'we' was, but he had a sinking suspicion he could accurately guess.

"I suppose I should explain their forms of entertainment." Jake's voice held a forlorn echo that made Bret's heart beat harder. "It was a sick form of dinner theater. They'd arrange fights to take place in the center of the room while they ate. Sometimes battles were fought until the first fall, some until first blood, and still others, though less often, were to the death. All of it was brutal.

"Another form of amusement was to perform slave punishments. There were many different ways this was done, but most often it was flogging and I don't mean a few lashes. They would whip those men bloody, until they passed out or died from the ordeal. I can still hear them screaming in my head…" Jake went silent, shaking his head as if to rid it of those memories. "I never did understand how those women could sit there and eat while a man screamed in agony and gore splattered around the room." Jake stopped again and a long silence followed.

Bret waited, knowing there was more and, though he wouldn't have complained if Jake decided to stop right then, he gave his friend time to decide. Jake would say what he needed to when he was ready…if he ever was. But Bret wouldn't push.

When Jake started speaking again a few minutes later, his voice was low and rough, as if he was having trouble controlling it.

"Their other favorite was to force slaves on each other…sexually. Man on woman, woman on man, man on man, it didn't matter. It was about power and control, to force someone to do something against their will. That isn't to say it was always against their will. Some slaves enjoyed it and were often eager to perform for the crowd. I wasn't one of them." Jake took a deep breath. Wringing his big hands between his knees, he released it slowly. "Even though I was so full of the damn drug I was shaking and queasy, I fought the guards who tried to lead me out into the room. They beat me with my own chains. I lay there on the ground while they hit me and decided it wasn't worth the pain. I agreed to follow them quietly. It wasn't until we got out there and they had my legs chained to the floor that I fully understood what they were going to make me do." He stopped and took another deep breath, and then another, and another. Bret could see a sheen of sweat on Jake's forehead and his hurt and fear transferred to Bret. His stomach churned at the possibilities.

Jake closed his eyes and started again, "I heard them bring someone out behind me. I didn't bother to look, I didn't want to know, at least not until I had to. When they told her to lie down on the table in front of me, I felt sick. It was… It…was…" He choked on his words and for a minute or two, he couldn't speak.

"It was Anna," Bret said gently, trying to make the telling a tiny bit easier, even though his heart pounded so hard it hurt.

"Yes." Jake sighed. "She was just a kid and they expected me to…to… They made me…"

"I get it," Bret murmured. Jake glanced up at him and Bret saw the pain and regret in his friend's eyes. "I get it." It was all he could say, the only way he could ease Jake's plight.

"I tried to stop them," Jake choked out, dropping his eyes to the floor again. "I told them no, but they started whipping me…us. I tried to shield her. I guess I mostly did, but it didn't last long. They said if I didn't do it, then they would hurt her and make me watch. You know what she said to me then?" He glanced at Bret, the shine of unshed tears in his eyes. Bret felt his eyes burn and simply shook his head, unable to speak. Jake's gaze dropped and he shook his head disbelievingly. "She told me to do it. 'Just do it,' she'd said. 'I'd rather it was you than someone who'll try to hurt me.' Can you believe that?" Jake fell silent again, air shuddering in and out through his teeth.

Bret didn't know what to say, but his friend didn't seem to expect an answer.

Jake took another long, shuddering breath and released it slowly before he continued, "I held out a little longer, but in the end, I had no choice…I did it." His voice sounded dead and Bret's heart went out to him. "I did it and I'm damned for it."

"There was nothing else you could've done," Bret said after a long silence, feeling the crushing weight of the guilt his friend carried as if it were his own.

"I should've done more. Held out longer. Something. Anything, but that!"

"It's not your fault, Jake."

"That doesn't change anything. I didn't know what to do, but I should have tried harder."

Anger pulsed in Bret's gut. His captors had forced Jake into that situation and he thought it was his fault? "And done what?" he asked harshly but softened his tone. He wasn't angry with Jake. "You were hurt, weak, and chained. You were at their mercy and they had none. What could you've done?"

"I don't know," Jake said softly, "but I shouldn't have given in." He peered up at Bret. "You wouldn't have, would you?"

Bret heard the desperation in his friend's question. "I don't know..."

"Maybe I should've let them beat me to death," Jake murmured, apparently not hearing Bret's reply. "It would've been easier..." He looked up at Bret again. "What would you've done?"

Bret had no idea what he would've done. What he did know was the experience had taken a devastating toll on his best friend. Jake was naturally an overprotective, big-brother-type, and he'd taken in Anna like a little sister, like family. He'd protected her and looked out for her, probably did a lot more than what he'd said to keep her safe. Darla forcing Jake to rape a girl he'd made that kind of commitment to would have torn him apart.

"I don't know, Jake." Then, because it was true and Jake needed to hear it, he added, "I may've done the same thing. God knows I've done things since the wars that I never thought I'd do. That wouldn't have been any different. But you need to believe that you didn't do anything wrong. They would've hurt you, probably killed you if you'd kept defying them, and Anna would've joined you. She seemed to have known that, and you've got to know it too!"

Jake nodded but remained quiet. Minutes past, but neither of them moved or spoke.

"So, do you despise me now?" Jake asked, finally breaking the stillness.

Bret met his friend's gaze with a confused frown.

Jake grimaced and lowered his chin as if Bret had struck him.

Bret's frown deepened. "Why would I do that?"

"I don't know," Jake said, dry-washing his hands again. "I know how you feel about men who abuse women...that way in particular, and I know why."

Bret's skin tingled and the knot in his stomach seemed to weigh a thousand pounds. "You do?"

4

BRET SHIFTED ON THE WINDOW LEDGE. His whole focus on Jake and the information he'd just revealed. He felt as if the rug had just been yanked out from under him to expose all of his deepest, darkest secrets. Jake knew most of them, but he'd never told Jake that part of his story. Could never bring himself to reveal what his mother had done to protect him from his uncle. Just considering what Jake might know made his pulse quicken and heat crawl up his neck.

Jake sighed as if exhausted and replied slowly, "Yeah, I've known for a long time."

"How?"

"Ruby."

"My mom?"

"Yeah." Jake sounded even more tired. "She needed to talk to someone, Bret. You spent a lot of time avoiding her and then when you did start talking again, you were still distant. When you moved over the mountains she was afraid you were gone for good."

"I told her I'd send for her when I'd gotten settled and had some money."

"Yeah, I know, but she was convinced you still hated her."

Bret paused, thinking back to that terrible yet freeing time in his life. "I guess a part of me still did. A little, anyway."

"She was afraid and asked me about it," Jake explained. "I didn't want to betray your confidence, but I didn't want to leave her to worry on her own either. It was eating at her, had been for a long time, and since I'd lost my mom so young, Ruby was the closest thing I had to one. And I didn't like seeing her upset."

"I *thought* you two were a little chummy before I moved," Bret said bitterly. It bothered him that his mother shared things with Jake that Bret couldn't bring himself to. He couldn't blame her though; they'd both needed something back then, he just hadn't been able to be the one to give it to her. "So, what happened then?"

"We talked and I tried to alleviate her fears without giving her too much. I knew you wouldn't appreciate it, which is why I didn't tell you back then. It wasn't a pleasant place to be, between you two, but I did the best I could for both of you." He paused and frowned up at his friend. "You didn't think it was strange that I never asked you about it again after that first time?"

"Well, yeah, I thought it was strange, but I just thought you were being a good friend."

Jake chuckled. "I was trying to be."

"You were... You are. A good friend, I mean."

"Does that mean you don't despise me...for then or now?"

Bret leaned back, surprised Jake even had to ask. "Hell no! Why would I? Back then, you did what I couldn't. And now..." He shook his head. "You were as much of a victim as Anna, Jake. What kind of person...what kind of friend would I be if I did that?"

Jake stared, his eyes showing Bret how very vulnerable his revelations made him.

Jake abruptly dropped his head and squeezed his eyes shut. He took a deep breath and released it in a shuddering sigh. "You have no idea how glad I am to hear you say that, Bret." He met his friend's gaze.

"Haven't you told anyone else this story?"

"No."

"Not Monica or Angel?"

"Angel a little. Monica more, but not all. I told you the most," he said. "I didn't want them to know. I was never sure how they'd react."

"Monica loves you," Bret said, "she wouldn't hold it against you. And Angel loves you, too. I have a hard time believing she'd ever turn against you for anything." That last was hard for Bret to say since he wasn't sure he'd receive the same treatment if their circumstances were reversed, and a part of him wanted that, badly.

"Yeah," Jake said, "maybe..."

"I'd say that's as close to a sure-thing as anyone could hope to get," Bret told him and felt another surge of jealousy. "Don't you trust them?"

"Yeah, I do," Jake replied. "I just can't get past the idea of either of them looking at me differently."

"Is that why you didn't tell me this before?" Bret asked.

"Yes." Jake shrugged. "It'd been a long time since we saw each other. I wasn't sure..."

"Do you think I've changed that much?"

"Like I said, I wasn't sure. Not at first."

"And now...?"

"Now I think you're still hurting, Bret. You're harder in some ways and exactly the same in others. I think you hide some of who you are because you're afraid of being hurt more. But despite all of that, I know you're still the good man I used to know. You're still my friend."

Bret's lips curled up, embarrassed by Jake's insight. "I'm glad you think so," he said, "because as far as our friendship is concerned, nothing has changed for me."

Jake returned his smile.

"So, what happened to Anna?" Bret asked tentatively, hoping she'd somehow escaped that life as Jake had. But the crestfallen look that crumpled Jake's face told him he was wrong.

"She died..." Jake murmured.

"How?" Bret asked, unable to suppress the question.

Staring at the wall, his eyes distant as if looking inward, Jake's voice sounded toneless as he replied, "She killed herself about a week later."

"Oh, man. I'm so sorry, Jake," Bret rasped through the lump in his throat. "That had to be…hard."

"She wouldn't come near me after…" Jake cleared his throat, wiped at his shiny eyes, and continued, "I tried to look out for her, but I couldn't be there all the time. The man who'd tried to hurt her when she first arrived finally got what he wanted." Jake paused. Head hanging low, a soft sob escaped him. "She came to me after, more shattered than before, but there was little I could do. That's when she told me it wasn't my fault. That she didn't blame me. I couldn't accept that, but I didn't argue with her… She was dead by morning."

Bret swallowed hard, unable to speak.

"I shut down after that," Jake said wearily, his eyes locked on something outside the window. "I didn't care what they did to me anymore. I fought everything they wanted. About three weeks later, I finally went after Darla when she tried to make me the entertainment at one of her parties. I wasn't going to go through that again! I almost made it to her, too." A broad, brutal grin split his face. "I finally scared her enough that she banished me to the lower cells."

"But you survived," Bret reminded him.

"Yeah," Jake said with a bitter laugh, "but not because of anything I did. I was rotting away down there, freezing and starving in the dark, for I don't know how long. Days…? Weeks…? I wasn't in any condition to notice time passing, but it was a long time that felt longer. Then one day I had a visitor, an older woman with gray-streaked black hair and stern but kind eyes. Her name was Jewel and she was a member of the governing council. I didn't care why she was there. I was dead inside and thought I'd be just plain dead soon enough. So I didn't care about anything."

"What did she want?"

"She asked me if I liked living there."

"What?" Bret asked with a disbelieving chuckle. "That was a stupid question. You were in a dungeon, right?"

"As good a word for it as any, I guess, and, yeah, that's where I was, but I think she was trying to make a point. When I said no, she asked if I'd like a chance to leave for a few months. If she'd told me I *had* to do something, I would've fought her, gone after her, but getting out of that place was the only thing that could've interested me at that point."

"Did she get you out?"

"Yeah," Jake said. "She asked me a bunch of questions about what I did before the wars. She must have liked what she heard, 'cause she said there was a job at another home for a few months if I wanted it."

"You took it?"

"Of course," Jake said, again with a bitter laugh. "I was going to die in that hole and, as much as I kept telling myself I didn't care, I didn't want to die."

"What was the job?"

Jake smiled and his face softened. "Monica. She needed someone to finish building her house. She also needed help with her ranch and farming operation. Her previous foreman had an accident; he fell while working on the house and broke his neck. I never got the whole story. Didn't really care."

"And they found you…"

"Yeah, lucky me."

"How did they know about you in the first place?"

"I have no idea," Jake said with a shrug, "but it wasn't a secret. One of Darla's decent guards must have told someone. That would've been a short list to go through if I'd gotten the chance to figure it out, but I never did. I left that day for my new temporary home. I didn't plan to go back…ever."

"And that's when you met Monica."

"Yeah," Jake said, his smile growing a little as he explained about his time on the ranch, getting to know Monica and the others, letting his guard down. "Monica seemed…nice, but after a while, I started to suspect there was more to the conversations we had."

"She didn't seem overly subtle to me," Bret said and Jake gave him a questioning look. "We talked a bit at Angel's party. She seemed too frank to be subtle; friendly, but outspoken."

Jake laughed softly. "Yeah, that's Monica. She was…ah…feeling me out, so-to-speak. Until she finally told me she was interested." He laughed again and this time, it was a happy sound. "I'd never had a woman do that before, just tell me she found me interesting. It was…"

"Refreshing?" Bret offered when Jake struggled for the word.

Jake smiled at his friend. "Yeah, exactly. That's how it started and even though I already knew I didn't want to go back to the hell I'd left, I soon realized I didn't want to leave at all. Not because it meant I'd be going back to Darla, but because I'd have to leave Monica. I told Monica I wouldn't go, that I'd run before Darla's people came for me. She said she'd talk to Darla."

"But that didn't work."

"No, it didn't work. She couldn't afford me. When we got word that Darla had sent her guards for me, Monica sent me to the one person who could help."

"Angel," Bret said and Jake nodded.

"She made some ridiculous offer for me and, after some debate— which was more like a lot of threats and screaming—Darla finally took it. Darla hates Angel. They were already at odds, but it got worse after."

Bret cocked his head, curiosity encouraging him to ask, "Why did she do all that? She didn't even know you."

"Because Monica asked her to help. Because she felt sorry for me. Because she hates Darla and was willing to do anything that would annoy her. Your guess is as good as mine. She got me away from Darla and I could still see Monica whenever I wanted…well, whenever I could, so I didn't care.

"I know there are all kinds of rumors about me and Angel and Monica," Jake said, meeting Bret's gaze, "but most of it's crap. Angel's important to me and I'd help her through anything, but I'm not in love with her." He frowned at the strange look on Bret's face. "Do you understand now why I didn't want to leave? Why I'm willing to put up with Angel's strange moods and help her when she doesn't seem to want to help herself?"

"Yeah," Bret said slowly, "I guess I do."

"Can you see she's done the same for you?"

"Because you asked her to, Jake. She didn't do it for me."

"Bullshit," Jake said, sitting up a little straighter. "She agreed to buy you because I asked, yes, but she also wanted to help you. Don't make it into something meaningless just because it's you we're talking about. You have value, Bret. Don't let what your uncle told you make you think any different. He was wrong then and he's still wrong now."

Bret squirmed uncomfortably. Jake knew more about what Vince had beaten into him than anyone else. Sometimes, Bret regretted revealing so much, but then he'd be more screwed up now if Jake hadn't been around back then.

"It's not just that," he said, feeling defensive. "She pushes me away. Like today, she got mad because I wouldn't obey her, and now she won't even let me in the same room. That doesn't make me feel all warm and fuzzy inside."

Too late, Bret clamped his jaw shut. He'd said too much about what happened with Angel in the exam room. The implication was vague, but all Jake had to do was ask one question.

One corner of Jake's mouth crooked up. "Whatever it is," he said, "she'll get over it."

"She's still angry about my escape too," Bret said, allowing his frustration to show. "She's not going to get over that anytime soon."

"She will. You just need to show her you're willing to stay."

"Show her?"

"Yeah." Jake smiled again. "Help her. You already said you were going to do that. Do it and she'll see it. It might take a little while, but she'll get past everything else. She's fair, Bret. Give her a chance."

"Yeah," Bret mumbled. It was the least he could do. His actions had led Jake into the hell he just described. He owed Angel for saving him. Monica may have fallen in love with Jake, may have even brought him back from the brink of complete hopelessness—for which Bret was also grateful—but Angel had saved his life. Angel had rescued him from the dark hole that would have destroyed the man that Bret had known, and at no small risk to herself either.

Now she needed someone to help her and the one person she'd always been able to trust was leaving.

She must feel so alone. Bret knew that feeling all too well, but could he give her what she needed? He cared about her, knew that without a doubt and she'd said she was fond of him, but she also said she could never love him. Was he willing to risk the price he might pay? The broken heart he'd promised himself he'd never feel again?

Yes, he thought, and it didn't matter if she ever felt the same. Things between them could always change. She *was* attracted to him—the way she melted in his arms every time he kissed her was evidence of that. He could make her want him more, but that's not what he wanted. He wanted her to come to him on her own, not because he'd seduced her. Maybe if he tried, maybe if he let her see that he cared enough to help her when she needed someone so badly…

"You're going to stay, right?" Jake asked and he jumped. He'd been so lost in thought, he'd forgotten Jake was there.

"Yeah," Bret replied. "I said I would."

"But will you take care of her? Let her know she can depend on you?"

"Yes," Bret murmured, knowing he could do nothing less. "I'll do the best I can for her, Jake. That's a promise."

5

ANGEL WOKE TO THE FEEL OF HER BED beneath her and sighed as she lay on her back. Sunlight filtered through the shade of her eyelids. She had no idea what time it was or how long she'd been home, but it didn't matter.

I'm home.

A fire crackled in the fireplace and she heard voices outside working in the garden. Esther called to one of the kitchen staff to be sure to get some green onions for breakfast. *She must be making Denver Scrambles*, Angel thought, distracted by the idea of food and smiled to herself. She liked Denver Scrambles.

Other people moved in and around her house, but a rustling closer at hand heightened her awareness. She was cold. Shifting uneasily and reaching for her blankets, she struggled to open her eyes. It took a moment for her vision to focus, but when it did, she was surprised to find Bret beside her. Feeling a little groggy, she thought she might be dreaming. She blinked, but he was still there.

The sun's rays slanted into the room, lighting everything with its early morning light, which made Bret easily discernible. She wasn't seeing things and she wasn't dreaming. His handsome-self sat on the edge of her bed, concentrating on the items in his hands.

So distracted by his presence, her fuzzy mind hadn't processed beyond seeing him. When his lean fingers brushed the bare skin of her side, she started and inhaled sharply. He paused and his green eyes glanced at her face.

He smiled softly. "Ah, you're awake. Good, breakfast will be ready soon, a little late, but soon. The doctor said you need to keep your strength up."

"Doctor?" Her voice was scratchy, making the single word sound more like a croak.

"Yeah, he arrived about an hour ago. Checked on you and said you're doing fine, but you need to take care of yourself. He just left a little bit ago."

She glanced down at herself to see her nightshirt had been pulled up to expose her belly. It was pooled high on her ribcage directly below her breasts and the blankets that covered her lower half were folded diagonally across her hips. She lifted accusing eyes to his face.

"Oh, wait…" Bret said quickly and lifted a tube of some sort of ointment to show her. "It's the doctor's orders. He said your incision needed cleaning and re-bandaging. That's what I'm doing."

"I see." Angel's eyes dropped and heat infused her cheeks, which annoyed her immensely.

"How are you feeling?" Bret asked on the heels of his explanation.

"As good as can be expected, I guess."

"You look a little tired."

She glanced at him. "I feel tired," she admitted. "I can hardly keep my eyes open."

"That's probably from the medication," Bret said. "The doctor at the hospital said it will make you sleepy."

Angel merely grunted and closed her eyes.

"How are you doing otherwise?" he asked and she opened her eyes again. "Your side feeling okay?"

"It hurts a little, but okay, I guess."

Bret's gaze lowered to her incision. "It looks good," he said as his lean finger brushed her side again, and goosebumps prickled over her skin. "It's starting to heal."

"Good," she murmured, more than a little uncomfortable with the familiarity of his touch, not to mention her body's warm reaction to him. She closed her eyes and concentrated on the pain in her side. Anything to keep from staring at him and thinking about his hands on her.

With strong, gentle fingers he inspected her stitches, then slowly spread the healing ointment over the whole wound. She remembered how his hands had traveled with as much tenderness—but far more intimacy—over her whole body all those weeks ago, waking sensations inside her that had long lain dormant. She'd dreamt about the night of her birthday party several times over the last couple of days, and those memories rushed into her mind as she watched him treat her wound.

Intense clarity infused everything about that night and him. She could still feel his heat warming her skin, hear his heartbeat thudding in his chest, and see the splendor of his long, naked body as he lay next to her. Everything from his gentle hands to his muscular arms, his broad shoulders to his lean hips, his flat, muscle-ridged abdomen to his powerful thighs and sinewy calves had brushed, or pressed, or slid against her that night, and she had loved every minute of it.

As he had settled between her thighs, he hesitated, looking down at her, searching for something in her face. She'd seen the insecurity there, felt his indecision, but she'd also seen a burning desire that surprised and excited her more than she'd have thought possible. He'd driven her out of her mind with wanting him—and he seemed to have ridden that wave right along with her—but he'd paused before fully taking her body to look into her eyes. Though she wasn't sure what he'd been hoping to find, she could understand his uncertainty. But she'd stopped thinking. She hadn't wanted to think about what might happen, what her actions that night would mean for both of them. She had just wanted to feel alive again. And Bret had made her feel so very alive!

The path of her thoughts made her shiver as he carefully spread the ointment over her incision and his green eyes looked up into hers. The concern in his gaze touched her and she felt the familiar constriction in her chest.

"Are you cold?" he asked with a slight frown.

"A little," she said, telling herself that was the reason for her shivers, but she didn't believe it.

"I'm almost done," he said as he wiped his hands on a towel and then tossed it back over his shoulder. "I'll get you another blanket in a minute."

He went back to redressing her wound, opening the gauze pad and placing it over her stitches then taping it down. She watched him as he worked and felt another jolt of sadness course through her.

She'd behaved badly the morning after their glorious lovemaking, but she'd known how much of a mistake it was the moment she realized he was naked and in her bed. As much as she'd enjoyed feeling that alive again, loved being in his arms, as much as she now silently admitted she still wanted him, it couldn't be; the danger was too acute and, if she was honest, she didn't want to risk Bret's life just to fill the emptiness inside her.

It had been a mistake. She'd tried to explain that, to make it easy for him to walk away, but she'd hurt him instead. She had never expected it to affect him so strongly, or so negatively. He didn't believe her, accused her of being as bad as the other women who used their breeders as toys, which, of course, had angered and broken her heart.

Except for that hot, mind-altering kiss in his room a few days ago, he'd been distant ever since. Even when he'd been forced to spend time with her while she hid from the world and her pain, he'd been reserved. The only time that had slipped was the night he found her on the deck in the rain, but even what he'd done then was simply because she was cold. His cool attitude while he'd held her—shivering and disheartened—told her as much. The next morning was the same. If he'd felt anything for her, he wouldn't have tried to sneak out of bed. He'd simply been kind when she was weak, and that made her feel painfully unwanted.

So what's he doing here now? Could she trust him? He had once claimed to hate her. Did he still?

His fingers slid over the last piece of tape. Then he pulled her nightshirt down, dragged the covers over her, and went to grab the other blanket. A little quiver of disappointment struck her as he'd lowered her shirt. She ruthlessly squashed the sensation before it could flutter into anything more serious. Instead, she watched the masculine grace of his body as he moved across the room to her closet. Returning with the second blanket, he shook it out and arranged it over her.

Why is he helping me now? It was a logical question, but she didn't have a reasonable answer. He accused her of using him, didn't believe her explanations, and a part of her was still angry he'd denied her demands at the hospital. All she'd wanted was to be released from the pain she'd been carrying every day for almost seven years. A pain that never seemed to cease.

Thinking back to his refusal, her jaw clenched and her lips pressed together in annoyance as her anger with and disappointment in him flared anew.

Tucking the edges of the blanket around her shoulders, he met her gaze, and seeing her glower, he frowned.

"What's wrong?

"Why are you *really* here?" she asked, and he pulled back, surprised by the venom in her tone. She hadn't meant for it to sound so accusatory, but she couldn't help it. He'd lied to her before, and he'd do it again. She truly didn't understand why he was helping her. The only thing that made sense was that he planned to use it against her.

She watched him with suspicious eyes as he sat next to her again.

"I was cleaning your wound," he told her.

"Yes," she said, "but why are *you* here? Where's the doctor?"

"He's with Peggy," he replied, but at the sudden widening of her eyes, he amended his statement. "Don't worry. It's just a checkup. Nothing's wrong." He gave her a moment to let that soak in and then continued, "Since Jake's moved to Monica's, I told the doc I'd take care of changing your bandage."

"Do you even know what you're doing? What to look for?"

The strain of not responding to the angry challenge in her tone showed in the silvery glint of his eyes. "Yes, I know how to detect infection or blood poisoning. I know how to change a bandage, and I know when to have the doctor check it himself. I told you, he was here earlier this morning and had no problem allowing me to take care of you while he was with Peggy."

"Oh," she said and looked away.

SHE LOOKS PALE AND TIRED, Bret thought as her eyelids slid closed then fluttered open to glare at him again. *And angry, too.*

"You're still here," she said, her eyes shooting blue sparks. "Are you enjoying my pain? Why aren't you halfway to the mountains by now? Ah, right, you already had your chance to be free of me."

He knew what she was referring to, could see her still fuming over his refusal to help her leave the hospital. She didn't trust him or his motives now, and he couldn't blame her.

"Why wouldn't you just take me home?" her voice cracked and she sounded wretched as her sad azure eyes gazed up at him.

"You were sick," he told her., "I couldn't just take you home. You needed a doctor."

"I needed you to do as you were told!" She winced and pressed a hand to her side.

"I wasn't going to help you die, Angel."

"Why not?" she asked weakly but with no less heat. "I know you dislike me. I know you plan to run, so why not make it easy on yourself? No one would have known you were gone until it was too late."

"Because it would've been murder," he replied.

It was her turn to stare dumbfounded. Then she shook her head slowly, dismissing his comment. "It would *not* have been murder," she told him.

"Really?" he asked and felt his temper rise to the surface as he snorted derisively. "You don't get it, do you?" He paused a moment to see if she would respond. When she just glared at him, he stood, paced a few steps away, and then turned. "What would the doctors and nurses at the hospital have called it? Hmm? What about those women who serve on the council with you? And what about the people here, what would they've called it? What would Jake have called it?"

He'd thought mentioning Jake would give her pause, but it didn't.

"I don't care about the others," she said slowly, tiredly, "and Jake would've understood. The people here would've taken their cue from him."

Bret stood, arms dangling at his sides, green eyes gawking, his mind stumbling to a disbelieving halt at her stupefyingly inaccurate statement.

Did she actually *believe that?* He couldn't tell if she was being deliberately obtuse or if the pain-killers had something to do with it. It took him a moment, but when his mind kicked into gear again, he moved back to the bed to sit beside her once more.

"Darlin', if you believe that, then you don't know Jake at all," he said, choosing his words carefully. He rested his palm on her shoulder, but she shrugged it off and scowled at him. He dropped his hands in his lap and sighed, his gaze shifting away and then back again. "He absolutely would not have understood, Angel. Jake would've never forgiven me. And I wouldn't have asked him to."

Her eyes narrowed as she searched his face, clearly not ready to believe him. He could see exhaustion creeping in on her, but she obviously didn't want him to win this argument by default.

"You're so full of it," she said, shaking her head. "You don't care about any of that. You know Jake would've gotten over it—he loves you too much not to. You don't care about me or what others would have called it. The only reason you didn't help me was because *I made you a slave.*" Her voice took on a nasal quality for the last five words, mimicking his remarks from numerous times before. "Because I wouldn't let you leave. I wouldn't let you have your freedom, so you wouldn't help me have mine!"

His eyes narrowed and she smiled in triumphant satisfaction.

"What kind of man do you think I am?" Bret asked, every muscle in his body tense with irritation.

"One who wants his freedom at any cost," she retorted.

Heat washed through him at the ridiculousness of her accusation and he wondered if she disliked him as much as her cold reply indicated or if she really thought he'd harm her to get what he wanted?

Then his shoulders drooped and his fury deflated like a punctured balloon. He'd cultivated her opinion about him by his words and actions over the last several months. How could he condemn her now for what he'd given her every reason to believe?

"Almost," he corrected, his voice deliberately soft. "Yes, I want my freedom, but not at any cost. I do have limits."

"Right," she said as her eyes closed drowsily. "You're too selfish for limits."

"Angel?" he called, half-expecting to get no response, but she opened her eyes and met his gaze. "I don't hate you and I don't want to hurt you. If either of those things weren't true, I would've done what you asked long before you asked me to do it…and not by letting sickness kill you. I'd be a completely different man if I'd done what you asked. That's not me."

"You're a liar," she said, her sleepy eyes looking at him sadly and he was shocked to see a tear slide down her cheek. "You lied to me. I can't believe you now."

"I know, and I'm sorry about that," he said as he brushed her tear away with his thumb.

She grimaced at his touch and he pulled away as she shook her head.

"I *am* sorry," he tried again.

"I'm tired, Bret," she said and her eyelids slid closed. "Go away. I need to sleep." He watched for a moment, but her eyes didn't open and her even breathing told him she'd fallen asleep.

"All right, darlin'," he murmured, pulling the blanket back up under her chin. "You sleep. We'll talk later."

6

ANGEL OPENED HER EYES to a sea of ghostly shadows in a storm of silence. Nothing moved in the murky room, even the hearth had burned low and gone quiet. She blinked several times sleepily, still groggy, trying to clear her vision and get some idea of the time.

Something had disturbed her sleep. Maybe it was a dream, maybe the wind, maybe a coyote had howled nearby. She couldn't remember, but now that she was awake, the room felt gloomy and oppressive. Recognizing her own bed beneath her, warmth and safety replaced the dread that had crept over her.

She glanced around. A silver lining of moonlight showed faintly around the curtains drawn over the windows and French doors.

Who closed them? she wondered. *And how long have I been asleep?*

She caught movement out of the corner of her eye and her head snapped forward. A man stood at the end of her bed. She could just discern his tall, broad-shouldered form, arms crossed over his chest, a shoulder propped against the end-post of her bed frame.

A little frisson of fear swirled in her belly.

"Howdy," he said, and she sighed inwardly. She'd know Bret's voice anywhere.

"Hi," she replied, oddly disconcerted by his presence in the dark. Unsure what else to say, she pressed her lips together and kept quiet.

Eyeing him, she couldn't help but remember what she'd begged Bret to do at the hospital. She'd still been angry with him when she woke last, but now her mind wasn't so fogged with pain and memories.

She had wanted to blame him for her suffering, but it wasn't his fault. Strangely, when her mind cleared and she'd stopped blaming him, her resolve to end it all had also disappeared. Not that she felt any better than she had last year, but something inside her had changed.

Maybe Jake had been right and time had begun to heal her pain—or maybe the drugs that deadened the ache in her side had dulled her wits as well. Maybe she'd started to forget Michael and the fact that he'd saved her.

That night, years ago, when he'd found her tied to a tree, her dead family spread out around her, a part of her had already died and gone cold. Michael's patient affection had slowly melted the ice around her heart and brought her back to life. They'd been so young, so idealistic, thinking they could make a difference somehow, but they hadn't. In the end, their ardent fantasy had cost Michael his life and left her more cold and hollow than before.

Michael had loved her, but Bret was just an unreasonably handsome man who didn't give a damn about what she needed or wanted, or what she was trying to do, only how it impacted him. She knew that; yet, everything he'd said the last time they spoke had held a ring of truth.

She tilted her head. Maybe something had changed for Bret too; not that she would ask—he'd only use it against her. Still, he had seemed…different.

Staring back at him through the darkness of her room, she realized with a sinking sensation that she wanted to trust Bret. She wanted to know him. She wanted…

"How are you feeling?" he asked, still leaning against her bed, his deep voice breaking into her thoughts, warming her. Yearning washed over her and settled in her chest.

Through the shadowy gloom, she could just make out the hard contours of his chiseled face and wished she could see him better.

"Still sore and tired," she replied, suddenly thankful for the blackness to hide her unease.

"That's the meds," he told her, evidently thinking she didn't recall his earlier explanation. "The doc said it would make you tired."

She nodded and they fell silent once more.

"What time is it?"

"Late," he told her. "After eleven."

She frowned. "What are you doing here?"

He chuckled softly, and prickles pebbled her skin. She loved his laugh.

"Well, you seemed okay this morning, but I wanted to check in again before going to bed."

She nodded again, then blurted out the next intelligible thought that came to her, "How is everything?"

"Don't worry," he said, and she could hear the smile in his voice, "everything's fine. We'll take care of the ranch until you're feeling better."

That "we'll" struck her as odd, considering his desire to be gone from the place, but it made her feel warm in ways she didn't want to think about as well. Fortunately, she was too tired to think.

Silence fell once more. Then she remembered her conversation with Jake before he and Monica left the hospital.

"Jake told me you're going to stay and…help out." A fist clamped down on her heart as she waited for his reply.

He shifted his feet. "Yeah."

Almost what she wanted to hear, but not enough. "For how long?"

"For as long as you need me."

"What does that *mean*, Bret?"

"It means exactly what I said." He sounded puzzled.

She sighed in frustration. "But how long exactly?" Her voice gained in pitch as she spoke, her throat growing thick with dread. "Until I'm back on my feet? Until I can ride again? Next week. Next month. Next summer? When will you run again?"

He stared at her through the shadows and her nerves stretched taut.

"I'm here until you tell me to leave," he said a moment later.

"Really?" She sounded as dubious as she felt.

"Yes, really," he said, clearly perturbed. "I gave Jake my word, now I'll give it to you. As long as you don't abuse me, I'll stay until you tell me to leave. I give you my word." He said the last sentence quickly as if he didn't want her to interrupt before he could get it out.

Angel frowned, and her mouth hung open in stunned confusion.

Bret keeps his promises... Jake's voice from long ago echoed inside her head.

"Wh-Why?" she asked. "You've spent the better part of this year planning to run and trying to get away. Why trap yourself like that? Why give me your word?"

He smiled, his teeth flashing in the darkness, but Angel couldn't see him clearly enough to read its meaning.

"You may not have noticed," he said, humor rippling through his low voice, "but I'm a little...stubborn sometimes..."

Angel laughed at the obvious understatement and then, wrapping her arms around her midsection, groaned at the shooting pain it caused in her side. "Oh, don't make me laugh!"

Bret grinned at her again. "I see you've noticed." A hint of playfulness still imbued in his tone, but his voice grew grave as he continued, "Well, I am stubborn, and I know it. But when I'm wrong—even if it takes me a while to see it—I *will* admit it."

His admission left her speechless.

Staring through the murkiness, she silently wished for a light.

A moment later, his boots thudded on the hardwood floor and his scent of leather and hay and musky-man filled her senses. The sound of glass tapping metal hit her ears. Then the scrape of a match along her bedside table, and a flame sparked to life. Sulfur tickled her nose as the small flicker illuminated the strong, perfect lines of Bret's profile. Then the wick caught and spilled light over them both.

She blinked in the lantern's brightness. *Is he a mind reader now?*

He set the lamp's chimney back in place, then straightened to his full height. Stepping back, he braced his legs slightly apart and crossed his arms over his chest before meeting her gaze. His hair was mussed as if he'd been running his hands through it, and his blue shirt and jeans were wrinkled as if he'd slept in them. He looked tired and even a little sad, and it made her heart ache. He seemed so forlorn it broke her heart, and so damn gorgeous it made her mouth water. She wanted to say something, anything to hear him chuckle again, but her brain wouldn't form intelligent sentences and her voice seemed to have abandoned her.

"I know what you did for me," the solemn honesty in his words made her eyes burn, "and I know you didn't have to do it. My situation…" He paused, glancing away as if to find the right words, before refocusing on her face. "My life," he amended, "would be very different now if you hadn't bought me at that auction." His eyes were as genuinely open as she had ever seen them, and he didn't stutter over the phrasing for what had happened to him.

He wasn't lying or trying to manipulate her.

"But you've always known that," she said through her constricted throat.

"I knew things were bad, but I hadn't realized how…cruel and sadistic they could be."

"Ah," she murmured, "Jake told you about Darla."

"Yes," he said, shifting his feet, "but that's not the only reason."

"You know," she said, tilting her head as she looked up at him, "you mean more to him than you realize."

He frowned. "Why do you say that?"

"Because," she said seriously, "Jake and I are close, but he never told me the whole story of what happened to him at Darla's. I just put the bits and pieces together with what I know about her."

Bret nodded, not meeting her eyes.

"So, what's the other reason?" Angel asked.

Bret looked confused when he met her gaze again.

"You said, knowing how bad things could be wasn't the only reason. What's the other reason?"

BRET DROPPED HIS EYES and fidgeted, the internal argument he'd been having all day abruptly raging to life once more. Should he tell her how he felt? Should he keep it hidden? Should he make himself that vulnerable or put distance between his battered heart and this woman who had somehow wormed her way into it. He lifted his head and met her gaze. He'd already made his decision and now was as good a time as any to face it.

"I don't want anything to happen to you," he said, his throat dry as dust and he cleared it. "Not just because of what it would mean for me, but everyone else too." He thought about saying more, delving further into the abyss of his emotions, but his jaw clamped shut and nothing more came.

Angel's delicate brow furrowed and her lips rolled inward, doubt plain on her face. "And after everything you've said and done, that would indicate that's a lie," she said, "how am I supposed to believe you?"

He sat next to her, one arm braced beside her hip, and leaned toward her. "I told you, I was wrong. I care what happens here, what happens to everyone," he hesitated for the briefest moment, his uncertainty crushing his ribs, but he pressed on, "I care what happens to you, Angel. I don't want to see you hurt. I don't want to see you die. And I don't want to walk away tonight letting you think anything different."

Her eyes widened in surprise and guilt flashed across her face. She dropped her chin. "I'd thought you'd jump at the chance to be rid of me," she murmured. "It never occurred to me, until now, how wrong I'd been about that." She looked up and his heart clenched at the unshed tears in her eyes. "I'm so sorry I did that to you."

He frowned and trepidation tickled the back of his mind, unsure what exactly she meant.

"I shouldn't have asked you to...do that," she said with a grimace and a shake of her head. "I shouldn't have...demanded you help me leave the hospital. It wasn't fair of me, and it wasn't right for me to be angry with you afterward either. It isn't your problem and I shouldn't have made it be. I'm sorry. I'm sorry I laid that all on you." She looked up, her eyes pleading forgiveness, seeming so small and defenseless tucked into her huge bed.

As surprised by her apology as she had seemed to be by his admissions, his frown slowly slipped away and he swallowed mechanically.

"Look," he said, steeling himself, "I gave you my word that I'd stay, but I…need you to do something for me."

"And what's that?" she asked, narrowing her eyes suspiciously.

His mouth went dry and he remained quiet for several seconds, the tension building between them again as a mixture of emotions swirled inside him. *Should I do this? Am I ready?* He inhaled sharply and Angel did the same.

"Don't give up," he rasped, his concern for her pushing him to speak. "Talk to me, I can help you."

She stared at him, tears flooding her eyes, and then she turned away.

His gut clenched at the pain he saw on her face.

"I don't talk about it," she mumbled, then met his eyes again. "Ever. It…hurts too much."

"Angel," he said, soft and low as he reached out to brush a stray coil of her silky black hair from her cheek, but she shook her head and hurried on before he could say more.

"It's not your problem, Bret, and talking about it won't make it go away. It just makes it worse."

"You don't have to do it alone," he told her, curling his hand around her upper arm.

She was trembling, struggling with her emotions.

He smiled at her tenderly, wanting to let her know that everything would be all right. "I know you've lost something…someone important to you," he said, "we all have. But we don't want to lose you too. I have a little experience in dealing with loss, in case you don't remember."

"Your mom and dad?" she whispered and he nodded.

"I know what it feels like. Jake helped me, but now Jake's not here to help you, and that's my fault. So let me take his place. Let me help you."

She gawked at him as if he'd grown a second head. "Who *are* you? What do you want? And what happened to the arrogant jerk I've come to know?"

He chuckled and the corners of her mouth curved upward.

"Okay, if you can't talk about it," he said, "then just tell me when things get bad. Let me be there for you. I won't let you down, not now."

A long, tense few seconds ticked by, insecurity, doubt, fear, all building inside him, wondering what she would do. What she would say. Whether she would believe him, trust him enough to let him in.

Suddenly, the damn broke and huge tears spilled down her face. "Why?" she choked out, her body shaking. "Why do you care now?"

His shoulders drooped and he sighed in mild frustration. "Do you have to qualify everything?" he asked with a teasing grin, but then he sobered and answered her question. "Because Jake asked me to do it. Because I actually want to do it. Because I should've been more grateful sooner. Because you need someone. What else do you want to hear?"

She still looked pale and tired and in pain, but now her sorrow seemed to stretch her thin to the point of frailty. He reached out to wipe her tears away and frowned at her trembling.

"Are you cold?" he asked, placing his palm on her forehead, and then resting it against her damp cheek.

She stared back at him, her eyes big and soft and so blue he felt himself falling into that sea of vulnerable beauty. And this time, he didn't fight it.

Suddenly, she turned her face into his hand and kissed his palm, her tongue flicking out to tickle his skin.

A lightning bolt of awareness shot through his body and he inhaled sharply. His hand tingled and the sensation traveled up his arm, into his chest, warming him, and his skin suddenly felt too tight for his frame.

"I'm not cold," she murmured, her soft gaze locked with his. "And I shouldn't believe you, shouldn't trust you, but…I do." She stared up at him, her eyes big and wide and filled with something he couldn't quite define. Love, lust, promise, truth, he didn't dare assume what lay behind her actions.

"What was that for?" he whispered, the shape and petal-softness of her lips still burning his hand.

She gave a weak smile. "For the truth. For finally accepting that I only wanted to help you. For wanting to help me."

He sat stiffly, watching her eyes grow cloudy with anxiety the longer he remained silent.

Every part of him sensed her closeness, the way her side pressed into his thigh, the way her cheek nuzzled his hand, her slow inhalation, her silky hair brushing his fingers. All of it tempting, inviting.

He clenched his jaw but remained still. The air between them sparked with tension, awareness, and need. But he couldn't take advantage of her like that, not now that she'd opened up. If only a little, it was more than he'd ever gotten from her before.

He wiped away the last of her tears, sat back, and smiled. "You still look tired," he said, dropping his hand on his thigh. "You should go back to sleep."

"Yeah," she agreed, her eyes drifting closed. He pulled the blanket up to her chin and stood, intending to get some sleep himself.

"Bret?" Her murmur brought him up short.

"Yeah?" He leaned toward her.

She blinked sleepily then focused on him. "Thank you…" It was barely a whisper as her eyes closed again.

"You're very welcome," he said quietly.

He stood and gazed at her sleeping face, wondering if he was making the right choice for the right reason. His heart trembled at the thought that he was being a fool and fear pecked at the warmth that had filled his chest, but he wasn't going to change his mind. He'd given his word and he would honor it. He just had to hope that Jake— and his own instinct—was correct.

Bending at the waist, he blew out the bedside lamp. He glanced at the bed one last time, unable to see Angel, but comforted to know she was there. He took a deep breath of the lilac-scented air, then turned and quietly left the room. His thoughts still raced and his heart still feared the pain he may have just opened himself to, but his mind was made up.

Turn the page for sneak peak in *Masters' Promise*,
Book 3 of the Angel Eyes series.

Masters' Promise
The Angel Eyes Series Book 3

The Weeping Willow

1

ANGEL ALDRIDGE LAY ON HER BACK, staring at the canopy of her oversized four-poster bed, waiting for the man who'd been a pain in the rear ever since he'd come to live on her ranch. Bret had mentioned last night when he brought her dinner that Michelle would be bringing her morning meal because he'd be taking his breakfast in the dining hall downstairs today.

"I want to check in with everyone, see how things are going with the ranch," he'd said. She'd heard his words but had been mesmerized by his mouth, the perfect shape of his lips, wishing she could taste them, measure their texture once again.

Instead, she had dragged her eyes away and shrugged. "Sounds good to me."

That hadn't been entirely true. She'd grown accustomed to his company and a little pang of regret struck her when he'd told her his plan.

But it was now after noon of the next day, and her stomach had reminded her several times already that lunch was late.

What's taking him so long? A little niggle of guilt tugged in her chest at that thought, but she stifled it. Bret had brought his circumstances on himself. It wasn't her fault that he'd chosen to run and then get caught by the Section Guards. To protect the others on the ranch, Angel had done what was necessary. Though Bret chafed under the order, she'd picked the best option available to her to punish him for his escape attempt. No way would she resort to the physical abuse other women used to discipline their enslaved men, but banning Bret from leaving the homestead walls and assigning him to take over Jake's duties within those walls had created another problem for her to deal with. Having his tempting self around and up-close several times a day, wreaked havoc on her self-control, but what else could she do?

Nothing...

Rolling onto her side, she groaned at the pain that lanced through her lower abdomen. A couple of days had passed since she'd undergone surgery to remove her appendix. The incision was only a few inches in length, but every movement made it feel as if she'd been stabbed repeatedly with something very large.

Sighing with the frustration of being bedridden and for having to accept Bret's help to do the most menial of things—like using the restroom, brushing her teeth, or just sitting upright—she began to stack pillows against her headboard in preparation for his arrival with her afternoon meal.

Her appetite had increased over the last few days, a stark contrast to her total lack of it before she'd gotten sick. Still, darkness loomed on the fringes of her mood and sometimes she worried that it might overwhelm her again, make her do and demand irrational things.

Bret, please, let me go... Let me die... Her words from the hospital when they'd been alone rang hollowly in her mind.

Bret's gentle voice followed. *I'm sorry, darlin', I can't do that...*

Angel punched one of her pillows especially hard and moaned when another slice of pain ripped through her. It hurt, but not as much as the remorse that sat like an anvil in her chest.

She should've never demanded Bret's help at the hospital, but she'd been so lost, so tired and afraid, and the pain had been excruciating. At the time, she hadn't cared about anything but ending her suffering—

not from her inflamed appendix, but from the horror of her past. The physical pain had simply amplified the loneliness and guilt that she'd carried inside for so long. It had been too much, and she'd been sucked into the black hole of dread and despair. Bret had been the light that brought her back from the brink. Essentially, he'd saved her life. Again.

The pillows in place, Angel braced herself for the discomfort of pushing her body into an upright position. She didn't want to rely on Bret to help her again. Being in his arms, even for something so small, triggered things in her body she didn't want to deal with. Hell, just thinking about it had goosebumps running up and down her arms.

Stop thinking about it, she scolded herself as she struggled.

A few minutes later, upright and relatively comfortable, she pressed her hand to her injured side and groaned. Concentrating on her breathing, she waited for the ache to dissipate as she sat against the pillows.

Her stomach growled. Bret should be there any minute with her lunch. His tardiness wasn't normal, but considering how much time he'd been spending with her and not dealing with the ranch, she shouldn't be surprised catching up took longer than he'd expected.

Not for the first time, she wondered at his attentiveness. He'd been kind to her before, helped her through bouts of unhappiness and had refused to listen to her idle threats or allow her to act like a child. He'd fought with her, shouted at her, done everything he could to make her eat, and she'd never really thanked him for any of it.

Then she'd gotten sick.

Remembering their conversation after returning home, Angel squirmed in place, careful not to upset her wound. Bret had been so sweet when she'd awakened in her bed. And he'd finally admitted that she'd saved his life when she bought him at the auction. He finally understood that had Darla Cain won him, his life would've been filled with misery.

The real shocker, however, had fallen on the heels of that admission.

I care what happens to you, Angel. I don't want to see you hurt. I don't want to see you die. And I don't want to walk away tonight letting you think anything different.

Heat gathered in her chest and rushed upward. Guilt and shame still hounded her for her actions. Not only for thinking he would jump at *any* chance to be free of her, but for his offer of aid when they'd returned home. Only two days before, he'd sat beside her on this bed and practically begged her to allow him to take Jake's place.

Let me be there for you. I won't let you down, not now.

Her chest tightened. She'd been tempted, but she couldn't open that door where all her secrets lay, couldn't share the regret and pain.

Bret hadn't been discouraged though and, in the end, had pushed through her wall of doubt and moved her battered heart to forgiveness and hope. She hadn't wanted to believe him—he had lied to her, after all—but he'd been so sincere, she couldn't help herself.

She'd kissed his hand when he'd reached out to wipe her tears away and when their eyes met again, sparks of awareness and something else, something new, danced between them.

Warmth filled her chest and a soft, fuzzy kind of something swirled around inside it. Could he really be the man she'd fantasized about for all those years?

Angel shook her head and reached for the book she'd been reading earlier.

It was silly to think she and Bret could get past all the baggage between them, but there for a minute, as she'd stared into his beautiful green eyes, she'd been foolish enough to think so. Her heart had fluttered and the possibilities had seemed…real. Even their conversations since had given her the sense of amiability growing between them. Despite being too foggy-headed from the pain meds to really remember the last couple of days in detail, she remembered the lightness in her chest, the warmth of his gaze, and the smiles that he'd brought to her face with his friendly teasing.

He was more than just a handsome man, so much more, and she'd be hard-pressed to think of him as selfish now. Not after all he'd done for her and the ranch. Not after his admissions of caring for both.

Opening her book to where she'd left off, she shook her head and reminded herself to be careful. If she kept thinking down that path, she could easily fall in love with him.

As if you're not half-way there already, her conscious taunted, and she sighed, her shoulders slumping a little. Maybe that was true, but maybe the rest of it was too. His promises and additional offers of aid, his apparent willingness to put himself out for her in ways he never had before, had touched her more deeply than her old fantasies about him could.

Her stomach growled again and she glanced at the grandfather clock beside her bedroom door.

"Hurry up, Bret," she muttered, dropping her eyes to her book once more. Ignoring the flutter of expectation in her belly and the warmth that swirled through her whole body at the thought of seeing him soon, she tried to lose herself in her book.

Bret would come and she'd play her part as amicable friend, but deep inside, she knew what she wanted. What she didn't know was whether she would ever get past her grievous losses or if she could ever truly trust Bret enough to let him into her heart.

2

BRET MASTERS MADE HIS WAY up the stairs with Angel's meal on a large tray in his hands. Despite his internal compulsion to hurry, he moved slowly to keep everything he carried balanced. Upon reaching the second floor landing, he carefully rolled his shoulders to loosen the tension that had gathered there. He hated being late, especially with Angel. Even more so since he'd tied himself to her with promises to stay as long as she needed him. He had warned her of his absence this morning, but he hadn't planned to be late with her lunch and his conscious gnawed at him, spurring him forward.

His cowboy boots echoed quietly on the hardwood even with the long carpet that covered the hallway as he strolled toward Angel's bedroom. A wave of unease washed over him, chilling his skin when he stopped at her door. He expected to find an annoyed and hungry woman waiting impatiently for him to bring her meal. Would she start a fight? Or had she really accepted his word to help her?

Taking a deep breath, he knocked and entered at her invitation.

His muscles tightened as he went inside, preparing for the worst, but instead of an angry frown, Angel was sitting up in bed, a plethora of pillows stacked behind her back, wearing her white pajamas, and reading a book. He hesitated, a fit of nervous butterflies fluttering in his stomach as that lilac scent that always followed her invaded his brain and made his heart thud in his chest. When she smiled, marked her page, and put the book aside, everything inside him loosened and he breathed a little easier.

"Hi," she said, and he grinned.

"Sorry it took me so long," he said as he kicked the door closed and sauntered over to the bed.

"It's okay," she replied and patted the book now lying on the mattress beside her. "I was plenty entertained."

"How you feeling?" he asked as he set the tray in her lap and then crossed the room to quickly build-up the fire

"Sore."

He nodded as he tossed two more logs onto the dwindling flames. "That should get better soon. The doctor told me this morning that you should be able to move around on your own in a few days and be on your feet next week." Finished with the fire, he pulled the wing-backed chair away from the hearth and closer to the bed, then slouched back in it. "You still look a little pale to me though."

"I'm still tired too," she said before tucking a forkful of macaroni salad into her mouth. She'd already devoured half of her lunch.

"You need to rest," he told her. "You've been through a lot in the last few days."

"Yeah, but between that and the meds, I feel like I'm asleep all the time. I hate it."

"It'll only be for a few more days. Enjoy it while you can."

She nodded and kept eating, but he sensed she was holding back. Something in the way her body had tensed at his comment and the slight pause he wouldn't have seen if he hadn't been watching her closely made him wonder if she didn't have other reasons for not wanting to sleep.

"I meant to thank you," he said after a couple of minutes of her fork tapping against her plate and the fire licking at the new logs.

She looked over at him quizzically. "For what?"

He squirmed a little in the chair, suddenly uncomfortable with the topic, but he wanted to get it out. "For keeping Carrie's guards from tearing my arms off," he said half-joking and half-serious. After Jake's retelling of his time with Carrie, Bret realized what they'd done to him could've been much worse without Angel's intervention. "You must've been in a lot of pain at the time too."

"I couldn't let them hurt you like that," she said after swallowing the last of her meal and fixing him with a solemn stare. "Didn't matter how much I hurt."

He nodded. "Well, I appreciate it. So, thanks."

"No problem." Angel grinned but it faded in a blink. "She'll be back though. She'll want to punish you for what you did."

"She broke Jake's arm," he said more defensively than he'd intended. "What was I supposed to do?"

"I wasn't blaming you, Bret," she said pushing the tray aside, "just stating a fact."

He shook his head and sighed. "I know." Dread rolled in his belly like a marble in a shaken paint can, but he kept his voice steady when he asked, "What'll she want to do to me?"

"I don't know," Angel replied. "Nothing good, I'm sure."

When she met his gaze, he could see his fear of Carrie mirrored in her eyes, but something more too. Though, he had no idea what that could be.

"She has to get my approval first," Angel explained, almost impulsively as if needing to say something, "and I'll do the best I can to protect you, Bret. I swear."

He nodded and dropped his gaze to the floor. So, that's the other part of what she feared—protecting him. How was he supposed to feel about that? This friendliness they'd adopted over the last couple of days was all fine and good, but how far would it go? That look in her eyes squeezed the knot of apprehension in his chest even more, but something about hiding behind Angel didn't sit well with him. His jaw tightened just thinking about it. But how much choice did he have? If Angel was afraid of what Carrie would do for his lapse in judgment, he should be terrified.

"How's everyone doing?" Angel asked, interrupting his disturbing thoughts.

"Good," he said, meeting her gaze and then gave her a rundown on what had happened since she'd gotten sick.

She yawned and he wrapped up his report.

"I'm sorry," she said. "I was listening. I'm just getting sleepy." She blinked slowly.

Bret stood and went to gather the tray. "Don't worry about it," he said as he straightened. "I was done anyway." He gave her a grin and she inhaled sharply. Her eyes dilated and he glanced at her slightly parted lips—so plush and soft, he resisted the urge to kiss her. "Do you need some help lying down?"

"Yes, please." She sounded breathless.

"All right, hang tight," he said as he turned and set the tray down on the dresser near the door while she rearranged the pillows behind her. He returned to the bed and, seeing her grimace, stepped in. "Let me get the rest." He leaned in to move the pillows. "Okay, ready?"

She sighed. "Yeah."

"What's wrong?"

A small smile curled her lips as she shook her head. "Nothing's wrong. I just know this is going to hurt."

"I'll do my best not to hurt you. Okay?" The look she gave him unsettled his hard-won calm. There was too much need, too much trust, too much vulnerability in her eyes. He didn't want to hurt her, but he hadn't realized how seriously he'd meant it until he saw that look.

She smiled tiredly and stifled another yawn. "I appreciate that."

Heat crawled up his neck as he wiped his hands against his jeans and returned her smile as he leaned over her. "No problem. Now, put your arms around my neck." She did as he instructed and he wrapped his arms around her shoulders and beneath her knees. Carefully, he lifted and repositioned her on the bed. She gasped and her fingers tightened on his shoulders, digging into his muscles. He froze and pulled back to frown at her suddenly pallid face. Her eyes were closed, her breathing a little labored, and she trembled, but then her lids fluttered open and she met his concerned gaze with a weary smile.

"Are you all right?" he asked, his voice raspy.

She nodded. "Yeah."

"Are you sure? Maybe I should check your stitches."

She shook her head. "They're fine, Bret. It just hurt for a second. It's okay now. Will you help me lay back?"

"Sure." Resting his knee on the bed and holding her close, he slowly lowered her back onto the mattress, his eyes locked on hers. The lilac scent was stronger this close to her. He tried to ignore it and the emotions that fragrance stirred up inside him. Her body trembled in his arms and something inside him pulled tight.

Flat on her back, he propped himself above her, but couldn't make himself pull away. Their bodies were only inches apart, the soft pressure of her hip and thigh pressed into his side and her hardened nipples brushed his chest. Was she as turned on as he was right now? Or was it just the chill in the room her body was reacting to? He hoped it was the former.

Her arms brushed his ribcage and her hands splayed out over his shoulder blades. Neither of them moved, they barely breathed. Bret felt that irresistible pull again, a crackle of tension drawing them together.

Angel swallowed and then wet her lips with the tip of her tongue and his eyes followed the movement hungrily as his body tightened. The overwhelming urge to kiss her swept through him once more.

"Thanks," she whispered, breaking the spell.

He went cold then hot, mentally kicked himself for being distracted. She was still ill and needed rest. He was supposed to be caring for her, not lusting after her. Quelling the uproar in his body, he put all thoughts of kissing her out of his mind. Well, at least as much as he could.

"Sure," he said. "Anytime." He pushed back and delicately pulled his arm from beneath her, being careful not to tangle her hair around the buttons on the cuff of his shirt.

"Not just for that," she said, her words made him pause in his effort to get off the bed.

He lifted a curious eyebrow and she sighed.

"Thanks for the meals, the conversation, your report on the ranch, and all the time you've spent with me. It's hard to sit in here alone all day, not knowing what's going on and not being able to go and find out for myself. I really appreciate all you're doing…all you've done. I don't think I thanked you before."

"It's not a problem," he said, his chest warming and puffing up a little bit with her gratitude. "Just doing my job." He smiled again and pushed up to his feet. "Now, you need your rest and I'll let you get to it. I'll see you at dinner."

BRET CLOSED THE DOOR behind him, but in Angel's head, he was still kneeling beside her on the bed. Something had happened between them as he held her, she'd felt it and was certain he had as well. For a moment, she'd thought he was going to kiss her and she'd wanted him to, but she couldn't encourage that. She kept trying to remind herself why she couldn't accept what he had to offer. Carrie's impending retribution should've been enough, but it wasn't.

She could still feel the heat of his body inches from her own and how her body had trembled his touch. Her breasts barely caressing his broad chest had sent a thrill through her, sparking small prickles of anticipation all the way down to her toes. His body was so big, so firm, so different from her own, and she couldn't help but remember the long length of him lying heavily against her in the ultimate intimacy.

Biting her lip, she let her mind wander back to their night together. Just for a moment, heat suffused her skin, she tingled all over, and then she locked it all away in a dark vault in her mind.

A wide yawn cracked her jaws and she shook her head. *I've got to stop fantasizing about him.* Bret was no longer just a story about a smart, attractive, interesting man. He was real and she didn't want him to pay for her inability to keep her distance. If Carrie did come for him, and even suspected anything was between Angel and Bret, he would pay dearly, and she would be forced to witness whatever punishment Carrie imposed.

She yawned again and closed her eyes.

She had to forget how secure his arms made her feel when they were wrapped around her, and how his hot kisses made her body burn with long denied need. She had to stop dreaming about him altogether, both the fantasies and the nightmares, though she wasn't sure how she was supposed to do that.

Maybe if I stop thinking about him all the damn time, she thought and sighed again.

Weariness, took hold and she began to relax, and, as happier days of her youth danced behind her eyelids, sleep took her.

* * *

Gasping, struggling for each breath as if she were being strangled, her eyes snapped open to blackness. The constriction of her throat muscles kept her from screaming out her pain and fear for the whole world to hear. Luckily, she was choking on it instead. Covered in sweat, with her heart still hammering violently in her chest, she concentrated on slowing her runaway breathing. Sometime while she slept, she had risen and was now sitting on the edge of the bed, shivering uncontrollably. The tremendous ache in her side, most likely due to kicking at the blankets and moving under her own power, made her whimper and hold her hand over it protectively. Tears streamed down her face as she lifted her nightshirt to check her incision. Somehow, she'd managed not to pull any of her stitches and though there was a small amount of blood on the bandage, it was nothing serious.

She dropped her shirt and looked around, her hand once again pressed protectively against her side.

"At least I'm still in my room," she mumbled, though the heavy ball of dread in her belly didn't abate. Where did her sleep-dazed mind think it was taking her?

It had only been a dream, but she was fully awake now and she knew where she had been going, who she'd been going to find.

I am awake, she reminded herself, *and Bret is asleep, safe in his own bed.*

A little sob escaped as a tremor of foreboding shot through her. Her stomach roiled as the memory of her nightmare and what Carrie had done to Bret popped into her head.

"Oh, God," she mumbled to herself, tears still falling, "what am I going to do?"

Her uncertainty over her feelings for Bret wasn't a question anymore. She cared for him and not just as a friend. She wanted him! She wanted to hold him, have him by her side, see his face before she fell asleep at night and be the first thing she saw every morning. But having him with her was the one thing she shouldn't want.

She sighed again and carefully laid back on the bed. Her side shrieked with pain, but she ignored it as best she could while positioning herself. Physical exhaustion nearly matched the emotional turmoil inside her as she pulled the blankets up and quietly stared at the bed's canopy, afraid to close her eyes. What if her nightmare actually happened? *Carrie can be brutal... If she finds out how important Bret is to me...*

Another whimper of fear bubbled up from her throat. Angel would have to curtail Carrie's actions to keep her from killing or maiming him.

If she comes for him. A derisive laugh bounced off the walls of her room and Angel groaned, pressing her hand against her aching side. "Of course, Carrie will come for him," Angel murmured into the dark. "It's what she came for in the first place!"

* * *

Look for the rest of this complex continuing story in Book 3,
Masters' Promise.
Scheduled for release in 2021.
Or, if you haven't read it yet, check out Jake's Redemption.
Turn the page to find out more about it..

* * *

Award-winner in the Global Ebook Awards

An imprisoned cowboy.
An empowered woman.
When true love is forbidden,
opening their hearts could destroy them
both...

Chained and enslaved, Jake Nichols is convinced he'll die alone. In this new order where men are stripped of all power, he endures brutal torture at the hands of his female captor. But when he's hired out to build a ranch home for an outspoken beauty, his dreams of escape transform into visions of passion.

Monica Avery struggles to fill her heart in a loveless society. With marriage outlawed and romantic partners reduced to pawns, she's given up hope of finding her soul mate. But watching the rugged rancher hard at work on her shelter awakens deeply buried desires.

As the project comes together, Monica discovers a kindred spirit in the tenderhearted Jake. But despite their growing attraction, he still belongs to a cruel woman who'd rather see him dead than free.

Can Monica save Jake, or will their love lead to a tragic tomorrow?

Jake's Redemption is a full-length book in the Angel Eyes cowboy dystopian romance series. If you like scorching-hot chemistry, clever post-apocalyptic worlds, and star-crossed love stories, then you'll adore Jamie Schulz's captivating tale.

ACKNOWLEDGMENTS

I'd like to say a special "Thank You" to my editor Silvia Curry. I'd also like to thank all my beta readers and proofreaders especially Jan Bailey, Angela Cross, Kate Amberg, Lady Elizabeth, Cheryl Johnson, Rosemary Kenny, Amy Shannon, Sandy at the Reading Café, and all the others I may have missed. I'd also like to send a heartfelt thank you to my family and friends. Without all of you, none of this would have happened. Thanks, once again, to Sam and TJ, the Facebook groups, Miss N. for everything, Bryan Cohen, and everyone else!

ABOUT THE AUTHOR

Jamie was born and raised in the wonderful Pacific Northwest and she has always wanted to be a storyteller. As a child and young adult, she spent countless hours dreaming up stories to entertain herself and her friends. She kept long-running, developing stories in her head for years, knowing someday she would write them all down.

She still has many stories still floating around the back of her cluttered mind (and haunting her hard drive as well). She hopes they will all make their way out into the world for your enjoyment someday (soon)!

She still lives in Pacific Northwest with her family and her fur-babies.

You can learn more about Jamie and her books on her website:
www.thejamieschulz.com

And you can follow her on her social media pages:
Facebook (@TheJamieSchulz)
Twitter (@TheJamieSchulz)
Instagram (thejamieschulz)
Jamie's Amazon Page
Goodreads
BookBub

Made in the USA
Monee, IL
30 December 2021

87568713R00225